Praise for Chloe Neill's

CHICAGOLAND VAMPIRES NOVELS

Biting Cold

"Chloe Neill keeps readers right on the precipice of anticipation."
—Fresh Fiction

"Chloe Neill delivers another engaging plot, but better yet, *Biting Cold* reminds us this urban fantasy series is about strong, well-developed characters. Ones we can get invested in and wish were real so we could indulge in a pizza and sing-along movie night at their place." —Vampire Book Club

"[Merit's] a character I fully root for." —Hardcore Heroines

"I look forward to seeing what the future brings for Merit, Ethan, her friends, and Cadogan House." —Fiction Vixen

Hard Bitten

"Delivers enough action, plot twists, and fights to satisfy the most jaded urban fantasy reader." —Monsters and Critics

"A fast and exciting read." —Fresh Fiction

"A descriptive, imaginative, and striking world . . . rich with real-world problems as well as otherworldly creatures . . . roughly fantastic from beginning to end, with one of the best endings in urban fantasy history." —*Romantic Times*

Twice Bitten

"The pages turn fast enough to satisfy vampire and romance fans alike." —*Booklist*

continued . . .

"IF YOU LOVED NANCY DREW BUT ALWAYS
WISHED SHE WAS AN UNDEAD SWORD-WIELDING
BADASS, MERIT IS YOUR KIND OF GIRL."
—*Geek Monthly*

"There's a new talent in town, and . . . she's here to stay. . . . An indomitable and funny heroine . . . truly excellent." —*Romantic Times*

"Engaging, well executed, and populated with characters you can't help but love. It was impossible to set down." —Darque Reviews

"I can just about guarantee that readers will want to read more of this series. . . . Vampire fiction fans should be well served by this vamp-centric story, too." —LoveVampires

"GO BUY IT NOW! It's a great urban fantasy that reads a little like Charlaine Harris's Southern Vampire series." —Literary Escapism

"Chloe Neill . . . has created an interesting vampire mythology and a heroine who has spunk and daring; she's kick-ass without the hard edges." —Romance Novel TV

"[Neill has] created a unique vampire tale in a genre that's flush with look-alikes." —Undercover Book Lover (Not Really)

"Not only action-packed, it's hilarious. I couldn't put it down. . . . [Merit is] extremely charming . . . a great read."
—Wicked Little Pixie

"I didn't want to put it down . . . excellently written. . . . [*Some Girls Bite*] brings a fresh perspective on the vampire craze that is going around these days. The book has a little bit of Harry Potter in it, a little bit of the Southern Vampire Mysteries in it, but with a voice and perspective all its own. No offense to the *Twilight* fans out there, but the writing from Chloe Neill is IMMENSELY better than that from Stephenie Meyer. . . . I loved it entirely and am now very anxious to read more from Ms. Neill." —Pink Is the New Blog

OTHER NOVELS BY CHLOE NEILL

THE CHICAGOLAND VAMPIRES NOVELS

Some Girls Bite

Friday Night Bites

Twice Bitten

Hard Bitten

Drink Deep

Biting Cold

House Rules

THE DARK ELITE NOVELS

Firespell

Hexbound

Charmfall

A CHICAGOLAND VAMPIRES NOVEL

BITING BAD

CHLOE NEILL

NEW AMERICAN LIBRARY

NEW AMERICAN LIBRARY
Published by the Penguin Group
Penguin Group (USA) Inc., 375 Hudson Street,
New York, New York 10014, USA

USA | Canada | UK | Ireland | Australia | New Zealand | India | South Africa | China

Penguin Books Ltd., Registered Offices: 80 Strand, London WC2R 0RL, England
For more information about the Penguin Group visit penguin.com.

First published by New American Library,
a division of Penguin Group (USA) Inc.

First Printing, August 2013

REGISTERED TRADEMARK—MARCA REGISTRADA

LIBRARY OF CONGRESS CATALOGING-IN-PUBLICATION DATA:

Neill, Chloe.
Biting bad: a Chicagoland vampires novel/Chloe Neill.
p. cm
ISBN 978-0-451-41518-9
1. Merit (Fictitious character: Neill)—Fiction. 2. Vampires—Fiction. 3. Chicago (Ill.)—
Fiction. I. Title.
PS3614.E4432B55 2013
813'.6—dc23   2013015057

Printed in the United States of America
3   5   7   9   10   8   6   4   2

Set in Caslon 540

PUBLISHER'S NOTE

For Jeremy, who sometimes lets me win, usually lets me write,
and always shares his cinnamon roll.
You are the best.

It is not in the stars to hold our destiny, but ourselves.

—*William Shakespeare*

BITING
BAD

✣

CHAPTER ONE

THE WINTER SENTINEL

Early February
Chicago, Illinois

I stared at the sleek steel blade, its honed edge only inches from my cheek, and tried not to flinch. I was taut with nerves and anticipation, my fingers slippery around the handle of my own ancient katana, my gaze flicking between the weapon that threatened me and the man who wielded it.

"Nervous, Sentinel?" asked the blond vampire before me, who held not one but two ancient samurai weapons.

I wet my lips and readjusted my grip, trying not to let my prurient interest in my adversary—the sweat-slicked, half-naked physique; the stunning green eyes; the golden hair that just brushed his shoulders—distract me from my mission.

Bringing. Him. Down.

"Not in the least, Sullivan." I winked at him, and in the second his eyes widened in interest, I took my chance. I dropped to my knees and used the handle of my katana to unbalance Ethan's right hand, forcing him to loose his sword.

Well, one of his swords.

My opponent was Ethan Sullivan, a four-hundred-year-old vampire and the Master of Cadogan House, one of three vampire Houses in Chicago. He was the vampire who changed me, rescuing me from a vicious attack one spring night.

Now he was also the vampire who made me whole.

I was the twenty-eight-year-old former graduate student he'd shaped into an immortal warrior . . . and I loved having the opportunity to show him exactly what he'd created.

Tonight, that meant learning to battle with not just one but two gently curved katanas. Vampires loved katanas, preferring swords to guns—primarily because vamps were an ancient and snobby people convinced to believe in katanas' superiority to other weapons by a samurai who'd once roamed Europe.

History aside, wielding two katanas was a tricky venture. The katana was an elegant weapon, and brandishing it was supposed to be an elegant exercise—as much a dance as a show of cleverness and strength. That wasn't easily accomplished with two swords, which required learning how to rebalance my body . . . and not trip over my own weapons.

Fortunately, even Ethan was having trouble. Scowling, he picked up the sword he'd dropped onto the tatami mat on the floor of the House's basement training room.

The vampires on the balcony who watched our practice with eager eyes cheered as their hero, the Master of their House, prepared to fight again.

And they weren't the only ones watching.

My former teacher of swordcraft, Catcher Bell, a mutual friend and sorcerer, was absent from tonight's festivities, busy with other work. We'd found a replacement, albeit one who was less than impressed with our initial efforts.

"That was damned ungainly," said the auburn-haired vampire in front of us.

Grey and Navarre were the city's two other vampire Houses, and our teacher was captain of the Grey House guards. Jonah was tall, handsome, and was my partner in the Red Guard, a clandestine organization created to ensure the Houses and Greenwich Presidium, the ruling body for the North American and Western European vampire Houses, didn't overstep their bounds. We weren't technically a part of the GP anymore, having seceded when the group became too oppressive, but there was little doubt they still had the power to make our lives miserable. Guarding the guardians was never a bad idea, in my opinion.

Ethan had accepted my RG membership, but he was still working on accepting my partnership with Jonah. He preferred my loyalties remain solely with one vampire of the male persuasion— him. They'd reached an accord about me after working out their aggression in a sparring match at the House, even if they weren't exactly the best of friends. Ethan still scowled at Jonah's comment.

"It wasn't ungainly," Ethan said. "It was awkward."

"No," I teased, "it was the result of strategic tactics by yours truly." I put extra emphasis on the hard "c" sounds to underscore the point.

"It was luck," Jonah countered. "And it wasn't especially pretty. You've both got to think of the katanas as extensions of your body. I know it's awkward, but you'll get used to it. Try again."

I rolled my left wrist, which was beginning to ache. Vampires had greater than average strength, but we'd been practicing for an hour, and Jonah hadn't exactly been generous with the water breaks.

"Problem?" Jonah asked.

"Just a little soreness."

"You'll be fine. Reset."

I couldn't help but give him a look. It wasn't that I'd expected my RG partner would be an easygoing instructor. He was responsible for keeping the Grey House guards ready for action, after all. But nor had I expected him to be a total hard-ass.

"Reset," Jonah repeated, a little more firmly.

"Should I remind him I'm a Master?" Ethan quietly asked beside me, rolling the swords in his hands and bouncing on the balls of his feet as he prepared to spar again.

Jonah's hearing must have been acute. "You're Master of Cadogan House," he said, "not dual swords. *Reset.*"

The crowd of vampires hooted, spurring us on just as Jonah did.

"Two katanas are trickier than one," Ethan muttered.

The same applied, I thought, to vampires. Especially vampires of the male persuasion.

An hour and a shower later, we returned to the House's third-floor apartment, the small set of rooms that we called home.

My work night was done, but in a few minutes, I'd be heading into a frosty February evening. And since I was hoping to make a better impression than "sweaty vampire," I found myself in the closet amid Ethan's expensive suits and polished shoes, worrying over what to wear.

"Ankle boots or knee-high?" I asked.

Ethan leaned casually against the wall, one foot canted in front of the other and an amused expression on his face. "Does it really matter what you wear?"

I gave him a flat look.

"Sentinel, you are an intelligent woman, with a solid sense of honor, an excellent pedigree, and a master's degree—"

"Nearly a doctorate."

"Nearly a doctorate," he allowed, "in English literature, and yet you're worried about your choice of footwear. It's not as if you have a date."

And a good thing, since Ethan and I had been living together for nearly two months. I had a key to prove it, although I was still getting used to the idea that the Cadogan penthouse was also mine.

Still, date or not, it wasn't wise to underestimate a Chicagoan's love of good winter footwear. Frostbite was no one's friend.

"I know I don't have a date. This just feels . . . important."

For the fifth or sixth time, I sat down on a padded ottoman and switched out my shoes, exchanging ankle boots—cute, but not warm—for knee-high leather boots, tugging them over the jeans I'd paired with a shirt and sweater. The boots were dark brown leather and fitted perfectly, ideal for long and dark winter nights.

When I'd pulled them on, I stood up and posed in front of the closet's full-length mirror.

"It is important," Ethan agreed, scanning my reflection. "She was your friend for a very long time. You're both attempting to pick up the pieces of your relationship to see if they still fit together."

"I know. And it's still awkward. And it still makes me nervous."

The "she" in question was Mallory Carmichael. My former best friend and roommate, a relatively new sorceress attempting to redeem herself after an unfortunate period as a real-life wicked witch. She was currently atoning for her sins by living without magic and performing menial labor for the alpha of the North

American Central Pack. She seemed to be regaining control of herself, but neither Ethan nor I was entirely sure of her.

"You look nervous," Ethan agreed.

I sighed. "Not helpful. I was hoping for something a little more complimentary. Like 'Merit, you don't look nervous; you look ravishing.'"

"Trap," he said, shaking his head.

I met his gaze in the mirror. "It's not a trap."

"It is a trap," Ethan assured with a grin, "because there's no response I can give that you'll actually believe."

I gave him a dubious expression. "Try me."

Ethan, who looked devilishly handsome in his fitted black suit, stepped behind me, brushed the long dark hair from my neck, and planted a kiss at the crux of my shoulder, sending a delicious chill along my spine.

"Sentinel, you are always the most beautiful woman in the room, irrespective of what you're wearing. And most especially—and preferably—when you're wearing nothing at all."

How did men manage to offer a compliment that transitioned from sweet to utterly salacious in the span of a few words? Still, a compliment was a compliment, and Ethan Sullivan was a master complimenter.

"Thank you."

"You're welcome." He checked his large and undoubtedly expensive watch. "I have a call in a few minutes. You should probably get going."

I huffed at the doubt in his voice. "My steed is trusty and will get me there on time." I talked a big talk, but in fact I'd be driving a well-worn Volvo across Chicago in February. The odds were not in my favor.

"And now you're beginning to sound like Jeff," Ethan said.

Jeff Christopher was a friend and colleague, a lovable nerd and shape-shifter I'd met through my grandfather, Chicago's former liaison to all folks supernatural. Jeff was tech savvy and a fan of role-playing games—I'd recently seen him in head-to-toe ranger garb, from boots to hood—so my reference to a "trusty steed" was right up his alley.

"Jeff has saved our butts on a number of occasions," I pointed out.

"Well aware, Sentinel. But you must agree he does it with his particular flair."

"He does. His own furry flair. Oh, and speaking of, you still haven't paid me on our little bet."

"You didn't win our little bet, Sentinel."

"I guessed Jeff was a puma."

"And as I've pointed out many times, Jeff isn't a puma."

I gave him a sarcastic look. "He's also not a marmot, which was your guess. Mine was closer; thus I win."

"Close doesn't count. It was a draw."

I rolled my eyes. I wasn't going to give up my position, but I didn't have time to argue the finer points of animal taxonomy today.

"Either way, furry makes a nice change from stodgy vampire."

"Vampires are not stodgy," Ethan said, pushing his hands into his pockets and staring back at me, stodgily.

"You are, but that's *your* particular flair."

Ethan arched an eyebrow, a move he used frequently to portray many of the emotions in his arsenal—doubt, imperiousness, wickedness, among them.

"You do realize, Sentinel, that you're one of us?"

I let my eyes silver, an effect that appeared when vampires felt strong emotions, to demonstrate just how much like him I really was—and the depth of my emotion about it. "I never doubt it. Anyway," I said, changing the subject, "what's your call about?"

"Darius. Apparently there are rumors he's no longer strong enough to hold the GP together. Morgan and Scott wanted to talk."

"Because Darius was kidnapped?" I wondered aloud. Darius West was the leader of the Greenwich Presidium. Although we were technically Rogue vampires since we lacked GP affiliation, Ethan maintained friendly relations with Scott Grey and Morgan Greer, the Masters of Grey and Navarre Houses, respectively. It also helped that we'd recently saved Darius's life, rescuing him from an assassin hired by the city's new supernatural "liaison," John McKetrick.

"Exactly," Ethan agreed. "I understand the other GP members are pleased we saved him, but concerned he needed saving in the first place."

The GP was populated by vampires revered for their strength, if not their magnanimity.

"It doesn't surprise me they'd question his abilities," I said, grabbing a short camel trench coat from a hanger and shrugging into it. The coat had been a gift from Ethan, who was afraid the thin leather jacket I usually wore on Sentinel excursions wasn't warm enough for February. I didn't need him to ply me with gifts—I was plenty pliant already—but the coat was warm and fit perfectly, so I'd decided not to argue.

"You'll be careful out there?" Ethan asked. A line of worry appeared between his eyes.

"I will. But we're just going for pizza. And Luc knows where I'll be, just in case of a zombie apocalypse."

My chain of command was complicated. I stood Sentinel for

the House, a sort of soldier for Cadogan and all that it stood for. But I wasn't a House guard per se, which meant Luc, captain of the Cadogan guards, wasn't exactly my boss. Neither was Ethan, for that matter, since I technically had the authority to override him if he wasn't acting in the House's best interests. But Luc was at least my acting supervisor, so I'd filled him in on my plan for the evening.

"I know," Ethan said. "And I know you need a break. We've both been working a lot of hours lately."

"Well, I've been keeping an eye on McKetrick, and you've been—" I looked at him sideways. "What have you been doing again?"

"Running this House of vampires?" he dryly asked.

"Ah, yes," I said with a nod. "Running this House of vampires."

He grinned a bit, then slid a tendril of dark hair behind my ear. "In all seriousness, we should arrange to spend some quality time together."

I gave him a sly smile, because I happened to have anticipated his request.

"I agree completely," I said. "Which is why I've made dinner reservations on Friday at Tuscan Terrace, Chicago's finest Italian bistro. Homemade pasta. Fine champagne. Truffles. These little dessert cakes that are nearly better than Mallocakes. We'll celebrate in style."

Tuscan Terrace was an old-school Chicago restaurant, where waiters spoke mostly Italian, the rooms were dark, and privacy was guaranteed. It was delicious and expensive, the type of place you saved for a special occasion.

Ethan furrowed his brow. "To celebrate what?"

"You don't remember what Friday is?"

His stare went blank, and his expression had a decidedly deer-in-headlights look about it. I'd stumped him.

"Friday is February fourteenth," I said. "It's Valentine's Day."

I'd been single for so much of my adult life that Valentine's Day hadn't, in context, meant much. Sure, I'd occasionally been given tired roses in a green vase, or a heart-shaped box of mediocre chocolates. But those gifts had been few and far between.

This relationship was real, which meant I could—for the first time—experience a meaningful Valentine's Day. Not because of pink roses or nougat-filled chocolates, but because of *us*. Because I'd found someone who made me better, stronger, and because, at least I liked to think, I did the same for him. That was worth celebrating, treasuring, being grateful for.

It was worth tuxedoed waiters and delicate champagne flutes.

"*Saint* Valentine's Day, you mean," Ethan said with a chuckle. "I'm surprised you want to celebrate such a bloody day in Chicago's history."

He meant the massacre on Valentine's Day in 1929, when Al Capone took out several men from a rival gang in a Lincoln Park garage.

"You know that's not what I mean." I picked a bit of lint from one of his lapels. "Like you said, we deserve some quality time together, just the two of us. A few minutes of peace and quiet away from the House, where it won't matter if we're vampires."

"That does sound inviting," Ethan admitted. "A bit tempting of fate, perhaps, but inviting all the same. I look forward to it."

He smiled at me wickedly, suggesting it wasn't so much the dinner he looked forward to, but what he hoped might happen afterward.

Since imagining that scenario wasn't going to help us meet our obligations for the evening, I pressed a kiss to his lips. "I need to run."

BITING BAD ✚ 11

Ethan's expression fell. Putting a hand on his chest, I could feel his heart thumping—steady and sound—beneath.

"I'll be careful," I promised. "I'll have my sword and my phone. And besides, I'll be dining with one of the most powerful sorceresses in the world."

His eyes flattened. "I know," he said. "That's precisely what worries me."

CHAPTER TWO

+ ＝◆＝ +

THE EVENING STAR

The night air was cold, crisp, and fresh, but the streets and sidewalks were coated in a layer of dirty, frozen-solid snow that wouldn't fully melt for months. I headed to my car, parked on the sidewalk in a spot I'd circled the block three times to obtain, waving at the humans who guarded the fence surrounding the House.

Tonight, the gate was closed, a rare sight in my ten months as a vampire. But we'd seen enough violence lately—from supernaturals hired by the GP, from the assassin hired by McKetrick—that we'd tightened security all the way around.

When they saw me approach, one of the humans, a gun at his side, pushed open one of the slatted steel doors just wide enough to allow my exit.

The guard tipped her black ball cap as I walked through, acknowledging me, then closed the gate again when I was through, shutting off Cadogan House from Hyde Park—and the rest of the world—once again.

I climbed into my car, immediately turning the heat to full

blast, not that it helped. My new coat was warm, but this was still February in Chicago. When the vent began to knock like a card in a bicycle spoke, I turned down the heat, deciding an insufficient but functioning heater was better than a broken one.

Now that I was out of the House, I also decided it was safe to call Jonah to get an update on the latest in GP-affiliated House news. Since Ethan was the only Cadogan vampire who knew about my RG affiliation, and our training hadn't exactly been private, I'd kept our in-House discussions to a minimum.

I put my shiny new phone—a replacement for the beepers we'd once carried—on speakerphone and dialed him up.

He answered on the first ring, the buzz of noise behind him. "Jonah."

"It's Merit. What's new?"

"Since I last saw you an hour ago? Nothing. You're bored and driving, aren't you?"

"Not bored. Just interested in your thoughts and wisdom. And a training room full of vampires wasn't exactly conducive to conversation."

"I do have a life, you know."

"Do you?" I teased. "I find that surprising."

"Actually, I have a date tonight."

I blinked. The news, admittedly, hit me a little weird. I was very much in love with Ethan, but as partners, Jonah and I had a separate, unique relationship, one that required a different kind of trust and intimacy. I just found odd the possibility that another woman was going to figure into it.

But I could suck it up. "Who's the lucky girl?"

"A Rogue," he said. "Noah introduced us. I'm not sure if it will go anywhere, but I like her style. And her figure."

"And I'd like it if you kept the details to yourself."

"Merit," he teased, "are you jealous?"

I wasn't, not really. Just a bit weirded out. But I wasn't going to admit that aloud. "Not in the slightest. I just don't need the gory details. Be careful out there."

"I intend to. And I'd say the same to you."

"Nothing weird should happen, but in case it does . . ."

"You want me to come save you so Ethan doesn't drop a sizable 'I told you so' into your lap?"

"I don't need saving. But yes, please."

He chuckled. "Maybe we'll get lucky, and you'll see McKetrick breaking into a car or something. It wouldn't be the most satisfying tag, but at least we could put him away."

I could hardly agree more. McKetrick had been playing the desk-bound bureaucrat, but in reality, he had a nasty hatred of vampires and the willingness to act on it. Four murders later, we still had no evidence to pin on him, and no idea what he might do next.

"We've found nothing," I said. "Maybe Michael Donovan was lying about McKetrick hiring him." Michael Donovan was the vampire assassin who'd been hired by McKetrick.

"That we haven't caught him doesn't mean he isn't doing anything," Jonah noted. "If he's smart, he's lying low right now."

"Lying low, or planning?" I wondered aloud.

"We won't know until we know," Jonah said, clearing his throat as if preparing for something. "If you want to speed things up, we could bug his house."

That had been a common refrain by Luc and Jonah. They were convinced they could get in, bug McKetrick's Lincoln Park house, and get out. Considering the regularity of McKetrick's schedule— he was a city employee, after all—there was merit to the idea. But the risk? Considerable, which was why Ethan and Noah, the head of the Red Guard, rejected the idea.

"We aren't the CIA," I reminded him. "And if we got caught, the city would turn against us Watergate style. There's too much risk."

"So we wait," Jonah said. "Which is awesome, because you're such a patient person."

I wasn't, and he really knew me too well. "He won't stay silent forever. He has too much ego for that."

The cars in front of me had slowed to a virtual standstill, and I knew better than to chat about supernatural drama while navigating gridlock. "Jonah, traffic's picking up. I'm gonna run. I'll keep you posted on any excitement with Mallory."

"Do that," he said. "But I will not be advising you on any excitement on my end."

Thank God for small miracles.

Wicker Park was northwest of Hyde Park, and the traffic didn't ease up again even as I pulled into the neighborhood. Even in the dark of February, Division Street, Wicker Park's main drag, was hopping. Chicagoans moved between bars and restaurants, climbing over and around the mountains of snow piled high by snowplows, darkened with street grit, and thickened by freezing temps.

I drove around a bit to find a parking space—a task that probably consumed twenty to thirty percent of a Chicagoan's waking hours—and nudged the Volvo into it.

I looked for a moment at the katana in the passenger's seat. I didn't like the idea of leaving it in the car, but nor did I think it would be welcome in the mecca of Chicago-style deep-dish I was heading to.

"I can always come back for you," I murmured, slipping the sword between the center console and the passenger seat to make its presence a little less obvious. I took a final calming breath, then climbed out of the car and locked it behind me.

Compacted snow crunched beneath my feet as I walked toward Saul's, my favorite pizza spot in Chicago or outside it. I'd done my time in New York, and although I could appreciate the depth of New Yorkers' love for floppy pizza, I didn't understand it.

Bells attached to a red leather strap hung on the door, and they jingled when I opened it, a gust of wind sneaking in behind. I pushed the door shut again, shrinking back a bit from the growly expression on the face of the man behind the counter.

"You tryin' to let winter in here?"

I pushed off the door and headed across worn linoleum to the counter, which had been covered in the 1970s by faux-wood-grain plastic, presumably to add an "authentic" pizzeria feel.

"If I was trying," I said, "you'd know it." I put my elbows on the counter and took a good, hard look at the man behind it. He was older, late sixties, with a thick head of black hair and eyes that sparkled mischievously. He wore a heather gray sweatshirt with SAUL'S PIZZA across the front in faded red letters.

He was the only person in the small room—which served as the way station for orders and pickups, and led to the small dining room beyond.

He scowled, caterpillar eyebrows drawing together. "You got a smart mouth."

"Always," I said, smiling back at him. "It's good to see you, Saul. How's business?"

His expression softened. "Don't get nearly as many orders for cream cheese and double bacon as I used to." He looked me over. "You look good, kid."

My eyes cramped uncomfortably, the warning signal that sentimental tears were about to flow. But I held them back. "You look good, too."

"Things change, don't they?"

I glanced around at the restaurant, with its dusty décor and hanging menu board slatted with movable plastic letters. Mismatched plastic chairs with metal legs sat along one wall. The counter was worn from thousands of hands, elbows, credit cards, and pizza boxes, and the room smelled like dust, plastic, and garlic.

"Do they change?" I wondered aloud with a grin. "I'm pretty sure that poster for *Cool Hand Luke*'s been there since the movie came out."

Saul's eyes narrowed. This was always dangerous territory. "*Cool Hand Luke* is a classic piece of American cinema, Ms. Know It All. It was nominated for five—"

"Academy Awards, I know." I smiled at him—it was nice to hear that familiar nickname again and listen to the familiar argument—and gestured toward the dining room. "Is Ms. Blue Hair in?"

"She's at your booth," he said, then checked the old Schlitz clock on the wall behind him. "Pizza should be up in ten."

"Thank you, Saul. It's nice to be back."

"Shouldn't have waited so long in the first place," he grumbled, and headed into the kitchen.

Mallory Delancey Carmichael, recently designated and discredited sorceress, sat in a plastic booth, the kind with molded seat depressions. She wore a knitted cap with earflaps and a pouf of yarn at the top. The cap was pulled down low over her blue hair, which darkened to a deep indigo at the bottom of the complicated braid that sat on her shoulder. She wore a jacket over a sweater over a button-down top; the sleeves of the sweater ending in bell-like shapes that nearly reached the tips of her fingers.

She looked up when I walked in, and I was relieved to see she was looking more and more like her old self. Mallory was pink cheeked, with classically pretty features. Her eyes were big and blue, and her lips were a perfect cupid's bow.

The restaurant was packed, so I was lucky she'd nabbed a seat. I climbed into the booth across from her, pulling off my gloves and putting them on the seat beside me.

"Cold out there tonight."

"Freezing," she agreed. "I like your coat."

"Thanks," I said, unbuttoning it, then adding it to the stack on the seat. "It was a gift." And since I was proud of them, I stuck out a leg beside the booth and showed off my boots.

"Hello, gorgeous," Mallory quietly said, sliding a finger along one leathered shin. "If he's buying you gear like that, I certainly hope you're sleeping with him."

She looked back at me and grinned, and I saw—for a moment— the old Mallory in her eyes. Relief rushed through my chest.

"He didn't buy them, but he has no complaints." I cleared my throat nervously, preparing for the confession I hadn't yet made to her. "I don't know if you heard, but we're actually living together. I moved into his apartments."

Her eyes widened. "And I thought we'd start with some awkward 'How's your family' type stuff." She paused, looked down at the table, then up at me again. "You're living together?"

I nodded, waiting while she processed the information and reached a conclusion. Honestly, her deliberation made me nervous. She'd been there from the beginning; she had been in the room the first time I'd confronted Ethan. She knew our potential— and limitations—as well as anyone else.

After a moment, she linked her fingers together and gazed at me with motherly concern. "You don't think you're moving too quickly with him?"

"I've moved one flight of stairs."

"Yeah, into the Master's suite. That's the vampire version of a penthouse."

"It's also approximately ten times larger and more luxe than my former room," I reminded her. "Relationship or not, you shouldn't deny me fine linens and turndown service."

Mallory narrowed her eyes. "Darth Sullivan does not get turndown service."

"He does," I said. "With drinks and truffles."

"How very . . . *Sullivan*," she said with an amused smile. "Don't get me wrong. I like Sullivan. I think he's good for you in his way. And you two certainly have a vibe. A strong one."

"Strong enough that it could have become hatred as easily as love," I agreed.

"I think you did hate him for a time," Mallory said. "And love and hate are both strong emotions. Flip sides of the same coin. The thing is, he's just so . . ."

"Stodgy?" I offered, thinking of my earlier accusation.

"*Old*," she said. "Four hundred years old, or something? I just don't want you to rush anything."

"We aren't," I assured her. "For once, we're actually both on the same page about our relationship. What about you? How are things with Catcher?"

Catcher, Mallory's boyfriend, had moved into her town house right before I moved into Cadogan House, but they'd been off and on since her recent escapades. Understandably, he hadn't taken her magical betrayal lightly.

"They're developing," she shyly said, picking at a thread on one of her sleeves. Her hands still bore the faint scars of her attempt to unleash powerful black magic on the world.

A few weeks ago I wouldn't have pushed her to elaborate, mostly because I didn't want to raise uncomfortable subjects. But if we were going to root ourselves in friend territory once again, we were going to have to stop dancing around the tough issues.

"I'm going to need more information than that," I said.

She shrugged, but there was a hint of a smile in her eyes. "We're seeing each other. I wouldn't say we're back to where we were—he still doesn't trust me, and I understand that—but I think we're better."

My protective instincts kicked in. Mallory undoubtedly had her issues, but she was still my girl. "He's not being obnoxious, is he?"

Mallory gave me a flat look. "We're talking about Catcher. He's always obnoxious. But not the way you mean. He's moved into overly protective. Lots of checking in on me, lots of making sure I'm eating and sleeping well."

"He's worried about you," I said.

"And," she said, drawing out the word, "he's feeling guilty that he didn't intervene the first time around. He's such a hands-off person. I mean, not romantically. He's very hands-on, if you get my drift."

"I have no interest in your drift," I said, gesturing her to keep going.

"The thing is, I think he hates himself a little bit because he didn't see what I was doing."

In fairness, he had missed a lot. Mallory was working her bad mojo while she'd ostensibly been studying to become an official member of U-ASS, the sorcerers' union. She'd done a lot of the mayhem-making in the basement of the town house they shared, right under his nose.

"It still surprises me," I said honestly. "I'm not really sure how he missed it, either."

"Yeah," she said guiltily, "but then, why would you assume your girlfriend was attempting to destroy Chicago?"

You might assume it when Chicago was beginning to literally crumble around you, but hindsight was twenty-twenty.

"Okay," I said. "So he's being motherly. Have you talked to him about it?"

Saul marched in, wearing a giant oven mitt and holding a round pan that smelled—you guessed it—of cream cheese and bacon. He put the pizza on a trivet in the middle of the table, and as was his style, served up a piece for each of us.

My mouth watered immediately.

"Thank you, Saul," Mallory said, glancing at me with amusement. "You're fanging out."

I covered my mouth with a hand, glancing around to ensure no one else had seen it. There was no point in drawing any extra attention to my biology.

"Thanks," I said, digging into my slice when I was certain my body was under control and I wouldn't ravish the pizza in full view of the room. The taste was absolutely sublime. I'd had take-out from Saul's since becoming a vampire, but that was nothing like eating deep-dish fresh from the oven.

"I'm in the process of talking to Catcher about it," Mallory continued. "I have to tread carefully because, you know, I almost managed to destroy Chicago. And I don't mean to make light. I know what I did, and now I'm trying to live with it. To turn myself around so that I can actually use this gift for something more than utter selfishness."

Now that was more like it. "I like the sound of that. What about Gabe and the others?"

Gabriel Keene was the head of the North American Central Pack and Mallory's magical rehab sponsor.

"Gabe's good. He's spending a lot of time with Tanya and Connor—doesn't want to miss out on Connor's milestones. Berna's still playing mother." Berna was one of Gabe's relatives and the bartender at Little Red, the Ukrainian Village watering hole where the Pack hung out in Chicago.

"How long are you going to stay with them?"

"I'm not sure. They're building up their catering business, and they need help to get it rolling. Frankly, I'm not sure they've really thought about me long term." She cleared her throat. "And that's actually what I wanted to talk to you about."

"What's that?" I asked, cutting a chunk of pizza with the side of my fork.

"What I'm going to do when I'm cleared to use my magic again," she clarified. "I need a productive job. A mission of some kind. And I thought, maybe, I could help you guys."

I paused, fork midway to my mouth. "Help us?"

"Help Cadogan House. I need to do something good, Merit," she explained before I could respond. Which was good, because I had no idea how to respond. "I need to help people. I need to make good for what I did. And, frankly, you guys need a lot of help."

She wasn't wrong about that, and I agreed she needed a post-rehab plan. But I wasn't sure Cadogan House was the appropriate outlet.

"What, exactly, did you have in mind?" I asked.

"Well, I was thinking I could become permanently attached to the House—like a magical consultant. I could help you plan operations. Go out with you on missions. I've done it before, with the Tates. And that ended up okay."

She had helped with the Tates—twin fallen angels Mallory unleashed on Chicago. But we'd asked for her help primarily because she'd created the problem and was in a position to help solve it.

I didn't want to break her spirit or halt her recuperation, but I couldn't see Ethan agreeing to that. He wouldn't give her that kind of access, especially considering her history with the House.

But before I could answer, a *boom* shook the building.

My heart pounded with sudden fear, but before I could rise from my seat another *boom* sounded—a percussion that vibrated through my body with its bass rumble and prickled my arms into gooseflesh.

A vase dropped from a small shelf on the wall across from us, shattering into pieces on the floor. The human closest to it screamed with surprise, and most everyone else jumped up and ran to the windows.

Now in the darkness came a different sound, a rhythmic sound. It was nothing I could identify, but nothing that was accidental. And there was another thing out there I easily recognized.

Steel.

I could feel out guns and swords, a perk of having tempered my katana with my own blood. That there was enough of it outside the building to sense inside made me that much more nervous.

Mallory's gaze—narrowed, but not afraid—found mine. "What do you think that was?"

"I don't know," I said, dropping my fork, my appetite suddenly, and unusually, gone. "But I think we'd better find out."

✦ ✦ ⫸⫷ ✦ ✦

CHAPTER THREE

BEAT THE DRUM

Mallory dropped cash on the table and followed me through the crowd of patrons to the front of the restaurant. As we walked, I pulled on my coat and stuffed my gloves into my pocket.

Saul stood at the front window with the aproned members of his kitchen staff, peering into the darkness. He didn't take his eyes from the glass until I stood beside him.

"What in God's name was that?" he asked.

"I'm not sure. But I'm going to check it out. Stay in here and lock the door behind me until I'm sure what it is."

"I'm not going to stay in here while you go traipsing into trouble."

"I've traipsed into worse," I told him. "I'll be fine. I'm immortal, but you're not." I put a hand on his arm and raised my pleading gaze to his. "Let me take this one, okay?"

Saul looked at me, judging for a moment, before stepping aside and letting me through.

But I wasn't the only one who aimed for the door. Mallory was right behind me.

I put out a hand. "Where are you going?"

"With you," she said, petulantly as any teenager. "I have certain skills, as we've seen."

I glanced around, realizing we weren't exactly in the right place to have a discussion about her skills—or whether she should be showing them off.

"You're not supposed to be *using* your particular skills," I murmured, "and I don't want to initiate a war with the Pack because I let you do it." We had enough intraspecies animosity in Chicago.

Mallory leaned in. "And I'm not going to stand around while you walk out into trouble."

"We don't know it's trouble yet."

"You know," she countered. "Your magic's all over the place. You know something about what's out there. Something you haven't said yet."

I hadn't mentioned the weapons, because I couldn't confirm anything in here. Not for sure. I looked at her for a moment, weighing my options: using her as backup and risking Gabriel's ire versus leaving her inside and risking her ire.

"If nothing else," she said, "I'll need a ride back to the bar. I've got an hour until Catcher is supposed to pick me up. He and Gabe aren't going to want me waiting here without you if there's trouble out there."

Unfortunately, she was right. They'd both have my ass in a sling if she got hurt on my watch. "Fine. You can come. But you don't move an inch unless I tell you to."

She gave me a salute, and we slipped out the door. When we were free of it, Saul pulled it shut and clicked the lock again.

I scanned the street, looking for the source of the noise. But other than the worried faces of humans peeking through doorways and windows, looking for the source of the percussions, I couldn't see anything. There was smoke in the air, so the trouble was nearby, but not in my line of sight. Whatever it was, it grew closer; the rhythmic sound grew louder, and the sensation of steel grew stronger.

Sirens began to whine as two CPD cruisers sped past the restaurant, lights flashing.

"What is it?" Mallory asked.

"I'm not sure. But I think they have weapons." Weapons and a total lack of visibility meant I needed backup. I could be brave when necessary, but I tried very hard not to be stupid.

I took out my phone and dialed up the Cadogan House Operations Room, where Cadogan's guards (and I) investigated and strategized.

Luc answered on the first ring. "Sentinel? What's the good word?"

"I'm in Wicker Park at Saul's. We just heard two really loud bangs. I can't see anything, but I can smell smoke. And I think they've got weapons. Can you get eyes on it?"

I heard a click and then the sound of frantic typing in the background. I'd been switched to speakerphone, and the noise of computers and research was audible.

"We're checking the scanners, Sentinel. You there alone?"

"I'm with Mallory. And I'm thinking I need to get her out of here."

"No argument there, Sentinel."

"Merit, it's Lindsey." Lindsey was another House guard—Luc's girlfriend and my House bestie. "CPD scanners are talking about explosions. It sounds like they suspect Molotov cocktails blew propane tanks or something."

"Who's throwing Molotov cocktails in Wicker Park?" I asked. Mallory's eyes grew wide.

Cadogan House didn't answer. I could hear the static drone of scanner feed in the background, but I couldn't distinguish the words. They must have been listening.

And still, the sound of drumming grew louder, mimicking the acceleration of my heart.

"Guys, I'm going to need something here pretty soon."

"The CPD's reporting riots," Luc said. "There's a fire a few blocks west of you, and a cabal of rioters moving east."

That explained the noise. "I think they're chanting with drums or something. I can hear them moving. What was the target?"

"Looking," Luc said. "Oh damn."

"What?"

"They hit Bryant Industries."

I frowned. "I don't know what that is."

"It's the company that distributes Blood4You in Chicago. Each distributor is independently owned. They call theirs 'Bryant Industries' to keep a low profile."

In order to assimilate, most American vampires avoided drinking from humans or vampires and, instead, relied on bagged blood called "Blood4You."

What were the odds of rioters in this day and age *accidentally* bombing a Blood4You distribution center?

"The rioters are anti-vamp," I guessed, stomach tightening with nerves.

"That's quite possible," Luc agreed. "And, Sentinel, they're moving your way. I think now would be a good time to make a polite exit and get Mallory out of there. Little Red is closer than the House. Maybe stay there until we're sure the coast is clear?"

I glanced back at the door. "Luc, I can't just leave Saul here unprotected, not if the rioters are coming this way. What if they try to hit the restaurant?"

"They're anti-vampire, Merit. They probably don't pose a specific risk to Saul's *unless* they find out you're there. If they think he's harboring vamps, they might hit it on purpose. You're a danger to him if you stay."

That possibility stung, sending a sick feeling through my chest. To them, because of my biology, I was the enemy. And that meant I posed a danger to everyone around me.

"Luc—," I began, but he cut me off.

"You can't protect Saul, Merit. Get to your car and go."

Crap. "Luc, call my grandfather. He's still got friends in the CPD. Maybe he can get a cruiser on the building."

"Good thought," he said. "I'll call him as soon as you promise to get your ass to Little Red."

"On it," I promised. I hung up the phone but took a moment to send a warning message to Jonah. It was simple and to the point: RIOTS IN WICKER PARK. BLOOD4YOU HIT. KEEP WATCH.

My phone beeped immediately, and I assumed Jonah had already responded. Instead, I found an infuriating alert that my message hadn't gone through.

I slipped the phone back into my pocket. I'd have to deal with technology later and hope Jonah got the message.

I glanced at Mallory. She looked nervous, but her eyes were clear, and her magic seemed appropriately banked.

"How much did you hear?"

"Enough to know we should hurry."

I nodded and had to speak up to be heard over the increasing sound of drumming and chanting. "My car's only two blocks away, but my katana is in the car. They might be out for supernaturals, so we're going to pretend that we're just two girls out for a night on the town. We're going to walk to the car, get in, and drive as quickly as we can to the bar."

"And if they recognize you?"

My father, Joshua Merit—Merit was actually my last name—was a Chicago real estate mogul, and media outlets in the city thought it newsworthy that I'd been made a vampire. My photo had been in the papers, so I wasn't exactly anonymous.

"We hope they don't," I said. And there was no chance in hell I'd go down without a fight. And I'd make it a good one.

I gave Saul a heads-up and promised that help was on the way. He didn't look entirely convinced . . . until I told him the riots were anti-vampire and I was part of their target audience.

"I don't want you or your place to get hurt because of us," I said. Saul nodded, a little guiltily, and shut and locked the door again.

I knew I wasn't human, that I was separated from them by genetics, fangs, and bloodlust. This was a poignant reminder of that separation, of the differences between us.

I looked at Mallory, who nodded and plastered a smile on her face. "You said we were party girls out for a night on the town. So let's, like, totally get out of here. For reals."

"Are there valley girls in Chicago?"

"Tonight," she said, "there are."

We started toward the car, avoiding Division, darting from the restaurant into the alley across the street, then running through darkness to the other end, where we peered out to survey the source of the noise.

There were dozens of humans, maybe forty or fifty altogether, and they moved up the middle of Division in a cluster. In a *mob*. They ranged in age from young enough to be carded to their mid-forties, and they were obviously passionate about their cause, which they shouted loudly and often.

"Clean Chicago!" they yelled in unison. "No more fangs! Clean Chicago! No more fangs!"

They repeated the words like a mantra of hatred, yelled at people on the street, waved bats and hockey sticks in the air and against one another, and smashed car windows and streetlights as they moved.

These were modern-day villagers with torches, and I was Dr. Frankenstein's monster.

"What a bunch of assholes," Mallory muttered.

"No argument," I said. "And we need to get out of here before they get any closer." Escape in mind, I scanned the street for the Volvo. It sat safely up the block, no missing mirrors or windows, but we'd have to sidestep the rioters to get to it.

"Party girls," I reminded her. Mallory nodded, and I slipped my arm into hers. I stuck on my most human expression, and we walked arm in arm toward the car, just two girls returning from a night on the town.

I worked not to wince at every *tinkle* of breaking glass and volley of anti-vampire cursing lobbed behind us, and kept my eyes on the prize. But that didn't stop my heart from racing. There were more humans here than I could handle alone, especially without a weapon other than the blue-haired girl next to me, who was utterly off-limits.

Sirens sounded around us as the rioters destroyed store windows and set off alarms. As we reached the end of the block—only a few dozen more feet to go—we ducked around the corner, hearts pounding as the rioters drew closer.

Unfortunately, that only riled up my inner predator, which was more than willing to take its chances with humans. Bitchy, whiny humans.

"So, funny story," Mallory said, her back flat against the wall of the building, her arm tight around mine. "Once upon a time, I tried to have dinner with my best friend, and the apocalypse happened."

"No kidding," I murmured in agreement, wincing as sounds of violence punctured the night around us.

"Merit," she said. "Look."

I followed the direction of her gaze to the other side of the street, where two young guys had been stopped by rioters who'd split off from the main group.

The kids carried the awkward bearing of adolescence. One was hauntingly thin; the other was more heavyset. They wore ill-fitting clothes that didn't look warm enough for the cold night, but that was hardly the primary concern.

The rioters, who had six or seven inches and a lot of muscle over them, stood over the guys menacingly. The taller of the bullies had a pincushionesque haircut and a chain with a giant dollar-sign pendant in gleaming gold. His friend, who was four inches shorter, wore a satin jacket with a dragon embroidered on the back and a Cubs cap.

I considered that an insult to the Cubs.

The more heavyset kid must have said something the rioters didn't like, as they both reached out and shoved the guys' shoulders, sending them stumbling back a few steps.

"Merit, we need to help them."

I'd have liked to help them, but first and foremost I had to help her. I could feel the magic beginning to simmer around her, bubbles of it beginning to reach the surface. Soon enough, that magic would reach a full boil, and I might not be able to stop the transition.

"Mallory, I've got to get you out of here before something happens."

She gave me a flat look. "Before I go postal?"

"Frankly, yes."

"*Caroline Evelyn Merit.* I am not going to go postal."

So she said. But her track record wasn't the greatest. We'd managed to create an alliance with shifters, but it was fragile. I didn't want to be the one to knock it off-kilter.

I looked longingly back at the car.

"I'm not unsympathetic," I said, "but I have responsibilities, and right now you're the main one."

"Shut it," she said. "You love acting like a vampire hard-ass."

Without warning, she let out an earsplitting whistle. "Hey, assholes! Why don't you pick on someone your own size?"

All four gazes turned to us.

"Mallory Delancey Carmichael," I muttered, swallowing down a sudden bolt of fear. I might have been a vampire, but the rioters had inches and pounds on me, too. And a lot more hatred.

The guy with the pointy hair glared at us, lip curled. "You got a problem, bitch?"

The harshness of the word cut right through the fear. I gave him an Ethan Sullivan–worthy eyebrow arching.

"What did he just say?"

"Oh, no he didn't," Mallory whispered. "Go kick his ass."

Easy for her to say, since I wasn't supposed to let her do anything. But it was too late to back down now; she'd set the wheels in motion.

Resigned to my fate, I shook out my shoulders, blew out a breath to calm my nerves, and put on my best suit of vampire moxie. "Keep an eye on the main group, and let me know if they get too close for us to get to the car. We can't take on an entire mob, not alone."

Mallory nodded.

I rolled my hips into a saunter that kept their gazes on me as I approached them.

"Um. Did you call me a bitch?"

Haircut and Dragon looked at each other and snorted, then bumped fists like they'd scored points by using a one-syllable word.

"I did," Haircut said. "What are you gonna do about it?"

I ignored the question and looked at the kids. "These guys hassling you?"

"They like vampires," Dragon said, as if that explained and justified their attitudes.

Frankly, the kids didn't look like they cared either way about vampires. They just looked scared, and eager to get the hell out of Wicker Park.

"We just, you know, think people should get a fair shake," said the more heavyset kid, nervously scratching his arm as he did it.

I couldn't imagine the moxie it had taken to get out those words in the face of two bullies, and I wanted to reach out and hug him for the bravery. But that was not what I was here for.

"Fuck you," said Haircut.

"Yeah," Dragon agreed.

But the kid had spoken his peace; he had found his courage. He wasn't about to back down, either.

"You're an asshole, you know that?" He tugged at the front of his jacket. "You think beating the shit out of me makes you brave? It doesn't. It makes you an idiot. So beat me up if you want to, if that's gonna make you feel better. But at the end of the day, I know who I am. And you don't know shit."

Haircut might not have known shit, but he knew when he was pissed off. He reached out to grab the kid by the collar . . . but he wasn't fast enough for me.

In the split second before his fingers grasped fabric, I reached out and snagged his hand. He froze in shock—that someone had thought to defy him, and that I'd done it so easily.

"Here's the ironic thing," I said. "I'm a vampire. And these guys"—I gestured to the kids—"are on my side. You, as it turns out, are not."

I gave his wrist a gentle squeeze. Not enough to break bones, but enough to let him know I was really and truly different, and I was very serious.

"Bitch," he muttered, but he didn't move his gaze from his wrist. Beads of sweat had begun to dot his brow. "Do something, Joe!"

Joe, otherwise known as Dragon, lifted up his shirt, showing off bony hip bones and a matte black handgun stuffed into the waistband of his pants.

"Oh shit," said the second kid, the quieter one. "We don't want any trouble. We're just walking home."

My blood ran cold. How had I missed his weapon, the telltale vibration of the gun? Not that the reason mattered now. The only thing that mattered was getting the kids out of here safe and sound.

Bluff, I told myself, even as my heart beat so loud I could hear it pounding in my ears.

"Here's how we're going to play this," I said, gathering up as much bravado as I could muster. "I'm going to let this guy go, and you're going to lower your shirt over that gun again. And you guys are going to walk away."

Joe laughed. "You think I'm afraid of you?"

Alpha predator, I reminded myself. *Top of the food chain.*

I let my eyes silver and my fangs descend, and I looked back at Joe with hunger in my eyes. Since dinner had been interrupted, I didn't need to fake it.

His eyes grew wide with fear, but only for an instant. He was a guy in his twenties with a gun at the ready, and he was better at bravado than I was. His eyes grew cold, hinting at hatred.

"You okay over there?" Mallory asked. But being a good girl— tonight anyway—she didn't move from her designated spot.

Maybe, I thought, I could use her in this little game of ours. She'd started it, after all.

"Your little friend is calling you," Haircut said. But since he was still on the ground, his wrist bent in my hand, I didn't pay him much mind. It was Joe and the gun that worried me.

"You think I'm scary," I said. "Granted, I'm pretty strong. But I have nothing on her."

"She don't look that strong," Joe said.

I grimaced. "I guess you don't know what she is."

All four of them looked back at her, obviously not intimidated by the petite chick with blue hair. If only they knew the truth . . . Of course, I couldn't actually let them know the truth, so I fudged a little more.

"She's a death reaper."

"Bullshit," Joe said.

"Nah," said the guy who'd stood up to the bully, watching me closely. "She's—she's right. That girl is a death . . ."

"Reaper," I filled in, since he was obviously following my lead. I really did like this kid. "Death reaper. Talks to the dead, reanimates them if necessary, points out the evil men and women who don't deserve to live."

"And then what?" the quiet kid asked.

I answered with a gesture, a finger drawn across my neck like a blade.

"That is some serious bullshit," Joe said again, but he didn't sound nearly so convinced this time. "Girls can't really do that."

"That girl can," I said. I leaned forward and lowered my voice just a bit. "Have you ever been walking down the street at night, and you think you hear footsteps behind you? Maybe you walk a little bit longer while your heart beats like a timpani drum in your chest. You think you're imagining it, so you keep walking. But the footsteps start up again. Step by step by step. And you stop, and you turn around, and there's nothing there. No sign of anything in the street. Just lights and shadows. But you know, sure as you know anything, that you weren't out there alone."

They were frozen, eyes on me but glazed, as if they were remembering their own experiences. I pressed on.

"Or maybe you're home alone, and you talk to someone in the next room, because you saw their shadow pass. When they don't answer, you go look . . . and the room is empty. It had been empty the entire time. But in your spine, you can feel it. You know you weren't alone. And when you try to go to sleep, when you close your eyes, you can feel them—you can feel *her*—at the foot of your bed, watching you sleep."

Slowly, for maximum effect, I slid my gaze to Mallory. "She is the stuff nightmares are made of. She haunts the minds of the living and the dead, and she sees evil where it lurks. And now she knows who you are."

Because in this fictional telling of mine, Mallory was a Grim Reaper/Santa Claus mashup. That wasn't anywhere close to the truth, of course, but it was enough to change Joe's mind. He dropped the shirt over his gun again.

"You can't do this," Haircut said weakly, but the fight had gone out of him.

"I can, and I did," I reminded him. "I'm going to let you go, and I'll give you a ten-second head start. Because we like the chase," I added with a delectable whisper. "But remember—even if you don't see her, you'll feel the hairs on the back of your neck rise, and you'll know she's there."

I let go of Haircut's wrist. He jumped up and ran down the street, away from the rioters. Joe followed him without looking back.

For a moment, the kids and I stood there in silence.

"That stuff all true?" the talker tremulously asked.

I looked back at him. "Yes and no. The truth is much less scary, and much more scary at the same time. What's your name?"

"Aaron." He gestured toward his quieter friend. "That's Sam."

I nodded. "You said good stuff, Aaron. Honest stuff. You're one of the good ones. Don't ever let anyone tell you different, okay?"

Aaron nodded shyly.

"Merit!" Mallory said in a squeaking whisper from her corner, eyes darting to a threat I couldn't yet see. "They're coming. We need to *go*! Now!"

I closed my eyes to clear my head from adrenaline and silvering, then looked back at the boys when I was sure they were normal again. "You should get going. I gave the guys a scare, but I'm sure I didn't change their minds about vampires or the people who support them."

"Our car's right there," said Sam, his nervous gaze still on my mouth. I supposed the hint of fang had made an impression, and not one he was likely to forget any time soon.

"Then go," I said, and they took off. The boys ran up the block, then climbed into the smallest car I'd ever seen—clown cars would have marveled—and zoomed up the block with an engine that sounded like a vacuum cleaner.

My good deed done, I ran back to Mallory and peeked around the corner into the street.

It didn't look good.

The rioters had reached us, the world's worst parade.

I tried to put on a happy face, but there wasn't much point in it.

"Shall we haul ass?"

"Let's do it."

We popped back into the street and ran full out until we got to the car.

"Unlock it," Mallory said, jiggling the door handle on her side. As if that ever sped up the process.

"Working on it," I said, fumbling to get the keys into the door lock. But adrenaline and anticipation made me clumsy. We were so close. So close to zooming safely away, and to my getting Mallory safely home again without a magical incident.

But not close enough.

"Hey, ladies!" said a male voice behind us.

I glanced back. He was probably twenty-five, with pale skin, blond hair, and a skinny and mean demeanor. He carried a bowie knife in one hand and a hockey stick in the other.

We tried to ignore him, but he wouldn't be ignored.

"Hey, I'm talking to you! You good girls with us in our fight for human rights?"

His prejudices were so irrational he didn't even realize he was attempting to add supernaturals to his posse.

Mallory's eyes narrowed. Clearly, she itched to slap the stupid out of him.

"Human rights!" shouted two more humans nearby. "Down with fangs! Chicago doesn't need them, and Chicago sure as fuck doesn't want them!"

The guy looked at Mallory. "How about you, Blue? You on our side? Justice and truth and no more fucking vampires? Who needs 'em, right?"

His voice was teasing, his words flirty . . . and quite the wrong things to say. He reached out and put a wiry hand on the Volvo.

Mallory's eyes narrowed at the threat, and the air prickled around her. Her magic was rising.

"No more fucking vampires," I pleasantly agreed, then smiled at the guy, who was making himself at home on the hood of the car. Keeping my gaze on him, I made a blind effort with the key.

"You live around here?"

"Used to. Moved away." Finally, the key found home, and the lock clicked open. "Sorry, but we need to get going, so . . ."

He looked at me for a moment, eyes narrowing as he realized he'd been handily rejected. And because he couldn't fathom the possibility that anyone would reject him, he immediately decided there was something wrong with us.

He tapped the blade of the knife against the hood. "You like fangs? You think that's hot?"

"I think you should get off my car so my friend and I can leave."

He flipped the knife in his hand so its point was facing me, and he leaned in closer. "I think you need to learn some respect."

Mallory's hands began to shake, her body vibrating with energy. She crossed her arms, tucking in her hands. She gnawed on her lip, banked anger in her expression, all of it directed at the guy who was hassling me.

She wanted to kick his ass.

She wasn't the only one.

"I know plenty about respect," I said. "But really, we need to go."

"Who the fuck do you think you are? Do you know what we just did?" He gestured back toward the column of smoke rising behind us. "We brought a building down. They think they're powerful? The vampires? Fuck them. Fuck them. Clean Chicago!" he yelled out, raising his arms to gather more of the rioters around him—and around us. They came with their weapons and began to surround us, drumming them on the Volvo to the beat of their own hate-filled symphony.

"You ready to go now?" asked the hateful one, the man who'd started the drama.

He slammed his hockey stick down on the hood, leaving a two-foot-long dent in her otherwise unmarred steel.

"What the hell!" I said, my own emotions breaking through the faux-human barrier I'd erected. I squeezed my hands into fists to keep from throttling him, from attacking humans in the middle of a street surrounded by witnesses, and no matter the justification. "That's my car!"

"Yeah? What the fuck are you going to do about it?" He hit the windshield, a crack spreading from side to side.

"Maybe it's not her you need to worry about."

We both looked at Mallory, who'd spoken those ominous words. She'd pulled off her knitted cap, and the tendrils of blue hair that had escaped her braid floated around her face in the cloud of magic. That cloud wasn't visible, but I could feel it, as though I were standing inches away from high-voltage wires.

"You got something to say about it, blue hair?"

"Mallory," I warned, but she was staring at him, giving him a look you might have expected from a genius to the man who'd just asked the world's stupidest question.

"As a matter of fact," she said, "I do."

She blinked . . . and so did a streetlight across the street. It flashed and crackled with light, loudly enough to make even the fearless rioters flinch. Another second of staring, and the light exploded—sending a shower of green and orange sparks into the air. Chaos erupted, and we took full advantage.

I tossed her the keys. "Get in the car!" I yelled out, and as she unlocked her door and climbed in, I used my door like a blunt object, slamming it against the guy's knees until he crumpled to the ground.

My predatory senses now on full alert, I heard the *whip* of a bat behind me and ducked just in time. But it was already moving, and it smashed right through the driver's side window.

"Damn it, I just washed the road salt off this thing," I gritted out, grabbing the middle of the bat and thrusting it backward into the gut of the woman who'd tried to take my head off.

The woman grunted and fell to her knees. I dropped the bat, climbed into the car, started it up, and gunned it. Most of the mob dropped away to avoid getting run over; some were braver and made a run at us, one final attempt at violence. I put the accelerator to the floor to gain speed and hightailed it down Division past another set of screaming police cruisers.

We'd gotten away. But what were we heading into?

CHAPTER FOUR

SWEET AND LOW DOWN

The car was freezing. The driver's side window was gone, and the windshield, while still in place, was marred by a web of cracks. Fortunately, Little Red wasn't far away. The bar was located on a corner in Ukrainian Village, which was only a hop and a skip—and in this case, a freezing car ride—away from Wicker Park.

When I'd put a few blocks between us and the riot, I glanced over at Mallory. Her knit cap was in place once again, and her arms were crossed, hands tucked into her sides. She'd banked her magic again, only a whisper of energy flowing around her, and all of it melancholy.

"Are you all right?"

She nodded but didn't speak.

"You only used it for a second," I said, assuming she was upset because she'd used her power.

"I used it to damage property in front of humans. They're not even supposed to know sorcerers exist, much less see me threaten them."

Sorcerers were among the last of the supernaturals still unknown to humans.

"You were protecting me," I pointed out. "And it's not like you shot a lightning bolt into the streetlight. They probably think it was a coincidence."

Mallory sighed and rubbed her temples. "Maybe they do, maybe they don't. Either way, I'm not sure Gabriel will care. I broke. That's what it comes down to. I broke, and he'll know it."

"And you have to tell him?"

She gave me a flat look. "You want me to try to hide something from the Apex predator of the North American Central Pack? He's a werewolf, for God's sake. He could sniff out the lie, even if I didn't tell him, no pun intended."

"I'm sorry, Mal. But thanks for sticking up for me. And for the car."

"Don't thank me for that. It's not exactly in one piece." Mallory leaned forward and looked through the cracked window at the dented hood of the car. "The assholes took their toll."

"Assholes often do."

"That's a Billboard Top Forty song waiting to happen."

"Sung to the tune of 'There'll Be Sad Songs,'" I suggested, then offered up a lyric. "'There'll be assholes, to make you cry.'"

"'Assholes often *dooo*,'" Mallory sang. "You're right. That's not bad." She sighed and pulled up her knees, resting her forehead on them. "My life sucks."

"It sucks because you're trying to do the right thing, but the result isn't showing it. You're at the stage where good intentions meet crappy abilities. Welcome to my first eleven months as a vampire."

"You've only been a vampire for ten months."

"My point exactly."

She chuckled a bit, which had been my motive.

"It gets easier," I said.

"You didn't have to adjust under the watchful eye of Gabriel Keene."

"You're right. I only had to adjust under the watchful eye of Ethan Sullivan. That was an utter cakewalk."

"You're really going to try to outdo me on this one?"

"You're the one who coined the term 'Darth Sullivan,'" I reminded her. "Besides, I wouldn't have let you slide a year ago, before you got your magic. I figure I probably shouldn't let you slide now."

She looked at me and smiled, just a little. "I'm glad you're here."

"I'm glad you're here, too," I said.

We reached Ukrainian Village. My ears and fingers aching with cold, I gratefully pulled the Volvo into a parking spot in front of the brick building that housed Little Red.

The shifters must have had enough of cold, as the parking spots in front of the bar were empty of expensive, custom motorcycles.

"Closed down for the winter?" I wondered aloud.

"Only the transpo," Mallory said. "Shifters don't care to ride in icy wind and below-zero temps."

Having driven without a window for the last few minutes, I understood the sentiment.

I turned off the engine, but we sat in the car for a moment. "Are you ready?"

"Not really," she said. "But a woman's gotta do what a woman's gotta do, and all that idiomatic bullshit."

She blew out a breath and opened the car door, and I wished her the best.

The bar was a classic dive, with scuffed floors, beat-up tables, and hard-bitten customers. A low, sad tune played on the jukebox—a crooning country music song from the seventies or eighties, when buckles were big and hair was bigger.

The bar wasn't exactly easy on the eyes or the ears, but tonight it smelled deliciously of sweet and spicy tomatoes, probably the sauce for the Pack's signature barbecue, the pride of its new catering operation.

Gabriel Keene, who stood in front of the bar's large plate-glass window, was a predator personified. He was tall and square shouldered, with tawny, shoulder-length hair and amber eyes that gleamed when they caught the light. He wore jeans, a long-sleeved T-shirt, and black boots that looked like they could do some damage. Not that he needed the accessories. There was power in the sweep of his shoulders and his wide-legged stance.

Shifters were an odd breed. They were tough, and they loved fine whiskey and chromed-out bikes. But they also had a strong connection to nature. They were the hippies of the supernatural world—if hippies wore biker boots and rode asphalt-pounding Harleys.

Gabe carried his infant son, Connor, in the crook of his arm. Connor was beautifully angelic, with bright blue eyes and a ruff of soft, dark hair, and he blinked at me and Mallory with a child's innocence. God willing, he could keep that innocence as long as possible.

"Ladies," Gabe said, glancing at us. "I hear there's trouble afoot."

"Rioters," I said. "They firebombed a Blood4You distribution center and then headed down Division."

Gabe gestured toward the car. "I take it you got caught in the cross fire?"

I nodded. "We tried to leave and avoid the dramatics, but we caught their attention. The car took some damage, but we made it out. They're still rioting. Marching down Division with sticks and bats."

My report given, Gabriel turned his gaze on Mallory. The amber eyes swirled with quiet power. "You're quiet."

"I used magic," she said.

"Should we talk about it?"

Mallory nodded, and without being asked, walked toward the red leather door that led to the back room.

"A moment, Kitten," Gabriel said, readjusting Connor and following her.

While I waited, I took the opportunity to call Ethan.

"Sentinel? You made it out okay?"

"We're at Little Red. The Volvo took some damage, and Mallory used her magic, but we're fine otherwise."

"Did she?" Ethan asked.

"She did. We were surrounded by rioters, and she knocked out a streetlight to distract them and give us time to get into the car."

"Clever," Ethan said.

"Very," I said, glancing over at the red leather door. "Gabe and Mallory are talking. I doubt he'll be thrilled."

"He's not opposed to the controlled use of magic," Ethan said. "Whether her use tonight qualifies will be up to him. At any rate, I'm glad you're okay."

"Me, too. The rioters were still out there when we left, but we saw a couple more CPD units heading in."

"Most reports say the riot's been contained to an area, but not entirely quelled. The fire at the distribution center's been extinguished."

"How bad's the damage?"

"I haven't yet heard, but Scott and Morgan are preparing for shortages."

Cadogan House was one of the few American Houses that actually allowed its vampires to drink from people or vampires. Most other Houses used bagged blood in the hopes that tamping down on their biting instincts would help them assimilate with humans. A shortage of bagged blood might change that analysis.

"Speaking of rioters," I said, "their mantra was 'Clean Chicago.' I don't know if that's the name of the group or just a slogan, but Luc might want to start the opp research."

Opposition research was one of our key tactics. If you couldn't beat 'em, at least learn as much about 'em as you could.

"I'll advise him. Is the Volvo drivable? Will you be able to get home before the sun rises?"

"It will be a cold ride, but yeah. I should be home shortly."

"Be careful, Sentinel."

"Promise," I said, and hung up the phone.

With Mallory and Gabriel still ensconced in the back, I headed over to the bar that lined one side of the room.

Berna leaned over the bar, reading a book, her chin propped on her hand.

"Off-season for shifters?" I wondered aloud, taking a seat.

"Is cold," she said in her thick eastern European accent, not looking up from her book. "Is hibernate."

"Shifters hibernate?" I asked. Gabriel certainly seemed awake, and I'd spoken with Jeff only a few nights ago.

"Not in cave. But we feel the cold." She made a fake shiver that set her impressive bosom swinging. "We stay home. We cook. We have oatmeal and bubbles baths. Thick socks for feet."

"Bubbles baths, eh? The Keenes don't seem much like the bubble-bath type." Although I could pretty easily imagine Gabriel soaking in a tub. Bare chested. Maybe a few damp curls. Truth be told, it wasn't a miserable image.

Berna narrowed her eyes at me, and for a moment I was afraid she'd caught the lascivious direction of my thoughts. Sure, I was taken, but that didn't mean I couldn't appreciate a fine—and happily married—shifter.

But that was not what she wondered. "You could be fatter."

Berna was a constant critic of my weight; she thought me too thin, which had less to do with what I ate, which was plenty, than with my vampiric metabolism, which was fast. Had I not been a vampire and a lover of all things chocolate dipped and baconated, she probably would have given me a complex.

"I eat plenty," I said. Although in this case, I hadn't eaten in hours, and dinner had been interrupted.

Berna pursed her lips in obvious suspicion and stared down at me with a motherly look Mallory had probably seen a time or two.

"Fine. I guess I wouldn't mind a bite before I hit the road again."

There was a gleam of victory in her eyes.

Berna disappeared into the back room, and before the door shut fully again, I caught a few of Gabriel's words.

"Think, Mallory," he was telling her.

His tone didn't sound complimentary.

I worried my lip for a moment and decided to do something I rarely did—except in emergencies. I dropped the barriers that usually separated my working mind from my supersharp vampire senses, and I eavesdropped.

". . . it was the right thing to do," Mallory was saying.

"You think this is unusual?" Gabriel asked. "You think there won't come another time when you're driven to the breaking point, when you know using magic is the right thing to do? That's exactly what you said to yourself last time, Mallory, and that's the entire fucking point of this exercise."

"It's different this time," Mallory said.

"Is what the addict always says," Gabriel said. "Look, I'm not your father. I'm not even your warden, not really. You've got power; you could use it. I know that. You're here because you want your life to change. Because you want things to be better."

"How can they get better if I keep replaying the same scenario over and over and over again?" There was franticness in her voice, real and abiding fear. "That I'm going to fuck up everything again. That I'm going to fuck over everyone—again."

Gabriel paused. "That, Mallory, is the question you have to ask yourself. That's your work. Your struggle. Figure—"

Before I heard him finish the thought, the door opened and Berna emerged, a steaming bowl in her hands. I feigned interest in a soiled paper menu on the bar. What was a "Wolf Popper," anyway?

Berna placed the bowl on the bar in front of me, along with a spoon and paper napkin.

"What's this?" I asked.

"Stew," she said. "Eat."

I poked the spoon in. Although the bowl's chunky contents didn't look entirely familiar, they smelled delicious. I blew gently on a spoonful and took a bite, savoring the salty, smoky, tomatoey flavor.

"Tongue good for you," she said. "Much protein. You grow strong. Like oxen."

Of course it was tongue stew, and of course she wanted me to be an ox.

Fortunately, the stew *was* delicious, and I downed half the bowl before the door opened again. I expected to see Mallory, but Gabriel entered with Connor still in his arms.

Berna's expression softened, showing that hint of the motherly worry that was driving Mallory crazy. "She is good?"

"She'll be fine. I sent her back to the kitchen. The meat guys asked if they could come early today. They want to talk to you about the brisket order."

Berna murmured something in a language I didn't understand and slipped into the back room.

Gabriel took the stool beside me, Connor cooing between us.

"Is she in a lot of trouble?" I asked.

"I'm not her jailer."

"I know. And you did her a lot of good by bringing her here after Nebraska. I know she appreciates that."

"She's coming along. The routine, the manual labor, the monotony, keeps her from ignoring her magic, from pushing it to the back of her mind like she did for all those years."

That explained the chores he usually had her doing. "Before we figured out she had magic, you mean?"

He nodded. "Before she can learn to use it consciously, she needs to learn to *have* it. To just *be* with it, even if it's uncomfortable. Even if it feels wrong and ill-fitting."

"It seems like she's making progress. She said it was different for her this time. I think she was right."

"Is it different," he asked, "or is it exactly the same? She accessed the book because she was uncomfortable. Because she wanted to reunite good and evil. But isn't that also exactly why she acted tonight?"

"The rule can't be that she can't use her magic if she's motivated to use her magic. That's completely illogical."

Gabriel made a doubt-expressing sound. "Do you remember when Chicago burned?"

"Quite well," I said. "I helped put out the fire. I'm not defending her actions. You let her use magic with the Tates. You know she can help. We can't let her waste all that potential. What kind of life is that?"

Gabriel's expression softened. "It's a life where she doesn't destroy anyone else, including herself. She knew, even while she was crossing the boundaries between good and evil, that what she was doing was wrong. She knew the same thing tonight—that she shouldn't have used her magic to threaten a human you could have easily handled."

"Then when can she use it on her own terms?"

"I don't know. She has to be able to control herself before she can control the magic. That's her journey, and it's not gonna be a quick one. When she can use her magic and be at peace with it, she'll be getting somewhere."

I nodded and pushed around some chunks of unidentifiable vegetable—cauliflower, maybe?—with my spoon, my appetite gone again. Maybe Berna was right; magical stress didn't do much for the appetite.

What food couldn't fix, a certain boy could. I was ready to go back to the House, to go home to the familiar. I put down my spoon and pushed back the bowl. "I should probably get back. Can you tell Mallory I said good-bye? And thank Berna for the grub?"

"I can."

I stood up, but paused before heading to the door. "I'm not entirely sure why you took her on. Or me, I guess, since I come with her. For whatever reason you're doing it, in case she doesn't say it, thank you."

"You're welcome, Merit."

I walked to the door, catching a glance of the parking spots outside. My Volvo, beaten and weathered . . . was gone. Had the missing window given a thief easy access? Or had a rioter followed me here and stolen her as a final punishment?

I looked back at Gabriel. "My car's gone."

He rose and walked toward me. "Yeah. I'm having someone look at it. See if it's worth fixing."

My Volvo was undeniably "worth" fixing, since it was my primary mode of transportation. Still . . . "You're having someone look at it? Who?"

He smiled slyly. "I've got a guy."

Okay, so he had a guy, and his guy was looking at my car. What was the appropriate response here? Shape-shifter car repair etiquette was definitely not covered in the *Canon*, the code of vampiric law.

"Your katana's on the table there," he said, gesturing to a booth by the door. I walked over and picked it up, wrapping the loose belt around the crimson scabbard.

"Thank you, I guess," I said. But I still had to get back to Cadogan House. "Isn't there an El stop on Damen? I think I can get to the Loop, then catch a bus to get back to Hyde Park?" I couldn't remember the last time I'd actually ridden the El or worried about bus schedules. I was woefully out of touch.

"No need," Gabe said. "I've got a loaner."

"A loaner? Should I give you some money?" I asked, but Gabriel shook his head.

"It's on the house, Kitten. I'm doing a favor for myself, really."

My eyes narrowed suspiciously. "How so?"

"I'll get to hear about Ethan's reaction when he sees you in that."

He pointed at the window . . . and the curvy, silver roadster that now sat in the spot my Volvo had once filled, a shifter emerging from the driver's side. It was small and loaded with chrome, and a Mercedes logo sat neatly between its round front lights.

"What is that?" I asked, just managing not to press my nose to the glass like an anxious puppy.

"That, Merit, is a 1957 Mercedes-Benz 300SL with a brand-new V8 and about 350 horsepower. It is the car Ethan would stake a vamp to drive, pardon the expression. And I'm going to let you borrow it."

Ethan's prized possession, a sleek, black Mercedes convertible, had been the victim of a supernatural attack by the former mayor of Chicago. He'd attempted to replace it with a series of vehicles: an Aston Martin, a Bentley, and currently, a black Ferrari FF coupe. He was still looking for the "right" car, and I had a feeling this particular gem would come pretty close.

Still, actively trying to rile up a vampire wasn't exactly a shifter thing to do. "You want Ethan to be jealous of a car?"

"No," he said, rocking Connor a bit as he stirred. "I just think you'll enjoy his reaction. And I'll enjoy hearing about it."

Connor gurgled happily. Even he liked the idea of riling Ethan up.

"Where do you even keep a car like that?" I glanced back at the bar. "Surely there's no garage here?"

Gabriel nodded at the shifter who walked into the bar and dropped the keys into Gabe's palm. "We don't sleep here. We have a compound outside the city. Grass. Trees. Space to roam."

"Space to run?"

Gabriel nodded gravely. Apparently that was no small concern to a pack of wolves. "I like project cars," he added. "It's a weakness. It lets me kick back, enjoy a fine brew, and lose myself in the mousetrap of the engine."

He offered the keys, but I glanced up at him, worry in my heart.

"Are you sure about this? That car must be insanely expensive, and it's winter in Chicago. The streets are a mess with the salt and the snow—"

"Kitten, have you ever known me to do something accidentally?"

No, I guess I hadn't. With his confirming nod, I curled my fingers around the key, itching to walk outside and run a finger along the car's curves. The ride back to the House was going to be something.

Gabriel jerked his head down as Connor fisted his hands and began to screw up his face. I knew that expression. Trouble was coming, and Connor was going to be loud about it.

"And it's dinnertime," Gabriel concluded. "That means it's time for us to get going. Drive carefully, Kitten? I don't want to find out you've destroyed another Mercedes this year."

I actually hadn't destroyed the last one, but considering his generosity, I decided not to argue. Instead, keys in hand, I walked outside and climbed into the sexiest car I'd ever seen.

The Mercedes had the curves of a midcentury roadster, but it handled like a Grand Prix racer. A bare flick of the accelerator sent the car flying, and it hugged the curves like, to use the cliché, I was driving on a rail. The car was so responsive, it seemed to anticipate my moves before I made them. Hands clenched around the braided leather steering wheel, I felt like the heroine of a spy thriller, as if I were racing through Chicago on my way to a dead drop rather than returning home after a failed attempt at pizza, a riot, tongue stew, and my best friend's trip to the supernatural principal's office.

Maybe the damage to the Volvo had been a mixed blessing. It would get some much-needed TLC ... and I had a roadster to drive.

CHAPTER FIVE

G abriel trusted me with the car, but I wasn't about to trust it to the residents of Chicago, not where parking was concerned. The risk of an errant snowplow, gravel truck, or ice-related fender bender was too high for my comfort, so I rolled up to the gated entrance to the House's basement.

"Ma'am," said the guard through the speaker, "you don't have a basement parking pass."

I might have been sleeping with the Master, but there were some prizes even that couldn't win me.

"I know," I said. "My car was damaged, and I'm driving a loaner from the NAC Pack. I don't want to leave it on the street. If you can contact Ethan or Luc, I think they'll make an exception for the night."

The speaker went silent, and after a moment the gate rolled back and the basement door rolled up. I drove the Mercedes down the ramp and into the single visitor spot.

Ethan and Luc, curly haired and cowboyish, walked into the

basement just as I got out of the car. Their curiosity must have been piqued by my request, and for good reason.

They took in the Mercedes, eyes glazing over in manly appreciation. I bit back a smile as Ethan fumbled for words.

"What—where—how did you?" he asked as he circled the car.

In his black suit, hair pulled back at the nape of his neck, Ethan looked like the double agent who might have ridden with me to the dead drop.

Gabe's car was giving me illusions of grandeur. And spy fiction.

"Gabriel," I said. "The Volvo was beat up, and he offered to have a friend take a look at it. This was his loaner."

Slowly, Ethan looked back at me, eyebrow raised in shock. "He gave you *this* car as a loaner?"

I nodded and tried hard not to grin, and not altogether successfully. *He wanted to tweak you*, I thought. And he'd managed it very effectively.

"Is this the car?" Luc asked.

"This is the car," Ethan said. He put his hands on his hips and completed his circle, green eyes poring over every detail, just as a man might peruse the curves of a beautiful woman.

"Wait," I said. "*The* car? You know about this car?"

"We knew her once upon a time," Luc said, walking closer. He reached out as if to caress her, but then pulled back, perhaps loathe to mar her finish with fingerprints.

Ethan glanced back at me. "Gabriel won this car in a game of poker from Sonny DiCaprio."

I frowned. "I don't know the name."

"Sonny DiCaprio was what you might call a well-connected man," Luc said. "He had a pretty nice establishment in Chicago in the eighties. Larceny with a side of protection racket. He also ran an illegal poker game downtown."

"Gabriel wasn't yet in charge of the Pack," Ethan said, moving to stand beside me. "His father was, and he was friends with Lou Martinelli, Sonny's arch enemy. Gabriel thought he'd show his old man a thing or two and arranged to join Sonny's game one night. He was just about out—having lost a lot of money and some of his father's territory—when he went all in on the final hand. He came away with a lot of money and Sonny DiCaprio's 1957 Mercedes."

"DiCaprio let him walk away with it?" I wondered aloud.

"They called DiCaprio the 'Gentleman's Mobster' for a reason," Luc said. "And that's probably why he didn't last much longer. He was taken out in a turf war a few months later."

Whatever I thought I knew about Chicago—or its supernaturals—there was always more to the story. Of course, having seen Gabriel shuffle and deal, I wasn't surprised to learn he was a cardsharp.

"That's quite a history," I said.

"Mm-hmm," Ethan agreed. "Did he mention why he's letting you drive this particular car?"

"Because we're friends?"

Ethan made a sarcastic sound. "You may be. But that's not why he's letting you drive it." He leaned forward and flicked a bit of dust from the clear coat. "He's doing it to piss me off, because I've been trying to buy this car from him for ten years."

Luc whistled. "That's quite a burn."

"Indeed," Ethan said, glancing at me with a dubiously cocked brow. "But I'm sure Merit had no knowledge of that, did you?"

"Of course I didn't," I said. "Not of the specifics, anyway."

Ethan gave the car one last, long look before gesturing toward the door. "Now that we've ogled, shall we get back to work?"

"Are you sure you can leave her here unattended?" I asked.

Ethan grinned. "I have no intention of leaving her here unattended . . . or letting her leave this House again."

"Let the battle begin," Luc said, clapping Ethan on the back, both of them clearly thrilled to have a different kind of battle to wage.

Boys and their toys, I thought, and followed them back into the House. But before we got to the Ops Room, Ethan stopped me in the hallway, a hand on my wrist. I glanced back at him.

"You're okay?" he asked.

I smiled up at him, and at the sweet concern in his expression. "I'm fine. Mallory, I'm less sure about, but I'm good. They didn't get that close."

Unless you considered "close" to be two supernaturals surrounded by humans with chips on their shoulders and weapons in hand. In which case it was significantly closer. But that would only worry him.

Ethan didn't seem to buy the lie, but he nodded anyway and pressed a kiss to my forehead. "Good. I was worried."

"It's your job to be worried," I said lightly, squeezing his hand. "That's why we pay you the big bucks. Which you are apparently going to hand over to the NAC in order to keep that car in the garage."

"Never fear, Sentinel. I will still be able to keep you in bacon."

"Damn right," I said. "You know your priorities."

Ethan rolled his eyes and slapped me on the butt.

The Ops Room, along with the training room and weapons storage, was located in the House's basement. Luc already sat at the end of the room's giant conference table, his booted feet propped up and a mug of coffee in hand.

The room's border was marked by vampires working at computer stations, mostly temps he'd hired to fill out the staff after our ranks thinned—and the first round of interviews produced really crappy candidates.

The official guards—Kelley, Lindsey, Juliet—were assembled around the table. Together, they looked like models from a beauty ad: Kelley had thick, dark hair and exotically slanted eyes; Lindsey was blond and wore a stylish ruffled coat; Juliet, a redhead, was delicate and dreamy.

Ethan and I took seats beside them.

"We've got the Ombud's office on the phone," Luc said. "Ombuddies—saddle up."

"It's Chuck and Jeff," my grandfather said. "Catcher is seeing to Mallory."

He must have gone to Little Red to check in on her.

"Hi, Grandpa," I offered.

"You're all right?"

"I'm fine. Things got a little heavy, but Mallory and I were both fine." At least until I left her with the shifters. I didn't think Gabriel would do her any harm, but given the closed-door conversation, I also wasn't privy to everything between them.

"And just when we thought it was safe to go back in the water," Lindsey said.

"As safe as it ever is, anyway," Luc said. He leaned over to tap a tablet in front of him and pop images up on the overhead screen. Pictures of the rioters with weapons aloft competed with the charred remains of a building.

"Forty-seven rioters," Luc said. "The Bryant Industries building sustained damage to sixteen percent of its square footage, including damage to its electrical and HVAC systems. They've got backups for the utilities, but the physical repairs are expected to take a few weeks."

"I've spoken with Detective Jacobs," my grandfather said. Arthur Jacobs was a well-respected CPD detective, and one of the few city officials who didn't have a vendetta against us.

"They've arrested twenty-three rioters, but no one's talking. They all asked for lawyers."

Luc looked at me. "Do you want to press charges for the damage to your car?"

"There was damage to your car?" my grandfather asked. I guess he hadn't gotten all the details from Catcher.

"Relatively minor. Gabriel's got a guy, and he offered to arrange for the repairs when I dropped Mallory off. And I definitely don't want to press charges. That would make Cadogan House a specific target. There's no need to make it personal. The rioters were chanting 'Clean Chicago,' and they made it pretty clear they believe we're the thing that needs cleaning."

"As if there's anything clean about hatred," Lindsey said. "But that gives us a place to begin the mocking. What rhymes with clean? Jean? Green? Scene? Bean?"

"'Mean Chicago' works intellectually," Jeff said. "But it's not that snappy."

"Nope," Lindsey agreed. "And we need something snappy to put the little shits in their places." She chortled. "Can you imagine how pissed they'd be if they knew vampires were sitting around mocking them?"

"Very pissed, I imagine," I said.

"And this conversation is no longer productive," Luc ruled. "Moving on."

"They went very violent very quickly," Ethan said. "I find it unusual we hadn't heard anything about this Clean Chicago group before today."

"Have we seen anything on the Web?" I asked, looking around at the vampires at the table.

"Not that we've found so far," Kelley said. "If they've got a Web presence, it's pretty well hidden."

"Point of order," Jeff said. "There's no such thing as 'well hidden' on the Web. If you put something on the Web, it's out there and it's available. 'Hidden' is just an issue of skill."

"We're all aware of your particular prowess, Mr. Christopher," Ethan said with a smirk.

"Damn right," Jeff said, and I could hear the smile in his voice. "Anyway, I looked, too, and I didn't find anything else. Which says to me they're new, or they're insular. They stay off the Web and keep to themselves."

"Staying private isn't necessarily unusual for hate groups," Luc said. "It depends on how unpopular they think their hatred will be. But there's usually some effort made to get new members and spread the word. Remember that organization in Alabama a few months ago?"

Lindsey nodded. "We've seen hatred and protestors before. But Molotov cocktails? That steps it up a bit."

"Molotovs are a hell-raiser's best friend," Luc said. "Not that I have any experience with anything like that."

"Chicago 'twenty-four?" Ethan asked dryly.

"That was a long time ago," Luc said, "if I was to admit I did anything in 1924, which I am not so admitting."

"They planned ahead enough to pick a vamp-related target and assemble bombs," I said.

"Maybe it wasn't just the vampire connection," Juliet said. Her hair was down today, waving softly across her shoulders, and she pushed it behind her ears with her fingertips. "Maybe there was something in the Bryant Industries building? Or some personal animosity against the owners?"

Lindsey nodded. "Maybe they've got enemies. Someone who wanted to put a little hurt on."

"Actually, I've got something," Jeff said. "We got an employee list from Bryant Industries."

"That was fast," I remarked.

"They were very cooperative," Jeff said. "I've got a hit on one of the women who works there. Does the name Robin Pope ring a bell?"

We all looked around the room, but no one offered anything.

"Not to us, Jeff," Luc said. "Who is she?"

"Former employee. She filed a grievance against the company a few months ago for"—he paused, and we could hear the clicking of keys—"the violation of her rights as a whistle-blower."

"That's interesting," Luc said. "What did they think she was tattling about?"

"Looking . . . looking . . . Okay, so her complaint says she believed the company was illegally assisting supernaturals."

Luc pursed his lips. "That's not a bad lead. She thinks supernaturals have it too good at Bryant Industries, maybe she's willing to put her money where her mouth is with a Molotov cocktail or baseball bat."

"Agreed," Ethan put in.

"Was she arrested with the rioters?" I asked.

"She's not on the list," Jeff said. "I'm running her pic against the videos and photos of the riots on the Web. That will take a little time."

"Even if she wasn't there, she could have a hand in it," my grandfather said. "Could be she's an officer, not a soldier."

"We should talk to her," Lindsey said. "We should also pay a visit to Bryant Industries."

"Good thoughts," Luc said, then looked at me. "Merit, you're the roaming guard. Assuming our liege here approves, those sound like assignments for you."

They also sounded like chances to drive the car I'd decided to name "Moneypenny" because it was James Bond–level cool.

I glanced at Ethan. He checked his watch. "We're an hour before sunrise. First thing tomorrow night, check out the facility and see what you can find out. If nothing else, we can improve relations with our suppliers." He smiled. "I'll give you a raise if you can get a discount for the House."

"One problem at a time," I said. "Jeff, would you or Catcher be up for a ride-along tomorrow night?"

"Quite possibly," Jeff said. "Let me check my sched and float the idea to Catcher, and I'll let you know."

"Appreciate it."

"Jeff, Mr. Merit," Ethan said, "I think we're done with you for the moment. Thank you for the information, and let us know if you need anything else."

"Roger that," Jeff said, and the phone clicked off.

Ethan looked at Luc. "If they start with Molotov cocktails, they probably won't stop any time soon. This is now our war room. Get as much information and background as you can on the rioters. Maybe we can tease from their backgrounds information about where they're organized. It would not sadden me to identify a principal location we can report to Homeland Security as a hotbed of domestic terrorism."

Luc leaned back in his chair, obviously pleased. "That's a mean little idea, hoss, but I like it." He grinned wickedly at me. "Keep doing whatever you're doing."

"*Lucas,*" Lindsey said, elbowing him in the ribs while the rest of the Ops Room twittered in amusement and my face turned crimson. "Inside voice."

Our business is our business, Ethan silently told me, activating the telepathic link between us, *but he's not wrong. Keep doing it.*

I was torn between melting from the heat of his words and crawling under the table in embarrassment. Fortunately, Ethan took the stage—and the attention off me.

"In the event this is not the first of the riots, talk to Margot," he told Luc. "Have her ensure our emergency food supply is stocked. Check the tunnels. Ensure access is available if we need it."

Margot was the House chef. Evacuation tunnels ran beneath the House to provide an exit in the event of an emergency.

"You got it," Luc said.

"What's the city's position on the riots?" Ethan asked.

"How pissed off do you want to be?" Luc asked.

Ethan's lip curled, and he sent out a burst of irritated magic. "What are my options?"

"Well, we can show you the video of the mayor's press conference, or McKetrick's."

Ethan's angry expression only stiffened further. John McKetrick was a particular sore spot.

We'd been assembling information about him on a whiteboard on the other side of the Ops Room. The most compelling item on the board was his picture. He'd had a military look about him, and a background, we'd learned, in military special ops. Square jaw, dark hair, piercing eyes. But he'd been horribly scarred when a weapon he'd tried to use against me backfired, leaving tracks and craters in his skin and costing him an eye. He was angry and bitter, and he blamed those emotions—and his injuries—on me.

So far, our research hadn't produced much. We knew he was employed by the city of Chicago as head of the Office of Human

Liaisons. We suspected he had a secret facility, but we hadn't found anything yet. As far as the city and county were concerned, his home in Lincoln Park was the only property he owned.

"McKetrick," Ethan decided, and Luc hit Play.

McKetrick's shocking visage filled the screen, a flag waving in the breeze behind him. He wore a suit and sat behind a desk like a politician, hands linked on the desktop.

"Good evening," he said, voice carefully modulated. "A tragedy has befallen our city, violence caused by the very thing that tonight's demonstration railed against—the destruction of the American way of life by supernaturals who do not care for our culture, our traditions, our values. We cannot condone the violence that has marred a neighborhood tonight. But we can fight back against the supernaturals' attempt to undermine our country. I am here for you. That's a promise, and I'll be making good on it. Beginning tomorrow, I'll be embarking on a series of town hall meetings across Chicago to get your thoughts on how we can make it the country's First City."

"The Star-Spangled Banner" began to play in the background. Luc paused the video, and McKetrick stared back at the camera, frozen in time.

"The supernatural threat is my boot up his ass," Lindsey muttered.

"He deserves it," Luc said. "That entire speech is nothing but a call to arms. He's going to incite another riot."

"He's blaming the rioters for the violence," I said, "all the while telling them the violence was worth it because we're a real and present threat."

"And hosting town hall meetings is only going to exacerbate things," Ethan said.

I squinted at the paused image of McKetrick, staring into his gaze as if I could find and eradicate the anti-vampire sentiment that had rooted in his brain. If his words were honest, he was truly afraid we were ruining things. Destroying things.

Frankly, there were bad seeds out there. Michael Donovan hadn't been a walk in the park, nor were half the members of the GP. But humans weren't immune to committing heinous acts, either; the riot was a perfect example of that.

So what drove McKetrick? What drove a human—strong, politically powerful, clearly well connected—to hate us so uniformly?

"There must be something to this," I said. My gaze was still on the screen, but I could feel the guards' eyes on me.

"What something?" Luc asked.

I looked over at him. "I'm not sure." I pointed at the screen. "But look at his expression, his gaze. He wasn't just reading words off a teleprompter. He was speaking from the heart. He doesn't just hate us," I concluded. "He hates us for a reason."

"We've checked his background," Luc said. "There's nothing out of the ordinary. No run-ins with the law, no obvious tragedies, no sudden disappearances."

"Exactly," I said. "We think he was in the military until he suddenly wasn't anymore, and there's nothing even mildly notable in his history after that. So maybe the tragedy happened while he was in the military."

Lindsey cocked her head. "You think he had a bad vampire experience while he was serving?"

"I don't know. But I think it's worth investigating."

"It might be," Luc said. "But we only confirmed his military background at all because Chuck called in a favor. That's probably all we're likely to get."

All we were likely to get aboveboard? Maybe. But Jeff always had a few computer tricks up his sleeve. I sent him a quick message and asked him about it.

"What about the mayor's press conference?" Ethan asked.

"It's largely the same," Luc said, flipping the screen over to a photograph of Mayor Diane Kowalcyzk with a Photoshopped Godzilla, werewolf, and cartoonish Dracula behind her.

"I see it was a well-attended event," Ethan said with the smallest of grins. Because if you couldn't find the humor in the drama, you only had the drama.

"According to Diane," Luc said, "the end of the world is coming, and we are the harbingers of all that evil. Not in so many words, of course, because that would cause public panic, leading to violence and riots against vampires." His voice was bone-dry. "And, to put a cherry on it, she doubts the riot was actually perpetrated by humans because they hate vampires, and suspects this was gang activity or an isolated incident."

"The woman is naïve beyond all measure," Ethan said. "And we are a political minority without an advocate."

"It may be time to discuss lobbyists and our friends in Washington," Luc said.

Ethan nodded. "Let's put that on the agenda." He put his hands flat on the tabletop. "I think that's it for now, unless anyone has anything else?"

Luc shook his head. "I'd like a hot shower and a bowl of predawn soup, but that's not really in your wheelhouse."

"No," Ethan said, rising from his chair. "Nor my jurisdiction."

My phone rang, displaying a number I didn't recognize. Curious, I stepped away from the table and accepted the call.

"Hello?"

"Merit, it's Jonah. Sorry—this is the first chance I've had to call you."

"Hey, I tried to text you earlier, but it didn't go through. Are you all right? I assume you heard about the riot. Did you get a new phone?"

"I didn't, actually," he said, a strange hitch in his voice. "I'm using a burn phone. That's why I'm calling you." He paused, which made my stomach knot with foreboding.

"You might want to give Ethan a heads-up—the GP has black-listed Cadogan House."

CHAPTER SIX

WE BUILT THIS CITY ON TYPE AB

"I don't know what that means," I told Jonah.

"It means, according to the GP—and therefore every vampire under the GP's control—you're the enemy. And you're to be treated like an enemy by the GP and every vampire under the GP's control."

Ethan had warned me once, before we'd considered leaving the GP, that they wouldn't take our leaving lightly. They suffered from a strong case of "if you aren't with us, you're against us."

"That's why my text to you bounced?"

"Yeah. We aren't supposed to talk to you," Jonah said. "Interact with you. Be seen with you. We do, and we get charged with treason."

I sat down in my chair again and found all eyes on me, phone pressed to my ear.

"I'm guessing that's bad," I said.

"The GP has feudal roots," Jonah said. "The punishments for treason are equally feudal."

I'd researched medieval torture in grad school. Some of the

methods were exaggerated, but some of them were very real and very painful. Metal spikes figured in surprisingly often.

"The GP wouldn't do this without a plan," I said. "What is it?"

"I'm not sure. Scott just got the call a few hours ago."

That explained why we'd suddenly gone from a training session to rejected text messages.

"You're going to talk to your friend who likes donuts?" I asked.

That secret friend was Lakshmi Rao, a member of the GP, and a friend of the RG. She also had a crush on Jonah, which made her an unusually strong ally. I'd met her in a donut shop in downtown Chicago.

"I am, if I can reach her. She's been quiet recently. I think Michael Donovan scared her."

Along with Darius West, the GP's head, Lakshmi had been one of Michael Donovan's near successes. We'd managed to find her alive, but it had been a close call, and the experience must have been jarring, especially for a GP vampire who probably believed herself generally immune to threats.

"Sit tight," Jonah said. "Even if Scott has to let this stand, the RG doesn't. I'll use burn phones to contact you, or I'll reach you through the RG. Just don't tell Darius. And keep a lookout. If the GP is going formal with this enemy-of-the-state business, there's no telling what they'll do."

"Okay," I said. "Be careful out there. And, hey, just in case, keep a lookout for a human named Robin Pope."

"Who's she?"

"We aren't sure. But possibly involved with the riot. She had a grievance against Bryant Industries."

"Noted. Thanks for the tip."

With that, he ended the call. For a moment, I stared at the phone in my hands, unsure how to break the news to Ethan and the others. I didn't look forward to advising them the GP was attempting to screw us again, and by a tactic we'd seen before—shrinking the ranks of our friends and allies.

Damn, I thought. But I sucked it up.

I put the phone on the table and looked up at Ethan.

"Merit?" he asked.

"We've been blacklisted by the GP."

The room went completely silent, at least until Ethan and Luc let loose a slurry of creative and invective-filled curses. Some were in English; some were in Swedish, Ethan's native tongue. And some made me wince.

"Since when?" Ethan asked.

"Tonight," I said. "That was a friend from Grey House." Although I trusted the vampires in the room, there was no need to give out Jonah's name, not when medieval torture was a possibility. "He doesn't know the impetus, just that the decision's been made."

"Since Darius was pleased we saved his life, I suspect the impetus is Harold Monmonth," Ethan said.

Harold Monmonth was a swarthy and smarmy example of a vampire, a man who treated humans as if they were disposable. He'd also previously attempted to steal a fairy artifact from our House to motivate them to attack us. I was the obstacle between his "attempted" and "accomplished," although we'd eventually turned the artifact over to the fairies anyway. He was untrustworthy and manipulative, and it wasn't hard to imagine he wanted to punish us for standing in his way.

"Scott believes factions are forming within the GP. Darius and his allies on one side . . . Harold Monmonth and his allies on the other."

"Your call earlier?" I asked, and Ethan nodded.

"Although neither mentioned a blacklist," he said with a frown. "This must have come down just after."

"That's not entirely surprising, given what we know about Monmouth," Luc said. "Although he probably cares less about whether Darius is or isn't capable of managing the GP than what he could get out of it."

"I would imagine you're right. Unfortunately, while I have no love for Darius, Harold is a worse option, particularly for humans, which means also for vampires. Harold Monmouth also isn't the type to believe vampires should have free will. If he ends up in charge of the GP, I doubt he'll see our independence favorably."

"So, exactly what does this mean for us?" I asked. I was pretty sure blacklisting a House hadn't been mentioned in the *Canon*. I wasn't sure if that was because the action was rare, or too awful, to merit a mention.

"It is intended to create a clear dividing line," Ethan said, tracing a line on the table with his fingertip. "GP Houses on one side. The blacklisted on the other. We are not merely apart from the GP; we are its enemy. It will be the American Revolution in reverse."

Just as Jonah had suggested. "So he's right—they'll punish anyone who talks to us?"

"Or does business with us, visits us, et cetera," Ethan said.

"To what end?" Juliet asked.

"Proving their mettle," Ethan said. "Demonstrating the GP is a force to be reckoned with. And for Harold Monmouth, flexing his power as a GP member, and proving he is the unqualified heir to that particular throne."

Luc clucked his tongue. "Every time you think you're out, they pull you back in, eh?"

Ethan looked at him blankly.

"It's from *The Godfather*. I'm paraphrasing."

"Is that a movie?"

"Seriously? *The Godfather*? Marlon Brando? Al Pacino?"

When Ethan shook his head again, Lindsey whistled. Luc was a bona fide movie buff, and *The Godfather* was often at the top of any movie buff's list. Given the look of utter shock and insult on Luc's face, I guessed his list was typical. We all needed our hobbies; Luc had definitely found his.

"That's a damn shame," Luc said, then looked at me. "Sentinel, I command you to host a movie night during which we educate this man on cinema classics—"

"I think Luc's point is," I interrupted, glancing at Ethan, "you thought you were out of GP politics, and you just got sucked back in."

"So it seems," Ethan said.

"What do you want to do, boss?"

Ethan checked his watch. "Tonight, very little. The sun is nearly on the rise. Go upstairs, sleep, and we'll try again tomorrow."

With the boss's permission, we quickly dispersed.

The Cadogan Master's apartments consisted of three rooms—a sitting room, a bedroom, and a bath. Four rooms if you counted Ethan's closet. Since the closet was bigger than my dorm room on the second floor, I counted it.

When we returned, we were greeted by soft lighting and the hum of a cello. Candles were lit, two bottles of water and a small box of chocolates were on Ethan's writing desk, courtesy of Margot, and the apartments smelled of gardenias and bergamot.

"I am glad to be home," I said, putting my katana on a table near the door and unzipping my boots.

"Before you leave a trail of clothing across the apartments and fall face-first into bed, you might wish to check the bath," Ethan said, taking off his suit jacket.

I ignored the insult and focused on the intriguing bit. "The bath?"

He gestured mysteriously toward the bathroom, so I made my way, pulling off one boot, then the other, hopping along the way.

The Master's bathroom was as luxe as the rest of the apartment, with a marble floor and vanities that looked more like furniture. A giant soaking tub sat in one corner, and tonight, it bore a surprise.

A bath had been drawn, the water steaming and scented, and full of bubbles. Small candles were lit around the room, bouncing circles of light across the ceiling.

My muscles sagged in relief.

"What's all this?" I asked, at the sound of footsteps behind me.

Ethan pulled the leather jacket from my shoulders. "You had a bit of an evening. I thought you could use a break."

I glanced back at him suspiciously. I didn't mean to question his motives, but in my experience a candlelit bath wasn't Ethan's usual method of coping when I'd been in a dangerous situation. He typically preferred a lecture about my having gotten into danger in the first place. In this case, of course, I'd been in the wrong place at the wrong time.

"Merit, I can all but see the gears turning."

"Sorry. This is just . . . unexpected. Very unexpected."

Ethan smiled, lips curving with sultry appeal. "On occasion, the unexpected is precisely what the doctor ordered. Or so the humans say."

"Since you, being immortal, have no need of doctors?"

"Precisely." He'd already kicked off his shoes, and he began rolling up his shirtsleeves.

"Are you joining me?" I wondered aloud.

"Patience, Sentinel. First, the bath. Then, the after."

I couldn't help but wonder about the "after."

Ethan stepped forward, and without preface, gripped my sweater by its hem.

"Arms up," he said, and when I obliged, he pulled the sweater over my head. He tossed it away, then centered his gaze on the silk and satin that covered my breasts, his lips widening in masculine appreciation.

"Patience, Sullivan," I said with a smile, and he growled out his objection. Ethan reached out and put his hands on my waist, sending goose bumps up my arms and a warm tendril of heat through my abdomen.

He cupped my face in his hands and kissed me, smelling of soap and spicy cologne, and my limbs tensed and relaxed at the same time. Ethan knotted his fingers in my hair, his tongue tangling with mine, turning up the intensity of the kiss until I was utterly relaxed—and taut like a bowstring. He put me there, at the knife's edge of tension, which was undoubtedly exactly his plan.

Ethan Sullivan rarely did anything without a plan.

He cupped my silk-covered breast in one hand, and my lips parted. His deft fingers unsnapped the buttons on my jeans, and my core went liquid from wanting.

How was it possible, I wondered, to want someone so much? To feel suddenly empty . . . and yet full of longing?

Without words, he pushed the jeans from my hips, and they pooled in a heap on the floor. His eyes burning like green fire, Ethan wrapped his arms around me and pulled me against the length of his body. He was still clothed, but that was no obstacle to his impressive arousal, which had vaulted between us.

As he kissed me again, I took advantage, arousing him through the slick fabric of his trousers until he pulled away, silver eyed and fanged. His hair had loosened, spilling spun gold around his face. The sight of him—aroused and predatory, all pretensions gone—was nearly too much to bear.

Ethan wet his lips. "I promised a bath."

"There's room for two."

He smiled wickedly. "Let's test that theory, Sentinel." He didn't bother with buttons, but pulled his shirt over his head, revealing his flat stomach and rigid abdominals, a chest that begged for touch, for fingertips drifting across curves and planes of skin.

His belt hit the floor, followed by his trousers. And then, wearing silk and cotton, we stood together in the steam, staring at each other, the heavy weight of anticipation between us.

"You first," he said, his feet planted, crossing his arms like a pirate on the swaying deck of a ship of the line.

I could just see the edge of the tattoo that marked the back of Ethan's calf. It was black script, words in a language I didn't recognize, and he'd been demurring an explanation for some time. It seemed unlikely he'd explain it now, and I wasn't about to waste time with unnecessary words or arguments I couldn't win.

I opted instead for a winning move. Playing coy, I turned my back to him, glancing over my shoulder as I freed my breasts.

"Playing the wicked Sentinel this evening, are we?"

"I'm always wicked. But most of the time, I hide it very, very well."

If vampirism had taught me nothing else, it was how to bluff when the time was right.

I removed the rest of the lingerie, giving him a good long look at my body before I dipped a toe into the bath water.

The heat was just shy of excessive, and utterly delicious. I closed my eyes for just a second as the heat sent a delicious shudder through my limbs. Before I opened them again, Ethan was behind me, utterly naked and aroused, his body pressed against mine.

He pressed his lips to my neck, to the spot that I'd sworn was more sensitive than any other on my body, as if vampires had been blessed by an additional erogenous zone, and cupped my breasts in his hands.

His fingers, long and nimble, toyed and teased until I was nearly breathless. But then he was gone, leaving my body cold again. In shock, I glanced behind me, and found his gaze, teasing and tempting.

"Now who's wicked?" he asked.

I humphed and sunk into the bath, the vessel large and deep enough that I could have almost swum to the other side. I found a perch in the corner and crooked a finger at him.

Ethan, smiling his pirate's smile, stepped in, steam rising around his naked body as if the water itself were aflame. Before a second had passed, he disappeared beneath the water, then rose again like an ancient god, skin damp and muscles taut.

Ethan had given me breath, and now he took it away again.

He moved toward me, eyes silver and shining, and captured my waist, pulling me toward him. He engulfed me in a kiss, magic rising as passion grew between us. Ethan wasted no time, claiming me as his own, claiming my body as his. He attacked with passion, using his body as a weapon—the long fingers that roused me to the line between pain and pleasure, the lips that tortured and tempted, the eyes that watched as he pushed me higher, until my body was aflame and pleasure blossomed through me.

I screamed his name, but Ethan didn't concede the victory. He pushed farther, twined my legs around his waist, burying himself inside me, and dropping his head to the nape of my neck to stifle his guttural moan.

"Merit," he whispered, teeth against my sensitive skin.

Ethan found his rhythm, challenging me to rise again, to give up rational thought for feeling, for pure and unbound sensation.

His speed quickened, his breath hitching, his fingers clenched in my skin as he sought his own pleasure, my name on his lips when he found it, grasping me like he couldn't bear to let go again.

For a moment, time stopped, and we lay together in the bath, candlelight dancing around us. And then I was airborne as Ethan lifted me from the water. He wrapped me in satin, heat steaming from our bodies, my eyes wide, my skin passion-flushed.

He placed me on the bed and tucked me into the cloud of soft and cool sheets, then lay down beside me. We held hands as the sun rose, pushing us under.

When the sun rose, we fell asleep in sensual bliss.

But when the sun fell again, we awoke in sloppy abandon.

We lay on our backs, sprawled sideways across the bed. The blankets were tangled around Ethan's feet, and I'd slept with a hand across his face.

Ethan nibbled at my finger to wake me. I pulled my hand back, lest it become vampire breakfast. "Sorry about that. I was out."

"Evidently," he said, sitting up and arching an eyebrow at our positions. "Did we wrestle during the day?"

"Not that I recall," I said, reaching over to pick up pillows from the floor. "Maybe we're having day terrors."

"God forbid," Ethan said. "The night terrors are bad enough."

"Speaking of," I said, "any riot developments while we were asleep?"

Ethan groaned. "To business already, Sentinel? So much for, 'Good morning, Liege. I love you, Liege.'" He managed a remarkably bad imitation of my voice, then feigned sweeping hair over his shoulder.

"I don't do that."

"You do," he said, grinning. "But my larger point still stands."

I rolled my eyes but sat up, sheet strategically around my breasts, and smiled at him. "Good morning, Liege," I said in a husky voice. "I love you, Liege."

"That's more like it," he said, then snatched up his phone from the nightstand and scanned it. He might not have appreciated the abrupt change of subject, but he knew my question was a legit one.

"Nothing new," he answered after a moment. "They're still cleaning up Wicker Park. There should be plenty for you to peruse tonight."

"Fortunate for the rioters they didn't make their way to Little Red. That wouldn't have gone well for them with Gabriel in residence."

"I imagine you're right," Ethan said. "The shifters avoid drama when they can, but they are not afraid to face a foe head-on. It would have been bad for the humans and, in the aftermath, the Pack. Violence, in my experience, only begets more violence."

I picked up his free hand and ran a finger over his knuckles, noting the scars that mottled the skin there. Ethan had been a soldier in his human life, and the scars might have come from his military service. As quickly as we healed, some scars remained. The pucker on his chest where a stake had punctured his heart was evidence of that.

"Is the city heading toward something?" I wondered aloud.

He stilled. "You feel it, too?"

His response shocked and scared me. He was supposed to say my question was silly. Overreactive, even. That he didn't dismiss the feeling only validated it, and I found I didn't want my paranoia to be validated.

"It feels like things are building to a head," he said. "The pressure rising. I don't know when the inevitable explosion will occur, and I'm not sure who will be involved, but there seems little doubt the violence will continue to rise. We have asked humans to put up with much. Celina. Tate. Mallory. And they've demonstrated they will not go gently into that good night forever."

"They certainly weren't going gently in Wicker Park last night."

"No," he agreed. "And perhaps we are being overly pessimistic. Perhaps Wicker Park was an isolated incident. Perhaps the tide has not turned completely, and will not turn at all. But if it does . . ."

He didn't finish the thought, which didn't need finishing at any rate. Humans had a long and bloodied history of destroying perceived enemies, even if the perception was only that.

"I hate to bring up another unpleasant subject," he said, "but there's an administrative matter we should attend to."

"Administrative?"

Ethan reached out and pulled a cream linen envelope from his nightstand. "I didn't want to mention this last night, given what you'd been through." He handed the envelope to me. "Open it."

Curious, but also nervous—he was building this up quite a bit—I slid a finger beneath the envelope's flap and pulled out a card in the same thick, cream-colored stock.

It was an invitation to dinner at my parents' house.

For both of us.

I made a low whistle. My family and I weren't close, owing

largely to the tense relationship between my father and me. He was controlling and manipulative; I was the rebel daughter he hadn't quite wanted. He was also the reason, at least indirectly, that I'd been made a vampire, and without my consent.

On the other hand, I'd promised my father that I'd visit my older brother, Robert, and it would be nice to see my sister, Charlotte, and her brood again.

Still. Dinner at my parents' house? With Ethan? That would mean a lot of Merit eyes on our relationship.

Ethan, who'd been silent while I mulled over the invite, tapped it with a finger. "What do you think?"

"I'm not entirely sure." I glanced over at him. "Dinner at my parents' would be two hours of pure and unmitigated discomfort."

"Because you and your father have a history?"

"And because they'll probably spend the evening dissecting our relationship."

"I believe that only makes them human, darling."

"And it would be formal," I added, pointing for emphasis. "With fancy food and cocktail attire. We'd have to use salad forks."

"Instead of eating a sandwich out of a napkin, you mean?"

I elbowed him but smiled. I hadn't exactly adopted my family's formalisms. I appreciated the advantages I'd had growing up as a Merit in Chicago, but unlike Charlotte and Robert, I'd found the lifestyle—and the strictures of wealth—completely stifling. Pumas and jeans and Chicago red hots were much more my style than Emily Post manners and crystal goblets.

"I'm unfussy," I said.

"I know. And I appreciate that about you. But try as you might, you cannot choose your family or give them back. I think we should do it."

"I don't know."

"You could wear a cocktail dress."

"You're not selling this very well."

"I could remove the cocktail dress afterward as a reward for good behavior."

I paused. "You're getting warmer."

"I'll throw in a sneak peak at the new House pendants."

I sat up. "They're done?"

"They are. And they're quite lovely."

Now that was an interesting offer. When we left the GP, we'd turned in our House medals, the gold pendants that provided our House position and number. They were the equivalent of vampiric dog tags, and I felt naked without one. (Granted, I had an inadvertent backup copy in the bottom of a drawer, but since I couldn't let anyone else know it existed, much less wear it, it didn't really count.)

Ethan had promised us a replacement, something to mark our House membership, even if we were no longer members of the GP. He and Malik, his second in command, had been researching and pricing options, but they hadn't yet announced their decision. And he was offering to let me be the first to see? Granted, I'd get to see the pendants eventually, but as he well knew, I was not a patient person.

"Throw in a box of Mallocakes and you've got a deal."

Ethan arched an eyebrow. "Mallocakes? That's the best you can do?"

Mallocakes were a favorite snack cake. "World peace is out, Gabriel probably won't let you buy Moneypenny for me, and I've already got these sweet digs."

"Moneypenny?" Ethan's lips twisted in amusement.

"She looks like a James Bond car. I think it's only appropriate that she get a James Bond name."

"Notwithstanding that, you're correct. I cannot give you, *ahem*, Moneypenny. But a box of Mallocakes is a manageable deal."

"When is this nightmare supposed to occur?" I asked, glancing back at the invitation. "Oh good. Tomorrow. So I have plenty of time to emotionally prepare."

Ethan ignored that. "Shall I arrange for a dress?"

"I can dress myself."

He gave me a flat look.

I punched him in the arm, deservedly. "I can dress myself," I reiterated. "But we also know that you're unusually good at picking out formalwear." He'd arranged dresses for me—all in classic Cadogan black—on other occasions, when he still doubted I was mature enough to select an appropriately formal ensemble for a fancy party. This for a girl who'd had an official coming out and debutante ball.

"I believe the word you used was 'stodgy.'"

"And I meant it," I said with a grin, pressing a kiss to his lips. "I'm getting up. Feel free to ask Margot to bring up breakfast. Croissants? Crêpes? Café Americano?" I suggested, with exaggerated accents.

"You are officially spoiled."

"I prefer to think of it as honoring the system."

Ethan laughed, and loudly. "That was unusually politic."

I faked a look of dismay. "Maybe we've been spending too much time together."

He pinched my waist, which made me yelp.

"Kidding," I said. "Kidding. I clearly could do no better than to learn from your fine example of what it is to be a vampire."

"I don't like where this is going."

"An earnest vampire," I said, continuing to spread the love. "A leader of vampires. And one, perhaps, that is open to unusual arrangements."

"What do you want, Merit?"

"So, while we're discussing uncomfortable things, I had an unusual conversation with Mallory."

He looked at me, clearly waiting for the shoe to drop.

"She wants to work for Cadogan House."

Ethan stiffened. "No."

"I know," I said, holding out my hands in détente. "I know. It's worrisome. I'm only passing the idea along. That said, we'd be able to keep an eye on her, and we're still looking for guards."

"No," he repeated, just as firmly.

"I'm not going to mention you said that. Not until we can give her an alternative idea." I climbed off the bed and glanced back at him. "At some point, the shifters will be done with their intern, and the Order has proved they can't handle her. We need a backup plan."

Ethan scrubbed his hands over his face. "I hate it when you're right."

I bit back a grin that only would have gotten me into trouble, and let my mouth do it for me. "Then you must hate me often."

I disappeared into the bathroom before Ethan could throttle me.

The bathroom, like the bedroom, was a bit of a shambles. I picked up clothes from the floor before getting dressed for the night, brushing my fangs like a good little Sentinel, and ensuring my weapons—my thirty-two-inch-long tempered-steel katana and the smaller, double-edged dagger Ethan had given me—were clean and ready for battle.

Not that I planned on a battle, but since a visit to a crime scene was on my agenda, I was damn well going to keep my weapons in good shape.

The bedroom was empty, but the croissants had been stocked, by the time I was dressed and armed. I grabbed a pastry and nibbled the edge while I checked my phone for messages from Jeff, Catcher, or Jonah.

I had no messages, but the phone was bristling with warnings and alerts from Luc's newest invention—an app that sent House notifications and updates for news around the city.

Most of the notifications were mundane—information about House deliveries and visitors, traffic snarls, and weather reports. But tonight there was another little reminder—a news flash sent out by the *Sun-Times* reminding readers that the Office of Human Liaisons was hosting its first town hall meeting tonight at the Marquesa Theater.

Now that was intriguing. The Marquesa was in Lincoln Park, a neighborhood on the north side of Chicago. It also wasn't terribly far from Wicker Park and the crime scene I'd be visiting.

My phone beeped again, and I found a text message from Catcher: VISIT TO ROBIN POPE, THEN BRYANT INDUSTRIES?

I guessed Jeff had declined to play escort, and Catcher had taken up the standard.

I passed the phone back and forth in my hands, considering my options. I definitely wanted to talk to Robin Pope about Bryant Industries and the riots. I also wanted to visit Bryant Industries and take a look at the destruction myself.

But there was also another stop I wanted to make, a conversation I wanted to have with a man who'd caused plenty of pain and suffering to Chicago vampires.

SURE, I responded to Catcher. MEET IN 1 HOUR?

I figured I didn't need much time at the Marquesa Theater. Maybe just long enough to put in an appearance, and remind him we were watching.

Catcher texted me Pope's address, and he agreed to meet me there in an hour.

With Catcher on my mind, I sent a message to Mallory: EVERY-
THING OK, BLUE HAIR?

I waited for a moment for her to answer, but smiled when
she did.

GABRIEL POUTING, BUT HAIR STILL BLUE, she reported.

She'd be fine, I decided. At least until she could find a route
out of Shifterville.

When I was dressed and armed, I walked down to the first floor
and advised Luc and Ethan I was heading out for my site visits. I
also gave Luc Robin Pope's address, just in case of an emergency
that I hoped wouldn't arise.

I walked to the front door, nearly forgetting my Volvo replacement wasn't parked on the street, but was tucked into its basement space.

Its warm and snow- and ice-free basement space.

That was yet another bit of high living I could definitely get
used to.

CHAPTER SEVEN

ONCE MORE INTO THE BREACH

The Marquesa Theater was a souvenir from Chicago's history. There were baroque balconies, red velvet curtains, giant chandeliers, and murals galore. All of it, supposedly, built to give the moll of a Chicago gangster a place to sing arias no one else wanted to hear. The motive might have been regrettable, but you couldn't deny the beauty of the place.

Tonight, that beauty was marred by a mix of fear and suspicion. I stood in the lobby and watched people of every variety march into the theater, their expressions dubious, as if they might be attacked at any moment by lingering vampires and shifters, as if we weren't citizens who paid taxes and were as much a part of the town as they were.

Maybe they were simply ignorant. Maybe they'd been raised on prejudice. Either way, I doubted McKetrick would offer them solace or comfort, or remind them that we had coexisted in Chicago for centuries. McKetrick had made a deliberate and conscious choice to hate us, if the look I'd seen in his eyes last night was any indication. Tonight, he would probably raise questions. He would probably imply we were troublemakers, that Chicago was worse off with us, and subtly encourage them to reach the same conclusions.

My heart began to race, and my palms moistened with fear. I'd left my sword in the car, thinking it would be more a liability than help in a building crowded with humans. Maybe I also should have warned Luc or Ethan—or even Catcher—that I was coming. Maybe I should have considered what, precisely, I was going to do if I managed to corner McKetrick.

I glanced through the front doors as a black limo pulled to the curb.

My target had arrived.

Heart pounding, I walked outside through the current of people flowing into the building, the wind swirling briskly in the February evening. A blocky man in a dark suit opened the limo's back door, and McKetrick climbed out. He wore a well-fitted suit and tie, but the skin still stretched awkwardly across the scarred portion of his face, drawing the attention of passersby.

He steadfastly avoided making eye contact with anyone but the man who'd opened the door—likely a bodyguard, given the vibration of steel around him—and another guard who quickly appeared at his side. But it took only a moment for him to see me, to realize that I was watching him.

I was fifteen feet from the car, but when our gazes locked, the world seemed to shrink around us.

I'd met, not long ago, two fallen angels—one virtuous, one not— who'd been joined together by a freakish act of magic. In the instant McKetrick and I made eye contact, I had a distinct mental image of the eviler angel, Dominic, sitting on my shoulder, imploring me to step forward and end the man who'd caused so much pain to vampires. He was responsible for the deaths of men and women who'd done nothing more than exist, which he apparently took as a personal affront. He'd hired an assassin, and he was now engaged in spreading hate around the city.

He didn't deserve his position, or his limo, or his bodyguards.

My imaginary devil was insistent, but I knew better. Killing an unarmed man wouldn't make me better than him. It would make me just like him.

I wouldn't hurt him—not here and now. But that didn't mean I wouldn't do what vampires did best.

Manipulate.

McKetrick's jaw locked; his gaze narrowed. One of the bodyguards, apparently aware of his boss's sudden irritation, glanced at me.

"Sir?" he asked.

"She's fine," McKetrick assured them. "We're well acquainted. Could you give us a minute?"

The guards looked at him for a moment, obviously concerned by the request, but he was the boss, so they relented. McKetrick and I moved closer and they moved past us, creating a barrier between us and the rest of the crowd.

"I'm surprised to see you here," McKetrick said. "I'm glad you've come to hear what the rest of Chicago thinks of you."

"As you well know, we aren't a threat to Chicago or anyone else. We're trying to live, to love, to go about our business. You're spreading discord because you like being the center of attention."

"You think the violence in this city isn't because of you?"

"If you mean last night's riot, it had nothing to do with us. It had to do with humans. Humans who were willingly destroying their neighbors' property and businesses because they've been told we're the reason for their misery."

McKetrick buttoned up his suit coat. "And how do you know that, Merit? Were you at the riot?"

I had been, of course, but only inadvertently. But I wasn't about to admit it to McKetrick; he'd hardly believe the excuse.

"The riot was *against* vampires," I reiterated, "not because of them. You're helping fuel the fire, McKetrick, and one of these days, it's going to come back on you."

His smile was a dare. "Are you threatening me?"

"Not at all. Just reminding you." I gestured toward the theater. "The people in there might believe you. They might think you're here for them. But we all know the truth. You're here for you, and you alone. And maybe not tonight, maybe not tomorrow, but one day, they're going to realize the type of person you really are."

"That doesn't sound so scary," he said, smiling with reptilian ease.

I gave him back a smile that was equally predatory. "Maybe not. But do remember one thing." I leaned in. "Whatever happens between us down the road, I'm immortal. And you, Mr. McKetrick, are not."

McKetrick opened his mouth to retort, but before he could speak, the guards moved back to us.

"Time to go, sir," said the guard who'd opened the door, hustling him toward the theater.

McKetrick, I was pleased to see, had a little less swagger in his step.

My interaction with McKetrick wasn't a victory. It wasn't even a three-point lead. I'd been, at most, a temporary mild irritant. But maybe—hopefully—I'd reminded him of the stakes (pun very much intended) and the fact that we were paying attention. And specifically—paying attention to him.

That mission accomplished, I drove to Robin Pope's Greektown address, which wasn't far from Lincoln Park.

Robin Pope's building was a fairly new, sleek tower of condos, with coffee shops and other retail on the first floor. I didn't know much about her background, but it seemed an affluent building, not bad for a woman who'd given up her job over a personal dispute.

I parked on the street and left my katana in the car—there were too many cops undoubtedly suspicious about vampires right now to risk pulling it out—but double-checked my dagger was securely tucked into my boot.

I locked the door, glancing back to ensure I'd parked it close enough to the curb to protect it from traffic, but not so close I wouldn't be able to get out without marring the rims. Moneypenny, it seemed, was going to be a high-maintenance mode of transportation. For a moment—a very brief moment—I longed for my Volvo.

At the sound of a car door slamming, I glanced behind me. Catcher emerged from his sedan in jeans and a leather jacket. He was tall and lean, with a shaved head and pale green eyes. He was undeniably handsome, but since his features were usually pulled into irritated frowns or glares, it was sometimes difficult to tell.

Tonight, Catcher wore a typically grim expression as he looked over the building. I gestured toward it, ready to get the show on the road, and we fell into step together.

"I hear you're taking your vampire home to meet the parents."

A surprising revelation, since I'd heard it myself only a little while ago. "How did you hear about that?"

"Your grandfather told me. Ethan RSVP'd, and your father passed along the good news. You're a brave girl."

"Ethan will be perfectly well behaved. It's my family I have to worry about."

"Your father?" Catcher asked.

"More my mom and sister. They'll start obsessing about Chicago wedding locations and whether we should select gold- or platinum-banded china patterns."

Catcher snorted. "I'd almost pay to see Sullivan's footwork on that one. It's bound to be impressive."

"Probably so," I agreed. "Anything I need to know before we go in there? Is she a black belt in martial arts? Does she carry a crossbow? Is Buffy the Vampire Slayer her personal savior?"

"Because that would bum you out?"

"The slaying part would, yeah. Not the Joss part. We all love Joss."

"Her background's clean," Catcher said. "She's got a degree in human resources, but most of her jobs have been admin or lower management. She didn't last long in any one position."

"Sounds like she has trouble playing nice with others. Did she file grievances against anybody else?"

"Not that I could tell. She'd been at Bryant Industries for four months. We can get details on her time there from Charla."

"Charla?"

"Charla Bryant. Her family owns Bryant Industries." We reached the front doors, and Catcher opened one, gesturing for me to precede him inside.

The foyer was dark and sleek and still smelled like new construction: lumber, paint, and adhesives. I liked that smell; it reminded me of childhood trips with my grandfather to the hardware store.

We passed an empty security desk and headed for a bank of elevators. Catcher pushed a button, and we stood in silence until the elevator dinged and the door opened up.

"So what's our backstory with this lady?" I asked when we were in the elevator and moving upward.

"Backstory? What do you mean?"

"Well, we don't have badges, and we're both supernaturals. She isn't going to just up and divulge her nefarious rioting plot, certainly not to us. If we want information from her, we're going to need a convincing backstory."

"In other words, we need to lie."

"That sounds much less pleasant, but yeah."

"You really are a vampire, aren't you?"

That comment was worth the slugging I gave him. "We need to figure out if she's connected to the riots. So, we play like we're vampire haters?"

"Can you do that convincingly?"

I smiled with saccharine sweetness. "I'm sure you can cover for me if I can't. But yeah, I think I can pull it off. I'll just remember some of my initial hatred for Darth Sullivan."

"Have you ever told Ethan you called him that?"

"I have not. And you won't, either, if you know what's good for you. I'm not above biting a sorcerer."

"I'm taken," he flatly said, although I actually took that as a pretty good sign regarding his relationship with Mallory.

We reached the eleventh floor, and the elevator opened into a hallway with muted paint, and carpet in a complicated and probably expensive pattern. A round pedestal table sat in the middle of the elevator area, topped by a vase of very tall trailing flowers.

I followed Catcher to a door near the end of the hall. He lifted his hand to knock, but paused to glance at me. "You ready?"

I nodded, and he tapped gently on the door.

A few seconds later, she opened the door. She was an attractive middle-aged woman with neatly styled hair, blouse tucked into jeans, and high-heeled boots. Her makeup was impeccable, and large diamonds twinkled in her ears.

If this was Robin Pope, she wasn't exactly what I'd expected. Overt bitterness tucked into a VAMPIRES SUCK T-shirt, maybe. But the woman and the apartment behind her seemed posh and completely devoid of an anti–Bryant Industries or anti-vampire sentiment. There were dark wood floors and sleek midcentury modern furniture.

"Hi," I said. "Sorry to bother you. We're looking for Robin Pope?"

"That's me." She smiled a little. "What's this about?"

"We're really sorry to bother you. We just—we hoped you could help us with something. We understand you used to work at Bryant Industries?"

"That's right," she said, her smile fading. "But I have a lawyer now, so any inquiries regarding that situation should go through him."

"That's actually why we're here," I said, feigning discomfort. I gestured at Catcher. "We heard about your grievance, and, well, we kind of agree with you."

"Oh?" she asked. "About what, exactly?"

Catcher and I exchanged a glance and a nod.

"Vampires," he said. "We think they're getting special treatment, ahead of working-class folks like us, and we don't think that's fair."

"We saw your grievance online," I said, "and we thought, well, maybe she's someone we could talk to, you know?"

She looked at us for a moment, probably evaluating whether we were telling her the truth. Whether we were like her, or leading her on for some endgame she couldn't yet see.

"And you're who, exactly?"

Well, I should have prepared for that. "I'm Mary," I said, tossing out the first name that came to mind. "And this is my brother . . . Boudreau."

"Mary and Boudreau," she repeated, obviously dubious, so I laid it on a bit thicker.

"I was hurt by vampires before. Attacked by one of them one night, with no warning." That was the absolute truth. "I was hoping to find someone to talk to, someone who would understand. I ran across your case, and I thought—there's someone who *knows*."

She looked at us again. A door opened and closed a few apartments away, and her eyes flicked nervously to the sound. She peeked into the hallway and seemed satisfied when footsteps disappeared down the hall.

"Maybe we shouldn't talk about this in the hallway. You never know who's listening. I have to be somewhere soon, but you can come in for a minute."

It wasn't much of an invitation, but it would work well enough for vampiric purposes. I walked into the condo, keeping my eyes peeled for inflammatory propaganda or anti-vampire ninjas. Instead, there were tasteful Danish furnishings and décor. A lot of brass and wood and sparse lines.

Catcher followed me inside, and as Robin turned around to lock the door behind us, he mouthed, *Be careful*. They were words I intended to obey.

When she turned back to us, her expression had changed completely. Now, behind closed doors, there was a glimmer of obvious excitement in her eyes.

"I am definitely someone you can talk to," she said.

"Good," I said, only partly feigning relief. It would have been a relief to find the perpetrator of an anti-vampire riot on the first take. Opportunities like that didn't arise very often.

"It's all about special interest groups," she said. "It's about the money. The vampires have it; the humans want it. Having the money means they get to run roughshod over the rest of us, because all the human politicians want to get their greedy little sausage fingers around it."

The factual errors aside, and there were a number of them, Robin got through her entire spiel without taking a breath. Both made me downgrade my initial impression of her stability.

"Huh," Catcher said, crossing his arms and looking extremely interested in what she had to say. "And that's what was going on at Bryant Industries?"

"You think a place that supplies vampire blood could have been open for so long without being part of a conspiracy? Without the manager sleeping with the mayor, or significant payoffs?"

"Payoffs?" Catcher asked, lowering his voice to a conspiratorial whisper. "You have records of that?"

"Somewhere," she said, gesturing flippantly to another part of the room. "They thought I'd play ball, and when I didn't, they thought they could throw me out like trash. But I'm not about to cave to pressure. I know what's right, and I know what's legal. My sister is a lawyer."

"Is that why they pressured you to leave?" I asked, choosing my words carefully. I wasn't sure how much of her diatribe I believed, but she was clearly convinced.

"They *fired* me," she said, "because I found out who they were and what they were doing."

"And you confronted them," I said, "like any good citizen would do."

"Exactly," she said, pointing a finger at me. "That's *exactly* what I did. They think they can skirt the rules, while the rest of us have to follow them? Is that fair?"

"It's not fair," Catcher said. "I don't know if you heard, but there was an attack on Bryant Industries last night."

She stilled and looked at both of us again. "Who did you say you are again?"

"Mary and Boudreau," Catcher said. "We're just looking for folks who think like us, I guess you could say."

As far as I knew, we hadn't slipped up, and we hadn't given her any reason to doubt us.

She reached a different conclusion. She bolted, running for the front door.

"Merit!" Catcher prompted.

"On it," I said, racing after her. But Robin Pope wasn't unprepared for a vampire engagement. She reached a ceramic umbrella stand beside the door and pulled out a wooden stake as long as a baseball bat. Aspen through the heart was the only wood that could kill us, and I had a sinking feeling Robin Pope knew that quite well.

She thrust out the stake like a fencer trying to win a point. I dodged her first shot, but not the return slap, which slammed into my shin with enough force to bring tears to my eyes. I doubled over in pain, and Robin used my distraction to her advantage, flipping the deadbolt and opening the door. She ran into the hallway, the stake still in hand.

"Little help," I said to Catcher.

"Vampire fail," he muttered, running into the hallway after Robin. I limped after them, an electric tingle in Catcher's wake as he gathered his magic in preparation for an assault.

By the time I made it into the hallway, Robin had reached the bank of elevators and moved behind the pedestal table, plucking up the vase of flowers.

"Robin—Ms. Pope," Catcher called out, cautiously moving forward. "We just wanted to talk to you."

But Catcher's attempt at a détente didn't dissuade him from continuing to power up. My hair lifted in the cloud of magic he brought to bear, spinning it together in the palm of his hand into an orb of glowing blue light.

"Get thee behind me, Satan!" she yelled out, throwing the vase at us. It hit the floor hallway between Pope and Catcher, shattering across the floor.

He didn't wait for another attack but launched the magic at her.

Paranoid or not, Robin Pope wasn't helpless, and she wasn't about to go down swinging. She wrenched a round mirror from the wall near the table, then dropped to one knee, using the mirror like a shield.

Magic and mirrors didn't mix, a fact I knew all too well. I'd actually used the trick on Mallory during her Unfortunate Crazy Times, although Catcher hadn't been there to see the trick, and apparently didn't know about it.

The ball of blue energy hit the glass . . . and bounced right back toward us.

"Crap," Catcher said, yanking me to the ground just as the ball of magic flew over our heads. It grazed my ponytail, singeing the edges and sending the scent of burning hair into the air.

The fireball hit the fire door behind us, exploding with a sound like the firing of a jet engine, the force throwing open the door hard enough that it clanged against the back wall.

"Good Lord, man!" I said. "Are you trying to kill us?" I swatted at the sparks in my hair, wincing as the sparks bit into my fingertips.

"It would have only disabled her. The mirror must have distorted the magic."

"Yeah, well," I said, glancing up just in time to see Robin disappear through the fire door at the other end of the hallway. "She's getting away."

"Little busy here," Catcher muttered behind me. When I looked back, he was stomping out sparks in the carpet behind us.

Robin Pope was gone, and we'd just torched a hallway in a very posh apartment building. I could only imagine the shit we were both going to get when our bosses found out how poorly this particular mission had gone.

"So much for Robin Pope not having any fighting skills," I said.

Catcher stepped out a final bit of smoldering ash and glanced back at me. "I didn't know she did. It didn't turn up in her background search."

"I think it's safe to say she knows something."

He nodded. "She's involved in it. We don't have the resources to tail her. I'll talk to Chuck about getting Jacobs involved. I'll also have Jeff run a deeper background, see if she has any other connections to the rioters, a Web site, whatever."

I swirled a finger in the air, gesturing at the burn marks on the carpet and bubbled paint on the door. "I think we also let the condo association believe Ms. Pope was at fault here with all this. Pope's a cowardly racist; I'm not letting her off the hook for that. She can pay for a little paint and carpet."

"A lot of carpet, actually," Catcher grimly said. "And technically, she was at fault. The damage only happened because she attacked you and bolted."

A siren began to wail in the distance.

"And that's our cue to exit," I said.

"Agreed," Catcher said, glancing back at the crispy door. "Fire exit?"

"It seems appropriate." The pain in my shin was already beginning to subside, so I half limped, half ran to the fire door and followed Catcher down the stairs.

"Ha-ha," he said.

"Vampires have a highly developed sense of humor. What building would you like to destroy next?"

"None. But I want to visit the one that was nearly destroyed. Let's see what Ms. Bryant has to say about her former employee."

I got into the car and rolled back into traffic and away from the scene, trying my best to look completely uninterested in the CPD cruisers that passed me, lights blazing.

I hopped onto the freeway, heading northwest for Wicker Park, and didn't stop checking my rearview mirror until I'd reached the Milwaukee Avenue exit. I pulled into the first parking lot I could find, then took a breath and picked up my phone.

There was no message from Jonah, which I took as a good sign, even with the blacklisting. If he'd discovered something really important, he'd have found a way to get the information to us.

I called the Ops Room, hoping to get Luc, and possibly Ethan, on the phone.

"Jimmy's House of Vampires," Luc answered, in a really poor Bronx accent.

"That was unimpressive," I said, "but our visit with Robin Pope was not. She thinks the Bryants are involved in a conspiracy—paying off government employees and maybe sleeping with them to stay open—and she bolted when we mentioned it."

"That's good stuff," Luc said. "Except that when you say 'bolted,' it sounds like she got away from you and Catcher. A vampire and a sorcerer with extreme magical powers."

"Which, it turns out, don't work that well indoors," I said. "And she did get away from us, after a minor battle in her apartment building's hallway. But her behavior was suspicious enough that Catcher thinks the CPD will be interested. He's going to make the call."

"I like the part about the CPD involvement," he said. "I'm less crazy about the 'minor battle' bit. Did anyone see you there?"

"Other than Pope, not that I'm aware of. Security desk was empty."

"Where are you heading next?"

"The distribution center. I'm halfway there."

"Be careful," he said. "It sounds like you've already had a full night."

"Fuller than I'd intended," I admitted. "And feel free not to mention that to Ethan. He'd only worry."

Luc snorted. "He'll worry regardless. It's his job to worry. But you're right—no sense in adding to the night's list. And keep us posted."

I assured him I would, and I hoped the next report would leave me feeling considerably less guilty.

Unlike the hallway of the building in Greektown, Wicker Park actually looked better than it had last night. Broken windows had been boarded up, battered cars had been moved, and streetlights had been repaired. It was surprisingly quick work for a city often slogged by bureaucracy.

I hadn't seen Bryant Industries the night before, or ever that I recalled. The building was easy enough to spot—a large, low structure surrounded by a tidy hedge.

The damage was easy to spot, too. Half the front was a blackened husk, from the door, which sat right in the middle, across one side. Charred interior beams were visible through the gap in the front, and they hung down at odd angles. The rest of the building bore marks from the fire and smoke, and the small lawn in front was littered with blackened debris. Yellow police tape kept members of the press and curious onlookers away from the building.

I pulled into a parking spot on the street. Snow and ice crunching beneath my feet, I quickly crossed the street toward the building and the crowd. The smell of smoke and charred wood grew stronger as I moved, along with something else . . . the copper smell of blood.

I was walking toward a blood distribution center, and I hadn't bothered to drink blood before leaving the House. The croissant I'd grabbed on the way out wasn't doing much. I felt a sudden perk of vampiric interest, and my stomach rumbled ominously. I'd been so busy thinking about the motivations for the crime that I hadn't prepared myself for it. That had been thoughtless, but there was nothing to do about it now except try to maintain control and hope I didn't fang out in front of the human bystanders.

I sucked in a breath, promised myself a liter of blood when I made it back to the House, and waved at Catcher, who stood at the edge of the crowd, scanning it as if looking for clues.

"Enjoying the show?" I asked.

"As much as one enjoys watching idiocy," he grumbled, then gave me a sideways glance. "Do you notice anything unusual here?"

I glanced around, assuming I was being tested, and trying to figure out exactly what he was looking for. Ironically, I guessed he wasn't referring to anything present at the scene, but what was missing.

"There's not a single protestor here," I said.

"There's not a single protestor here," he agreed. "They went to the trouble to firebomb the place, and they didn't even show up to protest afterward? What's the point?"

"Grandpa said they lawyered up. Their lawyers probably advised them to stay away."

"Maybe," he allowed. "Or maybe this isn't about vampires, not really. Maybe this is about a crazy lady and her vendetta against her employer."

"I presume you told my grandfather about Robin Pope?"

"I did. He's calling Jacobs, thinking he'll be interested enough to at least bring her in for questioning."

"Excellent."

Catcher nodded and looked back at the smoldering building. "I suppose she's technically innocent until proved guilty, but innocent people, in my experience, don't tend to run. At least not when they're well-heeled northsiders living in a posh apartment building."

I nodded and stuffed my hands into my pockets, although that didn't help with the rest of my freezing body parts. The temperature was dropping, and my ears had begun to ache with cold.

"I assume we're out here because we're waiting for someone from Bryant Industries?"

"Ms. Bryant herself. And there she is," Catcher pleasantly added.

A woman appeared on the lawn. She was tall, with a wide smile, dark eyes, and ebony skin. Her straight hair swept her shoulders, and even while standing in the rubble of the building, she looked smartly dressed in a fitted red trench coat and black patent galoshes. She was, as far as I could tell, quite human.

Catcher moved forward through the crowd to the edge of the tape, and gestured to get her attention. At the sight of him, the woman nodded and walked toward us, raising the police tape so we could walk through.

"Charla Bryant," she said, extending her hand.

"Merit," I said. "I'm from Cadogan House. And this is Catcher. He's from—well, currently, my grandfather's house."

"We've met," Catcher said, and Charla smiled at me.

"We're well acquainted with your grandfather, Merit. He handled several issues on our behalf when he served as Ombudsman." She looked at Catcher. "It's a shame you aren't official anymore."

"We couldn't agree more," Catcher said, casting a glance back at the building. "I hope no one was injured?"

"Fortunately, no," Charla said. "We were between shifts, and in the middle of a company-wide meeting." Charla looked sadly back at the building. "No lives lost, but the building will never be the same. Let's have a look, shall we?"

We followed her toward the front door—or what was left of it. The smells of singed wood and plastic, and the low note of blood, grew stronger.

"The first bottle was thrown here," she said, gesturing at the door. "On its own, it wasn't terribly powerful. Less a blast than a source of fire. But they threw the second about fifteen feet away." She gestured farther down the wall. "The fire breached the building's propane line, which caused the explosions."

That explained the *booms* we'd heard.

"The fires eventually merged, and that's what caused most of the damage to the building."

"Do you have security tapes?" I asked.

"We do, although some of the cameras were damaged by the fire." Her eyes narrowed. "If you need a visual of the attack, it won't be hard to find on the Web. The protestors weren't exactly shy about taping their handiwork."

"So we saw," Catcher said. "But the videos could help us, if you can get them."

Charla nodded. "My brother, Alan, is also involved in the business. He has a biology background, so he handles research and development and oversees our lab work. He's also in charge of security. I'll see what he can do."

"How long have you been around?"

"In one form or another, since 1904. We've been in this building since the sixties."

"How many people know what you actually do?" I asked.

"Obviously all of our employees," she said. "But they stay quiet about it. We try to treat them well—pay them well—in return. That's part of our policy. If something had been off in that direction, we'd know it."

She looked back at us. "Did you see the mayor's press conference? And McKetrick's? Very disturbing stuff. How they think supernaturals would have been involved in this is completely beyond me. What benefit would they possibly have in endangering their own blood supply?"

"That's a very good question," Catcher said. "Which is why we tend to think this is about humans. We understand one of your former employees, Robin Pope, filed a grievance against the company. What can you tell us about that?"

Charla's expression shuttered, and the pleasant smile evaporated.

"Robin Pope, if you'll excuse my frankness, is an ignorant bully. If she didn't get her way on the smallest issue, she complained up the chain of command until someone finally caved. She cannot conceive of the possibility she's wrong, much less tolerate constructive criticism. She bullied her colleagues—even away from the office—and invented conspiracies to justify her behavior."

"You fired her?" Catcher prompted.

"We did. Her little grievance is the result of it. She claims she was fired because we love vampires and, thereby, hate humans, including her. That everyone else we employ is human didn't seem to cross her mind."

"That must have been irritating," I said.

"It was infuriating," Charla agreed. "Do you think she's involved?"

"I think it's an awfully big coincidence if she isn't," Catcher said.

"Do you think she's capable of it?" I asked Charla.

"I don't want to give her too much credit," she said, "but she didn't seem the violent type."

"You did say she bullied your employees," I said.

"Well, yes, but that was small scale. She left a nasty note on someone's car. Made a few unsettling phone calls. They were more about having uncovered the truth—and making sure that someone believed her—than violence. Firebombing the building because she was angry? I don't know about that." I wouldn't have figured Robin Pope for attempting to prick me with an aspen stake and then running like a fugitive, but I didn't mention that to Charla.

She scratched absently at a spot on her shoulder. "But maybe you're right. Maybe we were all fooled."

"What about any other threats against the business?" Catcher asked. "Harassing e-mails? Phone calls? Anything that would suggest you'd been targeted specifically?"

"Nothing at all. No communications, phone calls, anything. Not a single e-mail."

"What about union disputes?" I asked.

"We aren't unionized," Charla said, "and the union hasn't shown much interest because of our ties to the supernatural. They aren't really sure what to do with us."

"Supply chain issues?" Catcher asked. "Arguments with suppliers or vendors?"

"Our contracts are negotiated annually, and we're right in the middle of the term, so it will be six months before anyone starts complaining. Here's the thing—production is still running. So whoever hit us, if they meant to knock us off-line, didn't know anything about how we operate. They hit the front of the building—where the offices are located—not the back."

"Where the production actually occurs," I said.

"Exactly." She shrugged. "If they wanted to shut us down, they did a pretty crappy job of it. Thank goodness. Almost all of our employees live here, work here in the neighborhood. They take a lot of pride in what they do. We're a very family-oriented company. And speaking of family," she said, as a tall man with dark skin, glasses, and a goatee walked toward us. He was dressed in a perfectly fitting suit, which only added to the sense of business acumen.

"Alan," she said, putting a hand on his arm. "This is Catcher Bell and Merit. They're helping investigate the riots."

"Good to meet you," he said, shaking both of our hands. His handshake was strong, confident. "Thank you for your help."

"Of course," Catcher said. "We're sorry about the trouble and property damage."

"I was just telling them you'd get the security tapes," Charla said.

Alan frowned. "I'm not sure what help they'll be, as they aren't outside the building. They wouldn't show the rioters."

"Even if they don't," Catcher said, "they might help us eliminate theories."

Alan nodded. "I see. Of course. I should be able to get them onto DVDs. I assume that will work for you?"

"Perfectly," Catcher said.

"Charla said you handle the science aspects of the business?" I asked.

"He actually just finished his PhD in December," Charla said. "We're very proud of him."

Alan rolled his eyes affectionately. "It's no big deal."

"What's your degree in?" Catcher asked.

"Biochemistry," he said, gesturing toward the building. "You could say I grew up in the field. I've been heading our R and D division."

"New products in the works?" Catcher asked.

"Always," Charla said with a smile. "But not just new products. We've developed additives to keep blood from spoiling, products to keep the blood in suspension, nutritional enhancements."

"Stronger teeth and shinier coat?" Catcher asked, earning an elbow from me.

But Charla laughed good-naturedly. "That's not far from the truth. Fangs are important to vampires. No reason not to give them a calcium boost."

Catcher smiled. "I'm sure they appreciate it. We should let you get back to work, unless there's anything else you think we should know?"

Charla put her hands on her hips and frowned sadly at the remains of the building. "Only that I wish you could wave a wand, fix this damage, and turn idiots into humanitarians."

"If I had a wand that could do that," Catcher said, "I'd do nothing *but* wave it."

CHAPTER EIGHT

LIKE A GOOD NEIGHBOR,
VAMPIRES ARE THERE

Charla disappeared into the building, and without our escort, the cops shooed us back behind the police tape. We regrouped beside Moneypenny, and looked very sharp doing it.

"Thoughts?" he asked.

"I think we have to wait for the CPD to question Robin Pope. I'm curious to know exactly how pissed she was about losing 'most popular hot dish' at the company potluck."

"Hot dish? What's a hot dish?"

"You know," I said, moving my index fingers in the shape of a square. "A casserole. A hot dish."

"Nobody says hot dish."

I rolled my eyes. "People say hot dish. My roommate at NYU was from Minneapolis. She said it all the time."

Catcher looked far from convinced, but he let it go. For the moment. "Idioms aside, I think you're right, especially since we don't actually have any other leads."

The wind was picking up. I spied a coffee shop across the street; a man with a laptop sat at a table in front, sipping at his mug while he stared out the window. Aspiring novelist looking for inspiration in violence . . . or sociology student with a window on a natural experiment?

"It's cold out here," I said, gesturing toward the café. "Why don't we grab something warm? We can talk shop."

"Sure," Catcher said.

We walked across the hills and valleys of snow to the shop's front door, and then inside. The shop, which was new to me, was just the kind of place I'd have frequented in grad school. Dark and a little cozy, with shabby couches and mismatched chairs and the scents of coffee, cinnamon, and smoke from the roaster. A checkers set was on one small table; saltshakers and other random tchotchkes replaced missing pieces.

We walked to the counter, where Catcher immediately pulled out his wallet.

"Latte, half caf, extra hot, double foam, two shots, soy milk," he rattled off, then looked at me.

"I'm not really sure how I can follow that," I said, before looking over the chalkboard menu and picking something simple. "Hot chocolate?"

The barista looked suddenly tired. "Caramel, salted caramel, mocha, Aztec, dark chocolate, double chocolate, white chocolate, black and white, low cal, fat free, or regular?"

"Regular?"

The clerk seemed utterly unimpressed by my decision, but she rang us up. Ever the gentleman—or at least in coffee bars in February—Catcher paid for both drinks. We waited in silence for them to arrive, then picked them up and tucked into a sitting area along the back wall. Window views were nice, but not in Chicago in the winter. The cold inevitably seeped through, which left you only slightly less chilled than if you'd been outside in the first place.

I took a seat on the couch and curled my feet under me, then sipped my hot chocolate. It was tasty, although the residual warmth from the mug was more valuable than the drink.

"They're going to strike again," Catcher predicted. "The rioters, I mean. There was no event here. No trigger. They weren't reacting to a Super Bowl win or the beating of a civilian. And if there's no trigger, there's a groundswell of rage. That's not the kind of thing that just disappears."

Unfortunately, I couldn't disagree with him. "So how do we stop it? Get a handle on it?"

He shrugged. "By doing the stuff we've discussed. We'll follow up with the CPD, check the security videos. The key here may not be the riot itself, but why this particular place was targeted. This isn't exactly a public hot spot for vampire activity. It's not flashy. Not like Cadogan House, which would have been the obvious, big-name target. There's something to that—to picking this place. I just don't know what it is yet."

I nodded, and we sat quietly for a few minutes, sipping our beverages. "While we're here, can I talk to you about something?"

"What?"

"Our little blue-haired friend? She asked me for a job at Cadogan House."

Catcher looked surprised, which wasn't a common expression for him. "A job?"

"She's contingency planning. Looking for something to do when her time with the shifters is up. She hoped we might have something for her."

"I can't imagine Sullivan took that well."

"He's not thrilled at the idea. She violated the sanctity of his House. And his mind. But I think he also knows *we* need a plan for when she's better. What do you think?"

He looked away; whether it was in thought or fear, I wasn't sure.

"I don't know," he finally said. "I think she's making progress. I think *we're* making progress. I don't want to interrupt it." He paused. "We started dating so fast. Jumped right into it, and into living together. To be honest, when she used the *Maleficium*, I thought I'd made a horrible decision. That I'd totally misjudged her."

I hadn't known how close Catcher had come to breaking up with Mallory, and I wondered if she did.

"And then I saw her with the shifters."

Confused, I looked at him. "You mean washing dishes?"

Catcher made a sarcastic sound. "She's doing more than just washing dishes, Merit."

That was news to me. Everything I'd seen and heard indicated Mallory was doing manual labor while she learned to live with her magic. Neither Mallory nor Gabe had mentioned anything else, even last night.

"So what's she doing?" And why hadn't either one of them told me there was more to it?

"I don't know all the details." Catcher swirled the coffee left in his cup, and I waited him out. "Shifters have a connection to magic that we don't," he finally said. "I think they're helping her learn to channel her magic productively."

"I'm surprised Gabe hasn't told us that."

"He's been playing it off," Catcher said. "Shifters don't involve themselves in the affairs of others; at least, that's what they keep telling themselves. That rep's taken a hit lately, considering his friendships with you and Ethan. And if word got out he was actively helping Mallory, a sorceress, a lot more people would come asking."

I nodded. I understood the reasoning, even though the information probably would have gone a long way toward soothing Ethan—and everyone else who'd had an unfortunate run-in with Mallory.

"And how do you feel about it?" Catcher had been jealous of Simon, Mallory's former tutor. I wondered how he felt about Mallory working with Gabriel and the other brutally attractive shapeshifters.

"It's not my choice," he said. "But it's our obligation."

He offered few words, but they packed a punch. Catcher was letting her work outside his comfort zone in order to prevent the chaos he'd helped facilitate by being inattentive the first time around.

My phone rang, so I pulled it out and checked the screen.

"It's the House," I told Catcher, holding it up to my ear. "Merit."

"Merit." Ethan's voice rang through the phone. "You're on speakerphone."

His tone was serious, and my stomach turned with nerves. "What's wrong?"

"Clean Chicago has fired back up," Luc said. "They're in Wrigleyville. And they're attacking Grey House."

The breath stuttered out of me in shock—then fear. Had we done this? Had we caused this riot by visiting Robin Pope, cluing her in to the direction of our investigation, and letting her get away?

And what about Jonah? As captain of the Grey House guards, he'd be right in the middle of the violence, right in the line of fire. I knew he was capable of handling himself, but that didn't mean I wished him into combat.

"Scott's called the CPD," Luc said. "But they don't have control yet. They're estimating three hundred rioters. He also sent out an SOS for help from other Chicago vampires."

"The GP blacklisted us," I pointed out. "Are we even allowed to help?"

"Blacklisting is between Cadogan and the GP," Ethan said. "Not Cadogan and Grey. That Grey House has not come to our aid does not mean we won't come to theirs. We set the example; we set our own bar. Besides, you've already heard from one Grey House vampire, who risked the blacklist to tell us about it. The barrier's already been breached. They need help, and we'll provide it."

"But that doesn't mean we can be careless," Luc put in. "This is the kind of situation the GP will likely stay out of—too much bad press, too many ways for their hands to get dirty, which they don't care for. But keep an eye out anyway. Just because action by the GP is unlikely doesn't mean it's impossible."

"Luc and Juliet are about to leave for Grey House," Ethan said. "Malik will stay at the House, in the event the rioters are looking for other targets. Lindsey is not to leave his side under any circumstances. Kelley's got command of the guards in our absence. Notify the humans at the gate. I want them on full-alert status. The tunnels are prepared?"

"Cleaned, stocked, and ready," Luc answered. "I'm going to say good-bye to Lindsey; then I'm heading to the car."

My heart clenched. Luc was saying good-bye—not just because he was leaving the House, but because he was leaving the House for possible battle.

"What do you want me to do?" I asked.

"Wait for me," Ethan said. "I'm already en route, and I'll meet you there."

The last place I wanted my boyfriend—and the Master I'd taken an oath to protect—was in the middle of a war zone.

"I suppose there's no point in arguing with you about this?"

"There is not," Ethan said, his tone firm. "So don't bother."

"Where should I meet you?"

"I'll talk to Luc and select a spot. We'll text you coordinates. Where are you currently?"

"At a coffeehouse with Catcher, across the street from Bryant Industries."

"Stay put until we send the location," Luc said. "I don't want you heading in blind."

"Roger that," I said. I didn't want to head in blind, either.

The call ended, and I looked at Catcher. "I suppose you got the gist?"

He held his phone out, revealing a message from my grandfather: GREY HOUSE UNDER ATTACK.

"Word moves quickly," I said.

"As does violence," Catcher said. "And we all have our parts to play."

Fear in my heart, I looked at him. "Did we do this? By questioning her, by letting her get away, did we make this happen? Did we scare her into it?"

"Did we scare her, within an hour, to organize a riot of three hundred people? No. This would have been on the books before we talked to Pope, maybe even before the riot last night. It's too big to be anything other than a planned attack. But I'll bet your ass and mine that she's got a hand in it, and she knows how to stop it."

Catcher stood up and rebuttoned his coat.

"Where are you heading?" I asked.

"I can't use magic in the middle of the riot," he said. "Too many witnesses. But I can manage the perimeter. Pick off the stragglers now and again."

"Pick them off?" I asked. I assumed he didn't mean it literally, but I thought I should perform the due diligence.

"I'm not going to kill them," Catcher said. "Incapacitating them will be enough. And it's a creative venture that I'm going to enjoy. With gusto."

"I haven't seen you this excited about magic in a long time."

"The world is changing," he said. "The old ways don't work anymore. For better or worse, Mallory's been a good reminder of that."

I nodded. "Then good luck, and thank you for your help."

"You're welcome. Good luck at the House. And I wouldn't be a friend of your grandfather's if I didn't ask you to please be careful."

"I'm always careful," I promised. "It's other people I can't be sure about."

Ethan sent me the address of the rendezvous spot—a pharmacy a few blocks away from Grey House. From there, we'd get a sense of the scene from the other end of the riot, then plan our approach and how best we could divert the rioters from the House. Luc and Juliet would drop him off, then proceed to the House, or as close as they could get.

Wrigleyville wasn't terribly far from Wicker Park. I arrived at the rendezvous point before Ethan and got out of the car, belting on my katana and ensuring the fit was perfect. With an imperfect fit, I wouldn't be able to draw the sword cleanly from its scabbard.

The street was quiet, but I could hear the now-familiar sounds of the riot—chanting, glass breaking, rhythmic drumming—a few blocks away. A gut-wrenching column of smoke lifted into the sky, visible even blocks away from Grey House.

I was seeing only the margin of the violence, and it was still enough to make me nervous. After all, I was immortal, not invincible. But my fear was irrelevant. This was battle, and I was Sentinel of my House. Being brave meant fighting through fear.

It was unfortunate Mayor Kowalcyzk didn't see this for what it was—domestic terrorism at its finest. But she'd already decided we weren't the protagonists of this particular story.

"This story," I murmured, a plan beginning to form.

Maybe, if we wanted to combat Kowalcyzk and McKetrick and Clean Chicago, we had to write our own story. We had to remind the city we were hardworking Chicagoans who were out to make lives for ourselves, not to harm anyone else. We had to show Chicago what the violence was doing to us, and to the rest of the city.

And how could we do that?

We could call our favorite reporter to give him the story of a lifetime.

Being raised in a wealthy family had obvious advantages. Good schools, square meals, safe neighborhood, and access to people in high places. The members of the Breckenridge family were some of those people. They were old-money Chicago, having made their fortune in the steel industry. I'd gone to high school with Nick, one of the Breckenridge boys. I'd gone to college and grad school; he'd become a Pulitzer Prize–winning investigative journalist.

He'd also once tried to blackmail Cadogan House, but that was water under the bridge. Especially after he put me on the front page of the paper beneath the headline PONYTAILED AVENGER. That press had been good for the House. We'd see if it could be again.

So as I waited for Ethan, I dialed up Nick.

A woman answered. "Nick Breckenridge's phone."

"Is Nick there?" I asked, feeling suddenly awkward about the question.

"He's in the shower. Just a minute."

Her voice carried an accent—Italian or Spanish, perhaps—and I imagined a lovely and buxom brunette. And since I hadn't known Nick was dating anyone, I couldn't help but be curious.

"This is Nick," he said after a moment.

"It's Merit. Sorry to interrupt, but I've got something you might be interested in."

"I'm listening."

"Clean Chicago is rioting again. They've hit Grey House."

He paused. "That's the one in Wrigleyville?"

"It is. They've asked for vampire assistance, and we're on our way. Other vamps are heading over there as well."

"How many rioters?" His tone was serious, journalistic. I'd hooked him; I could hear it in his voice.

"Two or three hundred."

Nick whistled. "That's a lot."

"Clean Chicago is making this about humans. But it isn't. It's about vampires. Whatever Clean Chicago's supposed issues, I'd put good money on the possibility they've never met a single member of Grey House. And it's the Grey House vamps who will suffer. Who are suffering as we speak."

"I'm on my way. Good luck," he said, then ended the call.

I appreciated the sentiment, because I was afraid I was going to need it.

Ethan arrived a few minutes later, and he was dressed for battle. Or, rather, not in the fitted black suits he preferred for a typical night at Cadogan House. He wore jeans over boots and a black motorcycle-style jacket that was styled like mine, already zipped up against the cold. His blond hair was tied back, his katana in hand.

"You look ready for business," I said.

"I tried to be prepared. You're all right?" He pressed a soft kiss to my lips.

"I'm fine. Nervous. Catcher's here; he's going to move around the perimeter and try to thin out the crowd. How bad is this going to be?"

"I don't know," Ethan admitted, looking over the neighborhood. "It depends on the CPD. It depends on the mayor. It depends on whether they deem the rioters the assailants, or the victims."

My stomach turned at the possibility the Houses would be blamed for an assault against them. Now, of course, it was Nick's job to help them understand the full story.

"I actually hired some help in that area," I said.

Ethan looked sharply back at me. "Oh?"

"I called Nick Breckenridge and suggested he might be interested in a human, or vampire, interest story—our oppression by hate groups."

Ethan's smile was sly, his magic suddenly pert. "I love the way you think."

"Good," I said, "because we're waging a war against stupidity, and we're going to need all the thinking we can get."

"Let's get the war under way," Ethan said, gesturing toward an alley beside the pharmacy. "Let's go up to the next block and take a look."

We didn't get far. We'd only just made it steps into the dark when we spied a trio of cops in full riot gear marching past the alley. They paused to shine flashlights into the darkness, and we pressed our backs to the brick wall, waiting until they'd passed.

Sure, we weren't the enemies here, and they weren't exactly looking for us. But revealing our presence wasn't going to help anything.

For a few seconds, the beams of light danced back and forth across the passageway. Apparently satisfied it held no threat, they drew back their beams and moved on.

"Next idea?" I whispered.

Ethan looked around, then pointed above us. "There," he said. "If we can't go around, we go up."

I glanced at the rusty and rickety fire escape that stopped six feet above our heads. It reached up to the roof, seven or eight floors above us, in a tangle of landings and ladders that didn't look entirely safe.

"Are you sure?" I asked.

"It's our best option," Ethan said ruefully. "I'll go first. You can follow me."

Ethan jumped up and grabbed the bottom rung, pulling until the ladder released and clanked its way to the ground. He shook it, testing its mettle and metal. It didn't collapse, but bits of ice and rust flew to the ground like dander.

"And up we go," he said, stepping onto the first rung and climbing to the first landing.

Since this wasn't the best time to argue about safety, I kept my mouth shut and followed him, climbing upward, one foot over another. The climb became monotonous—climb the ladder, switchback around the landing, climb the next ladder.

I made it to the seventh floor—nearly to the top—when a *boom* shook the building and the fire escape—and the vampire upon it.

My heart stuttered, and my boot slipped on ice. My knee hit the rung below, singing out in pain, and I felt myself falling, without even time to call out Ethan's name for help.

He saved me anyway, reaching down from the landing above me and grabbing my wrist, holding it tight. "Steady now, Sentinel."

I nodded, ignoring the sound of the explosion and pursing my lips to slow my breathing, and felt for the rungs until I found my footing.

"I'm okay," I said when all four limbs were once again attached to the fire escape.

Ethan climbed over the ledge, then helped me over, and we dashed to the other side of the building to look down at the scene below.

A small part of me—the part that still believed in Santa Claus—wished we'd look out upon the city to find the fires extinguished, Grey House in pristine shape, and vampires and humans shaking hands on the sidewalk.

Instead, we found a war zone.

Flames rose from the front of Grey House, two blocks north of us. The path in between was filled with a boisterous mix of rioters and the CPD units trying to control them. Like the cops we'd seen in the alley below, they were outfitted in black, with helmets and shields, and they marched in a line toward the rioters from various directions, pushing them into a smaller and smaller area. But like putting a thumb over the end of a garden hose, condensing the anger only seemed to make it worse. The rioters yelled and raised their makeshift weapons—sports equipment, tools, kitchen knives—the tension only escalating as the camps moved closer.

"*Jesu Christi,*" Ethan murmured.

"There's a lot of them," I said.

Ethan nodded and pulled out his phone. He dialed Luc's number, holding the phone out so I could hear. "Where are you?"

"In front of Grey House," Luc said, crackling and noise in the background. "Fire department's here. The fire is nearly under control."

"We heard an explosion," Ethan said.

"It wasn't from the House," Luc assured. "It must have been

from somewhere else in the neighborhood. The cops have made a pretty good perimeter around the House, and Juliet and I are helping with the evacuation. It's clear Jonah's very good. The first wave of rioters had the firebombs, but he established a perimeter very quickly, set up a zone around the House."

"Molotov cocktails?" Ethan asked.

"Just like the first riot, yeah. At least three made contact," Luc said. "The fire department went through the roof to extinguish the flames; the atrium is toast. Water and glass and ash everywhere. Six vamps with severe burns, two currently unconscious. All were Novitiates; no staff."

I closed my eyes in relief. Jonah was staff, which meant he was okay. For now.

"We're on the roof of a building facing north," Ethan said. "The CPD's put a perimeter of bodies around the rioters at"—he paused to squint at the street signs—"Seminary and Cornelia, I think. The cops are trying to move them east, probably out of the residential areas."

Suddenly, a rioter carrying a mean-looking serrated shovel emerged through the knot of rioters and toward the police, raising his shovel against the closest cop. The cop used his shield to ward off the hit but still fell to his knees from the force of the blow. More cops joined the fray, pulling the attacker away, but creating a hole in the perimeter. Before it closed again, a handful of rioters slipped through the gap, heading north toward Grey House.

"When there's a gap in the perimeter, the rioters head for the House," I said, glancing at Ethan. "Maybe we should give them new targets."

He smiled, just a little. "That could work, Sentinel."

"Liege?" Luc said. "I'm not entirely sure what's going on over there, but I don't think I like it."

"There's no time for *like* tonight, Luc," Ethan said. "We're going to intercept the stragglers, try to lead them on a nice little goose chase."

"In that direction," I said, pointing to a cruiser parked a couple of blocks to the southwest.

"Agreed," Ethan said. "Help as you can, Luc, but keep a low profile. The GP could have spies about."

"Will do, hoss. For what it's worth, please be careful. Malik will have my ass if you go down in combat again."

Ethan's eyes shimmered with green fire. "I have every intention of staying alive."

He put away the phone and looked at me, and I'd have sworn there was a hint of a smile in his expression.

"Sentinel, I believe this dance is ours."

We decided to split up, giving us double the chance to redirect rioters away from Grey House.

Once on the street again, wearing my relatively tame leathers, I decided I needed to look a bit more dramatic. I flipped over my head and shook out my hair, giving it enough volume to add a Bride of Frankenstein vibe, then smudged some of the pink lip gloss in my coat pocket beneath my cheekbones. For the big finale, I let my eyes silver and my fangs descend. I was hoping for a "vamp on the prowl" look, with just enough ferocity to spark the rioters' interest.

A man wielding a very large, and very pointy, chef's knife picked that moment to dash around the corner. He stuttered when he saw me, trying to figure out if I was a full-on threat or a momentary obstacle.

His eyes stilled when his gaze reached my mouth and needle-sharp fangs; his eyes widened, the air filling with the heady scent of fear.

Of frightened prey.

"Going somewhere?" I asked.

It took only a moment for his fear to transmute into anger. He adjusted the grip on his knife, fingers flexing around the handle.

"Bitch," he said, and ran forward.

That was my cue. I turned and took off, running down the sidewalk. After a moment, footfalls and copious swearing sounded behind me. He'd taken the bait.

"I don't answer to 'bitch,'" I called out, jumping over a bench to cross the empty street, leading the rioter southwest toward the CPD cruiser we'd spied earlier.

I dodged around a parked car, and, pretending the bumper tripped me up, slowed just enough to let the rioter gain ground.

"You are mine now, bitch."

"Seriously, with the language," I muttered, moving with a faux hobble down the block, looking back and showing my fangs until he reached out with both hands to nab me, nearly grabbing the back of my jacket.

I skipped forward, feeling victorious, when karma bit me back.

He stuck out the knife and caught the back of my jacket. The leather split, freeing me, but the stutter broke my stride . . . and I hit a patch of ice on the sidewalk.

I slipped and fell forward, hitting both knees. Before I could rise again, the rioter was against my back, smelling of tinny sweat, his arm around my body, his knife cutting through leather and fabric and opening a line of hot blood across my belly.

I screamed in pain, elbowing him in the stomach to free myself as tears filled my eyes. He grunted and tried to draw the knife again, but I bent his wrist backward until he dropped the knife. I grabbed it up, wriggled away, and held it out at him, hand shaking with fear and pain and adrenaline, and from the crimson that bloomed across my stomach. He'd cut me, and deep.

The rioter's eyes, round and deep set, didn't waver. They were flat, devoid of emotion, as if I were less than human, an animal he'd trapped and nearly managed to kill.

My brain clouded. *Think*, I told myself, a hand pressed against my stomach to slow the blood loss until my body began to heal, trying to slow the crazy beating of my heart.

I had been running this way . . . because there was a cop around the corner.

Without looking back, I ran. It was a slow, ugly run, an arm against my stomach, the man's knife in my hand. I stumbled around the next corner, nearly running into the uniformed officer who stood beside his cruiser.

He looked up at the sound of the chase, caught sight of the blood on my abdomen, and put a hand on his gun. "Ma'am?"

Before I could answer, the rioter rounded the corner behind me. He saw me, and smiled—but then saw the cop and prepared to bolt again.

I stuck out a foot, and he hit the ground. The cop was on him before he could crawl away.

He put a booted foot on his back and glanced at me with concern. "Ma'am, you're bleeding. Did he cut you? Are you all right?"

"I'm fine," I said, handing over the knife. For some reason, it seemed important to get rid of it. "I don't think this is mine."

Stars appeared at the edges of my vision, and I managed a final thought before the world went dark.

Ethan.

CHAPTER NINE

REAL HOUSEWIVES OF WRIGLEYVILLE

I awoke hungry, greedy for blood. I knew nothing, remembered nothing, felt nothing except for the craving that clenched my stomach into knots.

"*Drink,*" he said, his wrist coming into focus in front of me, two lines of crimson across pale skin. I wrapped my hands around it and pressed my lips to the cuts he'd opened, and I drank.

"Be still, Merit." He stroked my hair.

I drank until the gnawing hunger in my belly receded, until rationality returned, until I could feel the chill in the air again. I drank until my vision cleared, until the fire across my belly was slaked. And then I pulled back from Ethan's wrist and sucked air into my lungs. As if by magic, the wound on Ethan's arm closed.

"I'm all right," I assured him, trying to take in my bearings.

I was sitting on his lap in a small bus-stop shelter only a few feet away from the police car. The rioter was in the backseat, and the cop stood on the sidewalk. The shelter gave us a bit of privacy, but he still watched us like a hawk as Ethan returned me to the land of the living.

He wrapped his arms around me. "Thank God. I thought I'd lost you."

I nodded but didn't attempt to climb off his lap. I breathed in the scent of him, the crisp scent of his cologne a relief among the smells of smoke and blood and battle.

"You passed out," he said. "I heard you call my name, but I couldn't find you. Luc traced your phone."

I rested my head against Ethan's chest, my body sated and suddenly lethargic, like a gourmand after a Thanksgiving meal. "New phone, new way to track vampires?"

"Precisely." He rubbed my hair again. "It was the perp?"

I nodded. "I tripped and he jumped me. He had a chef's knife."

"Odd choice of weapon."

I nodded again, still woozy and using words sparingly. "How long was I out?"

"Four minutes, maybe five, likely from the blood loss. The officer called for an ambulance, but I got here first."

When the world stopped spinning enough for me to glance down, I took a peek at my wound. My jacket was ripped, the shirt beneath a bloody ruin, but at least the wound was beginning to close, now a bright pink line across my gut.

"You'll heal," Ethan said.

"What about the riot?"

"Largely contained. The CPD did a solid job."

"I only managed to distract one rioter." I gestured toward the car, and the perp who was currently flipping us off with both hands.

"What a charming fellow."

"Charming *felon*," I corrected. "I kicked him off, but there's not a doubt in my mind he'd have killed me if he'd had the chance."

Ethan tipped my chin upward, forcing me to meet his gaze,

and scanning my eyes as if looking for the source of the sadness in my voice. "He's not the first with murderous intent."

"I know. But this feels different. More of a violation."

"Because he didn't see *you*," Ethan said. "He didn't assault you because of who you are or what you stand for. He saw only that you are fanged, and that was the only motivation he needed."

"What about you?" I scanned him for injuries. His jeans were dirty and torn in places, and there were scratches on his neck—like he'd been clawed by a set of fingernails.

"A group of rioters decided four to one odds were pretty good. I led them south and taught them otherwise."

"A war of stupidity," I reminded him. "This isn't just about protests and marches. They're willing to fight, to kill, individual vampires."

"So it appears," Ethan said. "Are you well enough to walk?"

Whether I was or wasn't was irrelevant. We weren't done here, so I would walk.

I stood and zipped up my jacket, wincing as I tightened it around my stomach. I chose pain over hypothermia.

"I could carry you?" Ethan offered.

I gave him a flat look. "I am a soldier," I said, putting a hand on his arm. "As much as I love these guns of yours, I would prefer not to be carried to a House of athletic vampires like a damsel in distress."

"Very well, Sentinel," he said, taking my hand, amusement in his eyes. Since my fingers were chilled into icicles, I didn't argue with the hand-holding.

Together, the cop's gaze on our backs, we walked toward Grey House, cutting through an alley and emerging in the middle of the next block. The House sat at the end of the street, but we found our progress blocked again.

Three women stood in front of a make-do barricade formed by patio chairs, baby gates, snow fencing, and other bits of garage ephemera. The woman in front had dark hair and dark tilted eyes, and she wore a heavy down coat, jeans, and sheepskin boots.

"What's your business here?" she asked us, crossing her arms as we approached.

"I'm sorry?" Ethan asked.

"She asked what's your business in this neighborhood?" said the woman beside her. She was a little older and a little heavier, and her hair had been combed into a very thoroughly hair-sprayed helmet.

"We're here to help with the folks who live in the warehouse," I said. "And who are you?"

"Wrigleyville Association of Concerned Neighbors," said the second woman, tapping a Cubs pin on her lapel. "We live here, we work here, we take care of our own."

"I see," Ethan said noncommittally. "And who, if I may ask, are 'your own'?"

The WACN representative looked suspicious. "Why do you want to know?"

"Because we're vampires," Ethan said, and the ladies' expressions suddenly changed. Instead of suspicion in their eyes, there was interest—very salacious interest in my very tall, built, and handsome vampire boyfriend. They scanned his body from snug jeans to leather jacket, stopping when they reached the eyes that shined with emerald amusement.

I guessed that explained whose side they were on.

"Ladies?" Ethan prompted.

They all blushed.

"Scott Grey and his people are our own," said the woman in front, her chin lifting stubbornly. "We've never had issues with

Scott or anyone else in the House. They're good neighbors. But these rioting jackasses? We don't know them at all. They don't live here, but they come into our neighborhood to start trouble? No, thank you."

"No, thank you," agreed the woman beside her.

"Well, we thank you for your loyalty," Ethan said. "I'm sure Scott appreciates it very much. We're here to help him and his people. If you don't mind, may we proceed?"

"Oh yes, yes," they variously said, moving a baby gate and a plastic chaise lounge to let us through.

Behind them, Grey House loomed. An imposing brick building, it was a warehouse transformed into living units and offices for the Grey House vamps.

Tonight, fire engines and other emergency vehicles sat at intervals around the block. Its front doors were broken, its brick covered with dark smoke. A line of vampires—all tall, all built, mostly men—stood in front of the building, probably keeping watch to ensure the rioters didn't make a second attempt.

I didn't see Scott, but Jonah stood in the middle of the line. Relief filled me. There was a gash across his temple and his shirt was singed, but he was in one piece.

"You're all right?" I asked, when we reached him.

"I'll live to fight another night," he said, glancing at Ethan. "But you aren't supposed to be here. The blacklist?"

"We do not answer to Darius," Ethan said. "But if you or Scott has an issue with our presence, we'll go."

"There's no need for that."

We turned to find Scott Grey, dark haired and somber, standing behind us. He wore one of the blue and yellow Grey House jerseys he'd selected in lieu of House medals.

Scott and Ethan shook hands—two Masters, meeting on a field of battle.

"We aren't here to create GP trouble for you," Ethan said cautiously.

"It's surprising how much perspective you gain in a crisis," Scott said. "And if the GP has a problem with our receiving necessary help in a crisis, I'd be happy to discuss that concern—very frankly—with Darius."

There was a glimmer of appreciation in Ethan's eyes. "Well put."

Scott glanced at the blood on my jacket. "What happened?"

"A rioter with a chef's knife," I said.

He nodded. "That jacket will never be the same."

I grimaced at the gaping hole in the front. "I know. And this was my favorite one."

"You've got injured vampires?" Ethan asked.

Scott nodded. "A few. We had no warning they were coming. The first wave was only three humans. It didn't even register with the guards that four people walking down the street in this neighborhood would be carrying Molotov cocktails."

"It was a smart decision by the rioters," Ethan said. "Hard to detect; easy to get close."

"The worst injuries were during the initial explosions," Jonah said. "The CPD got here in minutes."

"Any sign of Robin Pope?" I asked Jonah.

"The disgruntled employee?" He glanced at Scott, and both shook their heads. "Not that I'm aware of. Why?"

"Catcher and I went to her apartment. She ran when we asked her about the Bryant Industries riot. We suspect she's wrapped up in it."

Speaking of which, I realized we hadn't yet seen Catcher. I pulled out my phone in case he'd left a message; to my relief, I found one waiting: I KNOCKED OUT 32 RIOTERS. THEY'LL WAKE UP AND ONLY REMEMBER EATING BAD CHEESE. HEADING BACK TO CHUCK'S HOUSE.

I sent a note back: GLAD YOU'RE SAFE.

"Liege," said a breathless voice. Luc ran toward us, Juliet behind him. Their clothes were sooty, but they looked otherwise healthy and hale.

Luc and Ethan embraced like long-lost comrades, and Luc exchanged a pleasant—if tense—nod of acknowledgment with Scott.

"Merit, glad to see you took care of our Master," Luc said.

"Unfortunately, she took the brunt of it." Ethan pointed to the tear in my jacket, and Luc winced sympathetically.

"Katana?" he asked.

"Chef's knife."

Luc pursed his lips, apparently trying not to laugh.

"I didn't get to select my attacker's weapon," I pointed out.

"I know, I know. It's just not the weapon I'd have figured you'd take a hit from."

A group in Chicago Fire Department gear stepped out of the gaping hole in the front of Grey House and walked toward us.

The fireman in front raised his visor. "It's clear," he said. "The fire's out. But be careful of the glass. The ceiling took a beating."

"Thank you again," Scott said, shaking his hand.

"Just doing our job." The man reached into his pocket and fished out a small card, which he handed to Scott. "Got friends in the rehab industry if you want help with the cleanup."

"I appreciate the recommendation," Scott said, stuffing the card into his jeans pocket.

Scott and Jonah watched the firemen walk away, but I glanced back at Grey House. The middle of the warehouse was a garden atrium, shielded by an enormous glass roof and covered by a shutter that closed automatically at sunrise. If that shutter had been damaged . . .

The roof is glass, I silently told Ethan. *If the shutter is broken, they're going to need shelter when the sun rises.*

Ethan nodded ever so slightly and looked at Scott. "Between Navarre and Cadogan, we can house your vampires. Noah might also be able to offer some beds."

"The blacklist?" Scott asked.

"As we discussed," Ethan said mildly, "we came here anyway."

"I'm sorry," Scott said, holding up his hands. "I don't mean to seem ungrateful that you're here. But staying at the House would be stratospherically different than your coming here to help. The GP will be pissed, and it puts an even bigger target on your back. I don't want to invite additional trouble to your House."

The sound of shattering glass—a lot of it—echoed across the yard, probably more panels from the House's roof. The sun would be rising soon; one way or the other Scott was going to have to find shelter.

"On the other hand," Scott said, "I'm not sure we have another option."

"It's done," Ethan said. "We'll handle the Cadogan arrangements, but you might want to contact Morgan directly, considering the blacklist. I suspect burn phones are not his style."

Ethan meant Morgan, Master of Navarre House. "Speaking of," Ethan added, "I notice Mr. Greer is not here."

"Neither him nor his people," Scott said, equally unimpressed by the sound of it. "He's taken losses lately. We presume that's why he stood us up."

"Losses or not, one does not avoid one's obligations."

"No," Scott said. "You're right." He extended his hand toward Ethan. "We're no longer part of the same European family, but you offered bodies in support. We won't forget that. I can't guarantee anything until the GP situation is sorted out, but we're here if you need us."

"I appreciate that," Ethan said.

The momentary peace was interrupted by the sound of a woman's voice.

"Scott!" she screamed, running toward him. She was a human in her early thirties, with tan skin and long, dark hair.

Scott moved toward her, opening his arms; she ran into them. She was curvy but petite, and his embrace nearly swallowed her. She was followed by two children—a small boy and girl. They screamed with joy at the sight of him, running with as much eagerness as she had.

He released the woman and picked up the girl, holding her close, the love in his eyes obvious. My own bloomed with tears. It wasn't often that vampires displayed such human affection.

Vampires couldn't have children, but there was definitely something familial between Scott and these humans.

"I wasn't aware Scott had a significant other," Ethan whispered. "Much less a human one."

"That's Ava," Jonah said. "He doesn't tell many. He doesn't want them to be used against him, or for them to be seen as a liability."

"Darius would not be thrilled," Ethan agreed. "He has no great fondness for humans."

"No, he doesn't. That also figures in."

"I'd like to get back to the House," Ethan said. "We'll need to oversee arrangements." He glanced at the sky. "A few hours yet until sunrise, but there's much to do."

"We'll get there before the sun rises," Jonah said.

Ethan nodded. "If you'll excuse me, I'm going to speak with Scott for a moment." As we watched, Ethan walked away and greeted Ava and the children, then chatted with Scott.

"Were you able to salvage any of your stuff?" I asked Jonah.

"Yeah, most of my gear is fine. Waterlogged and smoky, but intact. We'll get it cleaned up. It'll just take time."

A vampire stepped into the hole in the front of Grey House, glanced around, and beckoned Jonah.

"They need me," he said. "I imagine I'll be seeing you later tonight."

"Vampire sleepover," I agreed. "We'll provide the sleeping bags."

"Bras in the freezer and shaving cream in the palm," Jonah said. "It's going to be a fun night."

Or a long one. We'd see how it went.

I took a glance at the building, trying to determine the extent of the damage, but it was difficult to tell in the dark. If the fire had been contained to the atrium, the vamps could move back in as soon as the roof and its complicated mechanics were fixed. If the rooms also had been damaged, they'd be bunking with us a little while longer. We'd deal either way.

But one thing concerned me: Double the vampires in Cadogan House meant double the targets if the rioters struck again. We were basically piling everyone they wanted to kill in a single building.

"You all right?"

I nearly jumped at the sound of Ethan's voice, and I was relieved to see him behind me. "Yeah. Just wondering how much worse this is going to get before it gets better."

"It's always darkest before the dawn," he mused.

I wasn't looking forward to any more darkness.

Ethan drove Moneypenny home. I fell asleep in the car, exhausted by the night's emotional turmoil and the loss of blood.

Vampires might heal quickly, but that didn't mean the wound didn't take a toll on our bodies. I'd been stressed and assaulted, and while I'd end up as whole as I'd been before it, I needed a break.

Hyde Park was quiet, the violence of the city's north side irrelevant here. The House glowed warm and golden, a beacon in the cold and unfeeling night.

We pulled into the garage and made our way to the first floor, where Margot manned a newly organized reception area. A giant silver tureen of hot chocolate sat beside one of warmed blood, and Helen, the House's den mother, was stationed behind a table already outfitted with a WELCOME, GREY HOUSE NOVITIATES! sign, welcome packets, and bags of toiletries and necessities.

"She is ridiculously fast," I remarked as we surveyed the setup.

"She is impeccably organized and efficient," Ethan agreed. "Did you know I stole her away from a former U.S. president? She was his social secretary."

"I presume you offered a signing bonus and immortality?" I asked with a smile.

"I did."

Luc emerged from the staircase, already wearing clean clothes, his face scrubbed of ash and soot. "Lindsey's at the gate with a list of Grey House vamps. Easier if she handles it, because she can ensure they're vampires without requiring them to vamp out."

"Good call," Ethan said. "Scott and the others should be here shortly. The ballroom is prepared?"

"And the library, much to the librarian's chagrin," Luc said. "We've got cots assembled and dividers up. They give a bit of privacy, at least. It will get them through sunrise."

"That's all we need to do," Ethan said. "I think I'd like to change clothes, and Merit will probably want a shower." They both looked at me, and I glanced down at the jacket I'd destroyed over the course of the evening. It looked even worse in the House than it had outside. Including the gash across the front, the leather bore patches of rust, probably scrapes from the fire escape, and flecks where sparks had nearly burned through it. Frankly, I looked like the victim of a zombie attack.

"I will definitely want a shower and change of clothes," I agreed.

Luc squeezed Ethan's shoulder. "Get cleaned up. We'll get everyone settled in. Probably also a good idea to get all the guards together to discuss protocol before sunrise."

Ethan checked his watch. "Very good idea. Let's say an hour, Ops Room?"

"You got it, boss. Hey, take care of our Sentinel this time, will you?"

"I'll do my best," Ethan said. "But I'm not sure even Merit could manage to get into trouble between here and the third floor."

Stranger things had happened.

We climbed the stairs, my legs heavy and achy like I'd just finished a marathon. I gripped the rail, pulling myself up one stair at a time.

Ethan did not look impressed by my efforts.

"I think the blood loss took a toll," I said.

"Yes, the laceration and your utter unconsciousness clued me in to that."

I couldn't help but laugh. "You sound like me. Maybe sarcasm can be transmitted by blood."

"God forbid," Ethan said. "You've more than enough for both of us."

"Would it be wrong to wear pajamas to a guard meeting?"

"It would be inappropriate," Ethan said. "But I think you're more than excused from leathers or a suit tonight."

"Sweatpants?"

"You're dating the Master of the House."

I took that as a "no" on the sweatpants.

I made it up the stairs, and he opened the doors to the apartments. The lights had been turned on, a tray of blood and healthy snacks on the side table. Luc must have given Margot a call about my unfortunate encounter with the chef's knife. Maybe, as House chef, she felt bad about the choice of weapon.

The snack called to me, but the shower called louder. I turned on the shower and peeled away my dingy clothes. I pulled off the jacket and placed it across the vanity. It had been a birthday gift from Mallory only days after I'd become a vampire and been appointed Sentinel of Cadogan House. It had been through a lot in the last ten months, and I wasn't keen to part with it.

"You're all right?" Ethan asked, stepping into the room.

I gestured toward the jacket and smiled sadly. "I hope Mallory got a good deal on this jacket. I'm afraid it's toast."

"This is Chicago. There are other leather jackets to be found."

"I know. But this one was meaningful. It was a gift—and it was before Nebraska."

"So much was," Ethan said. "I doubt Mallory will fault you for destroying it tonight. She'll be glad it protected you. At least somewhat."

I nodded. "In fairness, I didn't mean to destroy it. I got dragged into someone else's war."

"Isn't that always the way?" Ethan said philosophically. "I don't mean to be dismissive of your melancholy, but we're short on time. Shower, please. I'm going to give Breckenridge a call while you're underwater."

I didn't argue about either option. When I was naked, I climbed into the shower. The water was deliciously hot, but it stung the gash across my stomach. The wound was closed, but it had now begun to ache and itch as it healed.

I scrubbed blood and dirt and ash from my pale skin, then emerged from the shower and towel-dried my hair.

Ethan stepped into the doorway. "Now that's more like it."

"Sir, you're a dirty old man."

"I'm a dirty old *vampire*. There's a difference."

Since time was of the essence, we switched places. I turned the shower over to Ethan, deposited my clothes in the laundry drop—maybe the staff could have some luck rehabbing the jacket—and headed back into the bedroom to find something appropriate to wear. Sweatpants and pajamas were out, but Ethan hadn't mentioned jeans. Personally, I'd have preferred some slouchy yoga-style pants, but the meeting would be in mixed company, and I might as well try not to embarrass my boss in front of another House.

I opted for the softest jeans I could find and a fitted Cadogan House long-sleeved shirt. I brushed and dried my hair, leaving it loose. A pair of much-loved Puma sneakers—too light to wear in winter, but perfect for in-House movement—and lip gloss to combat the effects of winter, and I was ready to go downstairs.

"Ready?" he asked, meeting me at the door. Like me, he'd changed into jeans, but the relaxed dress didn't minimize the power and authority in his posture. He was still the Master of his House, even when other Masters had moved into his abode.

"Let's go," I said, then glanced back longingly at the bed and the cozy duvet and pillows. "I'll see you again soon," I promised, and closed the door behind us.

————

As we descended the stairs, we passed Grey House vampires heading upstairs. They carried large duffel bags bearing the Grey House logo, and they were led by Cadogan House vampires wearing black CADOGAN AMBASSADOR badges.

"Cadogan ambassadors?" I asked Ethan.

"Helen's idea. She thought it a good idea to appoint vampires to represent the House at unusual functions. She expected we'd have more of those functions since we're no longer part of the GP. She did not anticipate this, I imagine, but it's helpful all the same. Actually," he said, pausing on the second-floor landing, "let's visit the ballroom and library. I'm curious how they've arranged the beds."

We walked down the hallway toward two of the House's most glorious rooms—the very grand ballroom, and the two-story library. The doors to both were open, and Grey House vampires were beginning to stream inside.

We hit the library first. Normally, a bank of tables filled the center of the main floor. Tonight, they'd been moved out of the way. That space, and the rows between the shelves, were filled with cots. Cotton dividers hung from simple racks in the open areas to provide privacy.

"There are too many vampires breathing on my books in here."

We turned to find the librarian, shorter than either of us and with a rakishly thick crop of dark hair, giving the evil eye to the Grey House vampires who were arranging suitcases, phones, and shoes in the small spaces around their cots.

"They're breathing on your books?" I asked.

"Do you know how much carbon dioxide and water a single vampire breathes into the air every day? And now it's all contained in this room, sinking into my pages."

The librarian was very, very particular when it came to his job and his books. He prided himself on the scope and organization of the library, and he didn't take kindly to the exhalations of vampires.

"I'm sure the collection will be fine," Ethan said. "But, if not, we'll make sure to set aside House funds for restoration."

That must have satisfied the librarian, because he disappeared between a row of books without another word.

"He is a particular breed," Ethan said, and we slipped into the hall again.

The ballroom was similarly decked out, with rows of cots and dividers across the wood floor, the chandeliers above dimmed to cast a gentle glow across the room. A long table had been set up on one side of the room with more toiletries and baskets of bottled water, blood, and snacks.

"Seriously, Helen did an amazing job getting everything arranged so quickly. You should give her a raise."

Ethan snorted. "Trust me, Sentinel, she doesn't need one. We had to double her salary after your transition to vampire."

I slugged him gently in the arm, but I suspected he wasn't teasing. My change from human to vampire hadn't exactly been smooth—and Helen, unfortunately for her, had had the unenviable job of welcoming me into the dark. It hadn't gone smoothly.

Satisfied the Grey House vampires were being cared for, we retreated and continued our journey to the first floor.

We reached the foyer just as Scott, Ava, and the children walked through the door.

"Perfect timing," Ethan said, striding forward to meet them. "Welcome to Cadogan House. I'm sorry it's under these circumstances."

Ava nodded nervously, gathering her children around her. "Thank you for having us."

"Ditto," Scott added. "We appreciate the gesture. I know it's an inconvenience."

Ethan smiled. "Not at all." He turned to Helen, who still sat at the greeting station, and gestured to the new arrivals.

"Helen, this is Ava and her children, Abby and Miguel. They are Scott's particular friends, and they will be staying with us."

If Helen found anything odd in his announcement, she didn't show it. In her typically administrative fashion, she checked her clipboard.

"We have the injured vampires in the guest suite, and it will be a bit noisy in the ballroom and library, given the number of vampires. If you'd like, the children can stay in Merit's old room," she said, glancing at me.

I nodded my approval, but Ethan interjected.

"That won't do," he said. "You can take the Master's apartment. That way you'll be able to stay together, with the children. You'll need space of your own to breathe and plan, and you'll feel better if you can keep them close?"

Ava nodded with relief.

Ethan looked at Helen. "You can arrange cots for the children?"

"Of course," she said. "But what about you?"

"We'll stay in Merit's old room."

Since my dorm-sized room had only a twin bed, it would be a squeeze. But Luc and Lindsey managed well enough in her room. Besides, Ethan was right. It wasn't much of a sacrifice to us, and it would give them all peace of mind.

"Then I offer our thanks," Scott said.

"Margot, if you'll take the desk," Helen said, "I'll show them the way." When Margot nodded, Helen gestured toward the stairs with her clipboard and they moved forward. Ethan turned back to me.

"I hope that's all right with you."

"Of course," I said. "They'll want to be together. Especially after tonight."

"My thoughts exactly." He looked at Margot. "We'll be in the Ops Room."

Margot saluted with the pen in her hand.

＋・＋ ⚔ ＋・＋

CHAPTER TEN

THE SLUMBER PARTY

In the basement, the Ops Room buzzed with activity. Juliet, Kelley, Malik, and Luc were already inside, and the whiteboard was in position.

"Grey House guards?" Ethan asked, exchanging a manly patting of backs with Malik, who'd undoubtedly been worried for Ethan's safety.

"They're on-site and getting settled in," Luc said. "We gave them a few minutes."

Ethan nodded, then glanced at Malik. "Any trouble here while we were gone?"

"Not a hint. No rioters. No attempts to jump the fence. No crank phone calls. You four had all the fun." He glanced at me with concern. "You were cut?"

"Yeah, but I'm okay. Just a little sore."

Devilishness shined in Malik's eyes. "What was the weapon again? Paring knife? Melon baller?" He squeezed his thumb and forefinger together. "One of those cinnamon-flavored toothpicks?"

I gave Luc, the only one who'd have had time to tell Malik about the weapon of choice, a very flat look. "Really."

He winked. "I told him the rioter used a spatula. He got to the rest on his own."

"It was a chef's knife," I said, holding my hands about a foot apart. "And a very large one."

"That's what she said," Ethan murmured.

Maybe my sarcasm was catching.

"I did get a call from one Nicholas Breckenridge. He's asked about the riots' potential impact on the House getting a lengthy feature."

Ethan looked very satisfied. "That was Merit's idea. Our effort to change public opinion."

"Nice thought," Malik said, and I nodded.

"Thanks."

"Give him whatever information he wants," Ethan said. "I'll apprise Scott. No interviews with individual vampires unless they specifically consent, but he's welcome to ask within the halls of the House."

Malik nodded, then glanced back at the door. "Speaking of access to the House, look who's darkening our door."

I glanced back, expecting to see the Grey House guards, but found a pleasant surprise. Jeff, Catcher, and my grandfather stood in the doorway, still bundled up in scarves and warm coats. Catcher must have picked up my grandfather and brought him back to Hyde Park. I smiled and walked toward them, accepting a very squeezy hug from Jeff.

"We heard there was a party," he said. "And we decided to crash it."

"Actually, we heard you were discussing the riots," my grandfather said, giving Jeff an amused glance. "I'm not sure we'll have a lot to offer, but we thought we'd chip in what we could."

"It was nice of you to come all this way," I said. "We appreciate it."

Catcher looked over my ensemble. "Sullivan's letting you dress down tonight?"

I lifted my shirt and showed them the scar across my belly. My grandfather looked mightily alarmed.

"Some nights, I'm not sure if I should be glad that you're immortal, or rueful about it," he said.

"We often have similar thoughts," Ethan said, walking toward us. He shook my grandfather's hand.

"How'd you get the cut?" Catcher asked.

"Rioter with a blade."

"Paring knife," Ethan said.

"It was a chef's knife," I pointedly said, giving Ethan the evil eye. "I tripped, and he got the jump on me. Literally."

"I'm glad you're all right," my grandfather said, glancing at Ethan. "Perhaps a position change to House librarian?"

"That job is filled," I said, slipping my arm through his. "I'm stuck at Sentinel, unfortunately. But I do have a knight in shining armor. Ethan rescued me. Again."

Ethan smiled. "It's the least I can do."

"Here, Mr. Merit," Lindsey said, standing. "Take my chair."

I expected my grandfather to protest; he was in his sixties, but still proud and active, and he was a former cop, after all. But instead he nodded and smiled.

"Thank you, hon," he said. "I appreciate that."

Lindsey gave me a wink as she scooted from her seat and took a spot standing near the wall. My grandfather sat down, a little slower than usual, and with a little more relief in his eyes.

"You're all right?" I asked, concern in mine.

He patted my hand. "Perfectly fine. It's just been a long day."

He sought to soothe me, but the reminder was still poignant: As a vampire, I was immortal. My friends and family weren't. My grandfather, always vibrant and vital, would inevitably age, and eventually I'd lose him.

I looked away before my eyes could fill with tears, but my heart was heavy.

Be still, Sentinel, said a voice in my head.

I glanced at Ethan, who stood a few feet away. He spoke with Luc, but his thoughts were on me. He must have seen the fear in my eyes.

Be grateful for your immorality, but do not deny them the honor of their mortality.

I nodded, but the vise around my heart didn't ease.

Scott appeared in the doorway, six guards, including Jonah, behind him. I recognized a couple—Grey House guards named Danny and Jeremy. Most of the group wore navy blue peacoats over jeans and boots. A bit, I assumed, of the Grey House uniform.

"I think we're all here," Ethan said to Scott.

Scott nodded. "Then let's get this show on the road."

To be honest, the atmosphere was awkward. There were a lot of vampires squeezed into the Ops Room, and we played for two different teams. The Grey House guards looked tired and uncomfortable. The Cadogan House guards looked nervous: We were responsible for our House's security, and now the security of vampires we didn't know that well.

Kelley, Lindsey, Juliet, and I had nabbed seats at the conference table, along with a few of the Grey House guards. The senior staff stood in front of the projector screen like lecturers ready to teach their fang-bearing students.

"First of all," Ethan said, glancing among the Grey House guards, "welcome to Cadogan House. I'm sorry it's under such unfortunate circumstances, but you may consider yourselves at home here. If there's anything you need, or if there's something we can help you with, please feel free to ask."

A few of the Grey House guards looked around at one another in surprise at Ethan's magnanimity, which made me wonder how they'd perceived Cadogan House.

"This is our Operations Room," Ethan said. "You're welcome to be here, to talk to our guards, or to request information about House security. We recognize that, for the time being, we are housing your most precious commodity—your vampires—and we want you to feel as comfortable as possible about their safety." Ethan nodded and looked at Scott. "I believe that's it for my part, Scott, unless you have anything to add?"

Scott lifted his hands. "They've heard from me enough tonight."

Ethan nodded at Luc, and he and Jonah moved forward.

"We're going to review events while they're fresh," Jonah said. "Then we'll dismiss for the evening."

"Let's start at the beginning," Luc suggested. "Merit, you want to tell us what you found out about the first riot?"

I nodded. "The first riot hit Bryant Industries, a Blood4You distribution facility in Wicker Park. Catcher and I talked to Charla Bryant, the current CEO. She wasn't aware of any threats against the business before the attack, but we're keeping an eye on a potential suspect named Robin Pope."

"Robin Pope?" asked one of the Grey House vampires. "Trim brunette?"

Ethan and I exchanged a glance. "Yes," I said. "Do you know her?"

The vampire blushed. "Yeah. We dated for a little while. Real briefly. When I was human."

Now that was interesting. "How long ago?"

"Three years?" he said. "Maybe four?"

That was a pretty good span of time, and I wondered how long Robin Pope could hold a grudge. "How did the relationship end?"

The Grey House guard squinted bashfully and scratched the back of his head. "Not well. I mean, it kind of just ended. Except that she kept calling. What's her connection to all this?"

"She's a former Bryant Industries employee," I said. "Basically, she filed a complaint against the company because she thinks they're conspiring with vampires."

"She had a connection to Bryant Industries. A grudge," Jonah said. "And the rioters targeted that facility. It also appears she had a bad breakup with one of our own, and Grey House was attacked next."

"I don't like coincidences," Scott said.

"Nor do I," Ethan agreed. "The connections suggest she's had a hand in selecting the targets."

"She doesn't seem entirely stable," I said. "We went to her apartment to ask her some questions, feigning support for anti-vamp groups, and she ran. She clearly believes vampires are a threat, and she's identified a web of conspiracies no one else can see." I glanced at Catcher and my grandfather. "Anything else from your end?"

My grandfather nodded. "We advised friends at the CPD that Ms. Pope should be a person of interest in their investigation. They put a car on her building and an APB on her car. She returned home about an hour ago, and they picked her up. She's currently in an interview."

For the first time in a couple of days, I felt a weight lift from my shoulders. Her arrest wouldn't repair the damage at Grey House, but maybe it would slow the tide of future riots.

Ethan gestured toward my grandfather. "For those of you who don't know, this is Merit's grandfather, Chuck Merit. Otherwise known as the city's rightful Ombudsman. And his colleagues, Jeff Christopher—"

"The city's best computer man," I added.

Jeff blushed and did a faux hat tip.

"And Catcher Bell," Ethan said, gesturing to both of them in turn. "Thank you for reaching out to the CPD."

"Of course," said my grandfather. "As a warning, we're swimming uphill a bit where the CPD is concerned. We still have some allies there, but overall they're focusing on the rioters, not the riots. I understand the administration has decided this is just public reaction to vampires, to fears their way of life is at risk."

"We've been out of the closet for a while," Lindsey said. "That's not even logical."

"It is to the prosecutors," Catcher said. "After all, they can't put society on trial, not really. But they can prosecute the handful of people who throw the bombs. That's where the evidence is."

"Has the mayor issued a formal statement for tonight's riot?" Ethan asked.

"And McKetrick," Luc said. "Pretty much the same talk as the last riot. 'We're incarcerating the perpetrators of these crimes,' blah blah blah. The mayor's toned down the anti-sup rhetoric a little, which is something. Hard to blame two riots on internal sup conflicts when the perps are all humans."

"And McKetrick?" Scott asked.

"Still blaming it on sups, but part of that's just jurisdictional," Luc said. "If it doesn't involve sups, he has no authority." He glanced at Ethan. "As part of our protocol, we looked for connections between McKetrick and the rioters, but we haven't found anything."

"Not surprising," Ethan said. "Even if he was involved, he's remarkably careful. Consider Michael Donovan."

"I'd rather not," Luc said.

I looked at Jeff. "Back to Pope. Can we prove her connections to the rioters?"

"I haven't found anything yet, but I haven't started on tonight's batch of arrests. There were a lot more rioters tonight."

"Many more than in Wicker Park," Jonah agreed. "And with slightly different tactics. In Wicker Park, the firebombing and rioting occurred simultaneously. Here, they hit us in two waves. The first—too small to trigger security—bombed the House. The rest of the rioters—the larger group—formed the second wave."

I glanced at my grandfather. "Have the CPD interviews of the rioters turned up anything?"

He shook his head. "There's been no progress, as far as we're aware. They're still refusing to answer questions. They have been repeating what they claim is Clean Chicago's motto."

" 'Hate is the new black'?" I guessed.

"*Sic semper tyrannis,*" Catcher said. "It basically means 'Death to tyrants.' "

"That's what John Wilkes Booth said after he shot President Lincoln," Ethan said darkly.

"Are we the tyrants?" I asked.

"We aren't entirely sure," Catcher said. "We didn't find anything else on the Web linking the phrase to the riots or the movement, so it could just be something they came up with at the last minute."

"So their group's grown larger," Ethan said, "and they have a motto. How are they recruiting?"

"We still aren't certain," Luc said. Luc projected a Web site onto the wall screen—a social-media site with a Clean Chicago badge.

"This was posted about two hours ago," he said.

"Two hours ago?" asked one of the Grey House guards, a short-haired and broad-shouldered fellow muscular enough to have played offensive tackle in his former life. "After the riot?"

"We asked the same question," Luc said. "But the account is definitely new."

"Which means they had other ways to pull in participants before the riots," Catcher said.

"Yes," Luc said. "We still haven't found any other Internet sources, but they're clearly recruiting members through some kind of network. Could be military. Could be informal."

"Could be hate groups," offered one of the Grey House guards. "Preexisting network of humans who make a hobby of hatred. It can be easy to rile them up to fixate on another group."

"True," Luc said, then glanced at Jeff. "Anything like that pop up on Robin Pope?"

"Not so far. Her background is bland. Nothing suspicious. Nothing even interesting."

"Could it have been wiped?" Jonah asked.

"Sure," Jeff said. "But there's also nothing so glorious it looks fake. She just seems dull."

"General awareness of the riots is undoubtedly helping recruitment," Luc said. "Media reports are all over the twenty-four-hour news stations, the Web."

"We're actually hoping we have an ace there," Ethan said.

"Merit's family is friendly with the Breckenridges, including Nicholas, the reporter. She called him and asked that he consider preparing a feature about how the riots are impacting the Houses, the neighborhoods. The darker side of hatred, as it were."

He glanced at Scott. "I've offered him access to the House, but you can grant whatever access you'd like—or none, if you prefer—for your people. I know the spotlight isn't comfortable for all."

Scott nodded. "I'll think it over."

"While we're taking roll call," Luc said, "has anyone heard from Morgan?"

"He finally called," Scott said. "Said he wasn't able to offer room in the House. According to him, Will, the guard captain, is new and not equipped to handle an influx of vampires, and they're still reeling from the recent deaths."

Unappreciative silence followed that explanation.

"Each Master must make his own way," Ethan said.

"That's generous," Scott said. "I was willing to give him the benefit of the doubt for the first few months of his term, and when Darius tightened the reigns. But he is Master of his House, and he's not exactly doing it proud."

Morgan was an odd duck. He'd gotten control of Navarre House under unusual circumstances, and he hadn't exactly made the most of it, at least not with respect to the other Houses. He seemed to be well intentioned, but he was emotionally immature. I'd hoped he could grow into his position, but he hadn't gotten there yet. Unfortunately, each time Navarre House huddled farther into its shell, he damaged his relationship with the rest of us. Some night, that was going to bite him in the ass.

"Harold Monmonth also called," Scott said. "He 'forbade' me

from staying at Cadogan House. Said the GP would consider it a violation of our charter if we live in sin with blacklisted vampires who'd so recently defied the GP and all it stood for. He gave me a lengthy speech about loyalty and punishment."

Ethan blinked. "And how did you respond?"

"I reminded him Darius West was head of the GP, and Darius was the only individual who had the authority to forbid Grey House from doing anything. I told him I haven't heard from Darius, although personally I suspect that does not bode well."

"Monmonth or not, you may take heat for your decision," Ethan said.

"My decision was keeping my vampires safe from the rising sun. Any member of the GP who doesn't understand that is an idiot, and not worthy of the position."

I couldn't help but smile at that comment.

"Is this when we talk about taxation without representation?" asked one of the Grey House guards, a woman with cocoa skin and a gorgeous pouf of dark hair. She was tall and trim, so the jersey nearly overwhelmed her lean figure. But paired with short nails painted yellow and a bright pair of yellow Converse sneakers—both of which matched the yellow in the Grey House jersey, she pulled it off.

If it was appropriate to judge a person based on her footwear—and it obviously was—I decided I liked her immediately.

The other Grey House guards chuckled, but Scott looked less than amused by the comment. I guess it was still too soon for jokes about defecting from the GP.

"Back to the riots," Jonah said in a serious tone, apparently taking his cue from Scott. "Two riots, two nights in a row. It's not unreasonable to surmise they'll hit another location tomorrow night."

"And not necessarily a House," Luc said. "They hit a Blood4You distributor the first time. That means they like businesses with connections to vampires, and they have enough information to ferret out places that aren't commonly known to humans. We've put together a potential list of targets."

Luc switched the image on-screen, and the bulleted list popped up. Navarre and Cadogan Houses made the list, as did Benson's, Red, and Temple Bar, the official bars of Grey House, Navarre, and Cadogan, respectively.

The harbor lighthouse in Lake Michigan, which served as the Red Guard's headquarters, did not make the list. Probably because Jonah and I were the only two vampires in the room who knew its purpose.

"Anybody know if Robin Pope has connections to any of those places?" Jonah asked, glancing around the room, but no one offered an answer.

Luc tapped a spot on the screen near the Houses. "If these rioters were really aiming for maximum impact, Cadogan House would be the target. It's in a neighborhood they haven't hit before, and we're all here together."

"Maximum impact and damage," Jonah agreed. "You hit one place, and two Houses."

"Yeah, but that assumes these guys are doing anything by the book," Lindsey said. "They clearly aren't. If they really wanted to hit vampires and for maximum publicity, you hit Cadogan House first. We're more infamous."

"Which suggests Robin Pope is on the riot steering committee. She's picking the locations—not because they'll make the biggest bang, but because she's got personal vendettas." I glanced at Luc. "You might want to poll the House, make sure she doesn't know anyone here."

"And we'll keep looking into her background," Jeff said.

"Just in case," Ethan said, "we've doubled the number of guards outside. They're humans, but they have guns. At dusk, let's discuss how we can work together to increase our guard presence while we have the bodies to do so. Chuck, could you also apprise the CPD of the possibility the House may be a target?"

"Of course," he said.

"I thought the CPD wasn't exactly on our side right now?" asked one of the Grey House guards.

"They aren't," Grandpa confirmed. "But they are on the side of humans, and there are plenty in Hyde Park. In particular, there are wealthy humans who own sizable homes and contribute to the mayor's election campaign. That will probably spark some considerable interest on the part of the CPD."

"That's a good segue," Scott said, stepping forward again. "We're looking for temporary housing, but that's going to take some time. While we're here, we've got a good opportunity to work together. As I see it, our agenda is to find the source of the riots and cut it off. We can look into the rioters, the employees, whatever. I'm less interested in how we get there than the fact that we get there. We've lost our House. That will not stand. And we will find a way—and now—to stop it."

He looked at Ethan and nodded.

"Well put," Ethan said. "With that, I think we're done."

While the senior staff discussed the details of our inadvertent partnership, I said good-bye to the Ombuddies.

"Thank you for coming, although I hope you didn't come this way for such a short meeting?"

"Actually, we didn't," Catcher said. "As soon as I got back to the house, we discovered some ongoing hysteria on the police scanners about a chimera on Fifty-seventh Street."

"A chimera? Like the mythical monster?"

"Exactly like that," my grandfather said.

"And what did you find?"

"Cocker spaniel wearing many awkward Halloween costumes," my grandfather said with obvious amusement. "The owner's children had been playing dress up, and it escaped the yard in full regalia."

"Including one of those costumes," Jeff said, hands in action, "that looks like a saddle and has a little cowboy on top."

"And one of the chimera heads was born," Catcher said.

"Hey, better than the real thing," I said. "What do you even do with a chimera?"

"What *wouldn't* you do with a chimera?" Jeff asked. "They're like the Swiss Army knife of animals."

"Party in the front, business in the back," Catcher agreed.

That earned a snort and laugh from me. "Any animal that can be compared to a mullet is a good animal in my book."

"We should get going," Grandpa said. "Marjorie has phone duty while we're gone, and she gets irritable if we leave her alone too long."

"But she's the admin," I pointed out. "It's her job to answer the phones."

"She does not quite see it that way," my grandfather said with a smile. "But there aren't enough hours left in the night to have that discussion." He patted my shoulder. "I wouldn't wish violence on anyone, but I'm glad you and your House were out of harm's way tonight."

"Me, too," I agreed, glancing around the room at the Grey House guards, who still looked shell-shocked. "But we're not out of the woods. Not yet. If Grey House can be hit, Cadogan House can, too."

And this time, there'd be twice as many vampires in the cross-hairs.

The Ombuddies headed south again. My good-byes complete, I walked over to the whiteboard and looked it over. Two riots, lots of injuries, an entire House of vampires UnHoused, and untold property damage. And all because Robin Pope held grudges.

"So, you're Merit."

I glanced back. The Grey House vampire with the yellow Converses stood behind me, arms crossed over her chest.

"I am. I didn't get your name."

"Aubrey," she said. "I'm a friend of Jonah's. We all are, the guards. We're a very close-knit team." She looked me over, and her expression wasn't exactly friendly. More like analytical.

"I wanted to get a sense of you," she said, meeting my gaze again. "He had a thing for you, you know."

I had no idea how to respond to that, so I didn't.

Jonah had had a thing for me, at least briefly. He'd confessed as much when Ethan was gone, but I'd been too in love, and still mourning, to even entertain an offer.

She stepped beside me and turned toward the board, looking it over. "It was when Ethan was dead?"

"Yes," I said. I was mortified by the conversation, but if she was going to look at the board, so would I.

We stood there for a couple of minutes in silence, standing beside each other, staring at the board and trying to ferret out what was there . . . and what wasn't.

"Why these riots?" she asked.

"Exactly my question," I said, hoping we'd moved on. "It seems like a waste of resources and capital—and hatred—to hit little targets."

"I couldn't agree more. Something bigger's at issue here. Something we aren't seeing."

"But what?"

"I don't know." She shook her head, hair bouncing as she did it. I was instantly struck jealous by the volume of it. It was star-worthy hair.

"I don't know, either." I glanced over at her. "I love your hair . . . and Ethan. Jonah told me what he felt, and I was honest with him. I think he's a great guard and a fantastic vampire, but I'm not going to apologize for being in a relationship with someone else."

She pursed her lips. "Not much for subtlety, are you?"

"No. Much like you, apparently."

"Aubrey?"

At the sound of Jonah's voice, we both glanced back. He watched us for a moment, as if puzzling out our interaction. "You ready to go? I want to touch base for a few minutes before sunrise about the accommodations."

"Of course," she said, and when he turned away, she looked at me again. "You'll do. And I like your hair, too."

When she walked away to join him, I smiled a little.

When dawn closed in, Ethan and I headed upstairs for bed. I had to remind myself to stop at the second-floor landing, that we were heading for my old room, not the more lush accommodations I'd become used to.

On the door, as on the doors of all Novitiates' rooms, was a small corkboard. A placard bearing my name had been pinned to it, as had a photo from a magazine: two waifish young starlets stretched across a velvet chaise in front of a deep navy background. Lindsey had replaced the girls' heads with small, unevenly cut pictures of us.

With Ethan behind me, I unlocked the door and opened it. The room smelled faintly of dust and the rose-scented perfume I liked to wear in colder months. Since the bottle was upstairs, the fragrance must have lingered on my clothes.

There wasn't much to the room, especially compared to the splendor of the Master's apartments. It was a small rectangle of space. A twin bed sat in one corner, and there was a bureau on the opposite wall that still stored all the personal effects and clothes I hadn't yet taken to Ethan's apartments. Two doors led to a closet and small bathroom.

"Home sweet home?" he asked.

"Something like that." He walked inside, and I closed the door behind him. For a moment, I was struck at how truly different my life had become since I'd been made a vampire. In those early nights, I'd been convinced Ethan was my enemy, the vampire who'd taken away my human life without so much as a second thought. I'd actually been grateful my room was on the second floor, one floor removed from his, so I wouldn't have to face him any more than necessary.

And now we were lovers. Confidants. Partners. I'd come to admit that he'd saved my life, not taken it away, and he'd accepted that I wasn't one to blindly follow orders. Our romance had not been simple, and it hadn't been easy. It still wasn't easy, as there was always some kind of supernatural drama interfering with our lives.

But perhaps that was the point? That plans, however well-intentioned, were ultimately irrelevant? That we had to learn to adapt, and the best-case scenario was finding a partner who was willing to adapt alongside us?

If I hadn't adapted, we might still be enemies. I might still be refusing his advice and counsel, and he might have picked a

House consort to fulfill his needs. My Red Guard membership would be less about helping the Houses than spying on Ethan. We'd have been enemies, engaged in a private war against each other.

Instead, over the course of the last year, we'd joined forces. We fought together against factions that sought to tear apart the House. And even in this tiny, cold, and sparse room, I was home, because he was with me.

Ethan looked at me curiously. "Are you all right? You're making the room buzz."

"Just thinking," I said, smiling a little.

"About?"

"How much things change."

He walked toward me and pressed a hand to my cheek, smiling slyly. "You were thinking about us."

I nodded. "About what we were, and what we've become."

"And how I wooed you with my brilliance and sophistication?"

"Or your narcissism," I teased. "I'm going to change clothes."

Ethan lay down on the bed, one arm behind his head, ankles crossed. "All right," he said. "I'm ready."

"Dirty. Old. Man," I repeated. But he had a point. There was one small room, and not much privacy.

"I'm not going to strip for you," I said, turning to the bureau and flipping through a drawer. Everything in my current clothing rotation was upstairs. The bureau held the remainder—college and grad school T-shirts and slightly out-of-style numbers that I hoped would be more popular next year.

With minutes before the sun rose, I grabbed an old NYU T-shirt, pulled off my jeans and shirt, and slipped it on.

"That was hardly worth the cost of admission," Ethan commented.

"The cost of admission was free," I pointed out. "And I was changing for my benefit, not yours." I gestured grandly toward the room. "The stage is yours, my friend."

"I don't know what you expect me to do."

I sat down on the bed and mirrored his posture. "I expect you to take it off, and I expect you to shake it. In that order."

"Hmmph" was all he said. As I looked on, he stood up, pulled his shirt over head, and kicked off his shoes.

By my calculation, that left a Master vampire in the middle of my bedroom, shirtless and staring back at me with a predictably arched eyebrow.

"You aren't done," I pointed out, but with waning enthusiasm. Not for the subject—he was as hot as ever—but for consciousness. The sun was nearly on the rise, and sleepiness had begun to set in.

Either sensing my sudden exhaustion or faced with exhaustion of his own, he slipped off his trousers without a performance.

"Wait—I nearly forgot," he sleepily said. He walked to the bureau and picked up a blue velvet box I didn't recognize and hadn't realized was there.

"What's that?"

"The payment for dinner with your parents tomorrow."

"Dinner with my . . . Oh crap."

I'd totally forgotten about that, although in fairness the riots had provided a pretty good excuse.

"Are you sure leaving the House is a good idea? We all agree Cadogan's on the list."

"And we're having dinner with one of the most important men in the city," he said. "I'm not thrilled about the timing, but we agreed to go. Your father is clearly trying to mend fences. I'm not taking any position on that—it's between you and him—but we need friends, and we can't afford to be picky."

He sat down on the bed beside me, cradling the box in his hands. The opening of a velvet box usually led to something interesting, even if Ethan was going to have to make this "interesting" relatively quick. I could already feel the slow, flaming rise of the sun pulling on my eyelids like brass weights.

"Are you proposing?" I drowsily asked.

"When I propose, you'll know it."

My heart stuttered, pushing me awake again. "*When?* What do you mean 'when'?"

"I stand by my statement," Ethan said, opening the box and handing it over.

Inside sat a gleaming silver pendant shaped like a droplet, draped on a silver chain. Pressed into the back, like a jeweler's mark, was an elegant "C" surrounded by tiny but neat script: "Cadogan House, Chicago."

An immortal drop of blood, marked by our Cadogan membership. It was a perfect reminder of our origins, and our loyalties.

"It's beautiful," I said, wishing I could trace a finger across its curve, but loathe to mar the surface. "The House will like this very much."

"I hope so," Ethan said, closing the box and putting it on the nightstand. "Because they're going to have to wear them for a really long time."

Ah, vampire humor. Thank God it never got old, said no one ever.

"Bedtime?" I said, but I was already tucking into the sheets and flipping off the nightstand light.

Wordlessly, Ethan turned off the lights, and I shifted to make room. He climbed in beside me, and we spooned together to conserve precious space. Even so, Ethan's feet hung off the edge of the bed.

It was a small consolation that the sun would knock us unconscious, and we wouldn't much care how comfortable we were . . . or weren't. I moved closer into his arms and the warmth of his body, my eyes growing heavier as the sun began to rise, the stars faded, and daylight came again.

CHAPTER ELEVEN

MEET THE PARENTS

E leven hours later, the sun fell, and I awoke sweaty in a tangle of arms and legs.

Not the good kind of tangle.

The two-adults-sleeping-in-a-twin-sized-bed kind of tangle.

I peeled myself from Ethan's grasp, but I lost my balance in the process and tumbled to the floor in a heap.

It was going to be one of those kinds of evenings.

Ethan peered over the edge of the bed. "Trouble, Sentinel?"

I growled at him. "I'm fine. At the risk of sounding insensitive, how long will the Grey House vampires be here?"

"Long enough for you to incur at least two or three more moderate injuries, probably." He sat up and flipped his legs over the bed, then offered me a hand.

"In all seriousness," I said, when I was upright again, "do they have any leads on a place to stay? It's going to take a while to get the roof fixed. The mechanical gizmo was complicated." It sensed the rising and falling of the sun, and provided light or shade to the atrium accordingly.

"And it's February," I added. February was not a productive construction month in Chicago. It was simply too cold for it.

Ethan plucked up his phone from the nightstand. "I'm not certain. They'll probably have to look for something intermediate—a hotel—until they can find semipermanent housing while the construction's under way. They've not even been here twenty-four hours, Sentinel. Let's try to be gracious, shall we?"

I muttered a few choice words.

A knock sounded at the door.

"Answer it," I directed. "You're mostly dressed."

"You're already out of bed. Besides, it's for you."

"How do you know?"

"I'm psychic."

"No, you're arrogant. That's a different thing."

Since Ethan made no move to get up, and the visitor knocked insistently again, I walked to the door, smoothing back my hair before pulling it open.

Helen stood in the hallway, a black dress bag in her hands. She was already dressed in her signature tweed suit, pearls in her ears and around her neck.

"Good evening, Merit," she said, extending the bag. "For dinner with your parents."

I took the bag, and Helen turned and walked down the hall again, her pace efficient and businesslike.

I shut the door and found Ethan smiling at me with obvious amusement.

"I am not currently accepting commentary."

"Buck up, Sentinel," he said, rising and wrapping his arms around me. "You're about to don a ridiculously expensive dress that any number of Hollywood celebutantes would love to wear."

"Oh?" I said, glancing down at the bag with interest.

"As it turns out, a number of designers were thrilled at the possibility of being the first couturier of vampire fashion. You're quite the trendsetter."

"I think you have me confused with someone else," I joked, but couldn't help frowning.

"What's going on in that head of yours?" he asked.

"It's just—I worry about leaving the House when there could be an attack."

He tipped up my chin with a finger. "We are allowed to be ourselves. Ethan Sullivan and Caroline Evelyn Merit, without the obligations of our House between us."

"I know. But I feel bad gallivanting off in a party dress"—I jiggled the dress bag for effect—"when there are things to worry about here."

"We aren't leaving it alone," he reminded me. "The House is currently guarded by a full cadre of humans and two Houses of vampires, including Scott, Luc, Jonah, and both guard corps. If you and I are the two vampires that make a difference in any battle, then Scott and I have truly commended the wrong people."

I had to give him that, and not just because I'd seen Jonah wield two katanas. "And how does Luc feel about our leaving?"

"If you must know, Luc and Malik think it's a good idea."

"A good idea? Because of my parents?" I asked.

"No," Ethan said shortly.

It took me a moment to understand why they felt that way—and why it irritated him.

"They want you away from the House in case there's an attack," I said. "They want you safely on the other side of town instead of going down with the ship."

Ethan did not look thrilled at that possibility. "I would not go down with my ship. I would fight for it, as is my right. I am the Master of this House."

"I know." My guilt could hang around if it wanted, but Luc had a point. "They're your subjects, and you're their liege. You gave them immortality, and for that, they want you to keep yours. If I must take you away from danger," I said grandly, "then I must."

Ethan checked his watch. "As much as I love it when you talk duty to me, you're procrastinating again. Get ready. I want to check in with the guards before we leave, and you don't want to be late to dinner."

I definitely did not. The quickest way to exacerbate a dinner with my parents was being late for dinner with my parents.

Well, other than bringing zombies to dinner. Because who kept brains in the fridge?

"I'll shower," I said. "You find caffeine. I'm going to need it."

While Ethan was downstairs, I showered and brushed out my hair, then donned the necessary undergarments, and put on mascara and lip gloss.

The basics accomplished, I unzipped the bag and took a look.

Ethan, not surprisingly, had done it again. The dress fit the event perfectly. It was a tailored sheath made of layered silk, with a belted waist and capped sleeves. It fell to just below the knee, and the bodice was dotted with birdlike whispers of white across a black background.

I slipped the dress from the hanger, unzipped it, and stepped inside, carefully raising the silk inch by inch to avoid ripping the delicate fabric.

I managed to get the zipper together, but only halfway up my back before the sleeves fought back.

Ethan picked that moment to walk back inside, a steaming cup of what smelled like Earl Grey in hand. He found me standing in the middle of the room, the dress still hanging from my shoulders, my arm across my breasts.

"Well," he said, putting the drink on a table and his hands on his hips. "Sentinel, you are a sight."

"Can you please zip me up?"

"I'd rather stand here and enjoy this particular view." I nearly rolled my eyes, until I realized what he was wearing.

While I'd been in the shower, Ethan had dressed in a sleek black suit, with a low, five-button vest beneath his jacket. I'd said before he'd have made a delectable model, but this look cinched it. With his green eyes and golden hair, he looked like he'd stepped from an ad for a dark and smoky whiskey.

As I held up my hair, he turned around and fastened the dress, then stood behind me for a moment, his eyes on my image in the mirror that hung on the back of the closet door.

"Leave your hair down," he said, his eyes seeming to turn greener as we watched each other in the mirror.

"Down?" I asked, piling it atop my head. "I was thinking a top-knot."

"Down," he insisted.

I dropped the faux bun, and he ruffled my hair so that it fell across my shoulders, a dark curtain around my face and pale blue eyes.

He was right.

In this just-snug-enough sheath, with my hair down and the pale cast of vampire to my skin, I looked like a blue-blooded heiress. A vampiric aristocrat with an agenda and the will to see it through.

"Not bad," I said.

"Indeed," Ethan agreed, before nudging me aside and opening the shirt box he'd brought inside, revealing a half-dozen pocket squares that ranged in color from white to just slightly off-white.

While I looked on, he tucked one, then the other, carefully into his jacket pocket.

"What are you doing?"

"Selecting a square," he said, gazing at his reflection.

"For my parents?"

"For your parents, your siblings, your nieces and nephews," he said. "For you. Because I want to make a good impression."

"You've met my parents before."

"I have," he said, and met my eyes in the mirror. "But not like this."

There was a different kind of gravity in his voice. Not, I thought, from the weight of being a Master vampire, of caring for others and ensuring their safety, but from the weight of being *us*. Of having, for the first time in a long time, someone whose safety and happiness you put above all others. Even if that meant impressing her particularly stuffy family.

"Sometimes you make me swoon."

"If it's only sometimes, I'm not doing my job adequately." He made a final silken selection, put the square into the pocket on his jacket and adjusted it, and checked himself out in the mirror. "Not bad, Sentinel."

"Not bad indeed. I think we're ready."

"Shoes?" he said, glancing down at my feet.

"Ah," I said. I looked in the closet and found several pairs awaiting me. Helen must have brought them down from the apartments. I climbed into an appropriate pair, and turned around for Ethan's final review.

"And away we go," I said.

Ethan looked at my shoes with an expression of abject horror. Stilettos were definitely the right choice for the dress . . . but not for February in Chicago.

That's why I'd pulled on a pair of ugly, puce green galoshes to wear in and out of the car, and Ethan did not look impressed.

I put on an expression of pure, unmitigated innocent. "You don't like these?"

"You aren't serious."

"About what? The shoes?" I glanced down, stifling a grin. "It's February, Ethan. There's snow on the ground."

He watched me for a minute. "You're kidding."

"I was." I held up the pair of black lace stilettos I'd been holding behind my back. "Do you prefer these?"

He looked relieved. "All that drama for a bit?"

"It was a good bit." I did a little soft-shoe in the galoshes to punctuate the joke.

"Let's go, Ginger Rogers," Ethan said, pointing dictatorially toward the door. But he was grinning when he said it.

Dressed in our finest, we headed downstairs to the Ops Room to ensure the House was prepared and we could still make a getaway.

Luc, Lindsey, and Juliet were in residence, but the Grey House vampires hadn't yet descended. Margot had clearly prepared for them, as a giant tray of pastries sat in the middle of the conference table. My stomach growled—a few sips of tea hadn't done much for my hunger—but I resisted the urge to nosh, knowing I'd inevitably drip pastry cream or sugared fruit down the front of my expensive frock.

Luc whistled when she caught sight of us. "Merit, you are a sight."

"What's the occasion?" Lindsey asked. I guess she hadn't yet read Luc's reports for the night.

"We're having dinner with my parents," I said with a grimace.

"You are kidding," Lindsey said.

Ethan and I took seats at the conference table. "Not a bit," he said. "They sent a paper invitation and everything."

"I'm surprised you're going," Lindsey said, her gaze narrowing suspiciously.

"Ethan thought it was a good idea."

"So you're blaming me for this?"

"Whenever possible," I said with a smile. But that smile faded quickly. "Oh crap."

"What?" Ethan asked, alarm in his expression.

"Aren't we supposed to take something to dinner?" I asked, looking around the room. "Like a side dish or dessert or something. Don't people usually do that when they're, you know, adults?"

I didn't have a lot of experience with potlucks, as my fusty parents generally relied on Pennebaker, their butler, to make most of their domestic arrangements. But I'd accompanied friends to their parents' homes, and they always seemed to bring along cupcakes or dinner rolls or an extra bag of chips.

"Sometimes," Lindsey said. "But I don't think it's required or anything."

Maybe not, but I still imagined Robert and Charlotte arriving at my parents' doorstep with children and hot dishes in hand, and I'd show up with a beau on my arm, a borrowed car, and a lifestyle my parents undoubtedly found questionable.

"Wine," Ethan said. "We'll ask Margot for a bottle of wine before we leave."

"Good idea," Lindsey said, snapping her fingers. "Make it a red. Humans love red wine."

Luc looked at her askance. "Since when are you an expert on the human palate?"

"Since I *was* one," she sarcastically said.

Ethan rolled his eyes and tapped his watch. "Since we're down here, maybe we should discuss the protection of the House?"

"Right on," Luc said, looking to Ethan. "We've polled the House. No one claims to know Robin Pope or recognize her picture, so that gives us some hope. But obviously, we're still on high alert, considering the circumstances."

"The riot circumstances?" Jonah asked, appearing at the doorway. "Or the GP ones?"

Jonah took in our ensembles but didn't comment. I bet he *had* read Luc's daily report.

"Both," Ethan said. "Monmonth called a few minutes after dawn. He said he considers our harboring Grey House to be an act of war."

Jonah looked stunned; I did not. I might have been a newer, greener vampire, but I had a lot more experience with GP shenanigans and egoism. Grey House hadn't much been on the GP's radar; we had. Often. Which was precisely why we'd left, even if our leaving hadn't done much to eliminate the shenanigans. They'd pulled us back in.

"Just like in *The Godfather*," I muttered.

"What was that?" Jonah asked.

"Nothing," I said, turning to Ethan. "Can't Darius do something to stop him? He's still in charge."

"Technically in charge," Ethan said. "But his political capital is nearly gone. He all but pushed us out of the GP, lost us when we called his bluff, wasn't able to consummate an attack against us, and was injured by a Rogue vampire. That doesn't exactly inspire confidence among the world's most powerful vamps."

"Confidentially," Jonah said, "it appears Darius has become rather agoraphobic since his fight with Michael Donovan."

"Agoraphobic?"

"The encounter freaked him out," Jonah said. "He's not used to being weak, to feeling weak. Donovan got the jump on him, which completely screwed up his sense of self. The others, especially Monmonth, feel that weakness."

"To be fair, he was wielding a gun that shot aspen stakes," I said.

"Certainly," Jonah allowed. "But Darius is centuries old, and he's fought enemies before. And usually doesn't need a pink vampire to rescue him."

"Pink" in vampire terminology didn't refer to my gender, but my age. I'd been a vampire for less than a year, and it stung Darius that his rescuer had been less strong and skilled than he imagined himself to be.

"And the other members of the GP are exploiting it?" Lindsey asked.

Jonah nodded. "They are vampires in the most traditional sense. Old-school monsters. The type Van Helsing hunted. The type villagers killed. They do not let subordination stand in their way."

"Which is why they attacked Cadogan House," Luc said, "even if they stood to gain financially when we left."

We'd been required to pay the GP back for financial gains we'd made during our tenure in the GP, but because their attack breached our contract, we got to keep the money.

"So what do we do?" I asked.

"In the long term, ironically, we do what we can to secure Darius's position. If he remains head of the GP, this conversation is moot."

"How can we make him stronger?" Jonah asked.

"That will require some strategizing," Ethan said.

"And in the short term?" I asked.

"We keep an eye out. I don't think Monmonth has the allies for another full-on attack. The fairies got what they wanted, and our peace remains in place. I can't think he'd strike out against the combined Houses with only half the members of the GP at his side. But as to what he might actually do? I don't know."

"We're putting a guard on the widow's walk," Luc said. "They have a bird's-eye view of the yard. Jonah and I also have created a new schedule for the Cadogan and Grey House guards. You'll find an app ready to download, and you'll get a reminder fifteen minutes before your shift. It's cold as a witch's tit out there, so grab gloves, earmuffs, hot chocolate, whatever you need to stay warm. But get out there, and be alert. Oh, and one spot of good news—Saul offered to donate pizzas to feed the extra-large House tonight. A little thank-you since Merit got him some protection during the Wicker Park riot."

"Of all the nights we have dinner with my parents," I murmured.

Ethan squeezed my hand supportively. "You'll manage, Sentinel."

"If it makes you feel better, Sentinel, we've put you on the patrol roster for later, so you can freeze with the rest of them."

I smiled a little. "It does, actually."

"Saul's gonna deliver the pies directly into the basement," Luc said. "That way the guards only have to approve one truck, instead of keeping an eye on vampires and humans running back and forth into the House."

"Good thought," Jonah said.

"I have them occasionally," Luc said, with honest modesty. "Not often, but occasionally."

"If we're done here," Ethan said, "we do need to get going."
He rose, and I did the same.

Jonah stood up as well. "Ethan, Merit, could I talk to you for a
moment outside?"

Ethan nodded his agreement but looked suspicious of the request.

We walked out of the Ops Room and toward the basement
door, then stopped for the chat.

"Considering the threat by the humans and the GP, Grey
House believes it's time to consider an alternative method of protecting the Houses," Jonah said.

Ethan put his hands in his pockets. That was another signature
move, a gesture that looked casual but usually signified he was
paying very close, very careful attention. "Which is?"

"There are people in this town who are stronger than we are. I
think we should consider adding them to the mix."

"You mean the sorcerers?" I asked, referring to Catcher, Mallory, and Paige, a sorceress we'd brought back with us from Nebraska.

"I do."

"No," Ethan said. "We've talked about this. Mallory violated
this House."

"You're right," I agreed. "She damaged property and hurt people. But she's also skilled. She's more powerful than Monmonth or
McKetrick or anyone else that we know of."

"They aren't supposed to be practicing sorcerers," Ethan
pointed out. "Catcher got kicked out of the Order, and Mallory's
on house arrest. I don't believe Paige is official, either."

"Catcher's already used magic this week, and Mallory can't be
magicless forever. If she's going to use magic again, maybe it's not
a bad idea that we harness it for our purposes."

Ethan stood quietly for a moment, staring at the floor, brows knitted as he considered.

Jonah glanced at me, and I shrugged. There was no doubt—Mallory was a risk.

But maybe, if she had the support of her friends and a network of supernaturals, she could figure out a way to do it right this time.

I frowned. Had I really come around to thinking Mallory was the solution? Was I ready for her to use magic again? No. I wasn't ready for it. But it was inevitable. And the only way to keep that inevitability from coming back to haunt us was to control it in the first place.

"I'll consider it," he said.

We both looked over at him.

"You're sure?" I said.

"Definitely not. But, loathe as I am to admit it, Jonah's right. They are stronger than we are, and we are vulnerable now in a new and different kind of way. It would behoove us to consider all possibilities. I've been called a control freak," he said, looking pointedly at me. "Maybe it's time to hand over a bit of that control to our witchy friends."

"Let us know how we can help," Jonah said.

"Rest assured," Ethan said, "We will. I want this House secure, and I want it secure now."

After ensuring the House was in good hands and that Luc, Malik, Scott, and Jonah had Ethan's number, my number, my parents' number, and my grandfather's number handy, and after grabbing a bottle of red wine from the kitchen, we proceeded to the parking area, scabbards and shoes in hand.

Ethan opted to drive to Oak Park, which was fine by me. He

also opted to take his new, shiny Ferrari. It probably would have been even more fun in the summer than on ice- and snow-packed streets, but we made do. Because, again, it was a *Ferrari*.

It was clear when we exited the basement that security around the House was tighter than usual. There were double the usual number of guards at the gates, more humans posted along the perimeter, and vampires interspersed with them, keeping a supernatural eye on things.

After two bouts of stop-and-go traffic—the first because of an empty sedan on the shoulder with its hazard lights on; the second because of a piece of cardboard in the road—we made it to Oak Park, the western suburb of Chicago that my parents called home. Ethan pulled the Ferrari in front of my parents' blocky, modern house. It was the only one in the neighborhood built in that style, and that wasn't a compliment.

Ethan helped me out of the car, which was tricky, considering my body-hugging skirt. The wind was bone-chillingly cold, even with a coat, gloves, a scarf, and galoshes.

I stared up at the boxy house, preparing myself for a moment before we went inside. Before my sister, mother, and sister-in-law fell on Ethan like hyenas at a kill.

"Are you okay?" Ethan asked when the doors were closed and the car was locked again.

I glanced back at him, so ridiculously handsome in his three-piece suit, so unlike any other man I'd met. He was as awe-inspiring as he was frustrating.

"I'm fine," I said, glancing over at the luxury minivans in the driveway. Neither Charlotte nor Robert spared the expense for top-of-the-line kid carriers. "Nervous, which seems to be a common theme these days."

Ethan frowned. "I thought you and your father were making progress."

"We were, although with my father, it's two steps forward, twelve steps back. It's more the rest of the crew that I'm worried about."

"I will try to forgo their advances on your behalf, Sentinel."

I rolled my eyes, knowing he was baiting me to help me relax, and loving him more for it. "You're not that irresistible, Sullivan."

He stopped suddenly, one foot on the street and one on the snowy curb. "Now you've done it," he murmured. Before I could object, he scooped me off the ground and into his arms, and carried me down the sidewalk to my parents' front door.

"What are you doing?"

"Being irresistible," he said matter-of-factly, as if there were nothing even remotely unusual about a vampire in a sexy black suit carrying his woman down the snowy sidewalk to her parents' castle.

I guess I hadn't needed the galoshes after all.

My arms around his neck, his mouth pulled into a haughty smirk, I couldn't help but smile.

He walked up the steps as if my weight were negligible—impossible, since I was five foot eight—and placed me carefully on the stoop. But he paused there for a moment, on one knee, grinning up at me.

My heart nearly stopped. Was he . . . ? He couldn't be . . .

As casually as he'd picked me up, Ethan flicked a bit of lint from the knee of his pants.

"Just a spot of dust," he explained, rising again and grinning wickedly at me. "Did you think I was on one knee for some other reason, Sentinel?"

My heart began to beat again. "You are a cruel, cruel man."

"If it's any consolation, I'm your cruel man." He lifted my hand to his lips and pressed a kiss to my palm. "Forever," he added, and I smiled like a smitten teenager. Ethan Sullivan could play me like a Stradivarius.

"Let's go, Casanova," I told him, smoothing out my skirt and raising my fist to knock on the door.

My mother pulled it open before I made a sound, and I blushed, wondering how much of the front porch drama she'd seen. She wore a pale blue sheath dress and a string of pearls, her blond bob of hair perfectly arranged.

"Merit!" she said, her voice tinkling. "We're so glad you're here. You look absolutely gorgeous. So professional." She pressed a kiss to my cheek before immediately dismissing me for bigger and better prey.

"Ethan, you look absolutely dashing. That suit is terribly becoming." She squeezed his hands and pressed a kiss to his cheek.

"You look lovely yourself, Mrs. Merit." Slyly, he glanced between us. "I'd have taken you for sisters."

My mother waved him away, crimson rising on her cheeks. "Hush," she said. "And call me Meredith. I insist."

For a moment, my mother looked at us, a mixture of pride and relief in her expression. I wasn't sure which of those to find flattering.

"Where are my manners?" she asked. "Come in, come in." We didn't need the formal invitation—we'd been in the house before— but we nodded politely and stepped inside, pulling the door closed behind us.

My mother reached out a hand for our coats, then deposited them on a wooden coat stand by the door. "We've given Pennebaker the night off since the family's all here, so just make yourselves at home."

I found it remarkable she'd arranged a dinner for so many without him. It either meant she'd cooked, which would be unfortunate, or she'd hired in the food. I crossed my fingers for the latter.

My mother smiled and clapped her hands together as she took in our ensembles, at least until she saw the galoshes on my feet. Her smile faded quickly.

I held up the straps of the heels in my hand. "Don't worry; I brought backups."

"Whew," she said. "I was afraid you were going to ruin that dress with those shoes. If we're calling them that. Plastic mud clompers, more like."

She disappeared into the hallway while Ethan chuckled beside me.

"Plastic mud clompers," he repeated.

I made a vague sound, using his body as a brace while I traded galoshes for pointy-toed stilettos. When the trade was done, I'd gained three inches in height. Still not enough to be at eye level with Ethan, but a good deal closer.

My mother appeared again with champagne flutes in hand and gave one to each of us.

I took a heartening sip before noticing the goofy expression on my mother's face.

Please do not glamour my mother, I silently requested.

I have no need to glamour, Sentinel. I'm naturally this charming.

I kept the commentary to myself.

We followed my mother into the house as five children—three boys and two girls—ran past us, toys in hand.

"My nieces and nephews," I explained.

"And Elizabeth is expecting a third. We're just in the sitting room," she added, and we followed her through the front of the house to the main living area.

As we made the journey, I found a house utterly different from the one I was used to. I knew my mother had planned to redecorate—she'd been moving out the old furniture during my last visit. But the change was remarkable. The architecture was still the same—concrete, like the exterior—but she'd brought in furniture and décor that made it feel warm and inviting, not the cold and clinical shell it had been before. No small feat for a concrete box of a house.

The sitting room, especially, was completely different, now full of rugs and brightly colored furniture, ten-foot plants, and a bevy of family portraits. And on that comfy furniture lounged a bevy of Merits.

"Merit!" squealed the youngest in the family, the nearly two-year-old Olivia, my sister Charlotte's daughter. She was adorably dressed in a green velvet dress that matched her mother's, her hair in pigtails that poked from each side of her head.

She ran haltingly toward me and held up her hands, clenching her fists, demanding that I pick her up.

"Hello, Miss Olivia," I said, putting my flute on a nearby cocktail table and propping her onto my hip. "You are so heavy! How did you get so heavy?"

"I grow," she said simply.

"I think you weigh as much as your mother does."

"I'm taking that as a compliment to me, little sister." Charlotte, wearing a green sheath, her dark hair cut into a short, pixie cut, kissed my cheek. "How are you?"

"I'm good. And it looks like Olivia's good."

"I'm two," Olivia said, holding up the requisite number of fingers.

"That is really old," I said. "You're a big girl now."

Olivia nodded gravely, then took a shy peek at the man who stood beside me. Charlotte was much less subtle.

"Oh my God, you are gorgeous!" Charlotte exclaimed. She had a cocktail in one hand and, suddenly, Ethan's arm in the other. "I told her to nab you while she could."

Ethan beamed at me. "She nabbed," he said, apparently delighted by the familial attention.

"Maybe now she'll finally trust that I'm right about everything," Charlotte said. "She had a very difficult time with that growing up."

"She still has a difficult time with it. I'm nearly always right, and she seems to forget that fact rather often. It's unfortunate, really."

"I bet," Charlotte said.

"Where's Major?" I asked. Major Corkberger was Charlotte's heart-surgeon husband.

"On call, of course, as usual. He's a surgeon," she added to Ethan, as if the news was confidential. Ethan nodded politely.

"Here, Olivia, why don't we let Auntie Merit and Uncle Ethan say hello to everyone else?" Charlotte asked. Olivia held out her hands to be swept away by her mother.

Ethan didn't verbally object to being called Uncle Ethan, although he did look a bit paler than usual—a difficult feat for a vampire.

"Uncle Ethan?" he asked, when Charlotte walked away.

I slipped my arm in his. "Just keep breathing, Sullivan. Isn't that what you've been telling me?"

I introduced him to Elizabeth, Robert's sable-haired wife, who looked nearly ready to pop with child number three. Ethan helped her off the couch when she needed a hand, and he managed not to wince when she wrapped him in a hug.

"We are just so glad Merit's found someone who makes her happy."

"Thank you," he said. "I do my best."

Elizabeth looked back and forth between us, a knowing smile on her face. "Mm-hmm," she said, a hand on her belly. "There's a lot of potential here. I can see it."

I finished my champagne in a single gulp. "Another glass maybe, Mom?"

"Oh hush," Elizabeth said, giving me a playful slap on the arm.

I'd always liked Elizabeth. Where Robert was the spitting image of my father, physically and emotionally, Elizabeth was funny and grounded. She was still a society girl, her father a magnate in his own right, but she'd always seemed comfortable in her own skin, like she didn't need to show off in order to prove her worth to everyone else.

"I assume your intentions are honorable?" she asked Ethan.

"What answer won't get me in trouble?" he asked, and to a one, every human female in the room over the age of ten sighed.

I rolled my eyes, but inwardly, the entire conversation was kind of . . . awesome. For the first time in my life, I didn't feel like an outsider in my own family. I had a family of my own, a partner in my escapades. We were here—together—so I didn't feel like the odd duck out.

And then, on the other end of the spectrum, was the man who'd seemed to make it his life's purpose to transform me into something else. From shy teenager to socialite. From human to vampire.

"You're here."

We turned to find my father in the doorway. Joshua Merit walked in, utter confidence in his stride. My older brother, Robert, joined him.

Like me, my father had dark hair and pale blue eyes. Robert had my mother's fair coloring, but he and my father shared the same aristocratic features and square shoulders.

"Ethan," my father said, walking forward with a hand outstretched. They shook hands, but Ethan's posture didn't change.

There was no sense of sycophancy or toadying about him. He might have been a guest in my father's home, but he was a force to be reckoned with in his own right, not a politico eager to hop onto my father's coattails.

"Joshua," Ethan said. They shook on it, and my father turned to me.

"Merit," he said, a bit awkwardly, and without offering a handshake or a hug.

"Dad," I said, then looked at my brother. "Robert."

Robert seemed older than the last time I'd seen him. More mature, or perhaps simply with more weight on his shoulders. He stood in line to take over Merit Properties, so there would have been plenty of weight to go around.

"Hello, Merit," he said, then nodded at Ethan. "Robert Merit."

"Ethan Sullivan."

They looked at each other for a moment. I wouldn't have called my brother the protective type, but there was something vaguely threatening in his eyes. I wasn't naïve enough to think it had anything to do with me. Robert was protective of my father and the family name, and I imagine he hadn't yet decided whether Ethan was a threat.

After a moment of staring each other down, Robert's posture eased a bit. "You're looking well," he said to me.

I nodded. "Thanks. Congratulations on the baby. Elizabeth seems very happy."

He nodded the same way my father did. Just a bob of the head, as if he were too busy to waste motion on anything more excessive.

"We're very blessed," he said. "It looks like you're having a rough go of it this week."

"Our popularity waxes and wanes," Ethan said, "as it always has. At the moment, there is very clearly a vocal crowd of anti-vampire Chicagoans."

"Unfortunate," my father said, "that they would judge a man based on his physical attributes, rather than his deeds."

"Hear! Hear!" Ethan said.

My father nodded with approval at Ethan's approval of him. "Now that we've all shaken hands, perhaps a drink in the office before dinner? It will give us a chance to chat."

He glanced at my mother questioningly, probably to check there was time enough before dinner was served.

"Yes," she said. "Head that way and leave us to our chatting." She waved at them. "Shoo."

Ethan glanced back at me, and his expression was hard to gauge. Something between "Save me!" and "I am beginning to regret my enthusiasm for this dinner idea."

I gave him a mean-spirited wave. "See you in a bit, darling."

His eyes narrowed as my father and Robert shuffled him down the hallway, but he went willingly, a prisoner with no hope for escape, having accepted the inevitability of his sentence.

As he disappeared, the children ran through the sitting room, dragging wooden pull-toys behind them. Loudly. And with extreme prejudice.

"So," Charlotte said, putting a hand on my knee, "I don't want to get ahead of myself, but have you considered your china patterns yet?"

Called it.

CHAPTER TWELVE

❧

NOTABLE NOSTALGIA

Eventually, the boys' and girls' clubs came back together, meeting in the dining room at an enormous table (also new) for a meal of roast beast (undetermined origin), mashed root vegetable (undetermined origin), and other assorted dishes. The children were seated at a smaller table in the next room. While we dined on fine china, they got plastic plates decorated with robots and were probably discussing the latest toys and electronic gadgets. I guessed I could have pretty happily integrated into that conversation.

What did not make me happy was the mild buzz of irritated magic that flowed from Ethan as he came back into the room, my father and brother in tow.

I grabbed two glasses of wine from the buffet—my mother hadn't stocked Blood4You—and took one to Ethan.

"Are you all right?" I quietly asked.

He took the glass but didn't drink from it.

"Business was discussed," he said without elaboration. He sounded, frankly, a bit mystified.

"Do we need to step out and discuss anything?"

"No need," he said, squeezing my hand and, when he realized I still wasn't satisfied, glancing down at me.

"All is well, Sentinel. Your father made a business proposal of a kind. It was . . . unexpected."

I suppose I shouldn't have been surprised that my father had cornered Ethan and made a business play. I shouldn't have been surprised that we'd probably been called to the house on this February night just for that purpose, because I'd once agreed to talk to my brother about family business, and my father was collecting on the debt.

"Never mind," Ethan said, taking a sip of his wine. "How about you? How was girls' time?"

"It was odd. Unusually drama free."

He chuckled. "What had you expected? Hair pulling?"

I shrugged. "I've always been the odd one out. I just figured the transition would be harder than it is."

"The transition to society dame?"

That narrowed my eyes. "I am not a society dame."

"All right," my mother said, interrupting the parrying. "I think we're ready for dinner!"

Right on cue, women and men in black pants and crisp white button-downs emerged from the kitchen. That explained the food; she'd hired caterers. They took up positions behind the buffet and drink station, tools in hand, ready to meet our every culinary whim.

I wasn't sure I would ever understand my parents. But I understood dinner, so I let the caterers place food on my plate and sat down at the table beside Ethan, the tension between him and my father nearly palpable when everyone took seats.

"A toast," Robert said, holding his glass aloft. "To a family united, to our health and well-being, to our prosperity and happiness."

We said, "Cheers," and clinked together our very expensive glassware, and then began our meal.

The conversation was typical. My father and brother argued about politics and money, and my mother and sister discussed neighborhood gossip. Each set tried to draw me into the conversation, but I generally preferred to watch and listen. That was probably what made me a good research and graduate student: I was fascinated enough by other people and their drama that people watching kept me pretty entertained.

The family had better luck engaging Ethan. He wasn't shy with his opinions, and although he was respectful, he was a man secure in his skin and in the world. He didn't bother with waffling or sycophancy, not when there was honesty to be had.

So this is a family meal, he said after a while.

I speared a bit of asparagus with my fork. *Indeed. Welcome to the Merit home.*

They're very formal, aren't they?

They like to be fancy, I agreed. *It's part of my father's plan to distance himself from his upbringing.* That upbringing being his lot as the son of a cop. Fancy is as fancy does.

My sister caught my light smile and gave me a sly one. "What's so funny over there?"

"Nothing," I said. "Just enjoying my asparagus."

"Mm-hmm," she said, but clearly didn't buy it.

"Hush, Charlotte," my mother said. "They're in love. Let them have their moment."

Wearing my expensive heels and my designer dress, and sitting next to the most handsome man I'd ever seen, I stuck my tongue out at my sister.

"Enjoy the thrill of young love," my father said, as if suddenly an expert on emotional fulfillment. "Youth is fleeting. Well, perhaps not in your case."

My sister raised her glass. "Here's to never needing, shall we say, facial enhancement procedures."

"Amen to that," my mother said, flicking a delicate gaze to Ethan. "If it's not impolite, may I ask how old you are?"

"It isn't," he said, "and you may. I'm three hundred and ninety-four years old. Oh, and approximately three-quarters."

The table went silent.

"That such a thing could even be possible . . . ," my mother mused.

"The things you must have seen—experienced," Elizabeth said, eyes shining with curiosity. "World wars. New technologies. The advent of modern medicine. It's staggering."

"I have been lucky to sample much that is laudable among humans," he said. He reached out and put a hand on mine. "And to find a prize awaiting me at the end of four centuries."

I might have sighed, but for the glint in his eye that told me Ethan was playing his crowd, and with success. My mother, sister, and even pragmatic sister-in-law got dreamy expressions at the sentiment.

Kiss-ass, I mentally accused.

How dare you think the sentiment is anything less than genuine?

The sentiment was intended to woo my family. So much for thinking him not sycophantic.

Ah, Sentinel. So suspicious. He picked up my hand and pressed it to his lips in full sight of the rest of the table, leading to even more sighs and puppy dog expressions.

For a pretentious Master vampire, Darth Sullivan was pretty dreamy.

An hour later, we finished the evening in the sitting room, a warm and pliable Olivia asleep in my arms.

"It's amazing how limp she goes, isn't it?" Charlotte remarked.

"It really is," I said, wincing a little as I tried to gently shift my arms, which were stiffening from the sack of potatoes in my lap. And a beautiful sack of potatoes at that.

Olivia was as pretty as her parents; she'd leave any number of broken hearts in her wake. Teenage boys who dreamed of her from afar; frat boys too cool to approach her.

Not that her appearance would define her. She was the grand-daughter of one of the most powerful men in Chicago, the daughter of a heart surgeon and a philanthropist. Ivy League schools would vie for her attention. That would be a pretty fun battle to watch.

But as I smiled down at her, I couldn't help but feel saddened by my own limitations. Vampires couldn't have children. I wouldn't be a mother, and Ethan wouldn't be a father. And despite Gabriel's once-upon-a-time prediction, it wasn't possible that a child with eyes as green as Ethan's could be in our future.

Suddenly struck by melancholy, I felt my eyes fill with tears, and I stared down at Olivia until I was sure I'd blinked them back, and they wouldn't spill across my face like etchings of grief.

After a moment, I glanced up at Ethan and found sadness in his eyes. We hadn't spoken, but he'd watched me hold a sleeping child—and mourn for a future we couldn't have.

Olivia woke, her eyes suddenly wide and staring up at a person who wasn't her mother. She began to cry, and Charlotte rose and lifted her from my arms, leaving behind wrinkled silk and a bit of sadness.

"Stranger danger," Elizabeth said.

"No kidding," Charlotte said, hoisting Olivia onto her hip. She wrapped her arms around her mother's neck and plunked her head down, her eyes drifting shut almost immediately.

"I think that's our cue to get home," she said.

"We should probably be going as well," Ethan said. "We've some matters at the House to attend to."

My mother nodded and rose. "I'll get your coats."

My father stood and reached out to shake Ethan's hand again. "Nice seeing you again. And do remember our conversation."

Ethan nodded tightly and escorted me back to the door, where my mother had readied our outerwear. We slipped on our coats, and I pulled on my galoshes. The mood was suddenly somber, having shifted from awe of vampire longevity to sadness about our other physical shortcomings.

"It's lovely seeing you so happy," my mother said, embracing me, apparently oblivious to the change in mood.

"Thanks, Mom. You, too."

We exchanged hugs and promises to do dinner again soon, then Ethan and I walked down the sidewalk, our hands linked together.

I picked carefully across the ice to the car's passenger side and climbed in. Ethan started the Ferrari with a tantalizing purr, and his phone began to ring almost immediately.

"It's Luc," he said, then put the phone on speaker.

"Ethan and Merit," he answered.

"You're on speakerphone in the Ops Room."

Luc's voice was tight, which put my nerves on edge. He wouldn't have called unless it was important, but Luc's brand of important was rarely good news.

"What's wrong?" Ethan asked.

"The CPD is done with Robin Pope. They've released her."

"Released her?" I repeated, panic rising in my voice. "Why?"

"Because she's alibied for both riots," Jonah said. "She wasn't at either."

"But her complaint against Bryant Industries?" I asked. "Her relationship with the Grey House vamp? Those couldn't have been coincidence."

"They were," Luc said. "She hasn't so much as sent an e-mail to anybody arrested in the riots, surfed a Web page, anything. I realize it's not much of an update, but I wanted to let you know as soon as possible."

"Thank you, Luc. We'll be back to the House shortly."

Ethan hung up the phone and glanced at me. "Ideas?"

"Not a single damn one. I was certain she was involved, and now we're back at square one."

"We will deal with this just as we've dealt with everything else. The solution is there, waiting for us to find it."

I nodded. "We have to go back to the start. Visit Bryant Industries and see if there's anything to be learned. See what we missed."

"We spend enough money on their products that they could probably afford to give us a factory tour."

"It's late," I said. "Will they still be around? At least without a riot to attend to?"

Ethan nodded. "Bryant Industries works with us, so Charla tends to keep vampire hours. I'll send her a message and see if it can be arranged."

He did so, then updated Luc and pulled into the road and then into traffic. When we'd gotten some distance from my parents' house, I voiced the question I'd been pondering since Ethan had emerged from my father's study.

"Out of curiosity, what did you and my father talk about?"

For a moment, Ethan didn't answer, and I wasn't sure if he'd heard me.

"Your father wants to become an investor in Cadogan House."

"He what?" I boggled at the request. I presumed my father had wanted to discuss Ethan's putting in a good word about Merit Properties with other Houses. This was in an entirely different orbit.

"He has money and connections. He wants to offer us a rather considerable amount of money to join the House's board of directors."

I frowned. "We don't have a board of directors."

"No, we do not. Which is one of the smaller of many, many problems with his proposal."

"He wants to pay us to let him control the House?"

Ethan nodded. "Your father has demonstrated very questionable decision making in the past. Which means that power might be used in questionable ways."

I nodded. "We'd be trading one GP for another."

"I'm glad to hear you think so." There was relief in his voice that I didn't find flattering.

"You can't think I'd have supported the idea? Giving my father the key to your kingdom?"

"Your father is a powerful man, and with power comes protection. I wasn't afraid you'd support the idea, but I wondered if you'd find it attractive."

"I find peace and serenity attractive. Bringing my father into our House is not the way to accomplish either of those. No," I concluded. "There's no way."

I looked out the window, wondering how things had gone so sideways.

Charla Bryant agreed happily to another meeting; Ethan was one of her customers, after all. The police tape was gone, the debris had been cleaned away from the lawn, and new wooden studs and plastic sheeting were in place. Charla was definitely a woman of action.

We stood in front of the building for a moment and scanned the scene.

"The damage looks mostly superficial," Ethan said.

"I think it was. The fire didn't go very deep into the building, but they spread across the front."

Ethan nodded. "Let's go see what kind of trouble we can get into."

"Actually, Luc would prefer you not get into any trouble."

Ethan smirked. "Then you shouldn't have let me out of the House, Sentinel."

I guess I couldn't argue with that. But I could keep an eye on him, so I followed him to the make-do front door, now guarded by a beefy man in a security guard's uniform.

He looked at us suspiciously when we approached. "Can I help you?"

"I'm Ethan, and this is Merit. We're here to talk to Ms. Bryant."

The guard smiled, his grin wide, toothy, and completely disarming, and nodded at Ethan. "I know who you are, Mr. Sullivan. I'm a Rogue myself, but I'm acquainted with your House and your tribulations with the GP. I hope you come out on top."

Ethan offered him a hand. "We just hope to come out of it," he said, "but I appreciate the thought."

The guard lifted the plastic and we walked inside, where the coppery tang of blood filled the air.

At least I'd actually eaten this time.

A woman with short brown hair peeked in from a door that led farther into the building. "Can I help you?"

"We're here to see Charla Bryant."

"I'll just notify her," she said brightly, then disappeared again.

Ethan, apparently not content to stand by and wait, walked to the end of the hallway, which ended in a large window.

"Come here," he said over his shoulder, and I joined him.

The window looked in on the bottling room. There were giant vats and long conveyors of bottles being washed, filled, capped, and cleaned. Everything was automated, and the entire line moved so fast my brain could barely keep up.

"Very cool," I said.

"And very crucial," said a voice behind us.

We turned to find Charla in the hallway in a fitted navy sheath dress and kitten heels. Her hair was tucked behind a couple of thin navy headbands. She looked like the perfect business-woman—whether or not that business was supernaturally related.

"We supply the vampires of Chicago and much of the upper Midwest. We're one of the largest facilities in the country." She smiled at us and stepped forward. "Ethan," she said, extending a hand, "it's lovely to finally meet you in person."

"Charla, a pleasure. And I understand you've met Merit."

Charla nodded, then clasped her hands in front of her. "It looks like you've had an evening out. Except for the galoshes, perhaps."

"We've tried," Ethan said. "Per my note, we're here about the riots. We'd believed Robin Pope might have played a role in se-lecting Bryant Industries as her first target. But it appears she's unconnected to the crime."

"I see," Charla said, frowning. "So you're looking for another cause?"

"We're trying to identify the source of the riots so we can stop them from happening again," Ethan said.

Charla smiled, just a little. "Like the Supernatural Justice League?"

"Something like that," he said. "I don't suppose you've thought of any other reason you might have been targeted?"

"Honestly, I've been racking my brain. I wasn't convinced Robin had the capacity to organize people—she just doesn't think anyone is as intelligent as she is—but she is a very angry person. So from that perspective, the theory fit. But I cannot think of any other reason people would be upset with us, other than because we're associated with vampires, of course. No grudges, no family disputes."

My gaze kept flicking back to the production line, the blur of bottles streaming by.

"This is pretty amazing to watch," I said. "And it's so clean. Not that I expected it to be dirty, but when you're bottling a liquid, you expect spills. That room looks spotless."

"Oh, it is," Charla said. "We had a city inspection last week, so we've been extra careful about pretty much every detail around here, including security."

Ethan looked suddenly interested. "A city inspection?"

Charla nodded. "Department of Public Health. They inspect our facility as part of our arrangement with the city. They've known who we are and what we do for a very long time. They had to—it was the only way we could get operational permits." She frowned. "Although, come to think of it, this inspection was a little less than routine."

"How so?" Ethan asked.

"Normally, our inspections are scheduled a month in advance. We might have an unscheduled drop-in, of course, but the top-to-bottom reviews are planned. This last time, they gave us two days."

Ethan and I exchanged a glance.

"You said the inspection was a week ago," I said. "Just a few days before the riot?"

"I hadn't thought of that," Charla said. "But now that you mention it, yes. They did. Do you think that matters?"

"It's difficult to tell," Ethan said. "Perhaps it's coincidence."

Or perhaps, I thought, *someone wanted inside the facility*.

"Did anything weird occur during the inspection? Did they take anything, or look at anything they don't usually inspect?"

"I actually wasn't here that day," Charla said sheepishly. "I take a spa day twice a year, and I'd had it scheduled for months, so when they called about the inspection, I let my brother handle it."

I smiled politely. "Completely understandable."

She nodded but clearly wasn't convinced she'd done the right thing. "No one reported anything odd to me afterward, and the inspection report was fine. Do you suspect foul play?"

"We suspect the timing," Ethan said, gesturing toward the front door. "You might want to check with your brother, ask if anything unusual occurred he might not have thought to mention."

"I appreciate the suggestion," Charla said, her expression changing to the same all-business mode I'd seen in Ethan's. She wasn't a vampire, but she was a leader of humans, and a protector of her particular house.

"Also, you'd mentioned your brother might have security videos he could share?"

Charla pointed at me and pulled a phone from an invisible pocket at her hip. "Thank you for the reminder. I'll send him a note right now." She paused for a moment, looking at the phone, which then beeped in acknowledgment.

"Got it," she said. "He promises to send them tonight." She put the phone away and smiled at us. "I love my brother, but he's not quite as . . . *organized* as I am, if you catch my drift."

"We do," Ethan said. "And we thank you again." He put a hand at my back. "We'll get out of your hair so you can get back to work. Thank you for your time."

"You're very welcome. Thank you for paying attention." She dropped her voice to a whisper. "I know I shouldn't say this, but we talk, you know. The distributors. Most of us are human, but we like to keep an eye out, and not just because you're clients. It's a tough time to be a vampire in Chicago, especially when thugs like McKetrick are about. And we know about the GP, about how you stepped forward when others didn't. Being the leader can be a thankless job," she said. "It often just makes you a bigger target. But we see. We notice."

Ethan took her hand in his and patted it collegially. "Thank you, Charla. I appreciate that very much."

We said our good-byes to Charla and the guard, and walked back across crunchy sidewalks to the car.

"A last-minute city inspection?" I wondered aloud.

"It could be related," Ethan said. "But don't get too excited. We don't have any evidence yet."

"Okay," I said. "But I will say this. If the city administration knew this place was a bottling facility for vampires, there's a good chance McKetrick did as well."

After my Robin Pope disappointment, I was hedging my bets. But smoke usually meant fire.

"Perhaps," Ethan agreed. "Perhaps we can tie him to these riots, and this will be the thing that brings him down. Your task, Sentinel? Find me some evidence."

Security was tight—and rather bored-looking—when we returned to the House. Luc generally considered bored security to be ineffective security, but I'd take bored over "overwhelmed by marauders" any day.

Ethan went to his office to get back to business. I didn't bother changing clothes but went directly to the Ops Room.

I found Jonah and Luc at the conference table, mulling over materials. The temps were at the computers, but the rest of the guards were gone, probably on patrol.

Luc and Jonah looked up when I entered.

"Sentinel," Luc said. "What's the good word? How's the family?"

"It varies by person," I said, taking a seat at the table. "The children are adorable. The adults grow more ornery with age. . . . It does not appear the rioters have shown up."

"Not even a hint of a drive-by or look-see," Jonah said. "But there are hours to go before sunrise."

"That's actually something that's been bothering me," Luc said.

"What's that?" Jonah asked.

"The riots have only been occurring at night, when we're awake. But why? If you want to damage vampires, hurt vampires, why not riot during the day when we're unconscious? Talk about maximizing damage . . ."

That point echoed many others I'd heard over the last few days. If the rioters really meant to get media attention and do damage, they'd done a pretty bad job of it.

"I've been thinking the same thing," I said. Counting on my fingers, I offered my concerns: "They don't hit the most obvious House. They don't hit us during the day. They don't hit us as hard as they probably could, and they don't even show up to protest afterward. All that buildup, and for what?"

"Maybe they just aren't very good rioters," Luc said.

"Maybe," I said. "But I can't help thinking there's something else afoot here, and we're only seeing the symptom, not the real illness."

"Like what?"

"I don't know," I said, deflated. "I miss having a suspect."

"Indeed," Luc said. "Robin Pope, we hardly knew ye. And while we did, we thought you were a crazy weirdo." He shook his head in faux grief. "What did you learn from Bryant Industries?"

"We talked to Charla. No new information about possible threats per se, but she did pass along a very interesting tidbit."

I waited for a moment before the big reveal, giving everyone a chance to lean forward in anticipation. But no one did.

"Seriously? What's a girl gotta do to build a little tension around here?"

"Firebombs," Luc and Jonah simultaneously said, then congratulated their single-mindedness with a fist bump.

"The Chicago Department of Public Health scheduled a last-minute inspection at the facility."

Still, no reaction.

"Really? Nothing?"

"Their facility was firebombed," Jonah said. "Probably they just want to look things over, make sure the product isn't tainted."

"The last-minute inspection was before the riot," I clarified.

Finally, there was a pique of interest in their eyes.

"Before the riot?" Jonah asked.

I nodded. "The city of Chicago has taken an oddly timed interest in a vampire-service facility. Maybe the riot occurred at Bryant because they didn't get something they wanted at the inspection."

"Like what?" Luc asked. "If they wanted blood, they could buy it."

He was right. Anti-vamp sentiment or not, humans were more than happy to stock Blood4You in their stores. I guess profit trumped conviction for the store owners who didn't really like vampires.

"Maybe it wasn't blood," I said.

"Then what?" Jonah asked. "What else do you want at a Blood4You facility?"

"I don't know," I admitted. "But consider this—if Robin Pope isn't the one organizing the riots, maybe someone else from the city administration is. Maybe McKetrick is."

"You've got evidence of that?"

"Why does everyone keep harping on 'evidence'?" I whined. "And no, I don't have any. But we've got a vamp hater in a new position of power, and a sudden interest in a facility that's been providing blood to vampires for decades. The rioters hit Bryant Industries first; they must have had a reason for it. Why else that place? Why else now?"

"I'm not saying you're wrong, Sentinel," Luc said. "But you don't have anything yet to confirm you're right."

"I'll find something."

Luc checked his watch. "You'd better find it quick. You've got a turn on patrol coming up, and that dress isn't going to cut it. Go upstairs and get dressed. I'll call Jeff and Catcher, see if your grandfather has any connections at the health department."

"What time is Saul arriving?" Jonah asked.

Somehow, I'd forgotten it was pizza night at Cadogan House, the food thoughtfully delivered during vampires' prime eating hours. Not that I needed any more food. Dinner at the Merit house had been plentiful.

"Half hour or so," Luc said.

"In that case, I'll walk Merit upstairs," Jonah said. "All this discussion of blood is making me thirsty. I want to grab some before the pizza arrives."

Probably not a bad idea for me, too, since I hadn't had any yet today. And other than the few minutes at Bryant Industries, I hadn't even had a craving for it. The emergency drink Ethan had given me last night must have satisfied the lust.

When Jonah and I were alone in the hallway, I broached the topic I hadn't had time to discuss with my RG partner.

"So, I met Aubrey," I said.

"Yeah? She's great. Relatively new to the House. Not compared to you, of course, but new compared to the rest of us. She was one of the first women sworn in as a special agent in the FBI."

"Neat," I said. That was actually pretty awesome, but I was on a mission here. "The thing is, she seemed to think I'd somehow wronged you."

"Wronged me?"

"Regarding our relationship. Or the relationship that should have been?"

Jonah stopped in the middle of the hallway and blinked . . . like a vampire in headlights. "Oh?"

I screwed up my face. "So, did you tell all your guards that I broke your heart? 'Cause I gotta say, that's kind of awkward."

"No," he said loudly. "No," he repeated, a little softer this time, his stance growing more awkward. "I didn't say that at all."

"We don't need to get into the details; it's just—they clearly have some strong opinions about me, and if we have to work together . . ."

Jonah grimaced. "Aubrey is . . . protective."

"So I noticed."

"In all seriousness, I mentioned you, but also that you weren't interested, and there weren't any hard feelings. Maybe she took my disappointment as, you know, a pretty severe heartbreak. But it wasn't. I swear it." He shrugged charmingly. "Just ordinary heart-break."

I believed him, especially about Aubrey being the protective type. She was a guard, after all. It was her job to protect her House, including her captain of the guards from all enemies. Living or dead, as the oath went.

"See? This is why work and romance don't mix."

"We're the only RG partners who aren't dating each other."

"And this is why," he said. "See the drama it causes? You just can't win."

"There's drama because we're vampires," I pointed out as we rounded the stairs to the first floor. "Or because we used to be human, or more likely both."

"You mean your life hasn't been simplified now that you're fanged?"

"Ha," I said mirthlessly. "You're hilarious."

We stopped at the first floor. He was headed to the kitchen; I was headed upstairs to find clothes.

"Do you really think McKetrick is involved in this?" he asked.

"I don't know. But I know I really, really don't like having two nights of riots with no suspect at all. He's got the motive. He's got the opportunity. We just have nothing tying him to the crime."

"You have an anti-vampire motive," Jonah said.

"That's true," I said. "So we're thinking, what, that McKetrick tipped someone off about the building, maybe seeded a little anti-vamp rhetoric, and let the chips fall where they may?"

"It's within his MO," Jonah said. "On the other hand, the theory's got an inconsistency. Why half-assed riots? If McKetrick wants us out of town, he's already shown that he's willing to commit murder."

"True," I said, putting a hand on the banister and tapping my fingers on the finial. "And, McKetrick's allegedly got a facility, and we know he's got weapon development capabilities. Molotov cocktails aren't exactly professional."

"Nor were the rioters," Jonah said.

He had a point. The rioters hadn't looked like soldiers—too much facial hair and not enough muscle mass. More like hipsters than soldiers of fortune.

"Since this isn't going to resolve itself in the next five minutes," I said, "I guess I should get upstairs and change."

"Hey, for what it's worth, you do look pretty good in that dress." He winked at me. "You clean up good, Merit. Ethan's a lucky man."

Jonah gave me a nod, then walked down the hallway to the kitchen, auburn hair bouncing on his shoulders.

Luck and dresses were going to be irrelevant if we didn't stop these riots soon.

CHAPTER THIRTEEN

UPSTART COUNTRY

I trekked back upstairs, dumped the shoes into the closet, and peeled off the dress. Getting out of it was much less classy than getting into it, without an extra pair of hands to help with the zipper. Many contortions later, I managed, leaving the silk in a heap on the floor while I searched for something to wear.

It didn't take long.

My leathers had taken a beating in the Grey House riot, including the slash across the front of my jacket. But they'd been neatly repaired and were hanging in my closet again. The seams were virtually invisible, and the jacket looked brand-new.

I slipped them on, reveling in the feel of well-worn leather, which felt cloudlike compared to the fitted dress I'd been wearing. Boots and thick socks followed, and then my scabbarded katana, which was belted around my waist. Just in case.

Since I was now all business, I pulled my hair into a high ponytail, which would keep it out of my face in the event of a battle. Unfortunately, the hairstyle also provided a handle for attackers, but other than shaving my head, there wasn't much to be done about that.

I checked my watch. There was time yet before my shift started, so I decided to head to the basement. I wasn't anywhere near hungry, but I could at least say hi to Saul.

The entire basement smelled like oregano and garlic, not that I minded.

The tatami mats in the training room had been rolled up, revealing a hardwood floor that was currently dotted with round tables. A long table had been set up against the far wall, covered with white pizza boxes. Cadogan and Grey House vampires moved through the line, chatting as they selected pizza and sodas from a cooler at the end.

Saul himself, wearing dress pants, a button-down shirt, and a long black coat, chatted with Ethan.

"There she is," he said, patting my cheek when I wandered over. "There's a couple of Saul's doubles under the table for you."

"Thanks, Saul," I said, although I really hadn't done anything to deserve the treat. I'd just asked Luc to ensure my grandfather and the CPD kept an eye on Saul's; they'd done the rest.

"Why are you so dressed up?" I asked. "I don't think I've ever seen you without a Saul's shirt on."

"Granddaughter had a dance recital earlier tonight. 'Snowflake Revue' they called it. Lots of glitter and that white material that looks like window screen?"

"Tulle?"

Saul snapped his finger and pointed at me. "That's it. Tulle." He checked his watch. "I should get back. She's having a slumber party tonight, and her momma promised I'd stop by with a pizza and a kiss. I think I've gotten you all taken care of here."

"You did, Saul, and we're much obliged," Ethan said, extending a hand.

They shook on it. Saul picked up a couple of red insulated bags from the table, and Helen escorted him back into the hallway.

"Nice spread," Scott said, sidling up to us. He didn't have pizza in hand, and he looked exhausted. I'd seen Ethan in the same condition before. We might not have been human, but we weren't immune to human stresses. Fear, anger, and exhaustion ate away at us, too.

"It's all thanks to Saul's generosity," Ethan said, glancing at Scott. "How are your vampires faring?"

"The injured are nearly healed, but weak. There were pretty significant burns and internal damage there. The rest of us are feeling . . . displaced."

"Are repairs under way?" I asked.

"They are. Crew's already cleaning up the water and smoke. And glass, which there's a lot of. All the individual rooms have to be cleaned—the walls scrubbed, every sheet and pillow and piece of clothing aired out. Actually, it's the same company that cleaned up Bryant Industries," he said.

I supposed it was worth considering whether the rehab companies had any connection to the rioters—were the riots an attempt to get rehabbing work in a bad economy? But I quickly discarded the theory. After all, there was no guarantee the victims would actually hire the same rehab company.

"And the atrium?" Ethan asked.

"They're replacing and glazing the glass," he said. "Slow going considering the temperature—but it's in process. The mechanics are going to take longer. The water and heat did a number on the sensors."

"That's the trouble with technology," Ethan said. "Helluva lot easier to break."

"And so inconvenient when it does," Scott said.

"Have you found an interim place to stay?" I wondered aloud.

"So eager to kick us out, are you, Merit?"

"Just asking," I said. "Cots in the ballroom can't be all that comfortable."

"We make do," he said, sounding as much like a coach as a Master vampire. "We've got feelers out in the neighborhood, but we're getting a lot of 'no room at the inn' responses."

"No room for vampires?" Ethan asked.

"Precisely. We found an apartment building being remodeled; they're finishing up the interior work, and we offered a short-term lease for two of the floors. I think there's a possibility there, but the owners are going to have to get over their hesitancy about renting to vampires."

That hesitancy, I thought, might not be about the biology, but the risk of violence. We weren't exactly a good risk right now.

"Merit, your father's in real estate, isn't he?"

I gave Scott a faux smile, not looking forward to the question I knew was going to follow. Of course I wanted to help Grey House. But being indebted to my father was a bad idea; he always called in his debts. "Yeah, he is."

"Do you think he'd have any leads, or pull in terms of helping us nail down a location?"

I'll take this one, Sentinel, Ethan silently said.

"Joshua Merit can be a prickly sort," Ethan said. "And his prices are usually very, very high. We'll make inquiries as we can."

"I'd appreciate that," Scott said, gesturing toward the food. "I think I'm going to grab a bite. I'm starving."

"Do that," Ethan said with a smile, and we watched as Scott joined the rest of the vampires in line.

"I suppose I should have seen that coming."

"Me, too," Ethan said. "It probably wouldn't be a bad idea to make an inquiry. Although asking your father for a favor is only going to lead him back to his offer about the House."

"I hate to break it to you, but he's going to keep at it regardless of what you say to him in the meantime."

"I know," Ethan said. "Recall this isn't the first business arrangement he's proposed to me."

That was a chilling reminder of my father's last proposal—offering Ethan money to make me a vampire. Ethan declined, and that I'd become one anyway was a perfect bit of irony.

My phone beeped, so I pulled it out. An image of Luc's face flashed on my screen, his finger waggling. "Time to go outside!" it said. "Time to go outside!"

I tried to silence it, reduce the volume, and turn off the phone, but to no avail. Luc had definitely created a reminder for our outdoor guarding duties—and there was no way to turn it off.

I grimaced at the phone and showed it to Ethan. "We have a monster on our hands."

"I rue the day I authorized those study-at-night programming classes," Ethan said. "Perhaps you should get to it."

I nodded. "On my way," I said, leaving the vampires to their business.

I'd gone to college in California and done grad work in New York City. Both could have nasty weather, but neither city was as temperamental as Chicago.

It felt even colder outside now than it had a few hours ago. Cold enough to make fingers stiff and lungs tight and cramped.

I nodded at Kelley as she headed back into the House, arms crossed and teeth chattering. "Cold" was all she said.

Not exactly pleasant foreshadowing, but at least my phone stopped screaming when I reached the gate. Luc must have managed to tap into the phone's GPS. Which was just one more reason why his newfound programming skills were disturbing.

Two human guards stood at the gate, and others were posted every twenty feet along the perimeter. The guards at the gate were both men. Both broad-shouldered and tall, both with moustaches that cops and military men seemed to favor. Their clothes were head-to-toe black, thick, and quilted against the cold.

I'd brought out two extra travel mugs of hot chocolate and handed them over. "Thought you could use a drink."

"Appreciate it," said the one on the left, whose coveralls were stitched with "Angelo" in the top left-hand corner.

"Ditto," said the one on the right. He was apparently "Louie."

"Anything interesting out here tonight?"

"Not even a little," Angelo said. "Couple of dog walkers. Couple of passersby with cameras. Most of the paparazzi are indoors for the winter."

We'd been rushed with photographers a few months ago, but the novelty of vampires had worn off. Now we were a threat to public safety.

"The dogs were cute," Louie said. "Little white thing and some kind of skinny greyhound."

"It was an Italian greyhound," Angelo said. "I told you that."

Louie gave me a downtrodden look. I guessed Angelo and Louie had these conversations often.

"You think rioters will try to hit the House?" I wondered aloud. I was at the limit of my insight, after all. Might as well see what the experts thought.

"The rioters?" Angelo asked. "Hard to say. We're an obvious target, and they don't really seem bright enough to hit obvious targets."

"Right?" I agreed. "I just said the same thing a little while ago."

"Harder to get in the gate here," Louie added. "No gate at the other House—what was it? Green?"

"Grey," I said.

"Grey," Louie agreed. "No gate there, so it's easier to get in. No gate at that business at Wicker Park, either. If I can be frank—"

"You can't," Angelo muttered.

"—you don't have security at your place, you're asking for trouble. Here?" He gestured at the gate behind him, and the posted guards. "Here, you've got plenty of security. Obstacles. Live guards, and the closed circuit. It's a good setup."

"I'm sure Luc appreciates that."

"I'll tell you what he appreciates," Louie said. "He appreciates not having crazy people throwing bottles of Smirnoff through his fancy front door and into his fancy house."

"I have no doubt of it."

"It's a shame, too," Louie said. "People minding their own business, bothering no one, and then the rioters hit."

"Makes you wonder what the world's coming to," Angelo quietly agreed.

"But then, if the world was perfect, we'd all be out of jobs, am I right?" Louie asked, nudging Angelo for effect. Very little effect.

Having talked himself out, Louie went silent. For a few quiet minutes we sipped our hot chocolate. I swayed back and forth just to keep my blood circulating. I didn't think vampire blood was so organically different that it would freeze in my veins, but neither did I want to test the theory.

When the hot chocolate was gone, and I had nothing else to focus on but the nose-numbing cold, I put down the container and looked back at Angelo and Louie, who'd begun to argue about the Bears' failure to make the Super Bowl. Again.

Angelo said the team's offensive line was shit; Louie said the problem was coaching.

I could think of nothing else but the thirty-mile-per-hour wind that was seeping in through the fibers of my jacket.

"Guys, I'm going to take a walk around the block. I need to keep moving."

They nodded. "Good for the circulation," Louie said.

"Keeps you healthy," Angelo agreed.

Cadogan House took up a lot of space, but I wasn't sure walking the handful of blocks around the perimeter was really going to accomplish much from a cardiovascular perspective. But at least I'd be moving.

I stuck my hands into my pockets and tightened the scarf around my neck, then set out down the street. The streetlights reflected off the snow and a bank of low clouds above us, which made the evening unusually bright. It was bright enough to read by, if I didn't think Luc would have my ass for reading a novel while on guard patrol.

I walked down the block, being careful to avoid patches of ice, my sword slapping my thigh beneath my coat as I walked. I hadn't yet figured out exactly how to arrange coat and sword, and figured I could spare a second or two to rip off my coat and draw it if the need arose.

I nodded to each human guard I passed. They all seemed less miserable than I was. Most, but not all, were brawny men who, like Angelo and Louie, looked like they'd done time in a weaponized uniform. They all looked focused, with earpieces in place and weaponry shined and polished. I was out here because I'd drawn the duty; they were here because their jobs involved keeping us safe, even in freezing weather. I had to respect that.

I rounded the corner and headed around the block, the fence

extending the entire block on my right. On the left side of the street, nice houses where nice families lived glowed in the darkness, the families having dinner or watching television or preparing for another day of work or school.

Cars occasionally passed, but the streets were quiet enough that I could let my mind wander, and I could think about the problems before us with clarity.

It all came back to the riots.

The riots inconvenienced us and injured us, but they were almost secondary attacks. They hit structures, not vampires. If McKetrick was involved, it was a change from his last round of attack. He'd hired Michael Donovan to assassinate vampires and destabilize the Houses.

This time, he'd skipped killing vampires outright. Maybe this was another attempt to destabilize? Try to interrupt our blood supply, try to destroy our Houses, and motivate us to leave Chicago?

I kept coming back to that—if he meant to kill us all or kick us out of town, surely there were faster and more effective methods.

It all came back to the riots.

I reached the front of the House again and found Juliet standing at the gate, waiting for me. She was packed into even more outerwear than I was, including a full-length camouflage coverall. And because I was usually waiting for the other shoe to drop, seeing her standing there made me nervous.

"Is everything okay?" I asked.

She smiled. "Check your phone."

I pulled it out and checked the screen. Luc had taken it over again, this time his caricature waving a small white flag. TIME'S UP, PARTNER! HEAD INSIDE! TIME'S UP, PARTNER! HEAD INSIDE!

"I guess that means I'm relieved," I said. "Short shifts tonight."

"It's the cold," she said. "These guys prep for it, and they have the gear." She nodded toward Angelo and Louie, who nodded seriously. "Us?" she said, sticking out a foot in a designer sheep-skin boot. "Not so much."

"Stay warm," I said, then collected the empty travel mugs for the return trip indoors.

I hopped up the steps and managed again to finagle the door open with mugs in hand. The foyer was empty but for one vampire who was heading for the door. It was Scott, all by his lonesome. He wasn't wearing a coat, so I assumed he didn't plan to be outside long. Either way, I was glad I'd met him going out. I didn't care for the thought of a Master vampire running around outside on a potentially lethal night. If I'd had a chance to pull out my phone, I'd have called Jonah. But I had to suffice for the moment.

"Heading out?" I asked, dropping the mugs on a side table.

He glanced back. "Merit. Yes. I needed some fresh air. Are you leaving?"

"Just heading back in. But if you want to go out, I can accompany you."

"Do you really think that's necessary?"

"I think covering my ass is necessary. And if anything happened out there after I watched you leave and didn't offer an escort, there'd be hell to pay."

"So I'd really be doing you a favor?"

"If you want to think about it that way, sure."

He seemed distracted and didn't put up much of an argument, although that made it easier for me. We stepped outside.

If the cold bothered Scott, he didn't show it. He leaned against the side of the arch that covered the portico and stared into the darkness.

I looked up at the sound of heated discussion. A group of people walked through the gate, undeterred by the human guards and vampires.

I reached for my katana, ready to strike.

But it wasn't rioters.

It was the GP, Harold Monmonth leading the charge. He was swarthy and packed like a sausage into a very snug three-piece suit. His history with the House left much to be desired, and there wasn't much to recommend him in person, either.

He'd brought three of his closest vampire friends behind him, two men and a woman. I recognized them as lower-ranking members of the GP—vampires who hadn't done much but play Follow the Leader and Threaten Cadogan House during my tenure as a vampire.

Behind them on the icy concrete lay the bodies of Louie and Angelo, their limbs splayed in awkward angles, the scent of blood in the air. I was too far away to tell if they were still alive, but the positions of their bodies didn't leave me much hope.

Juliet was nowhere to be seen, and I feared for her; she wouldn't have allowed the guards to be taken without a fight, unless she hadn't been capable of fighting herself. . . .

A thousand exclamations of shock and grief ran through my head, but my throat was tight with fear. As the adrenaline began to speed the processing in my brain, the thoughts congealed and condensed into one central goal: *Get in front of Scott.*

I unsheathed my sword and stepped in front of him, offering my body as a shield. There wasn't even time to be afraid or to fear the consequences of what I'd done. There was only the act—protecting my partner's Master, and my Master's friend—from the obvious danger in front of us.

"Well, hello, dear," Harold said.

Ethan, Harold Monmonth is here. The guards are down, and I don't see Juliet. I'm outside with Scott. Gather the guards and get your ass out here. And call an ambulance.

"You're trespassing," I advised him. "The authorities have been notified."

"I seriously doubt that, Merit. You haven't had the time, and I doubt the authorities would be terribly concerned about more infighting among Chicago's vampires."

"What do you want?" Scott asked.

"We are here to take what's ours. GP vampires are not to intermingle with trash who've rejected our authority. By being here, you are rebelling against the GP, and we take that as an act of war. Leave this House now, or we will be forced to act."

"As I advised you on the phone," Scott said, "if the GP wishes to give us orders, Darius can contact me directly. I take orders from him, not from you."

"Ah," Harold said, lifting a finger, "but Darius is incapacitated. And while he is, we cannot simply allow this rebellion to go on without reprobation."

He looked at me, and the hair on the back of my neck lifted. McKetrick's hatred may have frightened me, but at least he was guided by principles, disturbing though they might have been. This man was utterly without moral compass. He was motivated only by his own avarice.

"I advise you, child, to step aside."

I refused to move. "Whatever rebellion you think has occurred has nothing to do with us. You're on the property of vampires not associated with the GP. You have no authority here."

Monmonth looked me over from head to toe, and I felt dirtier for it. "You are charming. It's unfortunate we didn't have an opportunity to get to know each other better the last time we met."

Get here fast, I warned Ethan, *or I will pummel this guy and enjoy doing it*.

I heard footsteps behind me, but they weren't fast enough.

Harold Monmonth may have looked out of shape, but he was so fast I didn't even see him move, just felt the bone-jarring impact of my ass on the sidewalk as he kicked my feet out from under me.

"That was disappointingly easy," he said, his face registering his disapproval.

He wasn't the only one disappointed.

My turn, I thought, arching my back, hopping onto my feet, and readying my sword. I gripped it in two hands, the leather cording tight beneath my fingers, my eyes now silvered with lust for battle.

"Didn't anyone ever tell you not to hit a girl?"

Scott also called out to grab his attention, but Harold didn't care. He'd deemed me his enemy, and he didn't waste any time. He moved forward, unsheathing his sword and spinning it like a dervish.

Move, I silently told myself, aiming for the only spot he wasn't guarding—his ankles. I made a low spin, bringing my own sword around in a perfect arc that sent him flipping backward to avoid it.

He hit the ground and spun the sword around his body. "You think I need weaponry to best you? You are a child, with the strength of a child. I am centuries old, with the strength of centuries." He dropped his sword to the ground, and it hit the ground with a *clang*. I winced sympathetically for the steel but readied myself for another attack.

"You, like the rest of your House," Monmonth said, stretching out his arms, "are garbage. You are the refuse of legitimate vampires."

"Screw you," I said, moving forward and slashing downward. But Monmonth had already moved, and the sword caught only air.

"Garbage," he muttered again, shifting his weight and executing a side kick that hit me square in the back with the force of a concrete block.

I fell to my knees, my brain registering only pain. I retched air as my body coped with the sensation, and I opened my eyes to see the other GP members spread out and begin the attack. The battle began.

"Monmonth!"

Ethan's voice roared across the yard.

Sentinel? he silently asked.

I'm fine, I told him. I put a hand on the ground to push myself up, but my body wasn't yet ready for movement. Pain radiated from my back, muscles spasming in waves.

I tried again to get up, to warn Ethan back, but as vampires battled around me, I couldn't find my footing. And I was too late anyway. Ethan had already advanced on Monmonth, with two katanas in hand.

Monmonth bent his knees, then leaped toward Ethan.

Ethan grunted as he spun out of the way, bringing both swords around and pressing the handles together at the blunt ends, the points out, like a staff Darth Maul would have appreciated.

As Monmonth hit the ground in a crouch, his sword poised in front of him, Ethan roared a sound of battle and advanced, spinning the knife-sharp staff back and forth around his body in a complicated pattern.

It was like staring into the blade of a psychotic steel turbine. Even Monmonth froze for a moment, as if not sure how to react.

He nudged away, but not quite fast enough. The chiseled tip of a katana just grazed his arm, sending a bright stripe of crimson to his skin, and sending the spicy scent of powerful blood into the air.

"You son of a bitch!" Monmonth roared. "Do you know who I am?"

He didn't wait for Ethan's response but answered his own question with moves that proved why he'd been chosen for the

GP. He became a dervish of kicks and strikes, a martial arts machine. Monmonth was faster than Ethan, but Ethan managed to hold his own. And two blades of finely honed steel didn't hurt.

Ethan spun the staff in a low arc, which Monmonth jumped to avoid. He flipped backward, but upon landing went immediately on the offensive. A spinning kick and series of punches had Ethan moving back and forth to block them. As they fought, they traversed the yard, moving into deeper snow that slowed them down.

Ethan stumbled and dropped one of his swords. Harold kicked the other a few feet away. I was too far away to help, and clapped a hand over my mouth to keep from screaming my fear.

"You have held court here for too long," Harold said, picking up the weapon Ethan had dropped. "You believe you are a king among the American vampires, but you are nothing more than a slave to humans who'd as soon have you dead as look at you. It is the Presidium that rules vampires, not an upstart soldier in the middle of an upstart country."

Harold raised the sword and lifted it, intending to strike downward, slicing Ethan from neck to groin.

"Ethan!" I screamed, jumping to my feet and running for the pair.

But as Harold's sword fell, Ethan managed to grab his. He wrapped his fingers around the handle and struck.

With a single slice of Ethan's sword, Monmonth's head was divorced from his body. It landed, unceremoniously, in the snow beside him.

Ethan tumbled to the side as the rest of Harold Monmonth, the former, fell to the ground.

Ethan climbed to his feet, bloody sword in hand. For a moment, clearly shocked by what he'd done, he stared down, wide-eyed, at

Harold Monmonth's lifeless body. His chest heaved, and his body steamed in the cold.

I watched from my spot in the snow, still too shocked to move. I wasn't the only one; the other battles stopped. Grey and Cadogan vampires who'd fought the other members of the GP stepped back, holding their enemies at sword point.

All eyes looked toward Ethan and took in with shock the body on the ground. A chilling silence fell over the yard.

"You've killed him!" yelled out one of the male GP members, a vampire from Canada named Edmund, who rushed toward his fallen colleague and wailed in what seemed earnest despair.

"Murderer!" he yelled, looking back at Ethan and pointing an accusing finger in his direction.

The show of drama seemed to break Ethan from his trance. "Enough!" he bellowed, and silence fell over the yard again.

He pointed his sword at Monmonth's body. "This man came into my House and brought violence, and for the second time. He has killed and threatened our friends and colleagues, to say nothing of his history of violence to the humans who came before us. He forfeited his life in the name of power and ego."

Ethan lifted his silver-eyed gaze to the remaining members of the GP faction who'd trespassed at Cadogan . . . and would be wearing the scars of their journey back to England.

Ethan pointed at Edmund. "Take home a message to Darius West. He gets his House in order, or we do it for him."

We found Juliet on the sidewalk, knocked unconscious by a blow to the head. Her sword was on the ground, and by the position of her body, it appeared the GP had snuck up behind her, probably using their glamour to keep their arrival a secret.

While Helen and Delia, Cadogan's resident doctor, attended to

Juliet, Ethan, Scott, and I stood outside with a handful of CPD cops in uniform. Fighting among supernaturals was one thing; the death of two humans on our watch was something entirely different.

I stood on the portico, watching Ethan and Scott point across the yard, diagramming for the cops the chain of events. I'd been numbed by the violence, by the GP's remarkable intrusion, and its grisly end. We were all capable of killing, and we'd all been in battles before. But I couldn't recall a time in which death had come so quickly to the House. And not just any death. Two innocent humans were dead. And a member of the GP was dead, and by our hands.

I stared out at the scene, the investigators who took photographs of the crime scene in front of the gate, the swirling blue and red lights of the ambulance that had arrived for Louie's and Angelo's bodies.

An arm slipped around my waist, and I nearly screamed in surprise. I found Lindsey beside me, circles beneath her eyes. She'd been crying.

"This is awful," she said, putting her head on my shoulder. "They were really nice. They had grandkids—both of them. They were talking about soapbox derby cars, how crappy their entries usually were, but how they had big plans this year." She swiped at tears beneath her lashes. "Stupid soapbox derby cars. Totally lame."

I put an arm around her, the sentiment bringing a new wash of tears to my eyes. "I talked to them a little during my shift. They seemed like good guys."

"They were," she confirmed. "Good guys. And not worthy of this end by that goddamn narcissistic GP nightmare."

We looked back at the spot where Ethan had killed Monmonth, his body removed but the snow stained by blood.

We stood silently together, sharing our grief. A few minutes later, the cops walked back through the gate, the ambulance drove away, and the investigators snapped their final photographs.

Ethan and Scott walked back to us.

"They're calling Monmonth's death self-defense," he said, and I felt a vise loosen around my heart. "Considering the violence already done by Monmonth, and the fact that he attacked you, they don't anticipate the prosecuting attorney will want to press charges."

"What about the other GP members?" I asked. They'd split at the sound of ambulances and police cruisers.

"They have private jets," Scott said, "and enough money to get them into the air, law enforcement be damned. They won't stop flying until they reach London."

Ethan put a hand on my shoulder. "It's freezing out here. Let's go back inside."

We moved back into the House, and Ethan called the vampires to the ballroom. Members of Grey and Cadogan stood alongside one another, sharing a moment of silence for Angelo and Louie, who'd given their lives in protection of the House. The swelling sense of worry was tangible, the magic that flowed from the roomful of vampires heavy and despondent.

When the ceremony was over, we returned to Ethan's office. The room was utterly silent, the mood and magic grim. In another time—perhaps in the era Ethan had been made a vampire—the mood might have been different. Vampires reveling in their victory, sharing mead and women and song in honor of having vanquished a foe, instead of mourning their losses and dreading the repercussions.

The Grey House guards, Scott and Jonah among them, stood in

one corner of the room. They undoubtedly discussed their future, and the ramifications of our actions on their lives as GP vampires.

Our concern was just as great. The GP already thought us enemies. Although their act tonight—or at least the act of Monmonth's faction—had been one of naked aggression, there was no telling how Darius would react.

Ethan had already tried to call, but he hadn't been able to get through.

One thing was sure: Of the seven members of the Greenwich Presidium other than Darius, Cadogan House was now responsible for the deaths of two of them. Harold Monmonth and Celina Desaulniers, both treacherous and egotistical, had taken on our Houses. Both had lost, giving their lives for the challenge. Yes, they'd both been the aggressors, but would that matter to the remaining members of the GP? Would they find Monmonth's death justifiable, or yet another act of treason on our part?

The Grey House group disbanded, and Scott stepped forward. "The events that transpired tonight were our fault, and I am sorry for it. I think, considering the circumstances, it's best we accelerate our search for alternative housing. We're simply putting you at too much risk."

"The events that transpired were solely the work of Harold Monmonth and his cronies," Ethan countered. "Neither your House nor your vampires had anything to do with it. We chose to let you stay here, and Harold chose his response of his own free will, and apparently without the consent of the GP proper. You bear no responsibility for that.

"But as for your vampires and their best interest, that is a choice only you can make. You are welcome to bed here as long as you need. But I understand your desire to find a home."

"They may seek retribution," Scott said.

"They may," Ethan agreed with a nod. "That is up to Darius or, more likely, an incestuous cabal of the remaining GP members."

I glanced up at Ethan. "This may sound cruel, but the faction that supports Darius might be appreciative of what went down tonight. They might be glad Harold's no longer a factor."

"They might," Ethan agreed.

"That's who?" Scott asked. "Darius, Lakshmi, Diego?"

"At most," Ethan said. "They're the only ones left." He shook his head ruefully. "We've saved Lakshmi's and Darius's lives," Ethan said. "That helps, although I don't presume their loyalty. Diego came to us when Darius was kidnapped, which suggests he sees us as an asset."

"That's three to three," Scott said. "Assuming Darius gathers the will to act."

I yawned, putting the back of my hand over my mouth to cover it up.

"Let's call it a night," Ethan said. "We can look at this with fresh eyes tomorrow."

"There's still pizza in the kitchen if anyone missed dinner," Malik said.

Everyone in the room looked at me.

"Seriously," I said flatly.

"Yes," most of them said.

"Apparently I've become predictable."

"At least something is," Jonah said, walking toward the office door. "I'm going to have a slice, then head upstairs, unless you'd like to talk, boss?"

But Scott shook his head. "Get some rest. We'll reassemble at dusk."

Jonah opened the door, offered a salute to everyone in the

room, and headed into the hallway. The rest of the Grey House vampires followed, with Scott at the rear.

"We'll talk," he said, and Ethan nodded.

"The same order goes for the rest of you," Ethan said, glancing around the room. "Get upstairs, get some rest. It's been a long night."

"Too long," Luc agreed, and everyone filed out.

When the room was empty, Ethan put an arm around my shoulders. I leaned my head against him, breathing in his cologne, which for biochemical reasons I didn't understand, always calmed me down.

"You're all right?" he asked. He'd been asking that often lately.

"I have no idea."

"Nor do I, Sentinel. So let us say nothing. Let us just be."

A few minutes later, I headed upstairs alone; Ethan begged off for a few minutes to try Darius again and close things down in his office.

In my room, I discovered Margot had found our new digs. Several white taper candles in silver candlesticks glowed on the bureau and nightstand, and a small silver tray—smaller to actually fit on the limited bureau space not already filled with candles—held bottles of sparkling water and wrapped chocolates.

Six minutes later, I was on the bed with a clean face and pajamas, when the door opened and Ethan walked in.

"Honey, I'm home," he said, jacket slung over his shoulder. His hair was loose around his face, and he looked weary and not a little depressed. He hung his jacket over the closet doorknob. Silently, he began unbuttoning his vest.

"How are you?" I asked.

"I've been better. I'm looking forward to oblivion."

The sun was on the rise, and a coherent response escaped me.

But it was unnecessary. Ethan slid into bed beside me, his body warm and ready.

"Yes," I said. And that was the end of all thought.

Ethan found me, prepared me, and took my body for his own, lust lingering with exhaustion, with sweat, love made tangible by palms and calves, with the curve of his spine and the apple of his shoulder, with my breasts and his fingers.

Love sparked and dissipated like sparks in the wind, and the sun rose high in the sky.

But night came again, because night, like death and taxes, was inevitable.

CHAPTER FOURTEEN

GROWING PAINS

I woke achy, but the pain in my back, at least, was reduced to a dull throb. The benefits of vampire healing couldn't be overestimated; the benefits of two adults of above-average height squeezing into a twin-sized bed could easily be overestimated.

But while the accommodations forced us to sleep like sardines, it was difficult to argue with an arrangement that put me skin to skin with a sexy blond vampire.

I was wrapped around him, naked from our predawn lovemaking and chilly. Cadogan House was many things, but warm it was not.

"Sentinel," Ethan said.

"Liege."

He trailed fingers down my back. "Considering our positions, I think we can dispense with the formalities. Happy Valentine's Day."

Despite having made the plans, I'd completely forgotten about Valentine's Day.

"Happy Valentine's Day," I said. "I'd actually forgotten."

"I didn't," Ethan said, "but I think a postponement is in order, considering . . ."

Intellectually, I knew he was right. If I was going to celebrate the miracle of my relationship with Ethan Sullivan, I wanted to do it correctly. I didn't want to be worried about whether rioters were going to attack my House and kill my friends, or the GP would send a herd of chimeras to destroy the House in retribution for Monmonth's death. I wanted to sit with Ethan and watch the sun rise over the lake, not rush back to the House out of fear we'd be burned to ash if we tarried too long.

In short, I wanted to be human. And that was not in the cards.

When I didn't answer, my disappointment keen even if totally irrational, Ethan explained.

"We can't afford it," he said. "Not considering what happened last night with the GP, and what might happen tonight. The rioters are still out there. I want Valentine's Day to be special, not a dinner in which we're worried the entire time about what might be happening here."

I was quiet for a moment. "Do you ever wish you were still human?"

Ethan paused, as if choosing his words carefully. "Are you wishing you were human, or that your life was simpler?"

I used one of his tricks. "Yes," I said, picking both answers. "I'll call and change the reservation. Give us a cushion of a few days. Maybe things will be less psychotic by then."

I pulled myself away from him, then climbed out of bed and walked to the bathroom.

"Where are you going?"

"To take a shower and get ready for the night," I said. "Because as you pointed out, there are likely nastier things around the corner."

I showered, brushed my teeth and my hair, then pulled my hair into a ponytail and then a topknot.

When I emerged from the bathroom, Ethan was gone, as were his watch and cuff links from the nightstand. He'd dressed and gone downstairs, without even time for a good-bye.

It was quite a beginning to Valentine's Day.

Since I was inevitably a vampire tonight, I walked down the hallway to the small, second-floor kitchen and snagged a bottle of blood and a bagel studded with raisins and topped with crunch streusel. I ate at the counter, reading through the announcements pinned to a small bulletin board along one wall. This news was surprisingly chipper: pearl earring found, owner wanted; small TV for sale; video games for trade.

I finished the blood, but managed only a few bites of the bagel. I was still discomfited by what had gone on last night, and my appetite hadn't come back. I also wasn't exactly eager to get started with the night, so I stood in the kitchen for a few more minutes, just in case my hunger fired back up.

It didn't. I was actually too stressed to eat.

I tossed the rest of the bagel, wiped my hands, and made for the stairs. I needed positive news and action. I needed progress, because I was beginning to feel like a drug dog that hadn't sniffed out a dirty suitcase in a while.

I walked to Ethan's office to check in before I left, but his door was closed.

Normally, I'd have knocked in warning and gone in. But there seemed a pretty good chance he was on the phone with people significantly above my pay grade and my interruption wouldn't be welcome.

Before I had time to wonder if I should eavesdrop, Jonah

emerged from the cafeteria at the other end of the hall, a glossy red apple in hand.

Excellent timing, I thought. I walked toward him, gesturing back toward Ethan's office. "What's going on in there?"

"I don't know. I assume Ethan's talking to the GP. Why?"

I shook my head. "Just being nosy."

Jonah crunched on the apple. "You're dating him. Don't you two pillow talk? Can't you seduce all the secrets out of him?"

"Who am I, Mata Hari?"

"You're Mata Hari enough to manage to snag the Master of the House." He lifted his eyebrows teasingly, then took a final bite of the apple before chunking the core into a small, decorative wastebasket on the other side of the hallway. He nailed the shot, which made sense, considering Grey House's athletic bent.

"You are hilarious, you know that?"

"I do," he said. "But seriously. Isn't there some kind of boyfriend-girlfriend privilege you can use to find out what's going on?"

"If there was, logically, it would mean he could tell me, but I couldn't tell you."

"Then my idea was poor," he said, crossing his arms. I could see the amusement in his expression slide right into concern. He might joke around, but he, too, was worried about the closed-door meeting.

I glanced around the hallway, ensuring we were alone. "Times like this make us perfect candidates for the RG, you know. We're suspicious by nature."

"And vampires are conniving by nature," he said. "Especially Masters. Or they wouldn't be Masters. Hey, isn't it Valentine's Day? Don't you two have big plans?"

"We did," I agreed. "At least until the city went boom."

"And the GP went bust," Jonah grimly responded.

Without ado, the door opened.

Ethan stood on the other side, gazing at Jonah and me like a schoolteacher who'd just caught two naughty children in the act of disobeying orders. Predictably, he shot up an eyebrow and gave me a visual dressing-down.

"Sentinel."

"Liege," I said properly, with a little head-bob for good measure. "We were just discussing business."

"Interrogation techniques," Jonah added. "Methods for extracting information from unwilling subjects."

Ethan looked dubious about the explanation. "There's no need for torture," he said, pulling the door open farther.

Nick Breckenridge, tall, with cropped dark hair, blue eyes, and the body of a rock climber, stood in the middle of Ethan's office, Scott beside him.

Nick wore a button-down shirt and jeans, with a tweed blazer over it. He carried a small reporter's notebook in one hand. The look was more professorial than I'd usually seen him, but he managed to pull it off. He looked like a very popular professor—the Indiana Jones of the journalism set.

"Nick," I said, walking in at Ethan's subtle nod. "Long time no see."

"Merit," he said, giving me an efficient once-over. It was journalistic inquiry, I knew, not interest, that made him check me out. We'd had our ups and downs, and although I assumed from the "Ponytail Avenger" story that we'd recovered from the blackmail incident, we definitely weren't bosom buddies.

"Nick, this is Jonah," Ethan said, "captain of the Grey House guards."

Nick reached out and shook his hand, and I saw Jonah's eyes widen—just for an instant—in surprise.

Like the Keene family, the Breckenridges were members of the North American Central Pack, although they didn't advertise their supernatural affiliations to many. I guess Scott, who did know, hadn't mentioned that to Jonah.

"Nice to meet you," Jonah said. "I hear you're doing a feature on the riots?"

"Their impact on Chicago's supernaturals, yes." He looked at me. "You're well?"

"I am, thank you. How are your brothers? And your parents?"

"They're well, thanks."

He didn't elaborate; I guess he wasn't up for chitchat.

"How's the investigation going?" I asked.

"Fine. Disturbing in certain ways. Enlightening in others."

"I think this story is going to go a long way toward educating the public about vampires," Ethan said. "You're doing us a profound service."

Nick nodded, by all appearances unmoved. "I'm here to tell the truth. I think I've got what I need from you," he said, looking at Scott. "If I could talk to some of the displaced vampires?"

"Sure. I'll take you upstairs. We're looking for temporary housing. We've got a line on a building, but we're hoping they'll negotiate a little more on the price."

Those prophetic words spoken, and before Nick and Scott even reached the door, chaos broke out in the hallway.

"You fucking asshole!" screamed a vampire whose voice I didn't recognize. We rushed into the hallway, where two guys—one of whom wore a Grey House jersey—were tumbling around on the hallway floor, absolutely whaling on each other.

"What in God's name?" Jonah said, trying to reach into the fight to pull the men apart. He got an elbow in the eye for his trouble, which only incensed him more.

Note to self: Do not piss off the captain of the most athletic vampires in the city's most athletic House.

Jonah let out another curse, then reached in again and grabbed the jersey-wearing vampire by the scruff of the neck and hauled him out of the fray.

He landed eight feet down the hallway, bouncing on his ass for good measure.

The other vampire, a young member of my Novitiate class named Connor—and a very brief fling of Lindsey's—jumped to his feet, ready to join the fray.

"Connor!" Ethan yelled out. There was magic in his voice—his ability, as a Master, to call the vampires he'd made. Obediently, as if returning to the Pack and the alpha male, Connor bared his fangs at Jonah and the Grey House vamp, but slunk back against the wall, and behind Ethan.

Jonah dragged the other vampire to his feet and was glaring daggers at him, daring him to move from that spot.

"I am going to ask this one time," Ethan said through gritted teeth, "and one time only. Connor, what is this about?"

"That asshole started in on our House, that we're a House of rejects."

"Bullshit!" called the Grey House vampire. "You were bragging about drinking, you egotistical little prick."

"I wasn't bragging," Connor said, chest puffed aggressively. "I was stating a fact. It's not my fault you get yours from bottles."

That was the wrong thing to say. The Grey House vampire surged forward, but Jonah used his body to keep him back.

"Enough!" Scott shouted, the second time that word had been used to quell violence in Cadogan House in the last twenty-four hours.

He strode to the Grey House vampire and stuck a finger in his face. "We are here because they have offered to shelter us, notwithstanding the risk we posed. A risk that obviously was valid, considering what happened last night."

"They brought the heat themselves," the vampire said. "If not for them, none of this would have happened."

"Last night," Scott said, his fierce eyes on his young Novitiate, "the GP indicated by its actions that it was our enemy. These vampires stood up for me, and for you, and for our House. I don't give a shit if Ethan Sullivan punches you in the face himself. You are a Grey House vampire, and you will show honor!"

"Honor!" Jonah shouted, pounding a fist to his chest. A half dozen Grey House vampires who'd gathered at the ends of the hallway did the same, shouts of "Honor!" ringing through the hallway. Goose bumps lifted on my arms at the display.

Scott having said his peace, it was Ethan's turn to discipline. He looked at Connor and offered a glance so full of anger—and worse, disappointment—that it made *me* feel bad. I thanked my lucky stars I wasn't on the receiving end of it.

"I am mortified," Ethan said. "Furious, disappointed, and mortified. They are guests in our home. And whether you condone their behavior or not, they are to be treated as guests. Is that clear?"

"Liege," Connor quietly murmured.

"I didn't hear that," Ethan gritted.

"*Liege,*" he said again, this time with conviction.

"Malik's office," Ethan directed, and Connor disappeared down the hallway.

"Upstairs," Scott echoed, gesturing toward the Grey House vampire. "The rest of you get back to it," he said, and the hallway cleared of vampires.

In the silence, we heard the scribbling of a pen, and we glanced back to the office doorway. Nick Breckenridge stood there, scribbling furiously, notebook and pen in hand.

Ethan sighed, and looked at Scott. "I suppose we asked for a story about the riots' real, unscripted effects."

"You get what you ask for," Scott agreed.

"Unfortunately," Ethan said, glancing at Scott, "I think it might be time to reconsider the offer on that building you found."

Scott nodded. "I think you might be right."

Nick followed Scott, Jonah, and the Grey House vampire upstairs, leaving me and Ethan alone in the hallway. He rubbed his temples for a moment before stepping back into his office. I followed him.

"Have you heard anything about Juliet?"

"She's awake and resting," Ethan said. "She wanted to be up and outside this evening, but Luc declined her offer."

A weight lifted from my chest. "That's wonderful news."

"This is one of those nights—one of those weeks—in which I think I could very much enjoy a mundane human life."

The admission, so close to what I'd been thinking, struck me in its honesty.

"I know," I said. "I've had nights like that, too. When a cubicle and a desk job and mind-numbing boredom seem preferable."

"I don't think a cubicle is our only other option. We could buy an estate in Scotland on the moors or in the wilds of Alaska where no one would ever find us."

"The grass is always greener," said a voice at the door. Looking up, we found Catcher and Mallory in the doorway.

Mallory's hair was in two long braids, a knit cap pulled over her brow. She wore a puffy down jacket and calf-high winter boots over jeans. Catcher, on the other hand, wore a thin barn coat over jeans, no gloves, hat, or scarf in sight. He was, however, wearing one of those expressions that said, quite clearly, "The world is an idiot." I guess his anger was keeping him warm.

"Looks like we missed some excitement?" he said.

"Too many vampires and too much testosterone in the House," I explained, earning an eye roll from Ethan. He could object to the phrasing as much as he wanted, but facts were facts.

"What brings you by?" Ethan asked them.

"We heard about what happened last night," Mallory said. "We wanted to check in on you." She gave me a head-to-toe look. "You look whole."

"I am," I said. "Just a little sore."

Catcher and Mallory stepped inside, and Catcher closed the door behind them. "I hear the GP didn't fare so well?"

At Ethan's gesture, we all walked to the office's sitting area. It had been a long time since we'd shared a casual chat at the House with the two of them.

Mallory and Catcher sat down. Catcher practically commanded the seat, arms on the armrests, one leg crossed, ankle over knee.

Mallory sat beside him, but she looked vaguely uncomfortable, perhaps because she hadn't actually been inside Cadogan House since Ethan's death. And that visit hadn't exactly turned out for the best.

"Harold Monmonth is no longer with us," Ethan confirmed. "And my blade is the reason for that."

"Can't say I envy your position," Catcher said, "although the guy attacks your House, he has to know the risks."

"One would assume," Ethan said. "But logic has often eluded the GP."

"How has the GP responded?" Catcher asked.

"They haven't," Ethan said. "We're awaiting their move."

"So the atmosphere around here is cool, calm, and collected as usual?" Mallory asked lightly.

"Pretty much," I said. "What about you? How are things with the Apex?"

"About the same."

I thought of my conversation with Catcher and the work Mallory and the shifters were doing together. I considered not asking her about it since she hadn't mentioned it herself, but playing subtle with Mallory had only ended in despair the first time around.

"I understand you've been working with the shifters on your magic?"

"I've been working on control," she said, meeting my gaze without blinking, which showed more confidence than I'd expected. Maybe she was ready to fan out her cards after all.

"They have a relationship to magic that's unique, and Gabe thought if I had a better connection to that magic, more sympathy for it, I might be able to balance myself a little better."

"Is it working?"

"It's not *not* working," she said with a smile. "But I use so little of it, it's hard to say."

Ethan leaned forward, elbows on his knees. By his expression, he was clearly fascinated by the concept. "They're letting you watch their rituals?"

"Some," she said carefully. "For some of the Keene wolves. I understand each type of animal has its own way to commune with the world."

"And that's what it is?" I asked. "Communing with the world?"

She tilted her head to the side and scrunched up her face, trying to gather the right words. "Magic isn't binary. It's not on or off." She glanced at Catcher. "Some folks say it's divided into keys, into segments." That was the way I'd learned about magic, the theory Catcher had espoused.

"But for me," she said, "it's more like a radio tuner. You can adjust the dial up or down until you get the station you want."

"And they're helping you get the station you want?" Ethan asked.

"They're helping me identify the stations," she said. "Feel them out. Figure out which stations are good for me, and which aren't."

"That sounds promising," Ethan said. I had to agree. It sounded better, at any rate, than her tuning into the magical "station" that was apparently intent on destroying Chicago.

"It is, I think," she said. "There's a way to go, but it's promising."

"What does the Order plan to do with you?" Ethan asked her.

"Pretend I don't exist?"

"They aren't good with punishment," Catcher said. "Yeah, they can kick someone out and theoretically ban someone from practicing in a particular area, but we've seen how well that worked."

Catcher wasn't supposed to be in Chicago; he'd been kicked out of the Order for coming here against Order mandate.

"They have methods," he said. "You might remember we can be stripped of our magic, but it's an . . . *unpleasant* process. Like the magical version of a lobotomy."

"Nullification, right?" Ethan asked.

Catcher nodded.

"And when Mallory's time with the shifters is up?" Ethan asked.

Mallory and Catcher looked at each other, and Catcher nodded a little.

"We've actually been talking about that," Mallory said. She linked her fingers in her lap and looked at Ethan.

She looked nervous and eager—like a job applicant at an interview—and it wasn't hard to guess what she was about to say.

"Catcher and I have been talking," she said. "And I've talked to Gabriel and Berna. With Berna until I'm blue in the face," she added. "And sooner rather than later I'm going to need to branch out on my own. They don't think it's wise that I don't use my magic at all—it builds up, and we saw how unpleasant that can become."

She paused, waiting for some commentary from Ethan, but he offered none. He stared back at her from his chair, his emotions completely unreadable. She might have been a stranger, not a woman with whom he'd felt a psychic connection.

"I have to prepare for my life," she said. "A life with my magic. A life in which I use it for something that makes me feel better about myself, instead of worse." Tears welled in her eyes, and she wiped them away.

But whether they were tears of embarrassment or guilt, she made herself look directly at Ethan, and the tightness in my chest eased a little bit.

For a long, quiet moment, they looked at each other. Magic rose and circled in the room, spilled by him and intentionally cast off, or so I thought, by her. I couldn't see the magic itself, but I could feel it. It swirled around us like the current of water in a stream. Their magic interacted, spun and danced and battled for superiority. Not because they were fighting each other now, but because they'd been so intimately connected. Because Mallory had been in Ethan's head, and he'd been a conduit for her emotions, her fears, her anger.

All the while, they watched each other. They looked oblivious to the magic, but it would have been impossible to ignore. Even Catcher eyed them as he sipped slowly at his cherry red drink, goose bumps plainly visible on his arms. Being a sorcerer, he was even more sensitive to the magic than I was. It must have been odd to stand in the midst of a vampire-sorceress battle of wills.

"Stop," Ethan finally said, and the magic swept across the room like a sudden peppery breeze, ruffling our hair and leaving a metallic tinge in the air.

"Magic doesn't lie," Mallory said. Had she been able to prove her motivations to him by using her magic?

"No," Ethan said, adjusting in his chair. "But people do, vampires or otherwise. How can I know you won't use this House for your own ends? That even if you earnestly believe you'd never go back to black magic, you won't succumb?"

"I don't believe that," Mallory said. "I'm an addict. I know that, and I live with it—and the consequences of what I did—every day. I can't promise I won't succumb, but I really, really don't want to. I hurt too many people that I loved, destroyed their trust, destroyed what little reputation I had. I don't want to go back to that place, but I can only try my best, one night at a time." She shrugged. "If you can't accept that, I understand. I don't deserve your trust."

She looked around at us. "I don't deserve the trust of anyone in this room. It's a miracle I didn't kill someone when I was high, and I realize that. I realize how close I came to really and truly destroying everything. All I can do is offer to make amends in the best way I know how. To use the gift I've been given for something more than parlor tricks and Order foolery. But the decision's yours."

Ethan's jaw was tight, his brow furrowed. He was concentrating hard about his options, and I honestly had no idea what he was going to do. I didn't envy him—not the burden of the choice. But at least he had a chance to consider it directly with her, to confront her about his fears.

And now, more than ever, it would pay to have a sorceress on our side. The fairies had defected, and the GP's recent intrusion proved again our vulnerability.

"I'll consider it," he said, "if Gabriel permits it."

Based on my conversation with Gabriel a few nights ago, he would permit it. He'd said Mallory would be ready to use her magic when she wasn't afraid of it. And although she was clearly intimidated a little by Ethan, she wasn't afraid of her magic right now. Not here, and not like this. Not when the lines between right and wrong were clearly delineated, and she'd be using her magic—like in the riot—against an enemy of the House. It would be a good first step for her, but only a first step. The next time, the lines might not be so clear.

"Thank you," Mallory said. "*Thank you.* I really, really appreciate it."

"Don't thank me," Ethan said. "Thank those who have been advocating for you. Those who know your heart, or hope they do, and those who know your power, and hope it can be used in support of the Houses. I hope, whatever happens, that you do not let them down."

Mallory nodded, swallowing down emotion.

"While we're here," Catcher said, "I also wanted to talk to you about your father. He's being a pain in the ass."

That, of course, was not much of a mystery, although it was a bit of a downer.

"He's pressuring Chuck to help convince you to let him invest in Cadogan House."

Ethan slid me a knowing glance. "We've heard about the offer."

"He must not have thought you'd go for it; he's called Chuck twice tonight. Barely talked to him over the holidays, didn't so much as wish him a Happy New Year, but is adamant it's Chuck's obligation to position Cadogan House to accept Joshua's largesse."

The disgust in Catcher's voice wasn't subtle, nor was he the only one who felt it. "His obligation?" I asked.

Catcher glanced at me. "Your father thinks you're in danger. He thinks this is helping."

"In danger from what?" Ethan asked.

"He didn't say," Catcher said. "Your grandfather, being your grandfather and a former cop, pushed him for details, trying to figure out if there was a specific threat. He didn't come up with anything. Chuck thinks the riots have gotten him nervous."

If you wanted to give my father the benefit of the doubt, that explanation was completely plausible.

I wasn't sure I was willing to give my father the benefit of the doubt. His motives were sometimes noble, but his means rarely justified the ends.

"What has Chuck told him?" Ethan asked.

"That he loves Merit, too, but that she can take care of herself, and she wouldn't want him to sacrifice the entire city for her safety."

I smiled, finally. That was exactly the kind of thing my grandfather would say.

"I don't think Joshua believed him," Catcher said.

Ethan nodded and looked at Mallory. "You're quiet," he said.

She nodded. "I don't really feel like I have much political capital to offer my opinion on stuff like this."

Ethan was obviously taken aback by the statement. Maybe he hadn't expected her to be so honest, or so self-aware of the damage she'd done to her relationships with others.

"That's very . . ."

"Accurate?" she finished. "Self-aware? Yeah, I know." She crossed one leg over the other, her booted foot swinging. "If you were to ask me, and I'm not saying you are, I'd tell Joshua Merit to take a long walk off a short pier. He can play buddy-buddy with Merit all he wants to, but he's a self-centered prick and we all know it."

Now that sounded like the Mallory I knew. I couldn't help but smile, even in spite of the unfortunate accuracy of her statement.

"I don't disagree," Catcher said. "But he's not taking the hint that he needs to leave Chuck alone."

"My grandfather would kick your ass if he knew you were over here trying to get help from us."

"He would," Catcher agreed. "I considered this one of those 'apologize later' rather than 'ask permission now' scenarios."

"I'll call Joshua," Ethan said. "Not to accept the offer, but perhaps to string him along just a little bit. Perhaps that will take the heat off your grandfather."

Catcher nodded. "I appreciate it. He's got enough on his plate playing secret Ombudsman without his son whining."

"More trouble with the nymphs?" I wondered.

"The River nymphs are calmer than usual this month," Catcher said. "The deeper the winter, the calmer they get. It's because of their connection to the water—it slows down, and they do, too." He shook his head. "No, in addition to the rest of the stuff he's working on, he's beginning to get calls from Detective Jacobs about supernatural issues."

"What kind of issues?" I asked. I knew my grandfather was smart and capable, but that didn't mean I wanted him in the middle of even more supernatural drama.

"It varies. Sometimes consultations. Odd one earlier this week— a body was found on the lakeshore on the south side, but Detective Jacobs had some questions about it. Something strange about it. I'm not sure of the details."

"Sounds like morbid work," Ethan said.

Catcher shrugged. "It's cop work. It's often morbid."

Mallory's face suddenly paled, and she reached out for Catcher's hand.

"Mal?" I asked.

She waved me off, her eyes closed and features squeezed together. "Prophecy. Coming up. Hold on. It's like a pre-sneeze—"

She stiffened, beads of sweat popping onto her forehead. Sorcerers had the discomforting ability to prophecy, although their prophecies were usually wrapped inside riddles and metaphors that required patience and imagination to figure out.

They were also hard work, requiring an outlay of energy that could weaken a sorceress pretty severely.

"Blood," she said, eyes closed, magic swirling in the room like an invisible twister and raising goose bumps on my arms. "The alpha and omega, the beginning and the end. The fount of life and harbinger of darkness."

She sucked in a breath, and a rush of words poured out in a string. "All is waiting. All is forever. All is before."

She stopped, clipping the end of the final word like the needle removed too quickly from a vinyl album.

But although the prophecy was done, her body hadn't yet released from the spell. She still stared blankly ahead, her expression utterly frozen.

"Mallory." Catcher called her name.

She didn't move.

"Mallory," Catcher said, more firmly this time, snapping his fingers in front of her face.

She shuddered, then shook her head. "Sorry. That one was heavy." She looked around the room. "What was it about?"

"Blood," Catcher said. "It was a treatise on how good it is."

Mallory brightened. "Oh, cool. Blood. Vampires. That makes

sense. At least it was actually about the right species this time. I had an attack last week while talking to Gabriel and ended up spouting off about unicorns and narwhales."

"Because both have horns?" I asked.

"God only knows why, or what it had to do with shifters." She shrugged. "I don't write the news; I just report it."

Catcher stood up, then offered Mallory a hand. "Come on, kid. Let's get you back to the crib."

"Hey," I said, "can you ask Gabriel about my car? Not that I'm totally eager to have the orange monster back, but he's probably going to want the Mercedes."

"Sure," Mallory said. "I thought I heard him say the repairs were done, but maybe I missed it. I'll check."

We exchanged good-byes, and they left the office. When they were gone, Ethan took my hands and looked down at me.

"What?" I asked. "What are you fretting about?"

"Mallory," he said. "I want you to be careful. I don't want you to get hurt."

"I'm not going to get hurt." I could hear the defensiveness in my voice, and I hated that.

"I'm not saying she's going to hurt you," he said. "But the possibility exists. She has made bad decisions before. Maybe she's on the road to recovery. Maybe this is her second chance at a good life. But in case it's not, I want you safe. I want you whole."

He dropped his forehead to mine. "I want both of us whole, Merit. I am trying to be patient, to realize that she was under the influence of something old and ancient and much larger and more powerful than she was, but she violated the sanctity of this House."

"I know."

"I do not love her the way that you do. She is your family, possibly more so than anyone else."

"Except you."

He tipped up my chin, his eyes wide with surprise. "Thank you for that."

"You're welcome. Somehow, you've become my family. But you're right. She's family, too, so she gets another chance."

"I want you happy," he said. "And I want you safe."

"I want to accelerate a few days and gorge myself on steak at Tuscan Terrace," I said with a smile. "Sometimes we don't always get what we want."

"And sometimes," he said, pressing a gentle kiss to my lips, "we get exactly what we want. Go get back to work."

"Dictator," I said, but felt the weight around my heart lighten, just a bit.

———— ✠ ————

CHAPTER FIFTEEN

JEFF'S HOUSE OF FUN

Ethan addressed and the internal riot momentarily quelled, it was (past) time to get back to business. Taking the stairs to the basement, I rounded the corner to find Lindsey blocking the Ops Room door, her arms stretched out across the threshold like a human baby gate.

Her hair was pulled into a ponytail today, and it sat stylishly on one shoulder. But the look she gave me was definitely not pretty.

"Stop. Fighting," she said.

Ethan and I radiated magic when we fought, but this time we hadn't actually been the ones fighting.

"I wasn't fighting. Connor got into it with one of the Grey House vampires. And then Mallory had a prophecy."

Lindsey grimaced. "Apparently we missed out on a lot. Fight first, then prophecy."

"Too many vampires in one House," I explained. "Connor's embarrassed, and he's probably going to get the vampire version of KP duty for mixing it up with Grey House, but yeah, he'll live."

"That sucks."

I nodded. "And the prophecy was something about blood and the 'fount of life.'"

"Weird."

"You should have seen it in person."

"I'll pass," Lindsey said. "She still gives me the heebie-jeebies." She looked at me askance. "But there's more. You and Ethan had some kind of something?"

"You're fishing. And we didn't have something or anything. We're just bummed it's Valentine's Day and I'm spending it with you guys."

"Yeah, well, tone down the magic. You're giving me split ends."

"I doubt that's even biologically possible, since you're a vampire, and regardless, no. What's got your undies in a twist this evening?"

Was it the entire House? Perhaps the angst of so many vampires packed into a small space, or worry about the riots or the GP, but everybody—me included—was in a mood tonight.

"The psychic sewer," Luc called out from the Ops Room. I considered that my invitation, and slipped around Lindsey and into the room.

"Psychic sewer?" I asked, taking a seat at the table.

Tonight, only Cadogan House vampires were in attendance. Luc was at the table, Lindsey now beside him. Juliet was still recuperating, and Kelley was probably on patrol outside, which left the temps at the computer stations.

"Because she's empathic," Luc said, "she gets the dregs of all the various emotions floating around this House. And trust me—with this many vamps stuck together, there are many, many dregs."

"That sucks," I said.

She shrugged. "I'll get over it."

"Since I'm down here, and dressed for excitement, maybe we could work on this rioting situation?"

Without prompting, Luc leaned over the conference phone and hit one of the speed-dial buttons.

"Jeff's House of Fun," Jeff answered.

"Jeffrey," Luc said, sitting back in his chair with a squeak and linking his hands behind his head. "What's the good word?"

"Indefatigable is a pretty good word. Lots of syllables."

"Not exactly what I had in mind, but I see where you're going. I'd give you a point for that."

"Hey, Jeff," I said.

"Hey, Mer. Sounds like you've had some excitement over there."

"True fact. But they haven't shut us down yet, so let's talk riots."

"There wasn't one last night," Jeff pointed out. "Maybe they're at an end."

"We can only hope," Luc said, "but I don't think we can bank on it."

"Although that does raise an interesting question," I said. "I've been thinking about the riots. What if they aren't about hating vampires, but about accomplishing something else? They had a House full of Cadogan and Grey House vampires. If they wanted to make a strike, a big strike, now would be the time to do it. But they didn't. Not a hint or a peep of violence. Two riots in a row, and then nothing."

"I think you are right, Sentinel," Luc said. "It's not just about vampires, or else we're looking at the most incompetent group of rioters to set foot in the Windy City. And God knows Chicago has seen its share of riots."

I nodded. "I think that's why we need to focus on Bryant Industries. It was the first place hit, and I think there's a reason for it. If Robin Pope wasn't that reason, then someone else must be. Charla Bryant's brother was supposed to get you some videos of the building. Have you seen those yet?"

"Not that I'm aware of. But Catcher's not back yet. Maybe they've talked."

"Yeah," I said, "he just left here a few minutes ago."

"Have you uncovered anything else that might indicate why the facility was hit?"

"Not a thing," Jeff said. "Charla's parents owned Bryant Industries initially. They had a nasty divorce, and Alan and Charla took over the business. That situation seems to have worked itself out. I also found a really old record for a CPD citation for a loud holiday party at the facility—someone spiked the punch. And about twelve years ago, a former employee got pretty livid when he didn't get a promotion he thought he deserved. He was paid a settlement and released his claim."

I frowned. "Charla didn't mention anything about that."

"It was twelve years ago. Maybe she didn't think it was relevant."

Especially not when Robin Pope's grievance was so fresh.

"What about the health department inspection?" I asked.

"From what we can tell, it's a coincidence. Chuck's got a friend at the health department. He said the woman who scheduled it was heading for maternity leave, and she wanted to get it done before she left."

"Okay," I said. "So let's say inspection's unrelated. The riot had to serve its own purpose. But what?"

"Let's brainstorm that," Luc said. He pushed back his chair, then headed to the whiteboard. "Possible motives."

"Maybe they needed access to the building?" I suggested. "Something they want from the facility?"

"Like what?" Luc asked.

"Could be anything," I said. "Their mailing lists, financial information, scientific equipment."

"Scientific equipment?" Luc asked.

"I'm sure they have some in the lab," I said. "Maybe somebody wanted it."

"Did Charla say anything was missing?" Jeff asked.

I frowned. "I don't think so."

"And I'm not sure about the access theory," Luc said. "A riot's a bad distraction for the place you actually want to get into— people would be everywhere, cops swarming, not to mention rioters. If you're going to use a riot as a distraction, it's because you want people's attention on the *riot*, not the place where you actually are."

"Then maybe to disrupt Chicago's vampires?" Lindsey asked. "To interrupt the blood flow?"

"But it didn't," I said. "Charla told us it didn't affect their capacity."

"Okay," Lindsey said, "but just because it wasn't successful doesn't mean that wasn't the goal."

"True enough," Luc said, writing "blood supply" on the whiteboard. "What else?"

"I don't know," I said. "If not access to the building, maybe access to the blood supply?"

"You're thinking poison?" Jeff asked.

"I don't know," I admitted. "Or maybe somebody was especially bloodthirsty?"

"We have the same distraction problem there," Luc said. "Bryant Industries is big, but not so big that starting a fire at one end of the building is going to pull everybody away from the production floor. I don't think it would work as a distraction."

"And besides," Jeff said, "you're all still here."

"The riot was only three days ago," I said. "How long would it take any adulteration to make its way into stores?"

"Yikes," Jeff said. "I am not digging this conversation. I'm going to send Catcher a note, ask him to double-check with Charla."

Luc recapped his marker and ran his fingers through his hair. "Or maybe all of this is just bullshit speculation. Maybe the inspection has nothing to do with anything. Maybe McKetrick made them move up the date because he's a self-centered prick. Maybe he hoped to catch them unprepared and shut them down."

"That would help drive vampires out of Chicago," I said. "If the inspection was clean, maybe the riot's just another attempt to shut them down."

Luc uncapped his marker again and scratched "Close them down" across the board with a series of squeaks. "Maybe it's that simple."

Maybe, but I doubted it. McKetrick preferred grandstanding when he could get it, and working indirectly to close down a blood supply facility seemed an amateur move for him.

"Got a message from Catcher," Jeff said. "I'm quoting: 'Charla thinks blood supply is safe. Frequent testing.'"

To say that was a relief would be an understatement. Poisoning the city's blood supply would be a quick way to end vampires en masse.

"I don't suppose Catcher mentioned anything else about the videos?" I asked.

"He said he asked her to check again."

"So there you go," Luc said. "We check the videos, and we see if they show us anything interesting."

They would, I silently thought. The question now was what.

As a graduate student, I'd spent a lot of time poring over books and manuscripts. Flipping through pages of centuries-old paper while wearing cotton gloves, staring through the lens of a microfiche machine at illuminated manuscripts. It was usually a slow and time-consuming process.

With that experience under my belt, you'd have thought I'd grown accustomed to being patient and methodical.

But where McKetrick was maybe, possibly concerned, patience was impossible. I sat at the Ops Room table, staring at the whiteboard from a distance and hoping that seeing the big picture would bring me some insight, suggest a clue I'd somehow missed that we could easily backtrack and find in order to secure all the puzzle pieces into the appropriate slots.

But that was easier said than done. You'd also think, having stared at the whiteboard for various mysteries and assignments, and having eventually resolved all of them, I'd get used to the pace. To the grind of looking for information—any information—while waiting for the flint to strike.

The process made me antsy and frustrated, and I found it difficult not to blame myself when clues and solutions weren't immediate, and when vampires were in danger in the meantime.

Before I could add anything helpful, the Ops Room door opened. Ethan and Scott walked in, Jonah behind them.

I had become a bundle of nerves, because even Masters walking through the door made me paranoid.

"Liege?" Luc asked. There was nervous anticipation in his voice, too, which made me feel slightly less crazy. "The GP?"

"Utter silence," Ethan said. "No members of the GP are talking to anyone, as far as we can tell. And I'm not yet sure if that's better or worse than a dressing-down."

"Maybe they're getting their own house in order before talking to the rest of us," Luc said. "But if they're still being silent, what brings you down here?"

"We've just finalized a contract for the apartment building in Lakeview," Scott said. "We've ordered some temporary furnishings while the House décor is being cleaned, and we're going to start moving people in within the hour."

Luc whistled. "That was fast. Congratulations on finding a place. Do you think it will suit you?"

"In the immediate term, yes. We still want to get back to the warehouse, but it's going to be weeks, possibly months, before the roof is finished and the repairs are done. This will give us a bit of breathing room, a bit of normalcy, in the meantime."

"Moving puts Scott and his people in a vulnerable position," Ethan said. "A lot of people coming and going, a lot of chaos. They're going to be busy with moving and making arrangements, so we're going to provide some assistance at the new location."

Ethan looked at me. "Merit, you'll take point. Coordinate with Jonah on the arrangements."

It couldn't have been easy for Ethan to hand me over to Jonah on Valentine's Day, but he managed to do it without sneaky comment. I had to respect that.

"Of course," I said, glancing at Jonah, and wondering if he didn't also have RG support in mind during the move.

"We aren't anticipating specific trouble," Scott said. "But we prepare for the worst, and hope for the best."

"That's practically our motto," Luc said, glancing at me. "Earbuds so you and Jonah can stay in touch?"

The earbuds were some of Luc's favorite toys, minuscule devices with microphones and transmitters, so we could communicate without bulky electronics or signaling our connections to our enemies.

"Sure," I said. "That would be great." I'd also take a full-length insulated coat and thermal underwear while I was at it, because it was probably freezing outside. But work was work, and there was no sense in complaining about it.

"We'll be here if you need us," Luc said, pulling the earbuds from a cabinet and handing them over.

I smiled and tucked mine into my jacket pocket. "Thanks. When are we leaving?"

"I thought you and I could head out first," Jonah said. "Take a look at the grounds and decide where to place folks. The Grey House guards will keep an eye on the rest of the vampires leaving here, and we'll keep an eye on them going in."

I nodded. "Sounds like a plan."

"In that case," Jonah said, clapping his hands together, "I think we're ready."

It made sense for us to drive separately; Jonah would be bunking in the House's new digs for the evening, while I'd head back home and again into the Master's suite.

Moneypenny still sat in the garage, dots of salt and grime on her exterior, but no less beautiful for it.

I'd just opened the door and put my sword into the passenger seat when the basement door opened behind me. Ethan walked inside, his gaze on the car.

"She needs cleaning," he said.

"Probably, although she's not going to get any cleaner tonight." It was useless washing a car in Chicago in the winter until the snow was gone and the forecast was clear.

Ethan made a vague sound. "You'll be careful."

"Always. And Jonah's no slouch."

"I know," he said. "And the irony of his spending the evening with you on Valentine's Day isn't lost on me."

"I didn't think it would be," I said with a wink. "You're very smart, for a vampire."

"You're very mouthy for a Novitiate."

"*Your* Novitiate," I said.

Ethan opened the door for me and gestured inside. "Go take care of Grey House, Sentinel."

I nodded. "Maybe, if you're very good, I'll bring back dinner."

Ethan smiled wickedly and pressed a hard kiss to my lips. "I'm rarely good, Merit. But I'm often spectacular."

He winked and shut the door, and disappeared back into the House.

It took a moment before I had the mental faculties to drive the car.

The housing might have been arranged on short notice, but the new temporary digs of the Grey House vampires were pretty nice.

They were in a building named the King George, and the décor involved lots of inlaid "G"s in the marble floors and gilded mirrors that lined the first-floor lobby.

I waited there a few minutes for Jonah, checking out the giant urns of tropical plants and the very expensive artwork. Whatever their other troubles, Grey House must have solid finances in order to afford a place this nice.

Jonah finally walked in, the breeze blowing his hair around like a model at a photo shoot, two paper cups in hand. He nodded at the security guard at the desk, then handed a cup to me.

"Martin," he said, gesturing toward the guard. "Rogue vampire."

I waved to Martin with my cup. "I guess he's on the night shift."

"Har-har," Jonah said, leading me to the bank of brass elevators. "Twentieth floor."

I sipped my drink, spicy hot chai, until the elevators dinged and we stepped inside. Even the elevator cars were fancy, with small televisions on each side above the buttons. One showed a news channel, the other commercials about Chicago and its nightlife. I guess the King George was selling not just condos, but a way of life.

"Did I mention this place was fancy?" I asked Jonah, as we waited for the car to complete its rise.

"It's what was available," Jonah said. "And unfortunately, we're paying for that fancy."

The doors opened, revealing a long hallway with thick, decadent carpet. A scroll "G" was centered in front of the elevator area, and flowers sat on a pedestal table nearby.

"The 'G' thing is fortuitous."

"Yeah, dumb luck there," Jonah said. I followed him down the hallway to the right, until he stopped in front of number 2005.

He fished a set of keys from his pocket, picked through them until he found the right one, and stuck it into the lock.

"And away we go," he said, loosing the lock and opening the door.

"Holy crap," I muttered, stepping past him into the condo. The condo was completely empty, but it was still pretty lush. Like the lobby, the floors were marble. The walls were painted in a pale, creamy yellow, with white wooden trim. There was a kitchen on one side of the giant living area, with marble countertops and dark wood cabinets. The opposite wall was lined with floor-to-ceiling windows.

"This place is gorgeous," I said, staring up at the coffered ceiling, which was painted three different tones of the same yellow color. "Very high end. Is this Scott's condo?"

Jonah chuckled. "Nope. This one's mine."

"Yours?" This place put my little Cadogan House dorm room to shame. "All this for one vampire?"

"You've seen my digs at Grey House," he reminded me. "Senior staff members get good rooms. That's part of the advantage of making your own House, instead of squeezing into an old building like Cadogan House." He gestured at the space. "You make your own home."

"I guess. Anyway, it's gorgeous. You could do some serious entertaining here. Hey, speaking of which, how was your date the other night?"

Jonah grimaced. "Not great."

"No chemistry?"

"No show," he said. "She stood me up."

"No way."

"Way. Haven't even gotten so much as a phone call since."

That couldn't have been good for the ego. I'd never been stood up, mostly because I'd rarely dated as a human. I supposed that wasn't much of a victory.

"That really sucks," I offered. "Sorry to hear it."

Jonah shrugged again. "It is what it is, you know."

"I do." I took one last gratifying look around the apartment, then gestured toward the door. "We should probably get ready."

Jonah nodded. "We should. Your earbud in?"

I popped it into place. "It is now. Can you hear me?"

"Yes, because we're standing in the same room."

"You're hilarious. Hey, I meant to ask: Did you recruit RG members to keep an eye out tonight?"

"I did. Four of them will be outside, but all in vehicles. Seemed safer that way. They stay warm, and no one gets suspicious if vampires are standing around outside, waiting for something to happen."

I nodded. "How would you like to work this?"

He pulled out his phone and pulled up an image of the grounds. The apartment building was a rectangle right in the middle.

"Two sets of doors," he said. "Front and back of the building. We've rented vans, and we'll be dropping off the vampires in the front. Furniture deliveries are coming through the back. We've got an RG car on each entrance."

He pointed to the front of the building. "Take point here. Keep an eye on cars passing by, the vampires coming in and out. Anything seems suspicious, don't hesitate to contact me. We'll stop at dawn, secure the building, start again at dusk if we don't finish." He glanced at me. "You good?"

"I'm good." I patted my scabbard. "I feel better when she's with me."

"I feel better when you're with me," Jonah said. "You've got a good head on your shoulders. Let's keep it that way, shall we?"

"I certainly intend to do so."

✦ ✦ ✦

CHAPTER SIXTEEN

A LITTLE B AND E BETWEEN FRIENDS

The move went smoothly. So smoothly, in fact, that I was already making plans to return to the House. Rioters might have ruined Valentine's Day, but I wasn't completely giving up on the possibility of dinner with Ethan. I could get Tuscan Terrace to go, and I hadn't yet met a man who could resist the siren call of their penne with vodka sauce.

The vans moved like coordinated dancers. One van dropped vampires off at the apartment building about every twenty minutes, while the other made the trip back to Hyde Park.

Grey House vampires weren't wilting lilies—they were mostly big, strapping guys—but they knew when to move. Like military recruits, they hopped off the van, duffel bags in hand, and jogged in line into the building, where Jonah sent them to their respective condos.

I saw non–Grey House vampires only twice. A member of the Red Guard—a cute girl in a Midnight High School T-shirt, the RG uniform—stepped out of the car and waved at me when I positioned myself outside the building.

I also saw a dog walker, a man with the largest Great Dane I'd ever seen. The dog pawed through the snow fearlessly and with obvious joy as his owner, muffled from toes to head, was dragged along behind him.

"This is the last one," Jonah said, a couple of hours and one chai later. "Last van approaching you now."

I put my hand on my sword, feeling a sense of inevitability strike. If drama was going to happen, it was going to happen now.

But the handoff came and went without so much as a stutter. The Novitiates disappeared inside, and the van driver handed me a receipt and took off into the night, no doubt seeking a warm bed. Jonah emerged from the lobby, looking tired but relieved.

I handed him the receipt. "I will not be paying this. But you can pay me for my services, if you'd like."

"I owe you a steak."

"That works." I chuckled and stuffed my hands back into my pockets, when a low moan echoed from the street.

I froze, squinting into the darkness.

Jonah must have picked up on it. "Merit?"

"Did you hear that?"

Jonah paused, silent. "I don't hear anything."

I heard it again, then spied a low, dark figure moving up the sidewalk. I didn't stop to explain, but I took off at a run down the sidewalk, my hand flipping open the thumb guard on my katana.

And then I reached her.

She was a vampire. A woman, blond and pale, wearing lounge clothes that had seen better days. And she was thin, brutally so. She didn't look sick; she just looked like she hadn't eaten in days.

"Good God," I muttered, hitting the ground beside her. "Are you all right?"

She moaned, and it was a pitiful sound.

I looked back at Jonah, who had nearly reached us. "Jonah! Help me."

"What the hell—," he began, then fell to his his knees as well. "Brooklyn? Brooklyn? Are you all right?"

I looked up at Jonah in surprise. "You *know* her?"

He looked up at me, completely bewildered and plenty afraid. "She's the girl I had a date with. Was supposed to have a date with, anyway. What the hell happened?"

"I don't know. But she looks like she hasn't had blood in a really long time."

I immediately thought back to the room where Michael Donovan, McKetrick's minion, had locked up the vampires he intended to kill. Michael was dead, but McKetrick was alive and well. Had he done this? Had this woman escaped death by his hands?

"We need to get her inside, and we need a doctor. Do you have someone on staff?"

"We do," he said, and then lifted Brooklyn into his arms as if she weighed nothing at all.

I ran down the sidewalk and opened the door, and he hustled her inside and onto a couch in the lobby, as the few remaining Grey House vamps who lingered there looked on.

Jonah looked at the guard. "Can you call Dr. Gianakous? He just went upstairs?"

The guard nodded and picked up the receiver.

Brooklyn looked even worse in the light than she had outside. Her pale skin stretched thin across bone and muscle; her eyes were shadowed and sunken.

"I saw her a week ago," he said, looking up at me. "That's when we met—had coffee. She was absolutely fine. Utterly healthy. Curvy, even."

"She couldn't lose that much weight that quickly."

Jonah shook his head. "Something else happened. Maybe that's why she didn't call me. She couldn't."

The elevator door dinged, and an attractive man with a head of thick dark hair rushed toward us.

"What happened?" he asked, instantly reaching for Brooklyn's wrist and checking her pulse.

"She walked up and collapsed on the sidewalk outside. We don't know why."

Dr. Gianakous leaned down over Brooklyn's head, presumably to listen to her breathing, then sat up again and checked her eyes with a small flashlight.

"What's her name?" he asked.

"Brooklyn," Jonah said.

"Brooklyn," Dr. Gianakous said, snapping his fingers in front of her. "Brooklyn, do you know where you are?"

"Jonah?" she weakly said.

"I'm here," Jonah said, grabbing her hand. "I'm here."

There was a sweetness and affection in his voice I hadn't expected. Not that I didn't wish Jonah well; I just hadn't gotten the sense when he'd initially told me that this date was anything more than casual.

"Brooklyn, do you know what's happened to you?" the doctor asked.

"Medicine," she said.

"You're taking medicine?" he asked, obviously surprised. Brooklyn was a vampire, with presumably the same quick-healing propensities as the rest of us. She shouldn't have needed medicine.

"Taking it," she confirmed with a weak nod.

The doctor looked at Jonah. "Why does she have medicine?"

Jonah shook his head. "I don't know. I mean, I don't know her that well. We were supposed to have a date earlier this week, but she didn't show up."

"Brooklyn, what medicine did you take? Brooklyn?" The doctor snapped his fingers again, but Brooklyn's gaze was unfocused.

An ambulance, lights and sirens on full, screamed to a stop in front of the building, and two EMTs rolled a gurney inside.

"Will they be able to help her?" Jonah asked.

"I'll go with her," Gianakous said. "I'll make sure she gets what she needs."

"Call me if there's an update?"

"Of course," he said, and began reciting her stats to the EMTs as they placed her on the gurney. Within seconds, she was in the ambulance, and it was roaring away.

Jonah looked completely out of sorts, shell-shocked by the quick turn of events.

I put a hand on his back. "Are you okay?"

"I hardly know what to think. I'm just—this just happened so fast."

"You haven't known her very long?"

He shook his head. "We met for coffee. That's all. Then she stood me up for the date."

And yet she showed up here, looking for Jonah, and at a location to which the Grey House vampires had only just decided to move. That seemed oddly coincidental.

"Jonah, if she was looking for you, how did she know to find you here?"

He looked at me apologetically.

"You told her you were moving," I said as the realization hit me.

"It's Valentine's Day," he said. "I was thinking about her, so I left her a message. I told her we'd be here."

The always cool, always careful captain of the Grey House guards sounded remorseful, guilty even.

"It was Valentine's Day," he said again, as if that justified and explained every stupid thing people did for love and companionship. To be fair, it probably explained a fair percentage of them.

It was time to be a friend, as well as a partner. "She came to you for help. If she hadn't known where you were, she might not have made it."

"It was such a stupid thing to do," he said. "To reveal where we were going."

"And it probably saved her life."

Jonah reached into his pocket and pulled out a set of keys. He held them out to me.

"What's this?" I asked.

"The keys to her apartment. I can't leave, but you can. See if you can find anything there."

I took the keys, and stared at them. Exactly what did "coffee" mean these days? "Where did you get her keys?"

Jonah rolled his eyes. "Her pocket, about three minutes ago. Merit, she's a good person, and a smart one. She's got military training. She wouldn't starve herself. Something happened to her."

"I'm not sure she'd be thrilled to learn I was breaking into her apartment."

"As you pointed out, she came here for help. We're helping. And you aren't breaking in. You have the keys."

I wasn't sure the CPD would find that argument compelling, but I agreed it was important to find out what had happened.

"What about my invitation? I can't go in without one."

"That's etiquette," Jonah said, growing exasperation in his voice. "I'm pretty sure she'll forgive the breach."

Under the circumstances, I guessed he was right. So I nodded and put the keys in my pocket. "Are the RG members still out-side?"

He nodded. "They're in the cars. They'll stay until I give them the all-clear."

I popped out the earbud and handed it to him. "Give this to them, so you have someone immediately accessible. I'll call you if I find anything."

"Thank you," he said, his relief obvious.

"No problem. This is what partners are for."

I just hoped I could find out something that helped him—and Brooklyn.

Brooklyn's brownstone was in Wicker Park, not far from Mallory's. It was narrow from front to back, and had windows along one side of the front façade. The windows were dark. A set of covered brick stairs on the other side led into the building.

I got out of the car and headed up the sidewalk. The front door was locked tight, so I pulled out the keys Jonah had given me, se-lecting the one I thought looked most like a building key.

"Sorry for the intrusion, Brooklyn," I quietly said, then slipped it into the lock and felt the tumblers shift and drop.

The door popped open, revealing a small foyer with a rack of mailboxes that led to a staircase. So the brownstone had been par-celed into apartments.

I walked inside and pulled the door shut behind me, feeling a little like the heroine in a caper movie. On the lookout for prying eyes, I quietly climbed the stairs, which squeaked beneath my feet like unintentional intruder alarms.

I heard steps on the landing above me and faked nonchalance as a guy in his twenties passed me on the stairs. He smiled, just a little.

"Hey."

"Hey," I said, politely but without interest, hoping that would be the end of it. When the door opened and closed downstairs, I breathed again.

Brooklyn's door was at the top of the landing, the brass "2" hanging sideways beside the "B." I unlocked the door and stepped inside, closing it quietly behind me again.

The apartment was nice, but small, with hardwood floors and arched passageways. The furniture was sparse, mostly vintage, but good quality. Nice chests of drawers and buffet tables, a long, low couch with a built-in table at one end. There was an inset area along one wall that probably would have held an old-fashioned telephone back in the day. Today, it held a vase of wilted flowers. Whatever had gone wrong, maybe it hadn't gone wrong here.

Otherwise, the apartment looked completely normal. Not too tidy, not too messy.

A kitchen was tucked beside the living room. The refrigerator was ancient, but humming steadily. I pulled it open. It was bare, but for two unopened bottles of blood and milk two days past its expiration.

A carton of orange juice sat on the counter. I picked it up and found it empty. An empty glass sat nearby.

I stepped on the trash can's pedal and peeked inside. It was empty. No evidence of drugs or empty bottles of juice from a "cleanse" that might have explained Brooklyn's condition.

Floors creaking beneath me, I walked back into the living room, and then into the small hallway off to the side. There was a small bathroom, mostly clean. The medicine cabinet held the usual suspects. Toothpaste, mouthwash, lotion . . . but there were no mysterious "medicines" a vampire wouldn't have needed, in any event.

Thinking the bedroom was at the other end of the hallway, I

tiptoed across the wooden slats, which creaked beneath my feet, and peeked inside. The bed was unmade, the sheets tossed around as if Brooklyn had had a few bad nights of sleep. The room smelled unwashed, as though the odors of many nights of sweaty bodies had collected there.

So she got sick, lay down in the bed, and didn't get up for days? How could that happen to a vampire?

I wandered back into the living room. How did a woman who seemed otherwise healthy just stop eating and drinking? As a vampire, her bloodlust should have kicked in long before she got to her current state. She'd have been biologically driven to drink, even if she didn't have the emotional capacity for it. I'd have expected a blood-drinking frenzy—even attacks on her neighbors—instead of the normalcy I'd found.

I looked around the room, searching for anything that might give me a hint about her condition, or the "medicine" she'd ingested.

I spied a pile of mail on a table behind the couch and walked over to inspect it. I flipped through the stack but found only bills, magazines, and solicitations from charities. Nothing that hinted about a problem.

A postcard fell from the stack that I tried to rearrange on the table in its previous position. I bent down to pick it up, when a glint of something on the carpet caught my eye.

I put the postcard back on the table and walked closer.

There, in the middle of her living room rug, was a silver and glass syringe, with an old-fashioned plunger of two circles of metal pressed together.

I was smart enough not to touch evidence with my bare hands. I walked back to the kitchen and searched through drawers until I found a box of zip-top plastic bags. I took one, apologizing for my thievery, and walked back to the living room.

The bag opened with a snap, and I turned it inside out, using it like a glove to pick up the syringe—and give it a closer inspection. Unfortunately, the plunger had been fully depressed, the chamber empty. Not even a drop of liquid remained inside. I wasn't sure it could tell us anything about Brooklyn's problem, but it was still the best clue we had at the moment.

I flipped the bag around so it enclosed the syringe, then sealed it shut. I locked up the apartment again and hightailed it to my car again as if monsters were on my heels.

When I made it to the car again, I pulled out my phone.

Jonah answered quickly.

"It's Merit. I found something. A syringe."

"A syringe? Of what?"

"I don't know. It's empty. It was lying on the living room floor. And it's the old-fashioned kind—glass, not plastic. Maybe that's the medicine she mentioned?"

"It could be, but I don't know. What was she doing with a syringe? She's a vampire."

"Could it be something, let's say, recreational?" A few months ago, a vampire drug called "V" had made its way around the city, but we'd shut down the supply.

"God, I don't know. She doesn't really seem the type. She's into clean eating and fitness. What was she doing with a syringe?" He asked me, but it was clear from his absent tone he was musing over the question himself.

"I don't know. Maybe we can ask Detective Jacobs to take a look at it. Catcher said my grandfather's doing him some favors, so maybe we can get a little quid pro quo."

"Yeah, maybe. Do you think someone broke in? And used the syringe on her?"

"I don't know. The apartment didn't look disturbed, and it didn't look like there was a break-in. Maybe she let them in?"

"Did you find anything else?"

"Not a thing. Everything else in the apartment looked completely normal. There wasn't much food. She hadn't had blood, as far as I could tell. There were untouched bottles in the fridge, and no empties in the trash. Wilted flowers in the living room, and the bed was unmade. I'm not sure if she's been gone, or stayed in bed."

"Thank you for checking."

"You're welcome. Have you heard from the doctor?"

"Only that she's checked in and he's running tests. He doesn't expect to know anything for a little while."

"Let me know what you find out. Are you okay otherwise?"

"Yeah, we're all tucked into Grey House 2.0. Security's set."

"Glad to hear it. Give me a call if you need me. And I'll let you know if we find anything with the syringe."

"Thanks, Merit."

The line went dead, but I still had calls to make. I needed to check in at the House and make arrangements to get the syringe to someone who could take a look at it.

"Ops Room," said Lindsey.

"It's Merit."

"Speakerphone?"

"Yes, please."

"And you're live," Lindsey said. "Luc and I are in the room with the temps. Say hello, temps."

"Hello, temps," they ridiculously muttered in tandem.

"The Grey House vamps are tucked in," I said. "Everything okay on your end?"

"Fine," Luc said. "The transition was smooth. Jonah's very good at his job."

"Yes, he is," I said. "But we've got a new wrinkle. A vampire wandered up to the new Grey House digs. She was nearly unconscious, and completely emaciated. Turns out, she's a friend of Jonah's. They were supposed to meet earlier this week, but she didn't show up. The Grey House doc rushed her to the ER."

"Does he know what was wrong?"

"Not a thing. She kept mentioning 'medicine.'" I cleared my throat, preparing for my confession. "So, I might have used her keys to get into her apartment. And I might have wandered around a little bit and found a syringe, the old-fashioned glass kind."

"I am surprised and pleased, Sentinel. You're getting some balls on you after all. No offense."

"None taken."

"I presume you grabbed the syringe?"

"I did, and in a plastic bag to keep my contaminates off, since I'm a forensic expert after hours of crime scene shows in Lindsey's room." We tended toward pizza and television for girls' nights.

"I'm going to see if my grandfather can get it to the CPD and figure out what might have been in it."

"Good girl. Random, though, isn't it?"

"It is. And that's what's bothering me. Even if she'd injected herself, or been injected by someone else, what was the point? She's a vampire. She'd have healed from any illness. As far as I could tell, she was in her apartment for days, then crawled out to find Jonah."

"Weird," Luc said. "That's an odd set of circumstances, not that we're low on those right now. Anyway, I'll tell Ethan."

"Please do. I'm going to call my grandfather and take the syringe over there."

"Got it," Luc said. "Stay in touch. Things are calm here for now, all things considered. But that could change at any minute."

I took that as a hint to get to work. Two calls down, I prepared to dial up the third. Catcher answered immediately.

"Catcher."

"Hey, it's Merit. Are you guys around? I've actually got something I'd like you to take a look at."

"What's that?"

"A syringe. We think it has something to do with a sick vampire that's also a friend of Jonah's."

"How does a vampire get sick?" he asked.

"Presumably from whatever was in the syringe. I checked out her apartment. It was on the floor. I grabbed it, was hoping you could get it to Detective Jacobs."

"You've escalated to breaking and entering?" Catcher mused. "I'll not mention that to your grandfather."

"Please don't."

"I'm out," Catcher said. "Jeff and I both left early. It is Valentine's Day, you know."

"I'm aware," I said dryly.

"Your grandfather was talking to Jacobs about their little forensic mystery, but he's home now. He'll be happy to see you. I'll check in when I'm done here."

"Roger that," I said, and ended the call, then sent Ethan a message: TAKING EVIDENCE TO GRANDFATHER. LUC HAS DETAILS. HOME AFTERWARD.

I tapped the screen for a moment, thinking about the surprise I'd planned and debating whether to tell him. But if I couldn't actually give him a decent Valentine's Day, the least I could do was tell him I'd tried.

I HOPED TO GRAB TT FOR DELAYED VALENTINE'S DINNER, BUT VAMPIRES INTERVENED.

TT? Ethan asked, and I sighed with pity.

TUSCAN TERRACE, YOU TROGLODYTE. SORRY AGAIN FOR POSTPONEMENT.

LIFE GOES ON, Ethan philosophically answered. EVEN FOR TROGLODYTES. AND UNLIKE TROGLODYTES, I'M NOT GOING ANYWHERE.

God, I loved that man.

Now that I had toured northern Chicago, it was time to head south. My grandfather lived in a working-class house in a working-class neighborhood, precisely the type of place my father avoided. Unlike my father, Grandfather didn't believe he had to prove himself by having the biggest or fanciest of anything.

The streets in this neighborhood weren't plowed as well as other places, and the street signs were in need of repair. But the people were good, and that was what kept my grandfather here.

The driveway held only my grandfather's giant boat of an Oldsmobile; Catcher, Jeff, and Marjorie, the admin, were gone. The living room light was on.

I pulled up to the curb and grabbed my katana and the plastic bag from the passenger seat. Maybe it was time to find a messenger bag to compliment my leathers, something I could transport my goods in. As I locked the door, I wondered if they made specialized messenger bags for vampires with straps for Blood4You bottles, hidden pockets for emergency weapons, and a flap for the registration cards we were required to carry.

I am a nerd, I thought to myself, slamming the car door.

I carefully navigated the ice at the edge of the street, then hopped onto a dry spot of sidewalk.

I was excited to see my grandfather, glad I had evidence in hand, and optimistic we might find something useful.

But in that excitement, I was oblivious.

The push came from behind, a strike that sent me reeling forward into the snow. I dropped the plastic bag and used my free hand to unsheathe my katana, but the push, like so much else, had been a distraction.

Time slowed to a crawl. I jumped to my feet, snow glinting off the steel in my hand, and ran toward the front door.

But they'd been ready, the plan under way. Three more ran from the back of the house to the front, the bottles already lit in their hands.

"Grandpa!" I screamed as they tossed the Molotov cocktails through the windows, still running through the snow.

The front of the house exploded, flames rushing through the windows and sending a spray of glass and fire and heat into the yard. The barrage hit me, full force, and threw me backward into the snow.

But I felt no pain, no fear.

There was no thinking, no rationalizing, no weighing of cost.

There was only *do*.

I dropped my sword, ran toward the flames, and leaped into the fire.

CHAPTER SEVENTEEN

+·+ ═◆═ +·+

HELL HATH NO FURY

The front of the house was gone. There remained only a curtain of rising flames and burning debris. I landed in the middle of a conflagration, the fire crackling and climbing the walls to the ceiling as if it were a breathing thing. Like the fire was made of a thousand hands, all grasping upward, all climbing from some hell down below.

I'd seen a fire before, but I'd forgotten how loud it was. Loud and hazy and chemical. The smoke was blinding and seared my throat with each breath, but that was irrelevant now. I was a vampire; he was not. I'd heal. I couldn't guarantee he would.

But that I was a vampire didn't mean the burns hurt less; they'd just heal faster. I covered my face with a crooked arm, but sparks flew like horizontal rain, peppering me with stinging ash.

I ignored it.

"Grandpa!" I yelled over the roaring of the fire. I stumbled through the living room, which was empty, and into the kitchen, hands outstretched, feeling my way through the house with clumsy fingers. Thinking he might have been in his bedroom, I searched for the wall that led to the hallway. "Grandpa! Where are you?"

I pretended I was a child, sleeping over for a visit with my grandparents, moving through the house in the dark for a drink of water. I'd done it a thousand times, knew my way around the house even in utter darkness. I closed my eyes and willed my mind to remember to search for the clues that would get me where I needed to go.

I remembered, as a child, fumbling for the light switch on the left-hand wall. I reached out, groping blindly until I found smooth plastic, and then empty space. That was the hallway.

As the fire grew behind me, and the smoke thickened, I advanced. "Grandpa!"

I stumbled over an obstacle and fell down, then reached back to figure out what it had been. My fingers found a sharp corner—it was a bureau, a piece of furniture that had once stood in the hallway, holding my grandmother's tablecloths and napkins. Sentimentality hitting me, I grabbed the only fragment of fabric I could feel—probably a doily—and stuffed it into my jacket.

One grandparent down, one to go.

"Grandpa? Where are you?"

"Merit!"

I froze. The sound was faint, but distinctly his. "Grandpa? I can hear you! Keep talking!"

"Merit . . . Go . . . *out . . . house!*"

I caught only intermittent words—"Out . . . house!"—but the meaning was clear enough. Those words also sounded like they were coming from far away. But I was feet from the bedroom. . . .

He wasn't in the bedroom, I realized. He was in the basement. The basement door was through the kitchen, so I'd have to backtrack and grope my way back to that side of the house—and then figure out a way to get him up again.

I dropped to the ground, where the air was still breathable and fresher, and crawled across the remains of the floor, ignoring the burning ash and glass beneath my hands. Adrenaline was pushing me now, sending me, regardless of the obstacle, toward the man who'd been like a father to me.

I crawled slowly forward, burned boards creaking beneath me as they struggled to hold up the remaining weight. I froze, not even taking a breath, before moving forward again.

My movement hadn't been light enough.

Without warning, the boards beneath me snapped, sending me free-falling to the basement.

I landed with a bounce atop a jumble of boards, debris, and the shag carpeting I was suddenly glad my grandfather had kept. The fall knocked the air from my lungs, and for a moment I sucked in air as my body remembered how to breathe again.

Unfortunately, the craving for oxygen gave way to pain as my senses returned. I'd fallen on my side, which was now racked by a piercing pain. Slowly, ignoring the stabbing sensation, I got to my feet to move again.

"Grandpa?"

"Here, Merit." He coughed, weakly enough that my heart nearly stopped.

"I'm coming, Grandpa. Hold on. I will be right there."

I searched frantically through smoke and ash, trying to fulfill my promise, but it was nearly pitch-black in the basement, and I couldn't find him.

The heat climbed as the fire roared above us. I pushed the most obvious question—assuming I survived this trip, how in God's name was I going to get him safely out again?—from my mind, and focused on the task at hand, on breaking it into its smallest components.

Step one: Find my grandfather.

A burst of fire suddenly rushed above my head. Terrifying . . . but revealing. A few feet in front of me I saw a glint of light—the firelight dancing on the face of my grandfather's watch. I dropped to my knees in ashy carpet, pushing aside half-burned books and pieces of what I assumed was Jeff's computer.

I grabbed his hands.

"Hi, Grandpa," I said, tears rushing my eyes.

He was on his back, surrounded by rubble. He squeezed my hands, which was a good sign, but across his abdomen was a gigantic wooden beam. It must have supported the basement ceiling and main floor.

Panic quickly set in, and I had to consciously remind myself to breathe slowly. A hyperventilating vampire would do no one any good.

One step at a time, I reminded myself. Step two: Put on a good face, and get him untangled from the burning remains of his house.

"What in God's name have you gotten yourself into this time?" I said with a mock laugh, brushing his hair from his face.

He coughed again, each sputter sending an uncomfortable torque through my gut.

"I need a babysitter," he said.

"Apparently so. You appear to have most of the ceiling on your legs. I'm going to try to move it now."

Like an athlete preparing for a dead lift, I squatted, knees bent, and tucked my hands under the beam. "All right, Grandpa. On three. One . . . two . . . three!"

I put every ounce of strength—biological and supernatural— into my arms and thighs, and I lifted with all my might.

The beam didn't budge.

Fear—and lack of oxygen—tightened my chest. It was getting harder to focus, and bright spots were beginning to appear in the corners of my vision.

This plan might go horribly, horribly wrong.

And for the first time, it occurred to me to actually ask for help.

Ethan? I asked, trying the telepathic connection between us. *Can you hear me?*

But I got no response.

"So, Grandpa, you've managed to get this thing pretty wedged. I'm going to try again." I tried again. And again. And again, until my fingertips were bloody and my arms and legs were shaking.

I reverted to screaming.

"Someone! Anyone! Get in here! I need help!"

The ceiling above us—what was left of it, anyway—shuddered and creaked ominously.

I covered my grandfather with my body, slapping at the embers that scattered my hair and jacket. A moment later, the ceiling stilled again, and I started a new set of dead lifts.

But I wasn't strong enough.

"Merit," my grandfather said, *"get out."*

His words and tone were forceful, but of course I ignored him. I was a vampire. He wasn't. I'd do what I could for as long as I could . . . and then I'd try again.

"You are crazy if you think I'm leaving you. I need help down here!" I yelled out.

I didn't want to leave him—wasn't going to leave him. Especially not when I could use my body to shield him if the roof fell. Hopefully, the house hadn't been constructed of aspen. Because, much like burning to death in a rather ill-thought-out plan to rescue my grandfather, that would be bad.

Okay, so terror and oxygen deprivation were making me even more sarcastic than usual.

"Merit!" Jeff's voice rang through the smoke. "Merit?"

Tears of relief sprang to my eyes. We weren't out of the predicament, but Jeff's voice—and his shifter-heightened strength—was a filament of hope. That was all I needed to hold on to.

"Down here! Grandpa's stuck, Jeff. I can't move him!"

Jeff dropped through the hole, hitting the ground a few feet away. He made the trip look stupidly easy, but I decided that would have been impossible without my having fallen through the floor in the first place.

"I was only gone a couple of hours, Chuck," Jeff said as he checked out my grandfather's position. "I want you to know I'll be seeking overtime for this."

"Only fair," my grandfather said, chuckling lightly. "Only fair."

Jeff pointed me into position. "There," he said. "On three. I'm not going to lift—I'm going to lever. When I do, pull your grandfather away." He looked at me, and I saw behind the boyish jokes and flirtations, the eyes of a man.

I nodded at him and took my designated spot a few feet away.

"Chuck," Jeff said, "we're going to lift this thing off you. I can't guarantee it won't hurt, but you know how this goes."

"I know how this goes," my grandfather agreed, wincing as he prepared himself.

I squatted again, this time reaching under my grandfather's armpits, ready to move him when the weight was lifted.

Jeff rolled his shoulders, moved to the end of the beam, and braced himself against it, one knee forward, the other leg extended back. He blew out three quick breaths in succession.

"One . . . two . . . three!" he said. He pushed the top of the beam upward, levering it just enough to lift the weight from my grandfather's abdomen. I dragged him away, his feet clearing the beam's path just as Jeff let it drop again.

My grandfather blinked. "That did hurt," he said.

And then his eyes closed, sending my heart racing again. "Jeff, we have to get him out of here," I said, but the last of my sentence was muted by a crash above us that sent a bevy of sparks over us . . . and covered the gap we'd used to get into the basement with flaming drywall.

"On it," Jeff said. He scooped my grandfather up and headed toward the back of the basement.

"Where are you going?"

"Back bedroom. Emergency window."

I hadn't even remembered there was a bedroom back there, much less a window.

"Right behind you," I said, listening for his footsteps in front of me, as I certainly couldn't see anything. I covered my mouth with a hand, smoke from the fire upstairs beginning to funnel down through the cracks in the ceiling.

Jeff moved swiftly through the serpentine basement hallway, around corners and into a small back room where, I now remembered, my grandmother had kept our Christmas presents before they were wrapped. My sister and I had dug through the closet on occasion, trying to figure out which one of us got the Lite Brite and the doll that wet itself.

But those presents were long gone. Instead, we fixed our sights on the small window that was about to become our escape route.

"Open it," Jeff directed, and I pulled a stool over to the window and unlatched the window frames, which opened into a window well.

"Get out," Jeff said. "I'll help boost your grandfather up."

I nodded, pushed myself up to the sill, and climbed outside, gulping in the first fresh air I'd had in minutes, then kicking away snow and debris to help our egress.

"Ready," Jeff said, maneuvering my grandfather's shoulders through the windows. I grabbed his torso again and pulled until I could cradle him in the window well.

"Let me help," said a voice above me.

I looked up to see a Chicago Fire Department member in a fire suit and hat on his knees at the edge of the window well.

As Jeff climbed safely from the fire and paramedics strapped my grandfather to a gurney, I said a silent thank-you to the universe.

The house was surrounded by vehicles—fire trucks, police interceptors, two ambulances. Their blue, red, and white lights shined across the yard, which was full of debris thrown out by the explosion.

I found my sword and cleaned away the smoke and ash, giving the EMTs room to work while they stabilized my grandfather, but I moved closer when they loaded the gurney into the back of the ambulance.

Tears welled in my eyes at the sight, and my throat constricted so tightly, I wasn't sure if I could breathe.

One of the EMTs stayed by his side; the other climbed out of the ambulance and shut the door.

"You're his granddaughter?"

I nodded.

"He's unconscious but stable," said the EMT, whose name badge read ERICK. "We'll take him to Southwestern Memorial," he said. "You wanna follow us in your car?"

"We'll get there," Jeff said, stepping beside me. He had a bandage on his head and another around his arm.

"You're hurt?" I asked, feeling suddenly numb and disconnected to the world. The adrenaline was wearing off, and fear and shock and pain were beginning to seep in.

"I'm fine. The guys said you were okay, too?"

I nodded. "Vampire healing. My lungs are sore, and I've got some minor burns, but they'll heal." I glanced down at my leathers, which were probably toast. They were pockmarked with holes from flying cinders and sparks.

"I ruined my clothes," I said, laughing. I sounded hysterical, even to me. Was I coming unglued?

Jeff put a hand on my arm. "Merit, I'm going to get the car, okay? I'll call Ethan and have him meet us at the hospital. He's probably on his way."

I nodded, and Jeff jogged away toward his car, which sat, untouched, at the end of the driveway.

I glanced around, refusing to look at the house, not ready to face the destruction or the loss of a place where I'd spent so much time as a child. A place where I'd grown up.

And what did I spy with my little eye? In front of the other ambulance sat a kid—no more than twenty—wearing a T-shirt that read CLEAN CHICAGO.

Rage coursed through me.

I picked up my sword, the handle damp with snow, and strode toward him.

"Who sent you here?"

He looked up at me and sniffed in disgust. "Nobody."

"Who sent you here?" I pressed, placing the tip of the sword against the beating pulse of his carotid artery. It throbbed just beneath the skin, a tiny echoing heartbeat that hinted at the satiation of my hunger, and the satisfaction of my sudden lust for violence.

It was a different kind of bloodlust.

I wet my lips and looked down at him, lusting for violence in a way I'd never experienced before. I'd needed blood, sure. I was a vampire. But I hadn't needed blood like this. I wanted to devour him, control him, sublimate him.

I wanted to end him.

I had sudden, new empathy for Mallory's black-magic addiction, for the mind-filling supernatural wanting that she must have experienced. Humans weren't any strangers to addiction, but this seemed almost more powerful, as if the addiction weren't simply foisted upon you by a drug, but by a living, breathing thing.

"Merit," Jeff said, "put the sword down."

"No, Jeff. This is the *last time* they hurt us. This has to be the last time. We have sat around for too long and let them get away with this. I say, fuck them, fuck this little shit. What's the worst thing that can happen?"

"Retribution," he said, more calmly than I would have. "Violence, martial law, litigation. I know you love your grandfather, Merit. I don't doubt it, and never would. But we have to consider what will help . . . and what will hurt."

I was a woman, a Sentinel, a vampire. A monster. But mostly . . . I was me. Irrespective of what else I might have been, I was me. I was my grandfather's granddaughter. I was a Cadogan Novitiate, from a noble House. And I couldn't dishonor either my grandfather or my House with murder in cold blood.

Biting was one thing. Biting bad was another.

I looked away, furious that Jeff wasn't going to let me have my way, my violence. I was a vampire, for fuck's sake. I wanted action. I wanted to sweat through my blinding fury, to let it find its home somewhere else, outside of me, where it couldn't gnaw at me anymore.

I walked away and threw my sword across the yard, then fell into the snow.

There, on my knees, in the middle of my grandfather's front yard, I looked at what had become of the home he'd shared with my grandmother. The house was virtually destroyed. The fire had spread from front to back, which was the only reason we'd managed to escape without worse injuries. The walls in the back were still standing, but the front had caved in, leaving a gaping chasm of charred wood and furnishings.

And the structure wasn't the only thing lost. The photographs and mementos had been burned. My grandfather's belongings had been destroyed. Even Jeff's computer was probably a pile of smoldering plastic toast right now.

The loss and fear and grief hit me, and I began to sob. I cried until my knees were numb and my eyes burned. I cried after a fireman covered me in a silver blanket for warmth, and until I doubted there was a tear left to shed.

I opened my eyes again and looked out over the yard. The work would have to start: rebuilding, finding a place for my grandfather to live, finding a place for the Ombuddies to work.

Work.

I realized, in my haste to get inside, what I was missing. The syringe. I'd dropped the plastic bag in the snow. We had to have it—it was the only piece of real physical evidence we had.

Frantically, I crawled forward, pushing through the chunks of ice and snow with my hands, sifting through rubble as I looked for the plastic bag—not an easy venture in the dark.

"Merit?"

Startled by the sound of my name, I glanced around.

Ethan stood behind me.

"I lost the syringe, Ethan. I can't find it."

His gaze softened. "Don't worry about that now, Merit. We'll find it."

"No, we need the syringe. It's our evidence. We need it, Ethan."

"Okay," he said, gently pulling me to my feet. "I'll look for the syringe, okay?"

I nodded, my mind still racing, my heart still racing. "It's our evidence," I repeated.

Ethan put his hands on my face and searched my eyes. "Merit. Breathe."

I shook my head. I'd already been overwhelmed once. I didn't want to be overwhelmed again. I just wanted a solution.

"I was so afraid," I said. "I thought I'd lost my grandfather."

Ethan smiled. "You didn't lose him. You saved him, Merit. You rushed into a burning building to save him, and I have never been so proud or so angry. You could have gotten yourself killed."

"I'm okay," I said. "I had to go in there. I couldn't not go in there."

"I know," he said, brushing bangs from my face. "And that's the only reason I'm not throttling you right now."

"The house was firebombed. There were rioters. One of them is over . . . there," I said, pointing to the second ambulance, but the rioter was gone.

"Jeff nabbed him," Ethan said. "He's in the back of the CPD car."

I turned around to check that out. Sure enough, the pouty rioter was in the back of the cruiser. I couldn't hear his words, but he appeared to be screaming at the top of his lungs, probably about the unfairness of his arrest and the injustices he was facing at the hands of vampires . . . after he'd firebombed my grandfather's house.

"My grandfather's house is gone," I said.

"But your grandfather is not," Ethan pointed out. He kissed me hard, reminding me that I had my own life to be grateful for, then wrapped his arms around me and held me tight. My tears began anew.

"I'm here," he said. "Be still."

Half an hour and one retrieved piece of evidence later, we sat in the dated waiting room of a hospital on the south side of Chicago. Grandpa was in surgery, and we were waiting for an update.

Chairs with pink tweed cushions and rounded wooden arms were grouped together in seating areas for family and friends, and televisions showing twenty-four-hour news channels played quietly in the corners. There was a small area for children to play, with a handful of wooden books and plastic toys with the decals and paint worn off. They seemed tired, and sadder for it.

I'd washed the soot from my face in the sink of the bathroom down the hall, using hand soap and brown paper towels. Soot was weirdly greasy, and it took a few tries before my skin was clean again. On the upside, I wouldn't need an exfoliating mask any time soon.

I sat beside Ethan, our hands entwined, my head on his shoulder. The rest of the Cadogan House vampires had stayed at the house out of fear the rioters might seek another target. They clearly meant business—whatever that business might have been.

Other vampires were also absent, but Jonah sent a text message: SOUNDS LIKE I MISSED ALL THE FUN.

YOU DID, I responded. BUT YOU SHOULD STAY WHERE YOU ARE. KEEP YOUR PEOPLE SAFE.

YOU'RE ONE OF MY PEOPLE, he messaged. AND I'M GLAD YOU'RE OKAY. BEST WISHES TO CHUCK.

My grandfather was well loved, and the waiting room was

stuffed with people who'd been able to check in and wish him well. Catcher and Mallory sat on the chairs across from us. Catcher looked guilty, I assumed because he hadn't been at the house when the shit went down. Not that that would have done anything.

Jeff and Marjorie were there, as were a handful of supernaturals I knew only through vague acquaintance—a couple of the snub-nosed River trolls and a small gaggle of River nymphs—but they kept to themselves.

Detective Jacobs and some of my grandfather's friends from the CPD were there. Ethan had passed the syringe over to Catcher, who in turn gave it to Detective Jacobs. He promised to have the lab take a look as soon as he could.

Gabriel, Tanya, and Connor even dropped by to wish my grandfather well. Connor was asleep in his father's arms, and Tanya looked sleepy, too. I hadn't realized how late it was—only a couple of hours from dawn, I thought.

"You're all right?" Gabriel asked, giving me a half hug and pressing a kiss to my cheek. That act of kindness, so personal and so unusual for Gabe, nearly made me break into tears again.

"I'm okay," I said. "Hanging in there."

"Only thing you can do," he said, shaking Ethan's hand.

"Your compatriot was a brave man tonight," Ethan said. "Jeff helped rescue him."

We glanced at Jeff, who was now cradling Connor in his unbandaged arm, Tanya looking over them both with a smile.

"He's a good man," Gabriel said. "And a good member of our Pack."

"Any word on my car?" I asked. "I don't want to wear out my welcome with the Mercedes, I mean."

Gabriel and Ethan shared a look I couldn't decipher, but I bet it was related to the car's history—and the fact that Ethan wanted it.

"As it turns out," Gabe said, "they're having trouble tracking down a windshield."

I frowned. "I thought Mallory had said it was repaired?"

"Only the hood," Gabe clarified. "That was easy enough to find. Intact glass for a Volvo that was manufactured before you were born is trickier. And don't worry about the car. You have bigger things to think about. Family things. That comes first."

"Agreed," Ethan said, slipping his hand into mine.

The Keenes didn't stay long, begging off in order get Connor home and safely tucked in. They were quickly replaced by my parents, who were the last to arrive. Both were formally dressed; she in sequins, he in a tux. They probably hadn't learned about the fire until after whatever event they'd been attending.

My mother was teary eyed. My father looked haunted, as if he'd suddenly been reminded of his own mortality.

We rose when they came in. My mother practically ran to me, embracing me in a hug strong enough to leave sequin imprints on my arms.

"You've talked to the doctor?" my father asked.

"Not yet," Ethan said. "He's still in surgery."

My father looked at me, and for the first time that I could remember, there was fear in his eyes. The man who'd bought his way through life had discovered that death always had a card to play and rarely lost a hand.

He wrapped his arms around me and squeezed. "You could have gotten yourself killed, Merit. You could have gotten yourself killed."

It was tragedy's unique ability to cross rifts between people, even deep crevasses between family members.

"I'm all right," I said, patting him on the back. I appreciated the hug, but that didn't make it any less awkward, considering our history. "I'm fine."

"How did it happen?" my mother asked.

"Rioters," Ethan said. "The same ones who attacked the vampire business and House earlier this week."

"What could they have against Charles?" she asked.

"I presume it's related to his work as a police officer?" my father asked.

"Possibly," Ethan vaguely agreed. "We aren't entirely sure. Why don't we sit down? It could be a bit of time yet."

Because he was right, we sat down in the chairs, and we waited some more.

I tried to rest, but my mind kept spinning with questions. Why had my grandfather been targeted? Because he'd supported vampires as Ombudsman? Because he was on our side? He'd been a cop for years; there seemed little doubt he'd made enemies along the way. Had those enemies become wrapped up in riots and anti-vampire hatred?

Most frighteningly, had he been targeted because he was my grandfather? Was I now a liability to my family?

Grief weighed on me, and I rested my head on Ethan's shoulder. *Be still*, Ethan silently told me. *Be still.*

I locked away the fear and the grief, and I did as I was told.

Every time the hallway door opened, I jumped, anxious for news, good or bad. But we were an hour in when a tall man with a head of thick dark hair and dressed in turquoise scrubs stepped into the room.

"Merit family?" he asked, his accent thick but the origin unknown.

"That's us," my father said, standing.

The doctor nodded and walked over, then sat down in an empty chair across from us.

"Dr. Berenson," he said. "I was Mr. Merit's surgeon. The surgery went very well, and we've moved him back into his room."

I closed my eyes in relief.

"What's his prognosis?" my father asked.

"Good. He took a pretty good fall. Shattered his pelvis and broke a few ribs. It was internal injuries from the beam's landing on top of him that did most of the internal damage. He has sensation in his legs, which is great, but his pelvis took a beating."

"He'll be ambulatory?" Ethan asked.

"He's not a spring chicken, and he's going to need some pretty extensive physical therapy. But, barring complications, we have every expectation he'll be able to walk again. We'll keep him until we're sure he's stable and healing, and then you can decide on a rehab facility or home-health nurse."

Jeff whistled. "Chuck is not going to like either of those options."

"Like is irrelevant," my father said quietly. "He'll stay with us."

Chuck isn't going to like that, either, I silently told Ethan.

I suspect you are right. But your father has room and resources to ensure he's well cared for. He'll adapt, as we all must do.

The doctor nodded. "You've got some time to make those decisions. He'll say in intensive care for tonight, and as soon as he's awake and stable, we'll move him to a room." He rose. "I think that's about it for tonight. You can check with the nurse anytime you have questions. And visiting hours are posted on the wall."

"I'll stay tonight," my father said, to the surprise of all of us. "He's my father, and I wasn't there when he was injured. It's the least I can do. I'll stay." He glanced at me. "Go home. Get a shower and some sleep. You look like you need both."

This time, I found I couldn't disagree with him.

————

We drove home in silence. Jeff and Catcher volunteered to get Moneypenny back to the House, which was an offer I couldn't refuse. I was mentally, physically, and emotionally exhausted, and in no shape to drive.

When we arrived at the House, less than an hour before dawn, we found security tight. Luc, Malik, Lindsey, and Margot met us in the foyer when we arrived.

"How is he?" Malik asked.

"He's okay," I said. "Long road to recovery, but he's alive. And that's something."

"That is something," Luc said, pulling me into a bear hug. It was definitely the night for unexpected shows of affection. "Glad you're safe, Sentinel."

"Thanks. Me, too."

"This is life," Ethan said. "This is Valentine's Day. Do not rue the tragedies; celebrate the victories."

"That sounds like something Merit's grandfather would say," Malik said with a smile.

"Are you hungry?" Margot asked. "Have you had time to eat?"

Not lately, considering my second effectively failed attempt at arranging a meal for Valentine's Day. I knew I'd be ravenous tomorrow, but for tonight, my appetite was gone.

"I'm not especially hungry," Ethan said. "But perhaps blood and wine?"

Margot nodded. "Absolutely, Liege. I'll get that ready for you and send it to your apartments."

That was at least a small relief—with the Grey House vampires installed at the King George, we could get our apartments and bed back. My body was going to need the rest, and I was pretty sure I'd be sleeping hard tonight.

And speaking of the new Grey House digs, "Any update on Brooklyn?" I asked Luc.

"Last we heard, she was stable," he said. "I don't have any more information."

Ethan put a hand on my back. "I think that's a sufficient update for now," he said. "It's been a very long night. Let's get ready for dawn, and we'll start fresh at dusk."

I couldn't have agreed with that more.

Upstairs, once again in Ethan's apartments, I dumped my ruined leathers on the floor and climbed into the shower without preface. I showered until my skin was pink, then pulled on the softest pajamas I could find. They were pink fleece, not exactly the sexiest ensemble, but they were comforting in a way that I needed.

When I emerged from the bathroom, I found Ethan in the sitting room. He wore nothing but silk green pajama bottoms that rode low on his hips, and he gazed down at a folded newspaper on the side table in front of him. Margot's tray was on the table beside it. Thinking both were worth a closer look, I padded across the room in my fuzzy pajamas, my hair still damp from the shower.

Ethan looked up with amusement. "Your coziest sleepwear?"

"Exactly. What did Margot bring?"

"Blood, wine, croissants."

I hadn't intended to eat, but my stomach growled ominously. "How long until dawn?"

Ethan glanced at his phone, which lay on the table. "Eighteen minutes."

"Croissant it is," I said. I bit into one while holding out my empty wineglass, waiting while he filled it with white wine from the carafe.

"Sometimes," Ethan said, filling his own glass when I took a sip of mine, "I think we're fortunate to make it through the night."

The wine was crisp and fresh, and it provided a nice, sharp contrast to the flaky, buttery croissant.

"You aren't wrong," I said, nibbling the edge of it.

"Here," Ethan said, holding out a hand for my glass. "Let's have a seat by the fire."

I glanced back at the onyx fireplace in one corner of the room, which I'd rarely seen lit. "I don't think we have time to get a fire going."

"Of course we do," he said. He walked to the corner of the room and flipped a switch behind one of the curtains. The fireplace roared to life, and Ethan looked back at me with a grin.

"Yes, yes, and yes," I said, joining him and sitting cross-legged on the floor. He handed my wineglass back, then did the same.

For the second time tonight, I watched a fire rage. But this time, I was safe at home, with guards outside to keep the monsters away. And, best of all, Ethan was beside me.

"Tell me more about this Scottish estate of ours," I said.

It took him a moment to remember the conversation we'd had earlier. "Ah, yes. Well, there would be much old wood and tall windows. And maybe a hound or two. We'd watch the wind race across the moors like Catherine and Heathcliff might have."

"But with a happier ending, I hope?"

"Absolutely. And without your Sentinel duties to attend to, you could learn to knit. Or embroider. Or perhaps tatting."

"I'll stick to reading, thank you very much. You could learn those things. Or how to cook."

"I can cook, Sentinel."

I looked at him, obviously suspicious. "You've never cooked for me."

"I've not yet done a number of things for you. That doesn't mean I'm not capable of doing them." He put an arm around me.

"We've many years to go yet, Sentinel. And many things to learn about each other. He clinked his glass against mine. "Happy Valentine's Day."

"Happy Valentine's Day, Ethan," I said.

—◆—≡◆≡—◆—

CHAPTER EIGHTEEN

ALL THE NEWS THAT'S FANGED TO PRINT

I was awakened by the shifting of weight in the bed; Ethan took a seat on the edge as he finagled cuff links into shirt-sleeves. He was forever adjusting cuff links. Maybe that was a potential belated Valentine's Day gift. Monogrammed hearts? Tiny silver katanas? Little male figures with tiny arched eyebrows?

"Good evening, Merit," he said.

"Grbarfulgorph," I said, pulling the covers over my head. "I'm not leaving this room tonight."

"That's unfortunate, as I think you'd get an inspirational kick in the ass."

I pulled down the blanket just enough to peek out with one eye. Ethan looked back at me with mild amusement.

"How so?" I asked.

"Your father just called. Your grandfather is out of intensive care and in a regular room. He's awake—sore, but awake—and they expect he's got a solid chance at a good recovery."

I closed my eyes in relief and put my hands on my face, shielding the tears that I knew would inevitably come. My eyes already ached from the anticipation, so it was almost a relief when they began coursing down my cheeks.

Ethan looked utterly flummoxed. "Isn't this good news?"

I wiped the tears away and smiled at him. "It's the best news."

"Then why are you crying?"

"Because sometimes women cry when there's good news. Tears of relief. You know, catharsis."

His expression was utterly blank.

"Haven't you ever cried when you, I don't know, you get a new batch of that fancy stationery you like with the watermarks on it?"

He looked bewildered. "That's what you think I'd cry tears of relief about?"

"You do like your office supplies."

Ethan closed his eyes and shook his head. "This conversation has taken an indecipherable turn. Nevertheless, I actually have more good news. Nick managed to get his story finished and online during the day, and it's been picked up by media outlets across the country." He reached out and picked up a folded *Tribune* from the nightstand. "They issued a special edition on the Houses."

I accepted it from him and flipped open the paper, which was sized like a magazine but on newsprint paper. VAMPIRES: THE COST OF OUR IGNORANCE read the headline, a shot of Grey House burning beneath it. I flipped it open and found the interior pages full of discussions about our financial and other benefits to the city.

"This is quite a coup," I said, folding it up and handing it back to him.

Ethan nodded. "I've no idea how much of it he actually believes, but it helps us either way. Perhaps he still feels guilty about the blackmail."

"Or he still has feelings for me," I said, putting a hand on my chest. "Ours was a forbidden love. . . ."

Ethan rolled his eyes and swatted me playfully on the leg with the newspaper. "That's enough egotism for you today. Get up. It's another night, which means another riot is possible, and we're running out of Houses to burn. Call Catcher. See if Detective Jacobs found out anything about that syringe. And follow up again with Charla Bryant and the videos of the facility. I want this solved!"

There was a knock at the door. Ethan and I looked at each other.

"They usually don't start rioting this early," I said.

"I was serious about the 'solving' bit, Sherlock," he said, and walked to the door.

While Ethan chatted with the visitor, I climbed out of bed and gathered up clothes. After a moment, Ethan closed the door again.

"Who was it?"

"Helen," he said. And when he stepped around the wall again, he looked confused.

"Well, don't leave me in suspense."

"Charla Bryant is downstairs, and Helen says she's inconsolable."

I stood up straight. "Inconsolable? About what?"

"I don't know. Apparently she waited outside on the portico until the sun went down, then started knocking until Margot opened the door. She's waiting for us in my office. Perhaps you'll want to get dressed."

"On it," I said, grabbing the pile of clothes and heading to the bathroom. "I apologize for the ensemble ahead of time," I yelled from the bathroom. "My leathers are toast."

When Ethan didn't respond, I assumed he'd decided to deal with it.

Eight minutes later, I was in jeans, boots, a black shirt, and the black jacket from my official Cadogan House suit. It seemed likely I'd have to leave the House for some ornery errand or other, and while I'd put on the suit jacket to make a good show while I was still here, I wasn't going to investigate crimes in a suit.

Only fifteen minutes had passed since dusk, and I already missed my leathers. They fit perfectly, and obviously had saved my skin in a number of battles.

But immortal, they weren't.

After nabbing water from Margot's dusk leavings—I decided against the blood until I learned precisely what Charla was crying about—we headed downstairs to Ethan's office.

Charla stood in the middle of the room. Instead of her usual suit, she wore jeans, snow boots, a sweater, and a parka. Like so many of us over the last few days, she looked like she'd been crying.

"Your grandfather?" she asked, rushing toward us. "He's all right?"

"He's in the hospital, safely out of surgery, and beginning the recovery process," Ethan said. "Are you all right?"

She shook her head and handed him a manila envelope. "The security tapes. I just watched earlier, and came over here as soon as I could. I waited outside." She looked at us. "This is our fault."

Ethan stilled, then gestured toward the couch. "Why don't you sit down," he said, "and we can talk this through. Could we get you some tea?"

She shook her head but walked over to the couch. Clearly troubled, she sat nervously on the edge of the seat, as if waiting for a bad verdict.

Ethan opened the envelope and pulled out a disk in its jewel case. While Ethan moved to the inset television on the opposite wall and futzed with the electronics, I took a seat by Charla.

"I could get you some water?"

She shook her head, tears gathering at her lashes again. "I'm fine. Let's just—get through this."

Ethan queued up the video, then moved aside so we could see the screen.

The video was in color and showed a clean, white facility that looked a lot like a kitchen. The tape moved haltingly, more like stuttering time-lapse photography than a video, but it was bright and clear, which made for a nice change. We didn't usually get high-fidelity evidence.

"What's this?" Ethan asked.

"The lab," Charla said. "The room where Alan does his research and we test samples. This is the two days before the riot. When I was at the spa."

A figure walked into the room. It was Alan Bryant, Charla's brother. He walked to a counter and reached beneath it, feeling around for something. After a moment, he pulled out a brown envelope that had apparently been stashed there. Another man approached him.

Ethan cursed in Swedish, his native language, an affectation he usually saved for big developments . . . like the fact that Alan Bryant and John McKetrick were chatting in the middle of the Bryant Industries lab.

I guessed that explained why Alan had taken so long to get the tapes to us.

According to the time stamp, they talked for four minutes, at which time Alan handed the envelope to McKetrick. They argued for a moment, until McKetrick handed a smaller one to Alan.

Their business done, both men walked out of the room.

The tape went to black.

"Keep watching," Charla said.

After a moment, another scene appeared. The lab was in the picture again, but the color had shifted, like the sun was at a different angle.

"When?" Ethan asked.

"Right before the riot."

McKetrick walked into the lab and began opening cabinets. He flipped through folders and papers, tossed aside beakers and flats of test tubes, clearly looking for something.

But what?

Ethan answered my unspoken question. "He's looking for the thing he and Alan were arguing about," he mused, eyes glued to the screen.

And he found it. With a grin we could read even on a security video, McKetrick pulled a blue folder from an open drawer he'd rifled through. He tucked the folder beneath his arm, pulled out a silver lighter, lit a cigarette, took a puff, and tossed the cigarette into the pile of papers.

The fire started immediately.

"Oh my God," I said. "McKetrick was covering his ass. He arranged the riot to cover up his attempt to burn down the lab."

"That's what it looks like," Charla said.

Ethan looked back at Charla. "What was in the envelope? What did your brother give him?"

"I don't know," she said. "But I think I know what McKetrick gave him." She cleared her throat nervously. "You may have learned in your research that our parents' divorce was messy. They were ready to retire, so Alan and I got the business to share. Alan wasn't thrilled about that. He wanted to buy me out, and I said no. His offer was ridiculously low, but that wasn't the real issue. I'd worked at my parents' business since I was sixteen; I wasn't going to just give it up.

"He started pressing me again a few months ago. I said no again, but he kept pushing and his offer was still too low. He wants to make the business international," she said. "Send the production overseas, rebrand, become the only global distributor of blood for vampires . . ." She trailed off and sat quietly for a moment. Ethan and I exchanged a glance but waited her out.

"After I watched the tape, I checked our accounts. There was an unscheduled deposit in our operating account two days ago."

"How much?" Ethan asked.

"Five hundred thousand dollars."

I glanced at Ethan. *McKetrick paid Alan Bryant half a million dollars. For what?*

That is the question, he silently agreed. "Charla, you have no idea what he might have given McKetrick?"

She shook her head. "Alan is a talented researcher, but I have no idea what McKetrick would want from us. We're trying to help vampires—to keep them fed and healthy. Those certainly aren't McKetrick's goals."

"Is it possible he wanted to adulterate the blood somehow?" Ethan asked.

"To be frank, if Alan wanted to adulterate the blood, he could do it. He has the access." Her eyes widened. "Oh, but information about the Houses, that he has." She glanced between us. "All three Houses buy blood from us. We have their account numbers, delivery dates—do you think McKetrick wanted that?"

That was a frightening possibility, but it didn't read for McKetrick, I thought. "McKetrick wouldn't pay money for information he could easily get," I said. "He's part of the city admin. If he wanted information about the Houses, he could get a warrant, comb tax records. He's got sources he wouldn't have to pay for," I said.

"I would tend to agree," Ethan said.

I glanced at Ethan. "Alan knows blood. McKetrick wants to wipe us out. Maybe McKetrick thinks Alan's got the information he needs to accomplish that with blood."

"Oh my God," Charla said, putting a hand over her mouth. "You think he's going to use us—our business—to hurt you?"

Ethan frowned. "We don't know enough right now. But it's clear McKetrick wanted information that Alan had. Information he was willing to pay for."

"Charla, why didn't Alan wipe the tapes?" I wondered aloud. "He's in charge of building security, right?"

"He thought he did," Charla said. "Our hard drive was clean, as was the backup we stored on-site. But when Celina announced your existence, I retained a backup service to store copies of the videos off-line, just in case things deteriorated. It was nearly a year ago. He must have forgotten."

She looked away for a moment, shaking her head ruefully. "He told me he watched the tapes, that there was nothing on them. That the inspection was just like normal, the same inspectors, the standard questions about packaging and quality control. He lied to my face about this. My own brother." She shook her head. "I'm so sorry. So very sorry."

Ethan shook his head. "There is nothing to feel guilty about, Charla. You didn't create this problem, or this drama. You undertook to do something we don't see others doing very often. Grieve for your family, for your brother. But know that you are the reason we will close this loop. Because you took the time to care."

Ethan knew how to make a speech, and he knew how to motivate. And by the sudden change in Charla's posture, he'd done the job effectively.

"That helps," she said.

"I'm glad, but I didn't say it to help. I meant it. Your family has provided for ours for decades, even when others would not. And now you've come to us with information you could have easily ignored. We need more people like you. Chicago would be better for it."

Charla's eyes welled again, but these were clearly the good kind of tears.

"Sorry," she said, waving a hand. "I'm just really emotional today."

"No apologies necessary," Ethan said. "Merit has told me about cathartic tears."

She looked at Ethan for a moment the way a person might inspect a beautiful, but confusing, piece of artwork. Then she burst out laughing.

"Right?" I said. "Four hundred years old and he doesn't know about relief crying."

"There are worse sins," she said, looking back at Ethan. "What should I do now?"

"We'll need to talk to Alan. Where can we find him?"

"The lab. He'll be in the lab. He's always in the lab."

"Are your people safe from Alan? Your employees?"

She nodded. "The irony is, I don't think he'd really hurt anyone on purpose. He's a vegetarian, for God's sake. He doesn't even want to hurt animals."

"Greed can make people act very irrationally," Ethan said. "Try to go about your business as normal, but perhaps keep an extra bit of security on the blood supply. If he tries to offer you money again for the business, perhaps you hear him out because he has so much more to give. Act like you're seriously considering the offer. That will keep him calm in the meantime, and keep him from making any rash decisions."

The plan in place, Charla nodded decisively and stood up. "I'll do that exactly. Thank you again for your understanding."

"Thank you for yours," he said. "And let us know if you need anything else."

She nodded, but she'd gone quiet. I could see her retreating into her head, mulling over what she'd seen, replaying conversations. It was exactly the kind of thing I'd do in the face of such betrayal.

We saw her back to the front door, then paused in the foyer. Ethan looked at me. "You were right about McKetrick."

"I was guessing about McKetrick. It just seemed his kind of operation. Too smart, too crafty for kids with bad attitudes."

"I'll grab the DVDs," Ethan said. "Go ahead downstairs and advise Luc. I'll be right down."

"Roger that," I said. As Ethan disappeared down the hallway, I made for the stairs, glancing back when the House's front door opened again.

Jonah appeared in the doorway, coat swirling in the winter wind. "Was that Charla Bryant I just saw leaving?"

"It was. What are you doing here?"

"Scott heard about your grandfather, sends his best wishes. And I think, instead of sending get-well balloons, he sent me to help with the riots."

I looked at him for a second. "How many balloons would it have been, exactly?"

"Smart-ass," Jonah said.

"Actually, you'll be glad you came," I assured him. "As it turns out, our paranoia has been validated."

"So I guess I'll have to respect you now."

"It would be a good start. Let's get downstairs."

The Ops Room became our gathering point once again. Luc and Lindsey were at the table, Kelley and Juliet outside.

Luc dialed up Jeff and Catcher as soon as Jonah and I walked through the door, apparently anticipating developments in the investigation, but we waited until Ethan walked through the door, DVD in hand, to get started.

"What's this?" Luc asked, glancing at it.

"It's a DVD," Lindsey said. "It stores videos or information."

"Hi-larious," Luc said.

"It's a video of the Blood4You lab," Ethan said, taking a seat at the table. I walked over to the whiteboard and erased our prior bad guesses. And as Ethan narrated the DVDs, I filled in the appropriate blanks.

"The video shows John McKetrick exchanging some sort of payoff with Alan Bryant, Charla Bryant's brother. But they argue, presumably because McKetrick doesn't get what he wants."

"That's something," Luc said.

"Oh, that's hardly the preface," Ethan said. "McKetrick comes back, takes a file, and torches the lab . . . right before the riot starts."

"Alan tried to erase the tapes," I said, "and obviously failed."

"Off-site backup?' Jeff asked.

"Off-site backup," I confirmed.

"What was the payoff for?" Luc asked.

"We aren't certain. Information that's worth five hundred thousand dollars to McKetrick, at any event."

"Good God," Luc said.

"Alan Bryant knows blood and biochemistry," I said. "So presumably McKetrick wants information to do with that. But what?"

It was a chilling question.

"And so we circle round again to McKetrick," Ethan said.

"I'm sending Detective Jacobs a message," Catcher said. "This is Chicago, so getting to McKetrick is going to take a little finessing. But I think we can have the CPD pick Alan up. I've only met him the once, but he strikes me as the type to flip easily. Maybe we can get something useful."

Ethan nodded authoritatively. "Thank you, Catcher. We appreciate it."

"Why is McKetrick doing this?" Lindsey asked. "Because he hates us?"

"He definitely does," Ethan said. "But he's also a public official in this city, and by all accounts, he's loving the attention and the ego boost."

"That's a good point," Jonah said. "He clearly likes the gig, and why risk his job? And even if he wanted something from Bryant Industries, why hit Grey House? Why hit your grandfather's house?"

"We now know the rioters hit Bryant Industries for a reason," I said. "So maybe he also hit Grey House and my grandfather for a reason. We just have to figure out what that reason was."

The room went quiet.

"Okay, then," I said. "We'll just mull on that for a little bit. Catcher, do you know anything about the syringe?"

"Nothing yet," he said. "There's a backlog in the forensics department. Might not be until tomorrow."

We all stared quietly at the board for a moment, irritated magic rising as we faced a problem we didn't have information to solve.

"I've got something," Jeff said, keyboard clacking in the

background. He must have found a replacement for the computer that had undoubtedly been torched in the fire. "I know why McKetrick hates you."

Ethan leaned forward. "We're listening."

"It's in McKetrick's military history. Turns out, when he was special ops, he was part of an operation in Turkey."

Luc screwed up his face. "Jeff, buddy, as much as I love you, and you know I do, are you about to tell us something we aren't supposed to know? I mean, this doesn't sound like the kind of thing you'd pull off the Department of Defense's Web site."

"I didn't do any digging myself," Jeff said. "I have a friend, who happens to also play 'Jakob's Quest.' Due to an unfortunate situation involving a winter elf, a pod of orcs, and a very nasty spell of dissolution, he owed me a favor."

Jakob's Quest was Jeff's favorite online role-playing game.

"Let it never be said that I don't support a man's God-given right to spawn," Luc said. "Continue."

"So, McKetrick was in an operation in Turkey in 'ninety-seven. Small group of special ops guys went in to deal with fallout from a national coup. The special ops team ended up in Turkey's Cappadocian region—that's the place where the fairy chimneys are, if you've ever seen them. Here, I'll send a picture."

Within a couple of seconds, Luc's computer had registered the message, and Luc was popping it up onto the screen. It was a photograph of an arid and hilly landscape, and sprinkled here and there were enormous rock formations that looked like pointy hats. Or something more lascivious, depending on your perspective.

"And why are we taking this detour through the geography of Turkey?" Luc asked.

"The special ops guys got into trouble there. Seven went in. Only one came out."

Dread tightened my stomach. "McKetrick was the one who came out?"

"He was," Jeff said. "The report is pretty heavily redacted, but it looks like the guys were lost over the course of a couple of consecutive nights. He made it out alive and started telling some pretty chilling stories."

"Oh shit," Luc muttered, apparently anticipating the same thing I was.

"Vampires?" Jonah guessed.

"Vampires," Jeff agreed. "They trained for this mission for six weeks, and special ops guys are always close. McKetrick was airlifted out, started telling stories about his friends disappearing, about these feral monsters who'd taken them at night. How they were strong, deadly, and no match for human weapons."

"No wonder he hates us," I said. "He thinks we're the reason his friends were killed."

"He thinks we *slaughtered* his friends," Jonah corrected. "And he's made it his personal mission to fix that."

"He's not going to stop," I said, looking at Ethan. "If that's his motivation, and he thinks he's a warrior bound to avenge his friends, he'll keep going until he's gotten all of us out of Chicago, dead or alive."

I walked to the whiteboard, uncapped a marker, and added "Lost colleagues to vampires" beneath the note we'd added about McKetrick's military experience. That done, I turned back to the group.

"He's trained, and he's got motive. We know he's willing to use his public platform to sway public opinion against us. We know he's willing to pay an assassin to take us out. We also know he has a facility," I said, "but we've never found any evidence of it."

"I'm beginning to wonder if that's just a rumor," Luc said.

"He's never gone there, at least not in the car we've tracked. And we didn't find any property records."

Jonah's phone rang. He pulled it out and checked the screen. "It's the doc about Brooklyn," he said, lifting it up. "I'm going to step outside."

Ethan nodded, granting permission, then gestured back to Luc. "Catcher, you might request Detective Jacobs ask Alan about the location of McKetrick's facility. Maybe he knows something."

"On it," Catcher said.

"That takes care of the 'where,'" Luc said. "What about the 'what'?"

"The syringe," I muttered, glancing at Ethan. "Brooklyn, a vampire, is sick because of some unknown condition. McKetrick's now interested in the lab work done by a blood distributor. Does that read as a coincidence to you?"

"It does not," Ethan said, "but I still have no idea what it means."

"Research means new findings," Luc said. "So, maybe it's not about access or facilities. Maybe it's about the blood itself. New things it can do? New technologies?"

"New means to our destruction?" Ethan suggested. "He invented a gun that shoots aspen—the ultimate weapon against vampires. The perfect way to best them. Figuring out a way to manipulate blood—to use it against us—would be well within his wheelhouse."

Jonah appeared in the doorway, face wan, his magic chaotic. Ethan and Luc, still debating McKetrick's murderous intent, were oblivious to the shock in his expression.

Slowly, Jonah walked to the table, but he didn't sit down.

"Are you all right?" I whispered.

Luc and Ethan, finally realizing something was amiss, looked up at him.

"Jonah?" Ethan said.

"I need to go—to see Brooklyn."

"Did something happen to her?" I asked.

"They can't figure out how to make her better," Jonah said, complete befuddlement in his voice. "I think I should go see her."

Ethan and I exchanged a glance, and he was out of his seat within a second. "We'll go with you."

"With me?"

"She's not sick," Ethan said. "This isn't a random illness. She could be the key. And that means she's ours to protect."

They looked at each other for a moment, something passing between them. Some unspoken exchange that had everything and nothing to do with me, and everything and nothing to do with Brooklyn.

After a moment, Jonah nodded. "Let's go," he said.

CHAPTER NINETEEN

THE CURIOUS INCIDENT OF
THE VAMPIRE IN THE NIGHTTIME

We drove together in Jonah's car. I rode shotgun, and Ethan took the backseat. There was nothing symbolic in the seating choices, but it still felt weird to be in a vehicle with Ethan in the backseat.

This time, the hospital was on the north side of town. It was new and shiny, with a two-story lobby and a sculpture of colored glass that hung down from the ceiling like a frozen waterfall. As hospitals went, it was lovely, but it was my second time in a hospital in two days, and I was nearing my saturation point.

Brooklyn's room was on the third floor. Jonah paused at the threshold, taking a breath and steeling himself to walk inside. He finally walked in, and I followed, Ethan behind us.

The room was as nice as the lobby had been—a private suite with a sitting area and a bank of flower vases along the windowsill. A silver get-well balloon rotated in the draft in front of the window.

Brooklyn lay on the bed, undisturbed by the wires or tubes that I'd assumed—dreaded—would have invaded her frail body. She looked just as pale and thin as she had before; a blue sheet covered her body, but it couldn't hide the outline of her skeletal form.

"She's stable."

We all turned, finding Dr. Gianakous in the doorway behind us. He walked inside and grabbed a chart that hung at the end of Brooklyn's bed.

The Grey House doctor, I silently told Ethan. He nodded slightly to acknowledge me.

"That's an improvement, right?" Jonah asked.

"In a sense, yes," Gianakous said. "She hasn't worsened, which is great. But she's a vampire. She should be healing, at least theoretically. If this was a wound, or even one of the few illnesses to which we're susceptible, she would be. But that's not what this is."

"Do you know what it is?" Ethan asked.

"Mr. Sullivan," the doctor said with surprise, apparently just realizing a Master vampire had joined the conversation.

Ethan nodded regally.

"Unfortunately, we don't." Gianakous walked to Brooklyn's bed and checked the readings on a monitor beside her. "We tried to provide her with blood, but she wouldn't accept it."

"She wouldn't accept it?" Jonah asked. "What do you mean?"

"She had no interest in drinking." He pulled a small printout from the monitor and put it in the chart, then flipped it closed. He looked up at us again, concern in his expression. "And we have no idea why."

"Do you have a theory?" Ethan asked.

Dr. Gianakous crossed his arms. "We've ruled out anything bacterial, common parasites. There are no drugs in her system. No toxins. Could be a virus, but it certainly doesn't match any we've seen before."

"What about a weapon?" I asked.

316 + CHLOE NEILL

His brows lifted. "What kind of weapon?"

"I don't know. Something created specifically to kill vampires. Something involving biochemistry. Something that could be injected."

"The syringe you found?" Gianakous asked.

I nodded.

"Once upon a time, with many years of medical training behind me, I'd have said magic and monsters and vampires were nonsense. And now I have fangs and a sunlight allergy. Far be it from me to say anything is truly impossible."

"Jonah?"

We all looked up. Brooklyn's eyes fluttered open; Jonah rushed to her side.

"Brooklyn? Are you all right?"

"I'm really sorry," she quietly said. Her lips were dry, and her words were rough.

"There's nothing to be sorry for. You're in the hospital because you're sick. Do you know what's happened to you? How we can fix it?"

I didn't expect she'd be able to identify the reason she was sick, or who might have caused it . . . but nor did I expect the guilty expression on her face.

"Brooklyn?" There was an edge of sadness in Jonah's voice that scoured my heart.

"I'm sorry," she said. "I'm sorry. I just wanted to go back."

"To go back?" Jonah asked, obviously flustered. "Go back to what?"

"To being—to being human."

The room went silent.

"What do you mean, 'to being human'? You aren't human, Brooklyn. You're a vampire."

"My father died," she said, looking back at Jonah again. "Three days ago. My father died, and my mother is gone. I don't want to be here alone forever. I'm not strong enough for that." She swallowed thickly. "I don't want to be a vampire anymore. I don't want to be an orphan, here when my entire family is gone. I made a mistake. And I thought I could fix it."

If the magic in the room was any indication, we all goggled at her confession. But Jonah was the only one who moved. He took a step back from the bed, eyes wide like he couldn't believe what she'd said, like it hurt him to his core.

As a vampire—and a vampire who'd been interested in dating her—maybe it did.

"I don't want to be alone," she said again.

Jonah didn't respond, but Ethan did. He stepped closer to the bed.

"Brooklyn, how did you mean to become human again?"

She shook her head.

"Was it the syringe, Brooklyn?" he asked. "Was there something in the syringe?"

For a moment, she didn't answer.

"Yes," she finally said, the word so soft it was barely more than an exhalation.

I looked at Dr. Gianakous, who was blinking back surprise. "Is that possible? And wouldn't you already know?"

He shook his head. "We didn't look at anything genetic, or even do a blood type. We just assumed she was a vampire. I'll have blood drawn. And tested. But as to your larger question—why wouldn't it be possible? If you can turn a human into a vampire, why couldn't you turn a vampire into a human?"

Why indeed? I thought. And while you were at it, perhaps you could invent an injectable serum that changed vampires into humans regardless of whether they consented to it. You could, quite literally, rid yourself of every vampire in the world.

I guessed that explained why Brooklyn hadn't wanted to drink blood.

"Where did you get it?" Ethan asked. "Where did you get the syringe to make you human again?"

"I don't know," she said, and began to cough violently. Dr. Gianakous moved to her, helping her sit up to ease the spell.

"Brooklyn, it's important we know where you got it," Jonah said. "It's made you sick."

She looked up at us, her eyes watery, but gleaming. "No. It's made me real again."

We walked back to the car in silence, through elevators and hallways and across parking garages. Ethan and I shared looks, but neither of us interrupted the considerable internal dialogue Jonah was obviously engaged in.

We climbed into the car, Jonah slamming the door shut as he got into the driver's seat and started the car.

Anger and grief and driving weren't going to mix well, so I interjected.

"I'm sorry," I said.

He shook his head. "It just came out of left field. I hardly knew her—but it stung. I'm not sure how not to feel like it's a betrayal."

"I hear how it could feel that way," I said. "But it sounds like she had lots of issues to work out, and none of them were related to you."

"I'm not sure that helps," he said. "But I'll deal regardless. In the meantime," he said, glancing up at the mirror to meet Ethan's eyes, "I assume we're thinking this serum was McKetrick's idea?"

"It's his," Ethan concluded. "What better way to eliminate vampires in your fair city than to turn them all back into humans?"

"Although it doesn't seem to be working very well," I said, shifting to glance back at Ethan. "Brooklyn seems worse for wear."

"So he's not good at transforming vampires back into humans," Ethan said. "That perfectly explains why he talked to Alan Bryant."

"The experiment wasn't working," I said. "He needed more work on the biochemistry, which I guess Alan was more than willing to give him."

"I'm not sure I should bash this guy's hatred of vampires or applaud his creativity," Jonah said. "I'd bet my ass there's a demand for this, although not the way he's thinking. Who hasn't imagined being human again, if for no other reason than so we wouldn't have to deal with this bullshit all the time?"

Discomfited by the question—and the questions it raised—I settled back into my seat, and I wondered . . . did I want to be human again?

I'd been made a vampire without consenting to it. Sure, I'd accepted the decision was necessary, but that was an easy choice when it was truly the only option.

But now, there was another option. There was, apparently, an out. A way to leave this life behind and enter my old life. Graduate school. Old friendships. Mortality. No more GP. No more McKetrick.

No more ignoring my first real Valentine's Day because I'd been pulled into other people's wars.

My phone rang, interrupting the meditation. I pulled it out and glanced at the screen. "It's Catcher," I announced to the car, putting it on speakerphone. "This is Merit."

"I've got something."

"So do I. You go first."

"Detective Jacobs just called. McKetrick's trying to make a serum that turns vampires back into humans."

"We know," I said. "We just met one of his victims. The transition isn't quite as smooth as he might have imagined. Did you get any other specifics?"

"Lots of biochemistry I can't follow. Alan was helping him with the details and his apparent initial failures. At first, McKetrick was talking about giving a choice to humans who'd been changed without their consent or as the result of an attack. But then the motive changed—or he drew back the veil. The rhetoric became stronger, more anti-vampire. And McKetrick's real motivation became obvious—creating a mass weapon that could turn vampires back into humans en masse. Denying them the choice by making it for them. Apparently, Alan got nervous about the anti-vampire rhetoric and decided he was done."

"Bryant Industries' livelihood is built on vampires," Jonah said. "They disappear, so does Alan's business."

"Exactly. But McKetrick kept pushing, and when Alan didn't help, he stole the information he thought he needed and torched the building."

"And found some haters to firebomb it and cover his tracks," I said.

"Indeed. Alan broke contact with McKetrick, so he doesn't know anything about his actions after the Bryant Industries riot. But he did say he's helped McKetrick order materials that were shipped to an industrial building near Midway. Former warehouse called Hornet Freight."

"That feels right," I said. "Can you ask Jeff to check on it?"

"He's already on it," Catcher assured. "I'll ask him to send the search results to you."

"Don't send," Ethan said. "Deliver. Can you meet us at the House?"

"To quote Jeff, is it secret-mission time?"

"It is," Ethan said. "And you might bring Mallory as well. I suspect we'll need all the allies we can get."

"What's on the agenda?"

"I intend to disabuse McKetrick of certain notions concerning vampires."

"That you're pretentious?" Catcher asked.

"That we're afraid of him," Ethan said. "We aren't. And by the end of the evening, I expect he'll know it."

Jonah drove us back to the House, and Ethan rewarded the effort—and his crappy night—with a parking spot in the basement.

We took a few moments to regroup. Jonah found a spot from which to call Scott and advise him what we'd learned and planned to do. Ethan and I went upstairs. He went to update Malik; I went to the kitchen for a bottle of blood I suddenly craved.

When I'd finished a pint and a piece of fruit for good measure, I met Ethan at the stairway.

"You're all right?" he asked, pushing a lock of hair behind my ear.

I nodded. "Just thinking."

"About McKetrick?"

"About the serum. If we're right, and it works, it could change a lot of lives. Would you consider it? Becoming human again? Giving up the drama?"

He gestured toward the House. "And giving up all this? No,

Sentinel." He took my hand, and we walked toward the basement stairs. "I gave up my humanity many, many moons ago. I've no interest in revisiting it."

We took the stairs to the basement but stopped at the bottom. Ethan looked at me, amusement in his expression. "What are you thinking, Sentinel? That being human again would solve all our problems?"

I'd been thinking about my problems, but I didn't let on. "Just that things would be simpler."

Ethan snorted. "Never underestimate the capacity of any living thing for drama, Sentinel. Human, vampire, shifter, or otherwise. We all have our fair share."

Having said his part, we made our way to the Ops Room. Jonah and the guards were already assembled, minus Juliet, who Luc decided wasn't quite ready for a field trip. Catcher, Jeff, and Mallory followed behind us.

Lindsey, Mallory, and I exchanged hugs. This was too nerve-racking not to prepare ourselves and take comfort where we could find it.

"Cool hair," Lindsey said.

Mallory had braided her ombré hair into Princess Leia–style side buns. She was one of the few people I knew—perhaps the only one—who could actually pull off the look.

"Thanks," she said, touching a bun. "Although I feel like I have cinnamon rolls attached to my head."

"Not that there's anything wrong with that," I said, pointing to the table.

We took seats around it, and when we were all seated, Ethan kicked things off.

"We believe John McKetrick has been manufacturing a serum intended to turn vampires back into humans. We believe he used

Alan Bryant, Charla Bryant's brother, to develop that serum. We aren't certain if he planned to allow vampires the choice to become humans again or not. But given his history, it seems likely he would have made the decision for us.

"Alan Bryant wouldn't provide the information McKetrick needed. So McKetrick stole that information, torched Bryant Industries, and induced a riot to cover up the evidence."

"It was a distraction," Jonah said. "Keeping us focused on vampire haters, not on what was really going on between himself and Alan Bryant."

"And the Grey House riot?" Luc asked.

"Perfecting the distraction," Jonah said. "One night of rioting is a riot. It's ne'er-do-wells in action. Two nights of rioting? That's a movement. That's political activism."

"And it spreads his larger message of anti-vampire vitriol," Ethan said.

Jonah nodded.

"But why my grandfather?" I asked. "He had nothing to do with any of this. He's only secondarily involved."

"Maybe he wasn't only secondarily involved."

We all looked at Catcher, who met my gaze. "He was looking at that body for Detective Jacobs. The one that washed ashore."

Ethan frowned. "Okay? So?"

"He called because they weren't supernaturally able to identify it—because they weren't exactly sure what it was."

We sat in stunned silence for a moment.

"It was a failed experiment," I realized. "McKetrick's been working on the serum, and he's had failures. That's why he kept going back to Alan Bryant. McKetrick must have known he was involved and thought he was getting too close." I looked at Catcher. "What did Grandpa learn?"

"I don't know," he said. "But he'd learned something. He was supposed to meet with Detective Jacobs for coffee the next day."

"McKetrick found out and decided to put a kibosh on that meeting," Ethan said. "And your grandfather was involved with vampires, so the rioting cover story plays."

"That sick, twisted, manipulative son of a bitch," I muttered.

"So he is," Ethan said. "And that's why we're putting an end to this. Jeff," he prompted. "The building?"

Jeff spread a map on the table. "It used to be Weingarten Freight," he said. "Now it's Hornet Freight, but the floor plan is online either way."

"What do they ship?" Luc asked, leaning over to get a better glance.

"According to their Web site," Jeff said, "pretty much anything you want them to. Retail goods, medical goods, sporting equipment, industrial stuff."

The building was essentially a large square divided into chunks: offices, loading area, warehousing area.

"Entrance here," he said, pointing to a door. "Loading bays along this wall. Emergency exits here and here."

He pointed to the back corner of the building. "The admin area was set up here, along the front-left corner, and the rest of the space is divided into the loading and unloading area and the place they stored the goods between pickups and deliveries."

"What's the goal here?" Luc asked, looking to Ethan.

"I want to go in," Ethan said. "I want to garner evidence of what McKetrick's doing, and I want to end his ability to do it."

"And the CPD?" Catcher asked.

"McKetrick is the ultimate slime. If we go in without them, he'll claim we attacked, and chalk it up to more vampire violence."

Ethan's gaze narrowed. "But I want my opportunity to chat with him face-to-face."

"Ethan—," Luc said, but Ethan held up a hand.

"No," he said. "This isn't about practicalities or safety. He has ordered assassinations, endangered my vampires, destroyed homes, nearly killed Chuck. And now he thinks he can play God? No." His eyes flamed silver and green. "I will have a shot at him first. After that, assuming he survives, the humans can do what they will."

Catcher and Ethan looked at each other for a moment, until Catcher nodded.

"A little late notice never hurt anyone," he said.

Ethan nodded. "We have to assume he'll have weapons, and many of them. Specifically, we know he's got aspen guns, so I'm proposing the first wave be non-vampires."

He looked at Mallory. "We need help tonight, and we'll hire you to join our team for this mission if you're willing. I've already checked with Gabriel, and he's approved."

Mallory had helped us before, including when we tackled a fallen angel and ended his reign of terror over the city. She'd done it to help, and because her magic had created the problem in the first place. So it wasn't that Ethan had asked Mallory to assist us . . . but that he was *hiring* her to do it. She wasn't being dragged into supernatural drama; she was being hired by Cadogan House as an employee and given the imprimatur of authority that went with it. Ethan was putting his stamp of approval on a girl trying to live with her magic—and that stamp would likely go a long, long way toward her having a real future.

By the expression on her face, she realized the boon he'd offered her.

326 + CHLOE NEILL

"Absolutely," she said. "Absolutely I will help. I appreciate the chance and the opportunity."

"It's dangerous," Ethan said. "Very dangerous, especially if you're the first line."

"I'm not afraid," Mallory said. And for the first time in a while, I think she actually meant it.

But Catcher was less than thrilled. He practically snarled at Ethan. "Do you have any idea how dangerous this is going to be?"

"I do," Ethan said. "I'll be fighting and sending my Sentinel into danger, and I realize precisely how frightening that proposition is."

His voice flattened. "I also recall it was dangerous in Nebraska, and that night on the Midway."

Ethan's meaning was unspoken, but still clear—Mallory had put us in danger before, and we'd responded despite it all. It wasn't any more unfair to ask her to pony up.

"You can be an asshole, you know that, Sullivan?"

Ethan smiled. "I do. We do what we must to protect our own."

Catcher looked at Mallory. "It's your call."

She nodded. "I already said yes. It's the right thing to do."

"We go in in two waves. Jeff, Catcher, Mallory, through the front. Me, Merit, Jonah, Luc, Lindsey, through the back. We find him. We capture him. We preserve evidence as we can. And we nail his ass to the wall."

"I assume you'll want us to lay down magical cover for the rest of you?" Catcher asked.

"If you can do it?" Ethan said, a dare in his voice.

"You know I can," Catcher said.

"You know what we need?" Jeff said, rolling up the map. "A rallying cry, like 'Avengers, assemble!' or 'Regulators, mount up!'"

"How about 'Bring back the head of John McKetrick'?" Ethan suggested.

"Grim," Jeff said, "but I think it works."

"For the sake of saying it, Liege," Luc said, "do you really think you should go? You know, for safety purposes?"

The chilling look in Ethan's expression left little doubt about his answer to that question.

"Alrighty then," Luc said. "Earbuds for all." He passed out the earbuds, which now rested in a jar on his desktop like the world's worst candy. "Good luck, and do try not to get killed."

"It's my nightly goal," Ethan said, rising from his chair. Jonah and I followed, and we walked back into the hallway and climbed the stairs.

We paused in the foyer when Jonah held up his phone. "I'm going to give Scott an update."

Ethan nodded and looked at me. "While he's doing that, you'll want to go upstairs and change."

I frowned and tugged at the bottom of my jacket. "I don't have anything to change into; my leathers were toasted in the fire."

"Just go, Sentinel," Ethan said, clearly with some other plan afoot. It didn't seem worth making a scene in front of Jonah, so I climbed the stairs again and headed back into our apartments.

Hanging inside the closet was a set of new leathers—sleek and black with crimson trim. A small white envelope was tied to the hanger with a crimson ribbon. I slipped out the card and read it.

"'To my favorite Sentinel,'" I read aloud, "'with love on be-lated Valentine's Day.'"

Smiling gleefully, I removed the jeans and suit jacket, then slipped the leather pants from the hanger. They were buttery soft and fitted, with a thin strip of crimson piping down each leg. I climbed into them and zipped them up. They fit like a glove, with the slightest flare at the bottom to cover the boot.

The jacket was heavier than my old version, although it had

the same segmented shoulders and elbows for freedom of movement. The crimson trim was subtle, but gorgeous, a secret vein at the edges of the leather. Ethan wouldn't have overlooked that, and he probably picked them particularly because of it. Because it hinted at who I was beneath the clothes, the fire that lurked inside the brunette.

I pulled the jacket on, and of course it fit perfectly. It wasn't hard to imagine that Ethan had learned the curve of my body and could guess my size. I modeled the ensemble in the mirror, more pleased than I probably should have been at how it looked.

It looked . . . perfect. Perfectly me, perfectly Sentinel, perfectly Cadogan.

Now, if I could just keep them from catching fire.

We met in the foyer. Catcher, Mallory, and Jeff would drive together, as would Luc and Lindsey. Neither my loaner nor Ethan's Ferrari was big enough for three, so Jonah volunteered—once again—to drive us in his vehicle.

We were going to have to start reimbursing him for mileage.

Jonah was a man on a mission, and he slalomed through traffic—nothing reckless that would raise the attention of cops, but enough to make the trip as efficient as possible.

The House was a twenty-minute drive from Hornet Freight. Jonah took the longer but faster freeway route to Midway Airport, then squeezed between taxis into the exit lane. But we diverged from the line of sedans and followed a second road through an industrial neighborhood.

Hornet Freight was on the left side of the road. A giant black and yellow sign bearing the business's name and a photograph of the bug lit up the night. It was a brick building, two stories tall, the last in a line of eight identical buildings. None of them appeared to have been occupied recently.

We parked in a row in a designated lot about a quarter mile away. "From here," Jonah said, "Hornet Freight looks legit."

"*Looks*," Ethan emphasized.

"Agreed." We got out of the car and belted on swords, the eight of us gathering behind our shield of vehicles.

"Earbuds in," Luc said, and we maneuvered the little buggers into our ears. Preparations made, we looked at Ethan.

As always, he was prepared to speechify.

"We are here for a reason," Ethan said, "because we've decided hatred and manipulation can only go so far. Be brave, but moreover, be safe. Bravery only gets you so far. Let's get into position."

There were nods all around, and we formed a sort of line, with the aspen-immune sorcerers at the front and the rest of us at the back.

"Tomorrow," Ethan whispered beside me, "we make time to celebrate Valentine's Day. But tonight, Merit, my Sentinel, my warrior, let's go find John McKetrick. And let's kick his ass."

CHAPTER TWENTY

VAMPIRES, ASSEMBLE!

We descended into the low—and thankfully empty—ditch that bordered the road, and we walked toward the building. We stopped when we were a football field away. From this distance, it looked utterly innocuous. It was an unremarkable building in an unremarkable part of the city, remarkable tonight only because it had become a bastion of hatred.

When we reached the parking lot, we separated into our groups and ran full out, dodging lampposts and ruts in the concrete. We separated from the sorcerer/shifter crew, running toward the back of the building.

"Luc, you and Lindsey take the door on the west," Ethan said. "We'll take the east. Don't let anyone out of the building."

"On it," Luc said. He kissed Lindsey, her eyes darting with surprise, and they ran low across the back of the building to the other side.

Ethan looked at me and Jonah. "You ready?"

We both nodded.

"Then let's go."

We moved around to the door, which was rusted and a couple of steps above the ground. We lined up against the wall, Jonah on one side, me and Ethan on the other.

Jonah moved closer, pressing an ear to the door, listening for anything on the other side of the wall. After a moment, he shook his head, then pulled two dangerous-looking knives from his jacket. Ethan and I drew our swords.

Ethan signaled us to move . . . and the battle began.

Jonah kicked open the door, and we rounded it, swords drawn.

The door led into an enormous open space dotted by processing equipment just like we'd seen at Bryant Industries—an assembly line of gleaming silver tanks and conveyor belts, currently still but clearly ready for action.

Yelling sounded from various points around the room. The people he'd employed to guard or work at his facility had seen us. They rushed forward, wearing Clean Chicago T-shirts.

"Something's wrong," Jonah said.

He meant with the attackers. They looked like mostly humans, but their eyes were nearly white, as if they'd lost all pigment, and their features were oddly stretched, as if someone had attempted to sculpt a human from clay and hadn't quite gotten the features right.

For a moment, we stared at them.

"I presume they've been given the serum," Ethan murmured, gripping his sword and preparing to strike.

"We'll find out," Jonah said.

They screamed at us, rushing forward, the attack begun. Ethan, Jonah, and I separated, driving them apart.

Three came toward me, waving arms and legs but with no

obvious weapons in hand. McKetrick wanted to build them, but maybe he hadn't believed in them enough to give them weaponry.

I dropped my sword to the ground, thinking it only fair that we fought on the same terms. The first one to make a move ran toward me, hand already fisted for a punch. I grabbed his wrist, twisted, and sent him to the ground, then used an elbow at his neck to knock him unconscious.

The next one launched, airborne and ready for a fight. I ducked to the ground, letting him sail above me and land behind. I swung around, offering him a kick to the ribs that sent him skidding across the room. He landed flat on his back.

I looked back at the third and smiled, just a little. "Ready?"

She bared her teeth and came running. I expected a strike, but she pummeled me like a linebacker, knocking me to the ground. She pulled my hair, and screamed into my ear—"Vampire whore!"—before clamping her hands around my neck.

Suddenly, I couldn't get oxygen, which made me panic.

I kicked beneath her, trying to roll and dislodge her away, but I couldn't get enough oxygen to make my limbs move.

I punched her in the stomach, then the ribs, but she ignored the pain. Was she human, but with the strength of a vampire? That, I thought, as my vision began to dim at the edges, was disturbing.

And then her weight was bodily lifted from me, and she was thrown across the room.

Before I could crawl to my feet, I was hauled upright and saw green eyes staring back at me.

I huffed for air and put a hand around my neck, feeling for the bruise I imagined had already popped up.

I saw the worry in Ethan's eyes, but his sarcasm masked it. This was a battle, after all. "Let's try to stay on our feet, shall we, Sentinel?"

I nodded weakly and got to my feet again. "Doing my best, Liege."

I glanced around, ensuring Jonah was all right. He pushed the hair from his eyes and seemed healthy; the floor was littered with minions we'd dealt with handily. But where, I wondered, was the main course?

A *boom* sounded in the other section of the warehouse.

"That's the sorcerers," Ethan said. "Let's go!"

I grabbed my sword. Ethan in front, me behind, we ran through the door and into an even larger space. This one held stacks and stacks of boxes. They contained syringes, if the box closest to me was any indication, and a lot of them.

A wall of blue smoke had divided the space in two. The smoke shifted, and Mallory, Catcher, and Jeff ran toward us through the smoke.

"They're behind us," they said, and we backed up.

"Make a line," Ethan said, and we did.

And when the smoke cleared, we could see the enemy. The proto-humans, with their milky white eyes, had assembled into a line, probably forty strong. We stood against them, our cadre of supernaturals.

They'd corralled us together.

Jeff whistled. "He's built his own army."

"The only kind he could stomach," Jonah said. "Vampires who aren't vampires any longer."

Jeff blew out a nervous breath. "At the risk of playing Anti–Little Mary Sunshine here, there are a lot of them over there."

Nervously, I adjusted my fingers on the sword. "Remind me why you didn't appoint me House librarian?" I asked Ethan.

"Because, Sentinel, you're so very good with a sword."

McKetrick emerged from the shadows in black fatigues, his face scarred and one eye milky white.

I didn't wait for him to speak first. "What have you done to them?"

"Has it ever occurred to you that not everyone chooses to be a vampire? That some, after becoming vampires, realize they have become monsters, and they want to go back?"

"We aren't monsters," Jonah said. "And they don't look entirely human."

"The catalyst is a work in progress," McKetrick said. "All science requires experimentation, mistakes. They were willing to sacrifice for the coming revolution."

"The coming revolution?" Ethan asked.

"When humans finally tire of your antics. Your demands. Your insistence that you be treated like everyone else, when we all know exactly what you are. Genetic rejects."

"Is that what you told Brooklyn?" Jonah asked. "Did you convince her she was a genetic reject?"

"Brooklyn wanted to live a mortal life. I respected her wish and provided her with a solution."

"Your solution poisoned her," Jonah said. "She's in a hospital bed right now, a sacrifice to your 'progress.'"

McKetrick didn't look moved.

"All this because of Turkey?" I asked.

His expression steeled. "Because of Turkey? That's how you refer to the sacrifices made by men who served this country, who were some of its finest warriors? You *freaks* killed them, and you know what I got? A citation for letting you get away. For not bringing vampires back so you could be studied and used as weapons." He slapped a hand to his chest. "My brothers were killed because of your greed, your insatiable appetites."

"We are sorry for your loss," I said, "but we weren't there. I wasn't even a vampire when that happened. How can you blame us for something we weren't even involved in?"

"I blame you," he gritted out, "because you carry the disease. And this city will not be safe from your appetites, your treachery, until you've been swept from it, wholly and completely."

McKetrick pulled a long-bladed knife from the utility belt on his pants and tossed the knife from hand to hand.

His army moved closer toward us, the circle growing tighter.

My stomach knotted with nerves, already taut from the spill of nervous magic that permeated the room.

"Catcher?" Ethan prompted.

"We're out of mojo at the moment," he said. "Currently refueling." Sorcerers had a limited amount of magical draw at any one time.

"Then I think we do this the old-fashioned way," Ethan said. "Novitiates?"

"Ready," we said together.

"Jeff, you want to get busy?" I asked.

"Done and done," Jeff said, and a blinding flash of light shot across the space, as human man turned into gigantic, stalking white tiger.

It was just the distraction we needed.

"Go!" Ethan said, and like the soldiers in a centuries-old battle, we rushed toward each other, weapons raised.

Ethan ran toward McKetrick. I took the minion closest to me. Creatively, he dodged immediately for my feet. Unfortunately for him, I brought the butt of my sword down onto his head, sending him flat to the floor.

Two former vampires, both in snug T-shirts and stylish sheepskin boots, came at me from either side, both with box cutters in hand. There was something pitiful about the weaponry, not just because McKetrick hadn't trusted them enough, but because he also clearly hadn't cared enough to make them anything other than expendable.

"You don't have to fight us, you know," I said, dodging one strike and sending my sword wheeling around to try to catch the other girl off-kilter.

"You're the enemy," she said, dodging the strike and kicking me in the ribs. "You think I wanted to be a monster? My family kicked me out. I got fired. You think this is any way to live? Crawling around in the dark like a snake?"

"You have immortality," I reminded her, as the other girl tried to box my ears. I got her in the stomach with the butt of the sword, a classic move, and offered the mouthy one a spinning crescent kick. She moved backward but stumbled over a box and hit the ground, skittering away. . . . Unfortunately, she skittered right into the face of a Siberian tiger, who dared her to move.

She fainted dead away, which saved us both the trouble.

But her friend wasn't impressed. "Vampire whore!" she screamed out, jumping on my back and wrapping her arms around my neck. I tried to shake her off, but she was strong and nimble.

"Mouth!" I warned her, maneuvering backward toward a stack of the boxes, and mashing her backward into them until she finally fell away.

Then she got a kick to the head for her trouble.

Sirens suddenly wailed outside, audible because the doors had been thrown open. A swarm of men and women in black uniforms with guns moved inside.

I guessed our time was up. The CPD had arrived.

"Chicago Police Department!" cried the leader. "All weapons on the ground!" they said. "Right now, all weapons on the ground. Hands on the back of your heads. All of you!"

To a one, humans and sups alike dropped their weapons.

Except for one man.

Ethan stood over McKetrick, sword in hand. "It would be so

easy, you know. So easy for me to do this, to take your life as you've taken the lives of so many others."

"Do it," McKetrick gritted out. "Do it." McKetrick dared him to murder, expecting, of course, that Ethan would oblige him. McKetrick might be dead, but his vengeance and his plan would be utterly validated. He'd have proved that vampires were merciless killing machines.

"The problem is," Ethan said, "I'm not you."

He tossed his sword away and stepped back, raising his arms as the CPD surrounded McKetrick.

"It's over," Ethan said. "And good riddance to you."

Detective Jacobs had given us a head start, just enough to work out some aggression against McKetrick and the others, but not so long that we'd have to make too many excuses.

Detective Jacobs whistled when he saw the processing equipment in the back. But despite the equipment, there wasn't a single syringe in sight. Apparently, McKetrick hadn't actually been able to get the assembly line working. He'd manufactured the serum a syringe at a time, and Brooklyn had gotten the last one.

A top-of-the-line computer sat on a top-of-the-line desk, and when Jacobs's tech guys booted it up, they found information aplenty: e-mails to and from McKetrick and the rioters, a copy of the chemical analysis Alan Bryant had given him, copies of the materials he'd stolen from Bryant Industries, and years of records regarding his attempts to sabotage and assassinate vampires across the country.

When the debriefing was over, with its very satisfying result, we were officially dismissed; we walked across the warehouse floor to the front door.

I happened to glance down, where a glint of silver caught my eye. There on the ground, resting halfway beneath a wooden pallet, was a single syringe, filled with a pale green fluid. It gleamed like a jewel and promised things I hadn't thought to ask for in a very long time.

Humanity.

The allure was stronger than I would have imagined, as memories plucked at my heartstrings: Sunshine. Summer boat rides on the lake. Morning jogs in the chill of spring. Shopping at noon on a Saturday. Spending my remaining human years with my family, instead of living long past them. Finishing my dissertation, becoming a professor.

Having children.

Generally, leaving my life as a vampire behind.

Leaving Ethan behind. For even if we stayed together despite our differences, I would age and die, and he would not. I would leave him alone to face the centuries, to find another. I would leave him in the hands of another Sentinel, someone who would have the responsibility of watching over him, of keeping him safe.

And not just Ethan. My grandfather. Mallory. My nieces and nephews. Their children, and their children's children.

I wasn't leaving their lives to chance. Not when I had the choice.

I had a choice . . . and I took it.

I picked up the syringe and hurried to catch up with the rest of them.

"Jonah," I said, getting his attention and handing it to him.

He looked quizzically up at me.

"For Brooklyn," I explained. "Maybe Dr. Gianakous can use it to find a cure for her condition."

He smiled. "Thanks, Merit."

The deed done, I took Ethan's hand, and walked into the life I'd chosen.

Malik met us in the foyer when we walked into the House.

"Congratulations on a successful mission," he said. "And Lakshmi Rao is on the phone."

"I swear to God, it never ends!" Ethan roared.

"Not when you're immortal," Malik agreed. "That's actually the point."

I covered my mouth to stifle a laugh, but Ethan got the gist and gave me a withering look.

"Better she call you than show up at your door unannounced," I reminded them, then glanced at Malik and pinched two fingers together. "Could you stall her for just a minute?"

He smiled. "For you, Sentinel, of course," he said, then disappeared down the hallway again.

Ethan looked at me expectantly. "Well, Sentinel?"

Ethan and I were both coming to grips with the fact that we weren't human, that our relationship would never be as simple as human relationships were. That we were supernaturals, and for the foreseeable future, drama would be an inevitable part of our lives. But that didn't mean it wasn't important to remember the little things, to make time for ourselves and our relationship, and to cherish what we had.

"We missed Valentine's Day," I said. "Even if we're vampires, I wanted to give us something special. I thought I'd arrange dinner before dawn."

"Meaning you'll have Margot order pizza."

I rolled my eyes. "No. Something better. Something special."

He looked at me for a moment.

"Benefit of the doubt," I dryly said.

"All right, Sentinel. You have your second chance at Valentine's Day. But I'll warn you in advance. I'm starving . . . and not just for food."

That comment made me light-headed enough that it was a miracle I didn't fall over in the foyer. That would not have helped the dinner planning, which was going to require a bit of teamwork.

I raced upstairs to the third floor and knocked on Lindsey's door. I found her toweling off from the shower.

"What's up, toots?"

"I need a favor."

"Oh?"

"I'd like to salvage Valentine's Day. But I need to do it within the next couple of hours. I've already decided on dinner—I can handle that on my own. I need something else. A treat."

Lindsey frowned, walking around her room a bit as she pondered the question. "Stores are closed, so there's no time for that. You've already planned dinner, so that's out, unless we can spice dinner up a bit?"

She turned back at me and winged up her eyebrows suggestively.

"He already gets *that*," I said.

She chortled. "Empathic, remember? Well aware of the twists and turns of your romantic life."

My cheeks warmed.

"No," she said. "I have something else in mind. Something Margot can help us with?"

"Oh?"

"It's simple," she said with a wink. "We'll let him eat cake."

Lindsey got dressed, after which I followed her downstairs to the kitchen. Ethan's door was still closed, but the magic seeping beneath the door didn't seem too crazed.

When she pushed open the kitchen door, we found the room empty but for Margot, who stood in front of one of her giant stoves in her chef's whites, her dark bob of hair peeking beneath her hat. She stirred a small saucepot with a tiny whisk, her gaze darting between the contents of the pot and the electronic tablet propped up beside her.

"What's cooking, toots?" Lindsey said, putting her bag on the counter and sidling up to Margot.

"Béarnaise," Margot said, frowning as she looked back at the sauce and began to stir furiously. "The sauce I cannot master."

"Can you buy it in a bottle?"

Margot gave her a skewering look. "A trained chef does not buy béarnaise in a bottle." She stared down at the sauce for a moment before letting out a sound of utter exasperation. She flipped off the heat and stepped back, rubbing her hands over her face.

"What happened?" I asked.

"The sauce broke. Again." Her expression forlorn and shoulders bent, she looked up again. "I could probably try to salvage it, but I have been beaten down by the French today, and I just can't do it." She glanced at me and Lindsey. "What are you up to?"

"Merit has a dilemma, and I think a cake might fix it."

It was like a light had turned on in Margot's eyes. Her entire expression changed, from defeat to the excitement of a new challenge.

"A cake will undoubtedly fix it," Margot said. "What's the occasion?"

"Valentine's Day. Well, belated, anyway."

Margot pressed a hand to her chest, "Oh, cute!"

"Right?" Lindsey said. "Isn't it, like, so normal of them?"

"They're such a cute couple," Margot remarked, crossing her arms and leaning a hip against the counter.

"That's why I love it. It's adorable."

"You know I'm standing right here," I reminded them.

"I was thinking you could make that chocolate torte," Lindsey said.

Margot's mouth formed an "O." "Oh," she said, "the torte."

"What's the torte?" I asked.

Margot glanced at me. "It's a very decadent, flourless chocolate cake. Velvety chocolate with just a hint of raspberry ganache. Very appropriate for Valentine's Day. It's a very sexy cake," she said. "And Ethan loves it. It's one of his favorites."

I had definitely come to the right place for help. "Is this possibly something we could do tonight? I was hoping for a meal before the sun came up again. It's been a long night."

She checked her watch and nodded. "It comes together really quickly. We've got just enough time to bake it off and let it cool. How does that sound?"

"Like a phenomenal plan," I said, beginning to smile a little. "Thanks."

"Oh, honey, I'm not actually *making* it for you. I'm just giving you directions." With a wink, she pointed toward a set of aprons hanging from a wall hook. "Grab your gear, and let's get started."

Start, we did. I'd thought, if just for a moment, that helping bake a cake would be a way to relax. And in a sense, it was. We were three girlfriends in a kitchen, mixing and measuring as we discussed boys and their various issues. But Margot took pride in her work. And just like every other vampire with the same trait, she was exacting in her methods and very, very particular.

The cocoa had to be measured in a very particular way. ("Sweep and scoop! Sweep and scoop!")

The cocoa had to be placed in the bowl in a very particular way. ("Sift it first!")

The sugar and butter had to be creamed just so, until the mixture was light and fluffy. ("It looks like concrete! Keep stirring!")

The pan had to be perfectly buttered, then dusted with cocoa, in preparation for the cake. ("If I can see metal, you're not done!")

The oven rack had to be placed just so, neither too high nor too low, to ensure consistent baking. ("Lower it! Lower it!")

Somehow, miraculously, we came through it still friends. And I must admit, I learned a lot. I hadn't done much baking in the past and really didn't have an urge to start now—I preferred dodging a katana slash to pressing the lumps out of cocoa powder—but in the short amount of time we worked with her, Margot taught us a lot.

The timer sounded, and Margot pulled a dark cake from the oven. She set it on a cooling rack, then stepped back to admire our handiwork.

"Ladies," she said, "it doesn't look awful."

It wasn't much of a compliment, but I'd take what I could get.

"You are the best." I checked my watch. "I have to run an errand. I'll be back in about twenty minutes. Is that okay?"

"Absolutely. I'll prep the raspberry glaze, and you'll be good to go. I'll make it work," she promised.

I had little doubt. She always did.

I'd missed my last chance to provide Ethan with the best pasta Chicago had to offer. So when the opportunity came around again, I didn't miss it. I drove to Tuscan Terrace, picked up aluminum containers of pasta, and hightailed it back to the House.

I found Ethan in his office, the door open, the aura relatively mild.

I stepped inside and held up the paper bag of food. "Dinner?"

He didn't look impressed. "In a paper bag?"

But I kept smiling, because I knew this man. I knew what he'd enjoy, and I knew that even if the packaging didn't impress him, the food would.

"In a paper bag," I confirmed. I closed the door and carried the bag to his conference table, where I opened the contents and set out a meal for each of us. Pasta, bread, and olive oil for dipping.

"You're sure about this?" Ethan asked, sidling behind me and putting a hand on my waist.

"Absolutely positive. I didn't steer you wrong about pizza, and I won't about this, either."

Of course I was right.

Dinner was glorious. Because the food, even in aluminum pans, was delicious. Because Ethan moaned with joy nearly every time he took a bite. Because we shared napkins and laughs and bread at the conference table in his office. Because we didn't need thousand-dollar champagne or caviar to prove our affection or the validity of our relationship.

"There is something to be said about the satisfaction that comes from a full belly," Ethan said.

"Couldn't agree more. We'll sleep well after this feast. Or we'll have weird carb coma dreams. Hard to tell."

Ethan chuckled, wiped his mouth, and tossed his napkin into the pile.

"So, the GP," I said, when I'd taken my last bite. "What did they want?"

"A tithe," he said. "Darius, through Lakshmi, has requested that we donate a sum to the GP in penance for our bad behavior."

"Is it a lot?" Bankrupting the House seemed like something the GP would want to do.

"It is surprisingly little."

"Little?" I asked. "Why?"

"Because, apparently, that's only the first half of their plan for our contrition."

"What's the second half?"

"I'm not sure. But Lakshmi is traveling here to tell us in person."

Before I could dive into the paranoia that upcoming event was going to foster, there was a knock at the door, and Margot peeked inside. "Special delivery?"

"Oh?" Ethan asked.

She opened the door fully and wheeled in a cart.

"Margot, how thoughtful. But you didn't need to go to the trouble."

"Oh, I didn't," she said, putting her hands on her hips. "Merit made the cake."

Ethan's eyes went dinner-plate huge. "*Merit* made it?"

"Sir, your tone is not flattering," I advised him.

"She did. For you, on Valentine's Day, because she's got a thing for you, I think." With that, she winked, and rolled the cart out again.

Ethan looked over the cake. "It looks surprisingly delicious."

"I am not above hitting you, you know," I said.

He chuckled. "I have something for you as well. Put on your shoes."

"My shoes? But there's cake."

He gave me a look that didn't allow argument. "Just do it."

I slipped my boots on again, then followed Ethan silently to the door.

The rest of the House was quiet, and when Ethan opened the

front door, the eastern sky was beginning to pinken with the first light of dawn.

But the sky was hardly the point.

On both sides of the front lawn, in the crisp, white snow, an enormous heart had been drawn in the snow with a thousand rose petals, a shock of crimson against the snowy ground.

"What is this?" I asked, putting a hand over my heart.

"A heart," Ethan said. "For you. My heart, which is very much yours."

He took my hand and led me through the snow, pausing at the edge of the heart. I picked up a petal and ran my fingertips across its surface, as soft as velvet, so soft it barely felt like I'd touched anything.

"I don't understand," I said, glancing back at him with wonder in my eyes.

"We aren't human," he said. "Nor are we average. We take on challenges and obligations that, arguably, are not our burdens to bear. We do it because it's right. Because it matters, and we've decided—you've decided—to stand for those who cannot stand for themselves. That means, unfortunately, that we don't always have the opportunity to enjoy human rituals."

"Valentine's Day?"

Ethan nodded. "Valentine's Day. But even if the rituals can't be the same for us, the symbolism is important." He cleared his throat. "You've asked about the tattoo on the back of my calf."

I smiled. "I have asked," I confirmed. "More than a few times."

"It was actually Amit's fault. We were in India, on a night train to Varanasi, and I lost a bet. A small bet, but a bet nonetheless."

I was stunned. That was so unlike him. "You got a tattoo because you lost a bet?"

"I did," he said, "and in Sanskrit, because those were the terms I'd agreed to. He graciously allowed me to select the phrase."

"What does it say?"

"Eternal life, undying passion."

"Oh, that's very nice." It was a beautiful phrase, and particularly appropriate for immortal vampires.

Ethan nodded and took my hands. "I had a sense of your passion when we met, Merit. When you first stormed into my House with fire in your eyes."

"That wasn't fire. That was sheer, unmitigated fury."

He chuckled. "Acknowledged. But a soul without passion doesn't feel fury. Or love. And there was definitely passion in your soul. I selected the phrase because I thought it lovely. Now, I feel lucky that I can deem it true."

Tears gathered at my lashes.

"I have eternal life," he said. "But you are my undying passion." He put his hands on my cheeks and kissed me deeply. There was passion in his kiss, in the nip of his tongue, but this kiss was about promise. About tenderness.

About love.

He drew back and pressed the softest kiss to my lips. "I love you, Caroline Evelyn Merit. Happy Not Valentine's Day."

"Happy Not Valentine's Day, Sullivan." I moved into his arms, surrounding myself with his body, his warmth, his crisp cologne.

The wind began to lift, then rushed toward us in a gust. As I glanced back, it scattered the heart, lifting the rose petals into the sky. I watched in awe as they circled around us, love rendered aloft by forces outside our control. A fitting metaphor, I thought.

"There is actually one more small thing."

"Is it diamonds? I like diamonds."

"No," he said. "It's actually about Moneypenny."

I perked up immediately. "Oh?"

"I talked to Gabriel. I was hoping against hope that he'd consider letting me buy her. Unfortunately, he wouldn't allow it."

My heart fell a bit. It's not that I'd been expecting it, but it certainly would have been nice to drive her more.

"He wouldn't let me buy her," Ethan said. "But he would let me buy her for you."

It took me a moment to realize what he'd said. "For me?" My voice came out in a squeak. "Are you serious?"

"Aspen serious," Ethan said. "She is parked in the garage, in her newly assigned parking spot. Gabriel is awaiting your direction as to the Volvo. It's an unkillable machine, it seems, so he'd considered donating it to a charity that accepts vehicles. If that's all right with you, of course."

The charity bit was awesome, but this was Chicago. "You're serious about the parking space thing? Like really?"

Ethan chuckled, then cast a glance at the sky, which was now marked by stripes of indigo, crimson, and orange. "The sun will be rising soon. Let's go inside."

He took my hand, squeezing it gently, and together we walked back into the House, the crimson wind swirling behind us. For night would come soon enough again.

Also, there was cake.

We made it to the front door before trouble found us again.

"Ethan. Merit."

We glanced back and found Detective Jacobs on the sidewalk. He was tall, with dark skin and short hair. He wore a suit and overcoat against the chill, a fedora placed just so on his head. His hands were tucked into his trouser pockets, his coat pushed aside for them.

Ethan frowned and walked back down the sidewalk. I followed behind him.

"Detective Jacobs. What brings you here?"

"Bad news, I'm afraid."

Panic set in. "My grandfather?" I asked, but he shook his head.

"He's fine, Merit. This is unrelated." He looked at Ethan. "This actually involves events that transpired here a few days ago—the death of Harold Monmonth."

Ethan's gaze widened, and my heart began to rush again, but for a different reason. "What about it?"

"The prosecuting attorney has determined you are responsible for his death. I'm afraid a warrant has been issued for your arrest."

I guess the GP's silence hadn't meant they were okay with Ethan's handling of the attack. To the contrary: They were angry enough—at least some of them—that they'd actually brought humans into vampire affairs. And made Ethan, a four-hundred-year-old vampire, subject to their justice.

"Harold Monmonth is no gentleman," Ethan assured. "As the CPD is well aware, he attacked this House and killed two human guards. We called the CPD, and officers took statements from everyone. They concluded it was self-defense."

"It doesn't matter what they think," Jacobs said frankly. "It matters what the prosecuting attorney thinks. But perhaps there is some flexibility here. Perhaps I came to the House and found you gone?"

Ethan and Jacobs looked at each other for a long, quiet moment.

"I understand you have powerful friends who live outside the city," Jacobs said. "Friends with strong connections?"

Jacobs meant the Breckenridge family.

Ethan moistened his lips, and nodded. "And if we did?"

"Then perhaps you pay them a visit for a few days until the appropriate conclusions can be reached, the appropriate reports filed. Otherwise, I'm afraid I'll have to take you into custody."

"Hardly a choice," Ethan muttered. "But I appreciate your hypothetical advice. And I'm sorry you came to the House and found me absent."

"In that case, my report will reflect that," Detective Jacobs said, touching the brim of his hat. He turned and walked out the gate, leaving Ethan and me silent in his wake.

"What do we do now?"

"Apparently," Ethan said, "we call Nick Breckenridge, and we ask him for another favor . . . and we hope to God he agrees to help."

Photo by Jeremy Dixon

Chloe Neill was born and raised in the South but now makes her home in the Midwest—just close enough to Cadogan House and St. Sophia's to keep an eye on things. When not transcribing Merit's and Lily's adventures, she bakes, works, and scours the Internet for good recipes and great graphic design. Chloe also maintains her sanity by spending time with her boys—her favorite landscape photographer (her husband) and their dogs, Baxter and Scout. (Both she and the photographer understand the dogs are in charge.)

CONNECT ONLINE

www.chloeneill.com
facebook.com/authorchloeneill
twitter.com/chloeneill